Mary's Moment

BY

SUSAN G MATHIS

smWordWorks, llc
Fiction

Mary's Moment by Susan G Mathis
Published by smWordWorks, llc

INGRAM:
ISBN-10: 1-7379366-6-4
ISBN-13: 978-1-7379366-6-4

Visit her at www.SusanGMathis.com
sign up for her newsletter
and please
consider writing an Amazon review.
Thanks!

PRAISE FOR MARY'S MOMENT

Susan G Mathis never fails to pack her books with memorable characters. In *Mary's Moment,* she gives us a fetching telegraph operator for a heroine and an irresistible fireman hero. Her attention to detail and rich history is classic Mathis, and no one does it better. While our two protagonists help battle the mysterious and devasting fires that sweep through the community, they soon learn that the hardest fire to put out is the one burning in their hearts. Highly recommended.

—Margaret Brownley,
N.Y. Times bestselling author

Mathis's extensive research into the Gilded Age Thousand Island Park community, its history, and the people of that time are evident in her charming story, *Mary's Moment*. Readers will enjoy this tale about a romance, an idyllic setting, a scoundrel, and events that forever changed the landscape of the area, both literally and figuratively. I applaud Mathis's painstaking efforts to include hundreds of historically accurate details about Thousand Island Park while weaving this most enjoyable story.

—Regan Brown,
Thousand Island Park Landmark Society

The Thousand Islands are a magical place! Through her impeccable research and endearing characters, Susan G Mathis takes readers on another journey back to the age of gilded society with its innovation and wealth, straight into the many dangers of this era and all its delights. Mathis introduced me to this beautiful region though historical fiction, and I enjoyed traveling to Wellesley Island via *Mary's Moment*, the latest book in her series.

—Melanie Dobson, award-winning author of
Catching the Wind and
The Wings of Poppy Pendleton

Susan G Mathis delivers again. With lively and multi-layered characters, Mathis whisks us once again into a historically charming and unique setting in the Thousand Islands Gilded Age. Her incredibly accurate and passionate knowledge of this vast area and its history makes the story not only a vivid journey back in time with a memorable protagonist, but also one that resounds with love, faith, and the tenacity to overcome.

—Jayme H. Mansfield, author of
Chasing the Butterfly, RUSH,
Seasoned, and *Portrait of Deceit*

Author Susan G Mathis has done it again with *Mary's Moment.* Her characters are real people I know and love, and I hate to say goodbye to them when I come to the end. Mary's pain is so real, my heart ached for her. And George—what can I say? He's the kind of man I want my grandsons to be like when they grow up. If you're looking for a great story to snuggle up with, this is it.

—Donna Schlachter, historical romance author

In 1912, life was different, with bucket brigades to fight fires, telephone operators at switch boards to funnel phone calls, and primitive medicine to heal the sick. Susan G Mathis' intriguing characters and exciting story will have you flipping pages to discover what happens next to Mary Flynn and George Flannigan. With Mathis' beautiful turn of phrases, always expect the unexpected. This book will become a favorite.

—Anne Greene, author of
Trail of Tears, The Story of John Ross

The Summer of 1912's island amusements and fiery tragedies evolve around a complexity of characters and wounded souls—with surprising results. I appreciated the many fresh, well-done character phrase descriptors throughout, learning about 1912 firefighting procedures, and imagining the horrors of rampant, sudden disaster. It was written deftly, like a nostalgic, old-time, silent film.

—Janet Chester Bly, award-winning author of
The Trails of Reba Cahill Series and
Grace Spilling Over/True Stories of God's Tender Mercies

Susan G Mathis weaves another tale of love and intrigue in *Mary's Moment,* book 4 of her Thousand Islands stories. Readers will not only enjoy the journey to Thousand Island Park in 1912 but may wish to never leave the gilded dreams of those glorious days.

—Davalynn Spencer,
author of award-winning western romance

In *Mary's Moment,* the tenth book penned by award-winning Susan G Mathis, the reader is transported to Thousand Islands Park during the sweltering summer of 1912. Fireman George Flannigan fights the horrific fires as he and his young son, Robbie form a friendship with Mary Flynn, the switchboard and telegraph operator at the Columbian Hotel. When she risks her life in a burning cottage and

v

loses all memory of George, he realizes how much Mary means to him and to his son, but is it too late? Susan skillfully shows us the best and the worst in people through twists and turns—and even some surprises near the end of her book.

—Carol Guthrie Heilman,
author of the *Agnes Hopper* series

Susan G. Mathis's tenth Thousand Island novel is nothing short of endearing. Once again, the author brings together fact and fiction for an enjoyable tale, this time in the unlikely romance between a spinster switchboard operator and a widowed firefighter with a young son. There's much for the couple to overcome amidst dangerous fires, including amnesia and a deceitful beau. I didn't want to put it down. Highly recommend for fans of Christian historical romance!

—Kathleen Rouser, award-winning
author of *Rumors and Promises*

DEDICATION

To my mother, Mary, who inspired this story. When she was a young woman, she spent two summers serving her aunts in the Thousand Islands Park. During my childhood, every summer she'd take me there for an ice cream at the Guzzle and tell me stories of her time there.

To the Thousand Islands River Rats and especially the Thousand Islands Park residents, my faithful readers who love the river as much as I do. Thanks for your support in reading my stories, sharing them with others, and writing reviews on Amazon and Barnes&Nobles. You bless me.

To my wonderful Beta Team, Judy, Laurie, Donna, Barb, Melinda, and Davalynn who inspire me with your kindness, faithfulness, and wisdom. You are dear friends, gifts, and a precious team.

Table of Contents

ACKNOWLEDGMENTS

I hope you enjoy *Mary's Moment.* If you've read any of my other books, you know that I love introducing history to my readers through fictional stories. I hope this story sparks interest in our amazing past, especially the fascinating past of the marvelous Thousand Islands. The Thousand Islands Park, the Columbian Hotel, and the fires are all real, and so are some of the amazing visitors to the Park, but please note that I took a bit of creative license in bringing this story to life, as some of the timing is a little different than recorded.

I'm so grateful for the book, *Thousand Island Park: One Hundred Years, and Then Some* by Helen P. Jacox and Eugene B. Keinhans, Jr. The information was invaluable, and I included many interesting details.

Thanks to you, my readers, for your faithful support and for staying connected. I love hearing from you. And special thanks …

To Judy Keeler, my wonderful historical editor, who combs through my manuscripts for accuracy. Because of her, you can trust that my stories are historically correct. And to Regan Brown, Thousand Island Park Landmark Society historical expert who read through my story for Park accuracy.

To my wonderful editor, Denise Weimer, for being a great friend and for sharing your talents with me.

To my amazing beta readers Laurie, Barb, Donna, Melinda, and Davalynn, for all your hard work and wise input.

And to all my dear friends who have journeyed with me in my writing. Thanks for your emails, social media posts, and especially for your reviews. Most of all, thanks for your friendship.

And to God, from whom all good gifts come. Without You, there would never be a dream or the ability to fulfill that dream. Thank you!

Please stay in touch at susangmathis@gmail.com

Chapter 1

❦

1912

Thousand Island Park, NY

"FIRE!"

Mary Flynn yanked off her telephone switchboard headset to confirm the shouts of danger. She sniffed a sulfurous odor, her heartbeat speeding to a sprint. Somewhere in the distance, a burning structure told the tale. One of destruction and pain—and possibly, death. For the third time in a month. A lump formed in her throat as she hurried toward the door and almost bumped into Mr. Wiseman.

Her elderly friend caught his balance by grasping tighter to his intricately hand-carved cane. Concern croaked in his gravelly voice. "It's the boathouses, Miss Mary. Better call for help. It's a one-alarm, most likely. A bucket brigade of linemen and town folk have already formed."

Mary nodded. "Right away, sir. I'll start with Clayton."

She hurried to the switchboard and rang the Clayton Fire Department, tapping out her nervous energy as she waited, drumming her fingernails on the smooth oak desk.

1

After far too many rings, a man answered. "George Flannigan here. How may I help?"

His deep, serene tone calmed her nerves. A smidgen.

She swallowed, willing her voice to steady and hide her fear. But it surged through her veins and snuck out her mouth. "Mary Flynn, Thousand Island Park telephone operator. We have a boathouse fire in progress. There's a bucket brigade, but with the wind …" Her quivering voice trailed off.

"I'll gather a crew and be there soon." With no further ado, he hung up.

Mary puffed out a breath, bowed her head, and prayed for the men, the fire, the town. It was all she could do at the moment, confined as she was to her closet-like office.

Just a month ago, a fire had destroyed five cottages on nearby Grenell Island, and another blaze had started at the Thousand Island Park Gardner Boat Shop a week ago. Nine boathouses leveled.

Worse, though, was the Frontenac Hotel fire on Round Island last August, less than a year past. That devastation had seared into the minds of all who loved the St. Lawrence River's Thousand Islands. If it could happen to such a magnificent, modern resort had the latest fire prevention inventions known to man, it could happen anywhere.

Even here, in this fine hotel.

She tapped her fingers again. If only someone would update her on today's fire. Her tiny switchboard and telegraph room in back of the Columbine Hotel suited her fine—until something like this happened. Then she yearned to be out in the thick of things, gathering information, helping others. And safe.

If a fire hit the hotel, she could jump out of her office's one small window if she had to, but the massive rose bushes beneath would make for a rather unpleasant fall. The front door was some distance from her office—through the large drawing room and long lobby. Smoke—or fire, God forbid—filling the grand foyer would block her way. She'd have to take a precarious route to the servants' entrance—or face the thorns below.

She looked out the window for evidence of the fire, but her view of the nearby kitchen building blocked everything else. Besides, the fire was in the opposite direction. Itching for information, she rang her aunties, who owned an adorable little cottage on Oak Street west of the hotel where she lived for the summer. The pink-and-white Queen Anne-style gingerbread matched Aunt Maude's sweet, feminine personality—the opposite of her sister, Stella's.

Unfortunately, Aunt Stella answered, her loud, curt voice grating on Mary's frayed nerves. "Hello? Who's calling? Mary?"

She groaned. "I am, Aunt. Do you have any information about the boathouse fire?" Mary chewed her bottom lip. "I'm confined to my workstation and am dying to know more."

"I smelled the smoke. Been on the porch all morning hoping to chat with a neighbor or two, but it seems everyone is still about their morning ministrations."

Aunt Stella huffed into the mouthpiece of her new candlestick telephone, causing an irritatingly loud sound. She'd only had the new device a few weeks and definitely needed coaching on how to use it properly. Like not breathing into someone's ear.

Mary pulled the headphone away from her ear. "Please let me know if you hear anything, okay?"

Aunt Stella guffawed. "You'll be the first to know. If there's a tale to tell, you can be sure you'll hear it from me."

"Thanks, Auntie. Hello to Aunt Maude."

Aunt Stella hung up just as Mr. Wiseman knocked. "May I update you?"

Mary nodded, motioning for him to take the small chair next to the switchboard. Besides that seat, her own workstation chair, and the switchboard and telegraph machines atop a large oak desk, there was nothing else in the tiny room. Thankfully, the electric light, small window, and warm cream-colored walls made the room somewhat inviting.

The chair creaked in protest as the older man sat. Small-framed and salt-and-pepper haired, the man possessed a smile that always seemed to rise to his lively blue eyes. But not now. He set his cane beside him and folded his hands atop his protruding paunch. "Clayton Fire Department just arrived, but the fire is spreading. It's taken out a few boathouses already. With the wind and all, I hope the men can stop it before it moves into the center of the Park."

Her heart took to trotting. "How'd it start?"

Mr. Wiseman clucked his tongue. "Don't rightly know, Miss Mary. There were fifteen linemen installing a new telephone line who saw it and started the bucket brigade. Good lads, all. Several of 'em let loose the boats nearest the fire. Likely saved a dozen vessels, though the owners will have to fetch them from the swift river current before they scatter to the four winds. Wee Tommie Roberts ran from house to house, alerting the owners."

Mary pressed her hand to her heart. "Oh, that's a mercy."

He shifted in his seat, which groaned under him. "Better fix this chair afore it collapses." He gave it a pat, and with much effort, stood and grasped his cane. "I'll head back to the veranda. If there be more to tell, I'll let you know."

Mary stood to see him to the door, but the wire from her headset pulled her back into her chair. She grinned, rolling her eyes at the blunder. She sheepishly removed it and followed him into the hallway. "Thanks, Mr. Wiseman. I can always count on you for the latest news."

He chuckled, tapping his cane on the shiny oak floor. "I suspect your Aunt Stella takes the lead on that one. She knows every piece of gossip from Lake Ontario to Singer Castle, that one." He shook his head, sending wispy shocks of hair flying every which way. He plopped his straw hat on his head and tipped it with a slight touch to the brim. "Be back with news when I hear more."

She patted his wrinkly hand. "Thank you, sir."

He brushed a kiss on her cheek and hobbled back toward his perch on the porch. The former minister had taken summer residence in the hotel ever since his wife of fifty years left for heaven. Every day the weather cooperated, Mr. Wiseman sat in the same spot on the veranda, watching the world go by, reading the Good Book, playing chess, and chatting with anyone who would visit.

She, for one, loved to spend time with him. He'd become a father figure of sorts, doling out wisdom and counsel with a large dollop of God's love. Unlike her aunt, who loved gossip, Mr. Wiseman spoke of higher things. Conversations with him were deep, thought-provoking, and sometimes challenging. And though his body showed the troubles of time, his mind was as sharp as a man her own age.

At twenty-eight, she'd become an old maid, just like her Aunt Maude. Not that Mary didn't desire marriage. It just never stepped across her threshold or even winked at her. Oh, she'd cast her eye on a boy or two, but they fled as soon as they learned she was a modern woman who enjoyed working outside the home.

No. She'd not permit a sink or a crib or any other domestic doldrum to chain her. She had too much to offer. Too much to accomplish.

Mary startled when the telegraph came to life. Dots and dashes danced in the air as she picked up her pencil and began deciphering the message as quick as a hummingbird's flight. "Alex Bay here. See smoke. Need help?"

Did they? She tapped out her reply. "Clayton here but please help. Boathouses burning. Wind strong."

She waited for what seemed a decade before the answer came, the clicks and ticks in the irregular succession of one unsure how to send a proper telegraph message. "Sending help."

Mary sat back in her chair, folded her hands, and sent up a quick prayer. Whether or not the boys needed it, aid was on the way. She grinned at the satisfaction of making such a lofty decision. If she were a housewife, dinner and diapers would be the only decisions she'd be making.

She stared out the window, wishing once again for a clear sight to the fire. Why couldn't she settle for the normal course of things? Marriage. Motherhood. Matronly attentions.

She ran her hand along the familiar machines in front of her. The telephone switchboard was a marvel, and she enjoyed connecting with others. But the telegraph suited her fancy best. She'd become quite adept at her work, speedily transcribing wires, even recognizing the senders by idiosyncrasies, much like the tones of a voice. Accuracy was critical in her translations, especially in times of sorrow and danger. Like now. And she'd found a level of satisfaction in her days, tucked away in seclusion with machines as her friends.

Still, if she was honest, she longed to be loved.

But by whom?

~ ~ ~

By the time George Flannigan and his three volunteer firefighters arrived from Clayton, the fire had consumed four boathouses, and five more were in peril. Despite the linemen and community volunteers forming a bucket brigade, their efforts were mostly in vain as they frantically tossed buckets of water on the flames without rhyme or reason. On the river, several launches and skiffs floated aimlessly as men swam out to retrieve them. Two burned boat hulls drifted like coffins along the shore.

Thousand Island Park hadn't yet established a formal volunteer fire department, but this was ridiculous. Surely, someone on the island knew something about firefighting. Where was the Park's equipment? He shook his head at the two chemical engines long ago spent and the unseasoned bucket brigade of men and boys.

A heavy-set man shouted to George and his companions, pointing to a sparkling new machine yet unused, partially hidden from his view around the corner of a nearby building. "Any idea how to use the steam engine? None of us have a clue."

They have a brand-new steam engine but don't know how to use it? Good Lord, help us! George nodded. "Aye. Burt and Manny will take care of that. Who's in charge here?"

A young teener spoke. "No one, sir. We ain't got no fire chief, nor a fire department, for that matter."

George patted his chest. As the only professional firefighter on scene, he must. "Then I'll lead this one."

He set Burt and Manny to preparing the steam engine and quickly made a plan to gather the volunteers into teams of three to five to fill specific jobs. The linemen could create a firebreak, but the wind kept whipping up embers, sending them aloft to land on the nearby boathouses.

He picked up the speaking trumpet he'd brought with him and put it to his mouth. "Listen up. You're doing fine work, folks, but we need to get better organized. We have to stop this fire afore it spreads throughout the Park." He pulled several strong-looking men from the bucket brigade, then handed them the shovels and axes his team had brought. "You five, make a firebreak. Dig a trench here, and let nothing past you."

They nodded and set to work.

George motioned to three others and handed them rag mops. "You men, take these and wet them in the river. Then climb atop the unaffected boathouse roofs. Put out any embers, sparks, or flames that come your way."

Next, he recruited three lanky teens from the bucket brigade to patrol the ground for stray sparks and embers. They saluted him and ran to their designated areas.

He grabbed two more men and handed them fire hooks. "Help me pull down the walls of the last smoldering boathouse." He pointed to the tenth boathouse that had caught fire and showed them how to use the hooks. Thankfully, they caught on quickly. "That's it, boys."

As they continued to fight the fire, George swiped his brow. His black rubber-lined duck coat and rubber boots held the heat like an oven. He baked inside, sweating until wet to his toes. But at least the material protected him better than the other poor lads in street clothes. Everything in him wanted to strip off his gear and hand his attire to one of them, but he knew better. He was in charge and had to be ready to go into the fire itself if need be.

After several minutes, Burt and Manny had the steamer spraying the eleventh boathouse, and an hour-and-a-half of furious work later, they'd finally gotten the fire under control. No one was seriously hurt, but May thirtieth would be a sad day in Thousand Island Park history.

As the fire smoldered, he thanked the men and boys who'd worked so hard and stationed Burt and Manny to oversee the cleanup operation. Four volunteers also stayed behind to make sure no spot fires popped up.

George, however, needed to alert the town they were safe. And he wanted to inform Mr. Wiseman himself.

He entered the vast green space along St. Lawrence Avenue commanded by the four-hundred-room Columbian Hotel, looming bright white against the blue sky. With the resort built in the shape of a Greek cross so that every room had an outside view, the best rooms looked out to the river with doors onto verandas for quick and safe exit in case of a fire. Heaven forbid that guests would ever need egress for such an emergency.

He'd inspected the hotel before and found it sound. Pressed tin ceilings in the hotel's common areas acted as fire retardants, and electric lights helped to avoid open flames such as had been customary with candles or kerosene or gas lamps. There were only three fireplaces, all in the main areas, which staff diligently oversaw when lit.

George shook himself from his focus on fire safety, a habit that overtook him far too often. Still, he acknowledged that the builders had constructed the Columbian to protect its patrons. George had visited there on several occasions, enjoying the hotel's orchestra during some of the daily concerts and evening dances. It was a fine place to come for entertainment, but he especially enjoyed visiting the old preacher, Mr. Wiseman.

As George climbed the hotel steps, he waved to his old friend. "Aye. The fire's under control. I have a few men mopping up, but the Park is safe."

Mr. Wiseman clapped his hands and then raised them to the blue sky. "Praise be to God! I've been imploring the heavens for every-one's safety. Anyone hurt?"

George waved a hand. "A few cinder burns and scratches, but nothing to be alarmed about. Still, before the fire gave up its ghost, eleven boathouses and three launches succumbed to nature's treachery."

Mr. Wiseman frowned and asked again, "But the volunteers weathered the storm all right?"

George nodded, patting the old man on the shoulder. "All are well."

Just then, the hotel manager, Mr. O'Shea, and a pretty young woman joined them. George reiterated the news, observing relief on both of their faces.

Who was this petite, raven-haired lass with her ivory skin and bright caramel eyes? When she grinned, one small dimple deepened on her right cheek, then disappeared as soon as her lips softened. But her eyes danced at his news. Somehow, she exuded a strength that bordered on sassiness, even before she said a word. He hadn't met such an intriguing woman… since Alma.

At her memory, George instantly sobered, turning his attention to the gathering crowd. Several dozen guests and residents cheered as the news passed from mouth to ear.

"Hurrah for Fireman Flannigan! Hurrah for the volunteers! Hurrah for Miss Flynn for calling for help!"

The chants increased until George wanted to slip through a crack of the veranda's plank flooring. He grew hotter by the moment, but he dared not take off his leather helmet or heavy duck coat. Without his uniform, he'd look even worse because he'd already sweated clear through his clothing. Enduring the unwelcome accolades, he swiped his forehead before sweat dripped into his eyes. He wasn't one for public displays of honor, especially when he didn't deserve it. He had saved no one today. He hadn't even singed his hair or burned his skin retrieving a priceless memento. He'd simply organized a ragtag group of volunteers as the wind and fire destroyed almost a dozen boathouses.

George gave a curt nod and turned from the gathering. "I should go."

Mr. O'Shea seemed to understand his angst. "Come with me and escape the crowds." The hotel manager led him to a hotel room and opened the door. "Bathe, and I'll fetch you clean clothes. You can return them on your next visit."

"Thank you, Mr. O'Shea. I really appreciate this."

He shut the door and slipped off his helmet and duck coat, smiling at the well-appointed white, tiled room. And how grand to have indoor plumbing. Before stepping into the bath, he thought of the pretty lass.

Who was the lovely woman?

He had to know.

Chapter 2

While waiting on the veranda to speak again with her old friend, Mary winced at the memory of the weary firefighter. Covered in ash, his prominent forehead bore the signs that he'd attempted, and failed, to swipe away the sweat. Even so, he was the most handsome man she'd ever laid eyes on. Filthy or not. Slightly receding hairline or not. A small scar above his left ear, down to his jawline, or not.

She hadn't wanted to stare, but with all the commotion of the gathering crowd, the opportunity afforded her just that. Something about him intrigued her. Because he was a heroic fireman? Perhaps.

Or perhaps it was his high cheekbones and strong jawline dotted with dark stubble. Or his broad shoulders and imposing stature? No, it was the man's piercing deep blue eyes holding a trace of melancholy—which most likely had taken up residence well before today's tragedy—that captured her attention. She sensed that melancholy came from something deeper. Something more intimate. But what?

The applause and adulation of the crowd had warmed her heart. Every firefighter deserved the highest tribute for putting his life on the line to fight a foreboding enemy that had no mercy. In truth, fire-fighters deserved much more than applause.

Perhaps if she lingered a bit now that her shift was complete, she might have a proper introduction to the man Mr. O'Shea had led into the hotel. The cheering crowd slowly dispersed, passing by her on their return to their prior activities.

Mary made her way over to her friend and grinned as she issued her challenge. "Now that the danger is past, would you care for a quick game of chess, Mr. Wiseman?"

He waved a hand at the chessboard. "Aye. How can I say no to such a pretty face? But be warned, I'll not favor you just because you pop that dimple at me."

Mary giggled as she sat to face her opponent. She'd learned the game well, but Mr. Wiseman was formidable. Indeed, he did battle on the chessboard like a general in a war.

She'd won two of his pawns, a rook, and a bishop before the fire-man stepped onto the veranda, duck coat and clothing draped over his arm, helmet tucked under it, and boots in hand. He'd cleaned up, shiny as a new penny, fairly gleaming in the afternoon sunshine. He wore a hotel's gardener's uniform, but he was as handsome as a wealthy gentleman going to a ball.

The man slipped her a gaze, and her cheeks instantly heated. Caught gawking at him.

He joined her and Mr. Wiseman and tilted his head toward the chessboard. "You're giving him a run for his money, I see."

When he winked at her, more heat rushed to her cheeks. Hoping to ease her embarrassment, she pasted on a bright smile. "Thank you for your service, sir. I'm sure your valiant efforts saved many structures and maybe even lives."

Mr. Wiseman grinned, a mischievous twinkle in his eye. "My fair lass, this is George Flannigan from Clayton. His father and I were good friends. He be a fine man and a fair chess player."

Mary sucked in a breath. "You're the man who answered my plea for help. I'm the switchboard operator."

Mr. Flannigan nodded, a kind smile rising to his baby blues. "You don't say. I'm glad you called. The volunteers made a valiant effort, but it was tough going with the dry wind tossing embers thither and yon."

Mary stood and put out her hand, but instead of shaking it, the fireman furrowed his brow as he stared at it. After several uncomfortable moments, he shifted his boots to free a hand, swiped that hand on his pants leg, and finally took hers, holding it rather than shaking it. "My hand is rather sweaty, miss. Sorry."

Mary grinned, giving him a reassuring shrug. "Understandable. You just fought a battle with burning buildings. I'll not fret about touching a little sweat." She shook his hand firmly and decisively, and his eyebrows popped up. "Honored to meet you."

He held her hand a moment longer than necessary, but she didn't mind. In fact, she rather enjoyed it. When he finally let go, Mr. Wiseman punctuated the interlude with a chuckle.

"George, I'd like to introduce Miss Mary Flynn, Thousand Island Park telephone switchboard operator and wireless telegrapher."

Mr. Flannigan blinked, a tiny smile crossing his lips. "You decipher telegraph messages? I thought only men—Well, I'll be jiggered."

Mary waved a hand, despite his assumption that only the male population was intelligent enough to decipher the complicated messaging system. "Oh, it's grand fun. All those dots and dashes. After a while, you even get to know who's on the other end by the style of their communication, and you can make friends from all around the world. I've actually communicated with someone in Ireland once, and she had the most delightful accent."

Mr. Wiseman interjected his opinion. "She's quite the find, and Irish like you and me, George. And she be a crackin' chess player, too. She might even outmatch you."

Her elderly friend winked at her, and she tossed him a knowing, scolding glance. Just like her aunties, Mr. Wiseman was always on the lookout for an eligible bachelor to make her life complete. Or so he'd said—more than once.

Mr. Flannigan slipped his helmet from under his arm, then waved it toward the shore. "I'd like to tarry, but I need to gather the lads and head back to Clayton. Nice to meet you, Miss Flynn. And good to see you, sir."

Mary nodded. "It was nice to make your acquaintance, Mr. Flannigan, and thanks again for all you did."

He left her with a gentle smile, his eyes like pools of deep, clear water on a sunny day. They reminded her of the ocean, which she had the thrill of seeing on a train trip and excursion to New York City last year.

Mary returned to the chessboard and knocked over her queen, conceding defeat. "I'd better get home to the aunts. If Aunt Stella hasn't heard all the news by now, I'm sure she's having a conniption fit."

"I'm surprised she didn't join the bucket brigade or come here to investigate." Mr. Wiseman patted her hand. "Farewell, my lovely lass. Until tomorrow."

She kissed his cheek. "Rest well, Mr. Wiseman. Hopefully, tomorrow will be free of drama and danger."

Mary hurried home and found half a dozen neighbors sitting with Aunt Stella on the porch. Aunt Maude carried a tray of glasses filled with her famous sun tea to her visitors. How she brewed it without even a hint of bitterness, Mary never knew. But it was delicious.

"Hi, everyone. And how might you be faring on this difficult day?" Mary climbed the stairs and took a glass of tea her aunt offered. "What's the news?"

Along with a chorus of greetings, their neighbor, Mr. Jones, answered. "Clifford's boathouse and launch are lost. Driscoll's too. But no one seriously injured."

Mary nodded. "I know. I spoke to the fireman from Clayton."

Aunt Maude set her tray down and gathered Mary into her arms. "And I heard you saved the day by calling for help."

Mary shrugged. "Just doing my job, as anyone would."

Aunt Stella huffed, swiping a lock of grey hair from her face. "Ain't fittin', I say. You should be married and caring for children as your job. Any of you fine folks know a young man who'd fancy an old maid to wed?"

"Aunt! Please!"

Mary's blood ran hot. The nerve of Aunt Stella to say such a thing in public. Instead of enjoying a few moments with her neighbors, Mary fled to her room, slamming the door behind her.

She threw herself on the bed and seethed. It was bad enough that everyone was constantly trying to marry her off. It was mortifying to have it be a topic of public discourse. But how could she end it, short of selling herself short? How could she …

Wait. The smell of smoke again? This time, a cloud settled halfway down inside her room. Choking, she tried to open the door, but it was locked. She pounded on it. Screamed for help. But no one came.

When she made her way to the window, she wasn't on Oak Street in Thousand Island Park. She was on the fourth floor of the famed Frontenac Hotel on Round Island. She darted back across the room, but the flames from the other side of the door heated her room like an oven. On the door, a map of the exits alerted her that her room was number 115. No! The man in room 117 had butted out his cigarette in an artificial plant in his room, causing the fire.

But how did she know that?

She tried to open the window, but it was one pane. She grabbed a vase from the dresser and swung it at the glass, but it simply bounced off as though the pane was made of rubber. Would she die here?

Just then, the door burst open, and fireman Flannigan entered the room, flames hot on his tail. The fire followed him in and lapped up everything in her room.

With a start, she woke up. A dream? No, a nightmare. The same nightmare she'd endured for almost a year, ever since she'd read the *New York Times'* account of the Frontenac Hotel's demise. But she'd never been rescued from the nightmare before.

Why now?

~ ~ ~

George hugged his son extra tight that night as he tucked him into bed. The tawny-haired six-year-old smiled sweetly as George trailed a tender finger over Robbie's abundant freckles. "Orion, the mighty hunter, and Leo, the great lion." He tapped Robbie's nose. "I'm glad the good Lord didn't splatter the scorpion or a crab on those cheeks of yours, else I'd be afraid to touch you."

Robbie wiggled. "Oh, Daddy. You're so silly. Guess what? I have a loose tooth, and I found a turtle today. Can I keep him? Please? I named him Timmy, and he can keep me company when Granny is having one of her spells."

Spells he'd endured as a child now and then. Indeed, George's mother seemed to have more and more of her episodes of late, ranting and raving like a crazy person. Scolding and screaming at his son, even in his presence. And accusing George of being a delinquent father because he hadn't yet found a replacement for Alma. Could he ever find a woman to equal the wonderful wife and mother she'd been? Extremely doubtful.

Ever since his poor wife had died, George had no other choice but to leave his precious son with his unpredictable mother, even succumbing to the two of them living with her. True, she'd always been a little unstable. But lately, she'd grown more and more sour and capricious, once leaving her four-year-old grandson napping alone on a blanket by the dangerous river while she went to tea with a friend. How much longer could he tolerate her carelessness? But if he moved out, who would care for his son while he worked? He'd have to consider that more deeply, sooner rather than later.

"Daddy? Are you listening?"

George blinked. "Sorry, son. I guess I'm pretty tired, as you should be."

Robbie frowned. "Was the fire very bad? Did you get burned?" He grabbed his father's arm and explored it for damage. "Does it hurt anywhere?"

"I'm fine, son. Just one tiny burn. See?" He revealed a small blister on the inside of his left wrist. Then he slipped Robbie's arms under the blanket and tucked the covers around him. "Snug as a bug in a rug. Now stop fretting over me and get some sleep. And yes, you may keep Timmy. I *was* listening, son."

The boy's big, brown eyes lit up. "Really? Yay!"

"Really." George kissed Robbie's freckled forehead. "I love you. Nighty-night."

"I love you, too, Papa." Robbie snuggled under his covers and closed his eyes. "Pray for me?"

George happily obliged. He implored the Lord to watch over his son, keep him safe, give him sweet dreams, and help him grow up to be a good, godly man. Before he'd even finished his prayer, Robbie was sleeping soundly.

He gently swept his son's bangs to one side and kissed him again. Such a treasure from heaven, his Robbie. The boy's hair, so much like his mother's. The freckles, too, came from Alma. Even his son's laugh reminded him of his departed wife. Grief gripped his gut and took his breath away. He stood, and with a deep sigh, left the room, nearly bumping into his mother.

"Has the child finally succumbed to sleep? I declare, that boy has more energy than a freight train. He's too rambunctious for his own good or mine, I tell you."

Mother. Never a kind word on her lips. Always complaining about one thing or another.

George stood his ground, willing his voice to retain a measure of esteem for the woman who lost his respect more each day. "He's a child, Mother. I'm sure I was even more rambunctious at times."

His mother waddled past him toward the staircase, a loud groan followed by her ever-liniment-tainted scent. "And I swatted that foolishness clear out of you more than once, if you'll recall, and I'll do the same with him. Spare the rod, spoil the child."

George ground his teeth to keep from answering.

She stopped at the top of the stairs and turned to him. "See here, son. I'm getting too old for this nonsense. I want to enjoy the latter years of my life with my friends, not chasing an incorrigible little scamp around until I die of old age. You simply must find a wife soon and free me of this burden—or put an advertisement in the paper for a nursemaid." She paused and lifted a fat finger to her cheek. "Have you ever thought about a mail-order bride? That might be our ticket out of this mess. Mark my words, you have until the end of the summer, and then I'm done."

Without allowing him to respond, Mother descended the staircase, moaning and groaning with each step as if she were on her way to her grave. Why, the woman was barely past seventy, but she acted as if she was Methuselah's peer.

Enough.

Even though George would have loved to sit on the porch and ponder the stars, he refused to join her downstairs and hear more of her tirade. Instead, he retreated to his room and read the Good Book, hoping to soothe his battered soul.

A soul battered by his mother. By today's fire. By loss so deep, he wondered how he'd ever move past it.

Indeed. How could he move on after losing the love of his life? Alma was his first love. His only love. Like losing a limb, leaving him half man. Half human. Halfway to nothing. Gone almost four years, but her passing still hurt like it was yesterday. Still stung and pained and grieved him. Not only for himself, but also for the little boy she had given him.

Robbie barely remembered his mother. He was only two when she went away. But *Mama* had been his first word, and the two had been inseparable. Alma had adored her son, and the toddler had revered her. Until that day when she didn't come home, and the preacher delivered the news.

A baseball slipped into his throat, and he broke into a cold sweat at the memory. He swallowed, but it wouldn't release. He couldn't breathe. Couldn't swallow. He could die right then and there, just like he always could when he thought of that day.

Oh, how he wished it would have been him instead of his dear, sweet Alma. She would have done such a better job of taking care of Robbie. Their little boy wouldn't have had to be relegated to the inferior care of his mother. As it was, every day he left Robbie with his grandmother, guilt niggled George's brain the entire time he was away. And during a fire, he had to be completely present and fully aware of the dangers around him, else he might risk the lives of others—or himself. Then where would Robbie be?

Perhaps his mother was right. Perhaps he should seek a mail-order bride. As far as he knew, there wasn't a woman in all the North Country who could compare to his Alma.

Just then, like lightning, Miss Mary Flynn's pretty face flashed through his mind.

Hadn't Mr. Wiseman introduced her as "Miss"? Could she fit the high standards his wife left behind? Probably not. After all, she was a working woman, serving as a telephone switchboard operator and telegrapher. Someone so accomplished would likely not be interested in raising another woman's child and caring for a home. Or entrusting her future to a fireman who might face danger every time he left the house.

A knock on his door signaled his mother wasn't through with her rant. Drat! He couldn't pretend he was asleep—the lamp burned brightly. He rolled his eyes and mumbled, "Come in, Mother."

His mother opened the door wide. "I heard Sally Ann Smith down in Cape Vincent lost her husband to a heart attack awhile back. Perhaps you should call on her. She has boys, so Robbie would have playmates. Tell me you'll see to it."

George shrugged, folding his arms over his chest. "I'll consider it, Mother. Good night."

"Good night." Mother cast him a triumphant grin.

Before she'd closed the door, George had considered it fully. He knew the Sally Ann Smith in question. Round as she was tall. Five, maybe six, beastly creatures who would surely end up delinquents before the year's end. Not in his lifetime would he allow Robbie within a hundred yards of those ruffians. What was his mother thinking?

Thinking of the easiest way to get rid of the both of them, that's what!

George readied for bed and plunked down on top of the covers. Crickets chirped through the open window, and a cool breeze calmed his frayed nerves.

Perhaps he'd call on Miss Mary Flynn, after all.

What could it hurt?

Chapter 3

Two days later, Mary returned from a long day's work to her aunts' little cottage. She shook her head at the incessant tapping of a woodpecker that had found a spot in her aunts' elm, searching for its food. He'd taken up residence before they opened the cottage and had been a nuisance ever since. She tossed a pebble its way but missed. "Go and find another tree to damage, you crazy bird."

She groaned as he cocked his head at her. Where were her aunts? All summer, they practically lived on the porch from sun up to sun down, the wicker furniture occupied by chatting neighbors, a pitcher of sun tea and a plate of Aunt Maude's shortbread gracing the tiny coffee table more often than not.

Mary climbed the steps and entered the feminine abode. A steep staircase ascended to the left, the pocket door to the right opened wide and welcoming to a frilly parlor. An abundance of doilies and knickknacks sat about, waiting to be noticed. She, however, had other things on her mind.

"Aunties? Are you here?"

Mary walked through the parlor and entered the dining room, fully set for a dinner party of five, lace and silver abundant. Fine

Rosenthal Continental china, with its gold trim and rose decorations, had been perfectly placed.

Aunt Maude's softly lilting voice beckoned her. "In here, dear."

In the kitchen, the two older women prepared a feast. Potatoes bubbled. Green beans steamed. Mary closed her eyes as if to better enjoy the scents, especially her aunts' herb-infused chicken and yeasty bread.

"Who's coming to dinner?" *Please let it neighbors and not another unwelcome suitor selected by my aunts.* They'd already invited more than her share, and the summer had barely begun.

Aunt Stella wiped her brow on her shirtsleeve, popped a green bean into her mouth, and chewed before answering. "Needs another few minutes. Mr. Archibald Richmond is coming. He's bringing a client from the mainland since their meeting ran late."

Hopefully, Mr. Richmond was coming to talk about insurance instead of being the victim of another attempt at matchmaking. She'd connected Mr. Richmond's business calls several times when he'd rung the switchboard. His voice was smooth, but there never seemed to be any joy in it.

Mary chewed her lip. "I see."

Aunt Stella dried her hands on the apron that skirted her ample girth. "Rather than canceling altogether, I told him to bring the man along. Don't know who, but I think we have enough for five."

Mary rolled her eyes before releasing a nervous chuckle. "You always make enough food for an army. What can I do to help?"

Sweet Aunt Maude waved her small hand. "Nothing, dear. Go freshen up, and then we can hear about your day."

Upstairs, Mary hummed as she changed her blouse. She refashioned her hair into a softer chignon, pinched her cheeks, and descended the stairs just as the two men stepped onto the porch. Observing them through the screen door, she looked twice at Mr. Richmond's companion—none other than the handsome fireman, Mr. Flannigan. Her heart gave a little skip, and she swallowed her excitement along with a bit of nervousness.

Mr. Richmond was handsome, too, but in a stern, rather austere way. The insurance man was tall and lanky, with black hair, a narrow face, and thick brows. Upon closer inspection, several scars dotted his cheeks and forehead. Perhaps from the pox? Or was it measles?

He knocked on the screen door, his small mouth set in a frown.

Mary pasted on a smile and answered the door. "Welcome, gentlemen, to my aunts' home." She stepped aside as they passed, and the fireman's grin rose to his piercing blue eyes.

He stopped just inside the door and removed his hat. "Hello, again, Miss Flynn. Fancy meeting you again so soon."

"'Tis a pleasant surprise, I must say. Please call me Mary. 'Miss Flynn' makes me feel old." Mary's cheeks heated at her bold admission. "Or should I say, older than I already am."

There, perhaps that nugget of information would remove her from Mr. Richmond's courting list.

Mr. Flannigan nodded. "Please call me George—for the same reason."

Mr. Richmond cleared his throat, motioning back and forth between her and Mr. Flannigan—George. His scowl spoke volumes. "You two know each other?"

George shook his head. "We met two days ago when I tended the boathouse fire. She called it in."

Mr. Richmond's scowl deepened. He glared down at her as if she were a worm to be squashed. "You're the switchboard operator I talk to?"

Mary squared her shoulders and stood as tall as her five-foot-two frame would let her. She put out her hand, but Mr. Richmond removed his hat and handed it to her instead of shaking her hand. Sure, many of the older generation didn't fancy a woman shaking an ungloved hand with a man, but this was a modern world, and he was of the same generation. Or so she assumed.

She willed her most exuberant confidence to carry her words. "Mary Flynn, niece to Mrs. Stella Everson and Miss Maude Armstrong. Welcome to our home." She took George's hat, set both on the hat rack, and motioned for them to enter the parlor, its mauve floral settee and matching Queen Anne chair seeming rather out of place as the tall men stood next to them. "Please sit. I'll inform the aunts you've arrived."

Mary hurried to the kitchen, wiping sweaty palms on her skirt. Aunt Stella at the oven. Aunt Maude at the sink. "They're here already. Shall I bring them into the dining room?"

Aunt Stella groaned, slamming the oven door a little too hard. "Ain't ready. Entertain them for a few minutes."

Mary returned to the parlor, her hands clasped in front of her. "May I offer you refreshments? Seems it'll be a few moments before dinner."

Mr. Richmond's eternal frown hung on his face like a dark, foreboding cloud. "I don't imbibe before I eat."

Mary glanced at George, who raised his brows. She glanced back at Mr. Richmond. "I didn't mean liquor, sir. Lemonade? Iced tea, perhaps?"

The insurance man waved off the offer. "We will wait for the meal."

Large and in charge, he didn't even bother to see what his guest thought.

How rude.

Time for small talk. Mary cleared her throat, choosing to ignore Mr. Richmond and turn her attention to George. "Any new fires since you were here, sir?"

He leaned forward, placing his forearms on his legs. "None, thank the good Lord. But we're always at the ready since it's so hot, dry, and windy of late. A perfect triangulation for trouble, and Ben Franklin's *Old Farmer's Almanac* predicts the entire season to be thus."

Mary smiled at the use of such an interesting word. She'd assumed a fireman would have limited education. "I've heard that the *Almanac* is more than eighty percent accurate. Amazing. It helps to know you're at the ready, but I pray you'll not need your skills here, there, or anywhere."

Mr. Richmond butted in. "Statistics say that will not be the case, Miss. As an insurance man, *I* predict there will be many fires this summer, perhaps even deaths. That's why fire insurance is so important. I offer the only guaranteed safeguard for that kind of thing."

What was she to say to that? It wasn't as if his insurance would prevent fires. True, folks would have the wherewithal to finance a new start in life, but nothing could replace lost keepsakes and mementoes.

An uncomfortable silence ensued until Aunt Stella appeared in the doorway. "Come, gentlemen, and enjoy a home-cooked meal."

She waved the men into the dining room, and Mary followed. *This may be a long, boring evening if Mr. Richmond rules the roost.*

After introductions, taking their seats, and saying a blessing, Aunt Stella employed her role as hostess. She bid the men to fill their plates, then she glanced around the room. "Do you know this very cottage was built on the original tent platform of the late 1880s?"

George's brows furrowed. "Tent platform?"

Aunt Stella nodded, poking a green bean into the mashed potatoes with her fork. "Yes. When they established Thousand Island Park as a church camp back in 1875, simple dirt-floor tents were people's summer abodes. As the years went on, many built platforms for the tents, and by 1894, more than five hundred families had built more substantial cottages."

George glanced around the room and smiled. "This is a beautiful Victorian cottage, ma'am. I love all the gingerbread trim and frilly enhancements."

"Firetraps, all," Mr. Richmond mumbled before swallowing his bite of food. "That's why everyone should have insurance."

Aunt Maude made a small choking sound.

Mr. Richmond drilled Aunt Stella with a narrow-eyed glare, pointing his fork at her, then waving it around. "What if this kindling-dry wooden cottage burns to the ground in one of the many fires predicted this season? All your things, gone. How would you replace them?" He set his fork down and tapped his finger on the fine crystal goblet for emphasis before continuing. "Your silver melted into nothing. Handmade doilies and lace destroyed. Family heirlooms lost to nature's terror. Perhaps even your lives. How would you navigate those steep steps in the dark of night with smoke or flames blocking your way? You ladies must consider the consequences immediately, or I warn you, you will sorely regret it."

George raised a palm and his voice raised with it. A slight pink mottled his neck and rose to his cheeks. "Sir, let us end this conversation, at least until after dinner, please. Let us only speak of pleasantries during our meal. 'Tis only proper to do so."

"As you wish." Mr. Richmond conceded with a harrumph.

Aunt Maude, ever the peace keeper, blew out a ragged breath and nodded toward her sister. Her porcelain complexion slowly returned to its usual tranquil pink. "Tell us of your family, sir."

Aunt Stella took the hint and turned to Mr. Flannigan, but the insurance salesman apparently misunderstood the nuances of dinner conversation. Rather than allowing the fireman to respond, Mr. Richmond shook his head, stabbing a piece of chicken and popping it into his mouth. "Got none."

George set down his fork and dabbed his lips before answering. "My family is small. I have a six-year-old son, Robbie. The two of us live with my widowed mother."

Mary giggled. "Six? What a delightful age."

She set down her fork in anticipation of learning more about the child.

And him.

~ ~ ~

George's blood fairly boiled at the pushy Mr. Richmond. How dare he scare these kind women and barrage them with thoughts of tragedy? And during dinner, no less. That was no way to win new clients. After this display of vulgarity, Mr. Richmond most certainly wouldn't have his or his mother's business.

Between the chatty Mrs. Everson and himself, the conversation would stay on safer topics. He wanted to pull Miss Armstrong and

Mary into the conversation as much as possible, so he turned to the former. He glanced at a picture on the sideboard of a tent and two women standing in front of it. "If you wouldn't mind, Miss Armstrong, I'd like to hear about the old church camp days."

Miss Armstrong smiled as she stirred her tea aimlessly. "Call me Aunt Maude and my sister Aunt Stella. Everyone does." She took a deep breath before continuing. "Reverend Dayan started the camp meeting association in 1875, but we didn't begin attending until a few years later. They established Thousand Island Park— no *s* on *islands*—for spiritual and physical renewal. The Sabbath was strictly observed, and regular religious services throughout the week saw abundant attendance. It was a marvelous way to spend the summer, to be sure. We leased this plot in '80, and then we had a platform erected in … when was that, sister?"

Aunt Stella continued. "In '83, Maude, the same year they opened the Thousand Island Park Hotel."

Mary jumped into the conversation. "Before I was born? I hadn't realized. I only remember coming to this cottage as a little girl and enjoying every moment here. It was a highlight of my summer vacation, to be sure."

The frail-looking Aunt Maude reached over and patted her hand. "We had the cottage built the year you were born, in 1886. Your mama loved it here, and your kind father was so good to let the two of you stay with us so often while he worked. Your visits were the best part of our time here."

George turned to Mary. "Where are your parents now?"

Mary frowned, her gaze lowering to her plate. Several moments transpired before she raised her head and answered. "They died of the influenza epidemic two years ago, within three days of each other. I was away at nursing school and arrived too late to help."

When she looked up, her caramel-colored eyes brimmed with tears as the little golden flecks in them seemed to swim around. She took a sip of her tea and gave an almost imperceptible shrug. Just then, she looked like a helpless little child, her pain tangible. Her words tugged at his heart.

George leaned toward her and spoke gently. "I'm so sorry for your loss, lass."

Aunt Maude took Mary's hand and squeezed it. "Even if you were there, you couldn't have helped them, dearest."

Aunt Stella patted the table, making her silverware clang together. She pasted on a wide, lopsided grin before tossing her niece a scolding gaze. "Happy thoughts only, remember? As requested by our guest."

Mary blinked several times and sat up straight. "Right. Sorry." She shook her head as if to rid herself of the unpleasant conversation before a full-blown smile blossomed on her beautiful features. "Did you know the Park is putting new benches along the pavilion, lawn, and docks? And they're painting the playground. I overheard the mayor inform a board member just today."

"What other news do you have to spill? Tell all." Aunt Stella cackled, leaning in.

Mary gave her aunt a chiding glare. Her thick, curly hair reminded him of Alma's. "You know I only share common information and not the private conversations."

Aunt Stella hooked a thumb toward Mary. "As the switchboard operator, she's privy to lots of fine gossip that she refuses to share, even though I often hear news from my own grapevine even before she gets home from work. She also knows how to decipher the telegraph. Can you imagine?"

The pride in her voice was unmistakable.

"I know. A telegrapher is quite a skill." George chuckled. "My neighbor is one, too, and I still can't figure out how he hears all those subtle dots and dashes. They run together in a big muddled mess when I listen to them."

Mary's gentle laugh rang like church bells beckoning worshippers to church. "It's a learned art, I must confess, but I love the challenge of it."

"But you said you were away at nursing school." Mr. Richmond scowled. "How are you now in such a different position? A *man's* position?"

A little groan escaped Mary's lips. Then she rubbed her left earlobe. "I couldn't abide the blood. Made me queasy every time. No matter how hard I tried, I never found the fortitude to be a nurse. After Mother and Father went to heaven, I started working at Bell Telephone in Watertown. Then I taught myself telegraphy and took the night shift in the telegraph office." She shrugged. "It kept me busy."

Aunt Maude laughed like a little girl at a tea party. "Then, when the TI Park job came open last month, we talked her into joining us here."

George grinned at Mary. My, such a vision of loveliness and a woman of talent, skill, and integrity to boot. Perhaps providence was shining down on them. His thrumming heart tried to leap into his throat, but he swallowed it back down.

Aunt Stella interrupted his daydream. "Dessert? Berry pie or pound cake with strawberries? I made both."

Mr. Richmond finished his third helping of potatoes before setting down his fork. "I'll have a slice of both, please?"

Where did that beanpole put all that food? He'd eaten twice as much as any of them.

A flicker of irritation crossed Aunt Stella's face, but she recovered quickly. "Certainly, sir." She turned to him. "And you, Mr. Flannigan?"

"A small slice of pie, please?" He smiled. "May I help clear the table?"

Aunt Maude popped up from her seat like the teener. "Certainly not, George. We'll tend it. You relax. Mary, stay and entertain the gentlemen."

"Are you sure? You've been working on this meal all afternoon. I can clear while you rest." Mary frowned at her elderly aunt.

"No, siree. You young folk chat." Aunt Maude waved off her offer. "Come, Stella, and help with dessert."

She piled the plates and placed the utensils on top like an experienced waitress before quitting the room with Stella close behind carrying the bowls of potatoes and beans.

Mr. Richmond cleared his throat, pointing a boney finger at her. "You must speak sense into those old ladies, miss. They simply must have insurance for this cottage, or they'll lose it all. And you'll be out of a summer home too. It isn't wise to ignore the inevitable."

Mary's brows shot up. "The inevitable, sir?"

Heat rose from George's neck to his face, and a small groan escaped. "The dinner table is not the proper place to speak of such things, nor is it appropriate to pit Mary against her aunts. Patience, Mr. Richmond." Before the man had a chance to retort, George shifted in his seat to angle away from the insurance man and face

Mary. "I, too, have dual careers. When I'm not firefighting, I manage the porters and shoremen at the Clayton train station."

Mary furrowed her brows. "I've been on the Clayton train, but the station is a confusing mess from a passenger's perspective."

"It can be for me too." George admitted. "The porters unload the luggage, and the shoremen unload the cargo and heavier goods like ore, lumber, and such. It's quite an intricate dance, to be sure. Steamships from the Midwest bring thousands of tons of coal and unload at the Clayton docks to be shipped by rail inland to the big cities. Grain, salt, iron ore, lumber, and thousands of tons of products pass through the area all the time."

"Truly, I had no idea all that came through this little town. How fascinating." Mary blinked before pulling at her left earlobe. Why did she do that?

Mr. Richmond joined the conversation, his irksome air of superiority tainting his words. "They also harvest ice from the river and ship it by insulated railroad cars to New York City. The work gives many men employment in the winter when they would otherwise be idle."

George nodded, acknowledging the information Richmond offered. "And recently, a new market for the farmers has emerged. Railroad cars shipping baled hay. New York Central now has one hundred locomotives, ninety-eight passenger cars, thirty-five baggage cars, and over twenty-five hundred freight cars going through Clayton every year."

Mary's eyes grew wide. "Goodness. For such a small village? No wonder they need management. Good for you."

Aunt Maude returned carrying a tray with dessert for everyone. For such a frail looking woman, she appeared quite strong.

Aunt Stella motioned to the coffeepot she'd carried in. "Coffee, gentlemen?"

George nodded, while Mr. Richmond motioned to his cup. "Of course. Thank you."

"I'll serve. You've done enough, Auntie." Mary smiled as she hopped up and took the coffeepot.

She poured Mr. Richmond a cup and turned toward George, her citrusy perfume dancing around her. She graced him with a gentle smile as she filled his cup, and he smiled back. The depth of her seemed bottomless, undergirded by a pleasant warmth mixed with a spark of joy.

And practical, pragmatic, and, well, pretty near perfection.

Chapter 4

Mary pinched the bridge of her nose as she stood and stretched. If only they could make spectacles that didn't bite. Waiting for a call or for the telegraph to tap out a message, she slipped on her reading glasses, positioning them carefully.

The familiar creak of the oak flooring and a groan from her chair as she sat reminded her that she was exactly where she wanted to be. Home, in her tiny office, doing what she loved. Even during the quiet times, she relished the silence and opportunity to learn.

She drew her hand over the morse code manual and picked it up. On Mondays, Wednesdays, and Fridays, she reviewed it. Not that she needed to. She could tap out a message faster than a butterfly's flutter. She just wanted to be ready. Ever ready, even though the telegraph served its purpose less and less as the telephone began to take its place.

Almost all the businesses in Thousand Island Park now had a telephone, and more of the Park's residents were installing telephones every month. When they did, Mary often paid them a visit and showed them how to crank the handle on the side of the box to ring her. Then she explained how she, or the other switchboard operator, would answer and connect them. She loved helping others move into the twentieth century of such wonders.

When she wasn't answering calls or reviewing the telegraphy manual, a small pile of books waited to be read. She thumbed her way down the spines. Papa's *Scofield Reference Bible*, her greatest treasure and a costly volume he purchased just months before he died. *Lady Molly of Scotland Yard*, a collection of short stories about Molly Robertson-Kirk, a fictional female detective. *The Railway Children* by Edith Nesbit, a children's novel, but a story she enjoyed, nonetheless. How she loved to read books from female authors and support their efforts. Perhaps she might write something one day too.

The switchboard lit up. Mr. Johnson. His hand-decorated china was lovely and all the rage. She inserted the phone plug into the appropriate jack and answered. "Good morning, sir. To whom may I direct your call?"

Mr. Johnson's soft voice was barely audible. "Good day to you, Miss Flynn. And how is everything at the Columbian?"

Mary loved the chit-chat with her callers, but two more lights lit up, beckoning her to connect callers. "Fine. Whom do you want to speak to?"

Mr. Johnson understood. When she had other callers, Mary was short; otherwise, she'd chat for a few moments before transferring the call. Only Mrs. Semper found offense when she shortened the conversation. "The Pratt House. A guest's china is ready to pick up."

She smiled, her voice rising to the occasion. "And a treasure your china will be. Here you go."

Plug and done.

"Good morning, Mrs. Cupernall. To whom may I direct your call?"

The librarian chuckled. "To you, my dear. Your request for Edith Nesbit's *The Magic City* is in. You may pick it up anytime. This is the second book of hers you're reading, yes?"

"Thank you. Yes. Sorry, but I have another call. I'll pick it up this afternoon. Goodbye."

Disconnect. Plug.

"Good morning, Mr. Oyama. To whom may I direct your call?"

The Oriental Art Store owner's English was surprisingly good. "Hello. May I have the Wellesley Hotel, please?"

"Certainly, sir. Good day."

Plug and done.

Quiet.

Funny how calls seemed to come all at once. There were always six or seven telephones on one line, so Mary often caught some of the conversations by chance or sometimes by choosing. Many times, the talk was so boring she'd remove her headphones, especially if it was personal. But other times, she found the conversation rather tempting—and interesting.

But the telegraph? She hadn't heard a peep from it in three days.

Oh. Another call? "Good morning, Mrs. Olson. To whom may I direct your call?"

"Martha Hill, please."

"Here you go. Have a great day."

Plug and listen. The two women often had interesting things to talk about. They were always gossiping about local events.

The caller led the conversation. "Martha, did you hear about the Gardner fire?"

Mrs. Hill's voice rose. "The one before the dozen-boathouse fire? What about it?"

The pride in Mrs. Olson's voice was unmistakable. The woman loved being privy to information that others weren't. "My husband thinks it was arson. Says they found circumstantial evidence. I hope we don't have one of those crazy people around who set everything ablaze. Although my husband says they can't help themselves."

"Oh, I do hope not." Mrs. Hill's voice trembled. "I'm sorry, but I must tend to baby Fred."

"All right." Mrs. Olson sounded perturbed. "But keep your eyes peeled for mischief."

The woman hung up, and Mary pulled the plug.

Arson? Mary glanced at the calendar on the wall. The Gardner Boat Shop caught fire on May twenty-third, just a week and a half ago. Nine boathouses went up in flames that day. Then a week later, the dozen-boathouse fire where she'd met George? Could they be connected—by an arsonist?

Surely, this small, faith-filled community of Thousand Island Park wouldn't have such a villain in their number. They were on an island, albeit a large one, so why would anyone who relied on secrecy for their evil deeds come here? And who would want to burn another's property and cause harm to others?

But the truth shook her to her bones. Fires happened far too frequently these days.

Mr. Wiseman interrupted her worries with a knock on the open door. The elderly man's silvery hair and bright eyes were always a welcome sight, though his grizzled eyebrows told the tale of a once-dark-haired gentleman.

Mary stood, slipping off her headset. "Come in, Mr. Wiseman. How are you today?"

His cane clacked on the richly polished wood floor as he approached and gifted her with a kiss on her cheek. Then he sat and clasped his hands over his pudgy middle. "Fine. Just fine, my dear. Are you going to the dance tonight? Please say you are, for I want the first spot on your dance card."

"Of course. I'd be honored." Mary giggled. How would he dance with that cane?

"Good. I want to dance with the prettiest girl in the Park. More than likely, George and Mr. Richmond and a slew of beaus will clamor at your feet and fill your evening with dancing."

Mary chuckled. "Oh, go on with you. Don't you know that flattery can get you in trouble?"

"Not if it's true. You *are* the loveliest beauty in town, Mary." He paused, challenging her with a gentle glare to not give a negative retort. "Have you heard about the possible arsonist? It's an ill wind that blows no good. I pray it isn't true." He guffawed, interrupted by a choking cough.

Mary wrung her hands. So it wasn't idle gossip. "I will join you in that prayer."

Mr. Wiseman gazed at the ceiling as if to recall something. "In 1890, a fire burned several homes and the first hotel that sat on this spot. They believed it to be started by an arsonist they called 'the tramp,' but they never found or prosecuted him. That was twenty-two years ago, but it's still a fearsome thought that someone would do such a thing."

Mary agreed just as the telegraph came to life. She stuck her forefinger in the air to urge him to pause, grabbed her pencil and pad, and jotted down the correspondence as fast as it came. The telegrapher on the other end was speedy, so she struggled to keep up. When she finished, she set down her pencil and turned to Mr. Wiseman. "Sorry about that. I should have this delivered to Dr. Wilbor at once."

"I'll let the front desk know to send you an errand boy. Be about your work, my dear. See you at the dance tonight." The elderly man stood and adjusted his cane.

He tossed her a wink as he left the office.

Ah, the dance. Would Mr. Richmond be there? She hoped not.

Would George?

She hoped so.

~ ~ ~

George adjusted his taupe herringbone slacks and dark brown vest his mother had carefully refashioned from his father's old suit. She'd done a marvelous job creating perfectly fitted, pleated pants. Mother would do anything to help him find a wife, he suspected. He buttoned his vest and tied his tie before slipping on his coat. Then he thumbed the two-button peak lapels and added a clean handkerchief. Finally, he slipped on his brown derby hat.

There. Ready for the Columbian Hotel dance.

Not that he was looking for romance or to marry again. Or was he? Yes, he was lonely, and if he admitted it, weary of his mother's overbearing ways. She scolded him as if he were a child and treated Robbie as if she were his hired nanny, not a grandmother. That infuriated him the most. And her opinions made his blood boil.

But could there be any woman as wonderful as his Alma? She was soft and gentle, feminine and kind. She had a heart of gold that lit up his world and cared for their child with love and affection.

Who gave you Alma? Is His hand too short to give you another chance at love?

George sucked in a ragged breath as he realized He'd just heard God's still, small voice deep in his heart. He bowed his head. "Could it be, Lord? I am willing."

A gentle peace blew over him as Mary Flynn's face passed through his mind. He swallowed hard and shook himself from the moment. Would she be at the dance? Perhaps he could capture a spot on her dance card.

George slipped into his son's room to find him already asleep. He bent down, brushed the boy's hair from his forehead, and planted a gentle kiss on it, as he so often did. As he closed the door, his mother appeared in the hallway, silent as a wraith as always, and eyed him up and down.

"You look handsome tonight, son. Beware of the vixens. You need a new mother for your child, not a wanton woman." She folded her arms over her ample bosom. "I'm getting too old to chase your rascal."

He exhaled. "I'm just going to visit friends, not find a wife. I'm not ready to entertain such thoughts yet."

Mother harrumphed. "You'd better, dear boy. I may not be on this earth much longer."

George waved a hand. "You're fit as a fiddle. I've got to go if I'm to catch the ferry. Don't wait up for me."

She shrugged. "All right, but if you find me dead in my bed, don't be surprised."

Reluctantly, he kissed her wrinkled cheek and hurried out the door before she could moan and groan and guilt him any longer.

When would she be free of her negativity?

~ ~ ~

George spotted Mary Flynn across the Columbine Hotel ball-room, even more stunning than she'd been before. She wore a soft pink cotton lawn dress with Irish lace trimming the collar, over-dress, and hem. He chuckled as she ran a hand over the wide, open collar and adjusted her three-quarter-length, pleated sleeves. Then she smoothed her fitted waist before pinching her cheeks to bring out the color. Apparently, she was just as nervous as he.

Why, he felt like a schoolboy at his first dance, not a strapping fireman who'd been married before. A twinge of sorrow flitted around him, pleading for him to follow like a moth to a flame. He had to turn his thoughts to the here and now. Somehow.

Mary.

He started her way, but Archibald Richmond stepped in front of him, took her hand, and led her onto the dance floor. Her lips pursed and brow furrowed, and with her free hand, she rubbed her earlobe and stood on the dance floor like a forlorn child. Suddenly, Richmond grabbed her waist rather roughly and twirled her around the room in perfect time to the music, his expression like a hungry scoundrel. As the music slowed, he bent and whispered something in Mary's ear. But instead of smiling, Mary dropped her hand, dis-engaged from him, and retreated to the bank of chairs where the maidens sat.

What had that uncouth insurance man said to make her so upset? Richmond also retreated, but to the smoking porch, a smirk wide on his face. He might be the son of a successful but now-deceased insurance man, but he'd not find fame and fortune with such a prickly personality.

George huffed his frustration. Should he go over and smooth her ruffled feathers or leave her to cool down? He didn't know her well enough to discern, so he waited and watched while she chatted with a tall blonde several years younger than she.

When a smile crossed Mary's lips, he decided to risk talking to her. He approached, and his right hand slid inside his jacket. "Good evening, Miss Flynn. And how are you tonight?" He bowed and smiled at her companion. "And who is your companion?"

Mary stood, a smile crossing her pretty lips. She waved toward the blonde. "May I present Miss Charlotte Mullins, the evening switchboard operator, and my friend." Then she nodded his way. "This is Mr. George Flannigan, Clayton fireman and manager at the railroad depot."

Charlotte stood and curtsied, bowing her head as a blush turned her young face crimson. "Pleased to meet you. If you'll excuse me, I'm going to get a glass of punch. Would you like some, Mary?"

"Please." She nodded, a sweet smile rising up to her warm, caramel eyes.

Charlotte turned to him. "Sir?"

"No, thank you."

After Charlotte departed, Mary blinked as she looked up at him. He towered over her tiny frame, but she didn't seem to mind. "Charlotte is quite shy until you get her behind the switchboard. Then she'll talk a hind leg off a stallion if she has the chance."

He chuckled. "She seems nice. She works at night?"

"Yes. Her father is the hotel's night manager, so he's nearby. They live in the hotel, just doors down from the office that closes at ten. So, it's perfect for her, and she loves it. I've been training her, and she's catching on quickly."

George smiled. "That's providential. May I ask if your dance card has a spot for me?"

"Actually, my card is open the rest of the evening. Mr. Wiseman had the first dance, and Mr. Rich … well, another gentleman took a spot, but the rest is open." Mary grinned wide, her eyes dancing.

George's heart sped up to a happy trot. "Very good. May I have the next waltz, please?"

"You may." She nodded, dipping a slight curtsy.

Charlotte returned with two cups of punch, and they chatted until the orchestra began to play, "The Blue Danube." George took Mary's hand gently and led her onto the dance floor as his nerves exploded into a frenzy of pleasant jitters. When her heady perfume almost made him dizzy, he placed his hand on her tiny waist, reckoning it couldn't be wider than both of his hands from fingertips to fingertips.

His eyes slid up to hers as he counted off the rhythm and started to twirl. The moment was … magic.

And time stood still.

~ ~ ~

Mary rested her hand in the crook of George's arm as he walked her home. They'd danced and talked almost the entire evening, and he'd insisted he escort her back to her aunts' cottage. Her heart had skipped several beats, and her cheeks had warmed at his valiant concern for her welfare.

An owl blinked from its perch on a large nearby oak, its head turning to keep watch over them as they passed. George placed his free hand protectively over hers as it rested on his arm, and a strange flutter tickled her stomach just as it had the first time she'd picked up a telephone and answered it.

"Will you return to your home in Watertown once the summer is over?"

She shrugged, her angst bleeding through her words. "I live with my aunts here and in Watertown. I had to give up our family home when Papa passed."

Dark blue flecks in George's light blue eyes shimmered in the light of the full moon, and tiny black dots of stubble darkened his jawline. Concern speckled his gaze as a small frown turned down his lips.

"As my father would say, I'm in God's good graces. When the time comes, I'll see what doors the Lord opens for me."

George smiled. "I like that. Listening to God's leading is the best way to live, I believe."

She gave his rock-solid arm a little squeeze. She had relished the feel of his strength while they'd danced and even more now as they strolled along the dark evening streets. But she longed to learn more of him, not just talk about herself. She wanted to ask about his deceased wife but thought the better of it.

"Tell me about your son. He sounds delightful."

George chuckled, deep and warm. "He's a charmer, that one. He already knows how to read and write and do arithmetic."

When speaking of his son, his words were as gentle as the soft velvet on a puppy's nose, causing warmth to travel from her neck to her scalp. George reminded her of her precious father, a kind and loving man she'd had the blessing to call Papa for twenty-five years.

"You must be very proud." Even as she spoke, her voice betrayed her melancholy over missing her father.

"Yes. Well, Robbie can also be a mischievous little boy too. Are you all right? You sound sad."

His musky scent tickled her nose as it had when they'd waltzed. Was it pomade, shaving cream, or cologne? No matter. She took another whiff and smiled. His manliness warmed her to her toes.

She shrugged. "I suppose I'll never stop missing my parents, is all."

"Nor should you. You should always cherish memories of loved ones." He patted her hand gently.

He seemed unaware that her heart pounded in her chest and her breath came out in little puffs. Aye, the man could take a lass's breath right out of her lungs.

But what if he didn't feel the same way?

She had to guard her heart.

Chapter 5

Mary handed Charlotte the Signal Corps Association Telegraph Manual before turning the switchboard over to her friend. "You're doing a fine job with the telephone switchboard. Now, I think it's time you learn the telegraph. In your free moments, I suggest you read through the manual, and then we'll work on your skills together. You can skip the first two chapters of introduction and history and start at chapter three."

Charlotte sighed as an uncertain frown crossed her full lips and smooth forehead. She was a pretty girl, just as she was sweet and kind. Her dark brown brows and deep-set coffee-colored eyes contrasted with hair the color of ripened wheat. Charlotte was surprisingly timid and naïve—and rather underdeveloped—for an eighteen-year-old girl living in a hotel. Indeed, she reminded Mary of a young teener. Had she remained cloistered in her room all her life?

Judge not lest you be judged.

Charlotte cut into her thoughts, pushing the manual back toward Mary. "I'm still unsure of myself when I answer the telephone. My voice quivers uncontrollably, and sometimes I'm not sure what to say. I don't think I'm quite ready for the telegraph. Another week, perhaps?"

Mary shrugged. Charlotte had been avoiding the telegraph like it was an alligator ready to snap. "All right, but try this to calm your nerves. When you look at the switchboard, imagine what's beyond each glowing light, and envision who needs you. Glad news. Sad news. People who need our help to secure information or share their lives. Business. Family. Life. Loss. It's all there in the telephone switchboard." She waited for a response or something to indicate the young woman understood. When she received none, she tried again. "We are the gatekeepers of important communications, Charlotte, and we should never take that for granted. But we also shouldn't fear it."

Had the girl swallowed her tongue?

Mary tapped a toe. "I've not worked here very long, but I've heard news of everything from war to peace, a new baby to the passing of a loved one. And you will too. Think of the telegraph as the voice of our community, Charlotte, only it communicates with sound instead of lights and voices."

Her passion for her job infused her with fresh energy, and she waved her arms, pointing to the lights and then the headset. "With the switchboard, we have to keep our voice regulated and not reveal any emotion. With the telegraph, we have to keep wits about us so we can decipher the message properly. To be a good telephone switchboard operator, we provide speedy, courteous, accurate service, and it's the same with the telegraph. If you can learn one, you can learn the other. Understand?"

Charlotte stood there with a blank look on her face for what seemed like hours. Bright sunlight filtered through the open window along with the gentle river breeze and the smell of the pines. Mary ached to be on her way to spend time in the fresh air and sunshine. But this poor, insecure girl needed patience.

Finally, Charlotte nodded. "I'll try to imagine it, and perhaps it will help. Thank you."

"Good. I'll leave you to it, then. Oh, and Mr. Richmond called to inform us he's expecting an important call from New York City. Be sure to transfer it to him quickly if it comes in."

Charlotte scrunched up her nose. "I don't like the man. When we danced the other night, he held me so tightly, I thought he might break my ribs, and he thrust me around the dance floor as though he was tossing a bale of hay."

Mary giggled at the image. "I had a similar experience, but we can only hope that what he lacks in social skills, he makes up with business acumen. He seems intent on insuring every cottage and business on the island since his father passed and left him his business last winter. But he didn't sign my aunts. They refused his services after he performed rather poorly at dinner last week."

Charlotte grinned. "Wasn't Fireman Flannigan at that dinner? He seemed quite taken with you at the dance. His face fairly glowed when he waltzed with you."

"Stuff and nonsense. He was just being polite. He's a widower with a small son. I'm sure romance isn't on his mind with all that he has going on."

Charlotte glanced at the open office door, then took a step closer to Mary as if she had a secret to tell. "Did you know the TI Park Association summoned Mr. Flannigan to create a plan for fire mitigation? Papa told me at dinner last night. He said Mr. Flannigan will be on the island daily to make assessments, and then he will draw up a plan of action, including developing and training a volunteer firefighting team."

Mary's heart took flight, beating like the wings of a humming-bird. Here every day? Oh, may it be true! She quickly took control of her excitement, tamping it down as though she was dousing a fire. She willed her voice to be steady. "That's a wise decision by our leaders."

"And you're not a bit excited? Come now. I also saw your blissful expression when you danced in his arms." Charlotte shook her head, folding her arms over her small bosom.

Mary blinked. Had she failed to hide her feelings that much? Heat rose from her chest to her neck to her cheeks, and she blew out a steadying breath. "Your schoolgirl imagination is running amuck, my friend. I was merely enjoying a good waltz."

Charlotte pursed her lips before shrugging and taking the switchboard seat. "If you say so. I'll read through the manual when I have time, but I don't think it'll do much good. Enjoy your evening, Mary."

"Thanks. You too. And don't forget about that important call for Mr. Richmond." Mary stepped toward the door and waved goodbye.

As Mary exited the hotel, her steps faltered. Mr. Wiseman and George sat on the veranda, engaged in a lively game of chess. The off-duty fireman let out a cheerful whistle, dangling a black chess piece in the air. "Got your knight, my friend. Your turn."

Mary swiped at a few wisps of hair that blew free in the breeze. She straightened her skirts and approached the chess players. "Are you being ungentlemanly, George?"

Her teasing tone stopped both men from concentrating on the game.

"May it never be, especially with an elder statesman like Mr. Wiseman." George stood and bowed to her.

He turned and winked at the old man, who struggled to stand, leaning back and forth as though gaining momentum was the solution.

"Don't get up for me. Please." Mary stopped him with a wave of her hands. "May I join you for a few moments? This late-afternoon sunshine is glorious, and the river breeze is heavenly."

Mr. Wiseman motioned toward an empty wicker settee. "Aye, please grace us with your presence. A little feminine loveliness is just what this old man needs to regain my composure and beat this lad."

She gave George a quick, nervous glance as she took her seat. "I hear you'll be working with the Park association on fire mitigation this summer, George. I'm glad. Fire has been a worry here for far too long. I hope you'll find lots of volunteers."

"Indeed." Mr. Wiseman moved his rook. "I was here when the Thousand Island Park Hotel burned to the ground back in '90. It took less than an hour for the fire to destroy the entire building. Bucket brigades drew water from the river and kept the fire from spreading. But before they finally got it under control, thirteen buildings went up in flames, and one man died."

His opponent groaned. "It happens far too often on these islands, I'm afraid. The Thousand Island Park simply must be prepared if another disaster strikes."

Mary shivered at the thought of the Columbian Hotel burning. Such a magnificent hotel with its elegant furnishings, gilt mirrors, and costly paintings gracing the walls, and all the well-to-do guests. She barely whispered, "May it never be."

"Checkmate."

Mr. Flannigan knocked down Mr. Wiseman's king and sat back in his chair. Instead of emanating victory, his handsome face shone with what Mary could only call an apology. He shrugged, then cleared his throat before confirming her suspicions. "Sorry, friend. You'll beat me next time, I'm sure."

"Good game, chap." Mr. Wiseman waved off his friend's angst. "You're a worthy competitor." Then he faced her. "And you, my dear Mary. How was your day?"

"Rather quiet. Just a few phone calls and no telegrams. I haven't heard a dot or a dash in days."

Mr. Wiseman reached over and patted her hand. "Your alliteration is refreshing, my dear."

Mary glanced at the low-hanging sun. "If you'll excuse me, I'd better get to the library before it closes. As quiet as it is, I need a new book to read."

Mr. Flannigan stood. "I'll join you, if you don't mind. I wanted to see what's new as well."

"Certainly, sir." Her pulse quickened. Goodness, he likes books, too? "Nice to see you, Mr. Wiseman. I hope you have a lovely evening."

"You two young people enjoy your evening too." Mr. Wiseman grinned.

Before she could protest that this was merely a neighborly stroll to the library, Mr. Flannigan offered Mary his elbow. She hesitated a moment, then she took it, descending the wide staircase to the walkway below. The library was less than a block away, so they strolled unhurriedly.

The breeze carried the pungent but pleasant scent of the river. What a lovely evening and even better company. As they turned onto the library boardwalk, she risked a quick peek at the handsome fireman. "So … you like to read?"

He squeezed the crook of his arm, pinning her hand to his strong chest. "Insatiably. Since I was a tyke. And my son is just like me. I can't find enough books to fill his curious little mind."

"That's wonderful. Children who are taught to enjoy reading are blessed. They learn so much, and their world becomes their oyster. As Benjamin Franklin put it, 'the person who deserves most pity is a lonesome one on a rainy day who doesn't know how to read.'"

"Well put, on both accounts. You're well versed, milady."

Handsome, Irish, and well read? Her heart did a little flip flop. So did her belly. Mary let out a tiny sigh as they ascended the library steps. But on the second step, her boot caught on the hem of her dress. She stumbled, losing her grip on his arm. Thankfully, George caught her, and his granite grasp took her breath away, his arms like marble under her hands, yet his eyes filled with compassion, as soft as a fawn's.

She quickly recovered, straightening her skirts and pretending to have the entire matter well in hand. But the reality of her feelings for him mocked her. Inside, she quivered in her boots.

His masculinity jostled her insides.

And her heart.

~ ~ ~

George said nothing about Mary's kerfuffle as he held the library door open to allow her to enter first. No need to embarrass her more than she already was. Her rosy cheeks betrayed her angst even as she acted as if nothing had happened.

Inside, he looked around at the ceiling-to-floor shelves of books. The TI Park library was small, but the vast array of books intrigued him. Philosophy. Religion. Science. Art. History. Fiction. Even a children's section. Mr. Wiseman had said that the wealthy patrons often leave most of their books when their summer retreat ended.

Mary ran her hands along a shelf of books, her smile so wide he couldn't help but smile with her. She opened her reticule and retrieved a pair of spectacles, wrapping the wires behind her ears and perching the eyepieces on the bridge of her nose. So, if the glasses were any indication, she didn't just like books—she loved them. He'd met few women who did.

His heart swelled to observe her joy. "I see they use the Dewey Decimal System. I'm glad you like books. Gives us something in common. With the many hours in between firefighting, not to mention the long winters here in the North Country, there's nothing better than indulging in a good story or an informational tome."

She giggled. "I have plenty of time between calls and wires as well. But I've loved reading since I was in pigtails. We lived on a farm, and I had my very own reading tree where I'd get away from everything and explore unknown places and people in the stories. But there was little to read where I grew up. By the age of ten, I'd devoured every book in our tiny one-room schoolhouse, and I begged and borrowed every book from anyone who had something for me to read. For the next few years, I was pretty frustrated reading the same books over and over again."

"Didn't you visit your library?"

"There wasn't one, even though Watertown had over twenty-two thousand souls. It was infuriating that the tiny villages of Alexandria Bay, Theresa, and Adams all had libraries, but we didn't."

"That's baffling. Clayton has one too. My mother was the librarian. I wonder why such a grand city lacked such a basic provision." He waved an arm wide. "Even Thousand Island Park has this."

Her eyes narrowed and grew stormy. "I know. I was fourteen when Watertown finally started a library fundraiser after asking for, but never receiving, funds from Andrew Carnegie's library endowments."

"Too bad Carnegie didn't help. I've read he's been building public libraries across the entire nation at an unprecedented rate."

A quick shake of her head countered his words. "The city petitioned him but never got a penny, so the city council finally decided to fund it on their own. The money came in a little at a time, a few dollars here and there. I even saved twelve cents from my egg money and gave it, though I was tempted to spend it on a dime novel."

George touched her forearm, patting it gently. "That was kind of you. And quite generous for a girl of fourteen."

She glanced at his hand and smiled. As if she welcomed his touch. So he held it there a little longer. "Thank you. I wanted to do my bit." She glanced at the ceiling to remember the details. "The *Watertown Daily Times* began publishing every donation to help raise the eleven thousand dollars needed to purchase the Emerson house on Washington Street, where they planned to put the library."

He chuckled motioning in the air as if reading a newsprint. "Hmm … I can see it now. *Miss Mary Flynn of the Flynn Farm donated twelve cents toward the library building fund.*"

Miss Mary pursed her lips in mock offense before giggling. "I gave it before the paper started publishing the donations."

"Pity. I'd liked to have seen your name in print." George scrunched up his face.

A half shrug brushed aside his fun at her expense. "Well, everything changed on April fifth, 1901. Mrs. Emma Flower Taylor gave sixty thousand dollars in memory of her father to the city to purchase the site, erect the building, and buy books."

"Goodness. That's a fortune." George blinked as his jaw dropped. He snapped it shut.

"She was blessed with a large inheritance. When I told my mother about it, I remember dancing a jig in the kitchen until Mama groaned, handed me a potato, and set me to peeling. It's funny how vivid some memories are. I imagined each piece of potato I chopped was a book I'd read. So I cut those poor potatoes into such tiny pieces that Mama mashed them instead of making what she had planned."

"That's funny." George guffawed until the librarian shushed him.

Mary scanned the books and pulled one from the shelf. But instead of turning her attention to it, she continued. "When the city accepted her offer, I was fifteen. It was a cold, rainy day, but I walked a mile and a half to be there at the ceremony. I stood in the back of the City Opera House and listened to the speeches and gazed at the generous woman who would make my—and thousands of other readers'—dreams come true. A few months later, she gave an extra fifteen thousand to purchase an adjacent lot and make an even grander library, and then a few days later, she gave another two hundred thousand to make it even more extravagant. Can you imagine?"

George's mind flooded with memories. He put his forefinger in the air. "I do remember reading about that. I'd forgotten."

"Do you remember that there was a competition for architects?" He didn't and shook his head.

Mary squared her shoulders, pride beaming from her sparkling eyes. "My father's employer, Mr. John Solar, got the job. As a carpenter, Papa worked day and night for a little over a year, telling us about the Greek style and the white Gouverneur marble, the large reading room with a fireplace and the children's room, the assembly rooms, and more. He described all eight thousand square feet of heaven until I could barely stand it." She hugged the book and closed her eyes, reminding him of an angelic child holding a teddy bear. "When it opened, I was transfixed."

Dare he ask? "Is that how you came to wear spectacles? Reading all the time?"

"No. I had scarlet fever when I was five. The fever damaged my eyes."

George nodded. "I had the fever too. It took my baby sister."

"I'm so sorry. We were at my relatives' in Cape Vincent when I got sick. My mother and my oldest brother fell ill also. But my youngest brother, Eddie, was fine. He was only two and wanted Mama, but the aunts and uncle didn't want him to get sick. So, my uncle put a pan in the doorjamb that held a disgusting, writhing eel to keep Eddie from entering the room. It worked, but oh, how he howled for Mama, and I had nightmares about that eel for months."

"Ugh." With a shudder, George pulled *White Fang* off the shelf and tapped its cover. "Have you read it?"

"No. My brothers loved it, but the Yukon Territory and Gold Rush and wild dogs and all that didn't suit me much." She paused and slid *Anne of Avonlea* from the shelf. "Have you read this and Lucy Maud Montgomery's other novel?"

He grinned. "Touché."

She showed him the book she also held. "This is my pick. *Women's Suffrage in Many Lands* by Alice Zimmern. This has contributed to the debate on the education and rights of women. I think I shall tackle its contents next."

"You're quite the unique woman, Mary. I've never met one so well read and informed." He paused for just a moment. "And you look beautiful in spectacles."

She grinned, a pink flush coloring her cheeks. "Nor have I met a man quite like you."

<h1 style="text-align:center">Chapter 6</h1>

Mary crossed the hotel lobby through the parlor on her way to her office. The richly carpeted common areas silenced the foot traffic. The plump chairs and overstuffed sofas welcomed lingerers, especially during afternoon teatime. But it was too early for that, so only a few guests sat reading the paper or chatting with one another. Several others meandered about the hotel, most likely on their way to breakfast.

Gilt-framed paintings and grainy photographs of the river lined the main lobby, sitting areas, and hallways. As she stopped and glanced at a photograph of the newly built hotel, she recalled the conversation of a few days ago and shuddered. The thought of this beautiful place burning made the oatmeal in her stomach turn into a hard lump.

No! George would make a plan so that would never happen. Thank heavens the association leaders hired such a wise and capable fireman to solve this dilemma.

When she entered her office, a light already blinked on the switchboard. The clock on the wall indicated it was only seven forty-five. Callers knew she didn't open until eight. With a huff, she inserted the phone plug into the jack and answered, pasting on a smile. That always made her sound more pleasant than she felt. "Good morning, Captain Brown. To whom may I direct your call?"

The captain's voice croaked. "Do you see the smoke? Has someone called in the fire?"

Mary's pulse skipped several beats and took off running, alarm surging through her veins. Not another fire. "What fire? I didn't detect it coming in to work."

"It's Harry Arthur's home next to my Arlington. Please call for help. I fear it may spread to mine—and others."

A large lump tried to constrict Mary's throat, but she swallowed it back as she hurriedly disconnected Captain Brown and called the Clayton fire line. It rang repeatedly, and no one picked up. She hung up and called Alexandria Bay.

"Hello?" The man on the other end wheezed, as if he was of an advanced age. "Sam Timberlane here."

Mary cleared her throat and gathered her nerves so she would sound professional—and calm. Her words clipped out in a staccato rhythm. "We have a fire on the north half of lot 213 in Thousand Island Park. Please send the fire scow, men, and equipment as quickly as possible."

Mr. Timberlane's voice rose an octave. "Goodness gracious. Immediately, miss. I'll send my grandson to sound the alarm."

"Thank you, sir. And please pray." Mary sucked in a deep breath.

"Will do, miss. Goodbye. Sammie, send for the firemen—" He hollered to the boy even before disconnecting.

Mary bowed her head and prayed for safety and help. Before she'd finished, Charlotte came running into the office. "Have you heard? There's another fire over at the Arthurs'. Fireman Flannigan is here, but there are few volunteers this early."

"Just called for the Bay to help."

Charlotte plunked down in the nearby chair. She scrubbed her face with her hands, sending wisps of hair around her hairline flying out of her chignon to stand straight up. It gave her a rather comical appearance, enough to calm Mary's nerves.

"There are too many fires this season. They give me nightmares. I dream I'll burn in my bed. Oh, Mary, what shall we do?" Charlotte shook her head, tears welling in her eyes.

Mary took Charlotte's hands and held them tight. She needed to be strong and reassuring for her more fragile friend. But before she could console her, another light signaled a call.

She put a finger in the air to beg Charlotte's patience, turned to the switchboard, inserted the plug into the appropriate jack, and answered. "Good morning, Mr. Green. To whom may I direct your call?"

Mr. Green almost shouted in her ear. "The Arthurs' cottage is in flames, and the Arlington has caught fire. A bucket brigade is working on it, but the wind is gusting something fierce. Call for help, please."

Mary sat straight up. *Be professional. Don't let him know your insides are kicking up a storm.* "Alex Bay is on the way. They should be there soon."

Mr. Green continued to shout. "*Soon* may be too late. Eight years ago, I lost my cottage to fire, and I don't think I could bear it if it burns again. If the wind changes direction, it's doomed."

Mary's voice cracked before she could will it to steady. "I'll pray it won't, sir. They should be there soon. Goodbye."

Disconnect. Another light blinked for attention. *Please, let it not be another cottage owner, distraught and in danger.* Plug.

Mary smiled, though she'd rather sigh. "Good morning, Mrs. Evans. To whom may I direct your call?"

The woman whimpered like a small, helpless child. "We just got here from Utica late Monday evening and spent the night at the Arlington. Now it's on fire. I fear our Pansy cottage may be next. Please call for help."

"Help is on the way. Take heart, Mrs. Evans. The Bay is sending its new fire boat to help." Mary ached for the woman.

"Take heart?" Mrs. Evans bordered on hysterical, heaving words in between sobs. "I spent all day yesterday preparing to open the cottage. Worked my fingers to the bone along with the rest of my family. The linens are still piled on the dining room table. The silver is out on the table too. And my mother's fine china. All of our clothes are tucked away in the dressers and closets. What if it burns? What if I lose my mother's things? The wind … it's gusting something terrible."

Mrs. Evans let out a moan so pathetically troubled that Mary feared she'd join her.

Instead, she rallied her composure. "Let's pray the wind will settle and the firefighters can beat back the flames."

"I hope so. Goodbye." Mrs. Evans huffed as she slammed down the telephone receiver.

After Mary hung up and informed Charlotte what was happening, they prayed together for protection.

When Mary opened her eyes, another light flashed on the switchboard. "I think this is going to be a long, hard day."

Charlotte agreed, a frown casting a pall over her countenance. "I'll leave you to it, then. See you at five."

"Good morning, Mrs. Brooks. To whom may I direct your call?" Mary waved her off as she plugged the blinking jack.

"It's spreading ..." Mrs. Brooks muddled her words, making her message rather confusing. "Fire out of control ... the whole Park ... please help."

Mary summoned her strongest voice. "Steady, Mrs. Brooks. Alexandria Bay is on the way with its fire scow, firemen, and equipment. They'll get things contained soon. Be brave and pray."

"Pray?" Mrs. Brooks turned irate. "What good will prayer do now? This entire Park may burn to the ground. Where is God these days? I don't see Him around here anywhere. We should never have relaxed our rules and let the secular riffraff into our community. God is judging us and finding us wanting. It's His retribution, I'm certain."

"I must go, but I will pray for relief. Goodbye." Indignant, Mary wanted to be done with the woman.

Disconnect. Breathe.

Mary shook the woman's acrid words from her mind. Mary had heard all that doomsday, hellfire-and-brimstone chatter from a few old biddies for as long as she'd been at the Park. Mrs. Brooks and her kind seemed to only see God as a tyrant, not a gracious, loving Father. A small group of locals believed that the Association brought judgment upon them when they sold property to people not connected to the Methodist Church. Some thought it sacrilege, and despite the presence of the newcomers, many of the original rules remained intact. For example, the committee prohibited boating and swimming during church services, and on Sundays, boats still couldn't dock at the Park unless their owners were coming to church.

So what was all the fuss about? The Park was still a clean and moral place where families could enjoy a wholesome summer together, strengthen their faith, and enjoy the beauty of the Thousand

Islands and the St. Lawrence River. Religious gatherings continued to be a weekly event, and wholesome entertainment was often on the schedule. Children ran free in a safe and caring environment. Neighbors watched out for one another and made lifelong friendships.

Mary sighed, reflecting on the panic she'd heard in her callers. Had she kept her professional demeanor through it all? Rather well, she believed. She'd stayed strong and calm. But suddenly, her thoughts turned to her aunts. What if the fire spread and their cottage burned?

She rang their line, and Aunt Stella answered. "Stella Everson here."

"Aunt Stella, are you all right? Any smoke coming your way?" Mary had hoped for Aunt Maude's soothing voice. Her calming influence.

Aunt Stella shrieked. "What are you talking about, child? What smoke?"

Her aunties hadn't heard? Aunt Stella must still be in her nightgown, else she'd be on the porch and already well informed. Mary filled her in. "Please be safe. The wind gusts are dangerously strong."

"We will. The Arlington is blocks away, but I'll get dressed and stay abreast of the news. God bless you, Niece."

"Thanks, Auntie. Goodbye." Mary smiled as she disconnected the call. For all her salt and vinegar, her aunt loved her.

Aunt Stella would stay up-to-date, all right.

Or perish trying.

~ ~ ~

George swiped the sweat from his brow for the hundredth time. He'd worked on the fires for quite a while before the scow arrived. Alex Bay joined them just in time, helping to save many other homes.

Even so, four cottages had burned, including Pansy Cottage and the Arlington. Just like the five cottages that had burned on Grenell Island in early May. Just like so many other fires that destroyed homes and changed the lives of those who owned them. Firefighters saved almost nothing from any of these structures, and the cost would likely exceed twenty thousand dollars or more. So much loss in just an hour's time.

And no one knew how it started.

The fire underscored the association's decision to have him draw up plans for better fire safety, but it was too late for these poor folks. In two weeks, he'd report his assessment to the Park Progressive Club, so he had much to do between now and then.

A tap on his arm pulled him from his thoughts. Mr. Abernathy. "How about a bath and some breakfast, son? Since the fire started, the missus has been cooking up a storm. She always cooks when she's nervous." The man patted his fat belly and chuckled low. "And she's been nervous a lot lately."

"I'd be much obliged, sir. Both would be welcome."

The Alex Bay fire captain, Tom, slapped him on the shoulder. "Go ahead, George. I've got this. I'll watch for hot spots until you return."

George grabbed his satchel that he had earlier tucked under a tree. Ever since that first fire, he carried a change of clothing, and today, he was glad he did. The rubber fire coat kept him safe but also acted like a steam room, holding in the heat and wetting him from the skin out. He followed Mr. Abernathy to his home a few blocks away, bathed, and changed into clean clothes.

He shoved his sweaty clothing into the satchel and entered the Abernathy kitchen to a potpourri of wonderfully enticing smells. "Am I in heaven? Sure smells like it."

Just then, his stomach rumbled so loud, his hosts chuckled while heat rushed up his neck as though he'd stuck his head in a furnace.

"You'd better sit down and fill that belly. Have a seat, son." Mrs. Abernathy cackled.

George sat, and the plump woman filled his cup with strong coffee. After Mr. Abernathy prayed, they all partook of pancakes, sausage, eggs, fried potatoes, and warm blueberry muffins.

Mr. Abernathy poked his fourth sausage link before addressing George. "I'm glad you're here to help us with this fire problem. It's plagued us since the start, and if we don't get a handle on it, it'll be the demise of Thousand Island Park."

Mrs. Abernathy *tsk*ed. "God's trying to get our attention. The Park should have kept its original purpose."

"Let's not start that again. God doesn't bring destruction." Mr. Abernathy set down his fork and glared at his wife. "We live in a fallen world, and things like this just happen. It's dry. Hasn't rained in weeks. And it's hot. A perfect storm for fire."

"Yes, but—" Mrs. Abernathy shook her fork.

Mr. Abernathy stopped her with a raised palm. "Enough. We'll not discuss your views on God's wrath at the breakfast table." That ended, he turned to George. "So how shall we prevent fires in the future, sir?"

George set down his fork and patted his lips. "Well, currently, Thousand Island Park only has two small chemical engines and a few extension ladders, not enough to fight a large fire. There are thirty-five hydrants around the Park, but with the pipes a mere two inches in diameter, the water pressure is barely enough at the best of times. There are fire extinguishers in the hotels and businesses, and most of the cottages have firebombs, but they are only for small blazes like cook fires and the like."

"Been meaning to get one or two." Mrs. Abernathy turned to him, her eyebrows raised. "Could you please help me understand these firebombs? My neighbors have them in their cottages, but they're a mystery to me."

"Certainly. The fire extinguisher bombs are glass bulbs filled with a special liquid. As you know, they are shaped a little like an incandescent lightbulb and stored on metal brackets on the wall. If there is a fire, you simply take it out of the holder and throw it at the fire. The fire will either be put out, or it will help to manage the fire until you escape the flames."

Mr. Abernathy set down his coffee cup. "I hear they're quickly going out of service because they don't really do much, so I've procrastinated. Do you think we should invest in them?"

Took another bite before answering. "Either a bomb or two or an extinguisher, yes. You could even bring them with you when you go back to your home and return with them each summer. They're a wise investment, if you ask me."

Mrs. Abernathy grinned. "See, Theodore? I told you. If you had the brains of a chicken, we'd already have them in our cottage and at home."

The crestfallen man before him ducked his chin. What a terrible thing for a woman to say to her husband. Particularly in front of a guest. No wonder he was overweight and unsure of himself.

George cleared his throat. "Thank you for the bath and the delicious meal. That should take me through to tomorrow. I'd best be back to work and let the Alex Bay crew return home."

"Would you be so kind as to take Mr. Wiseman a plate?" Mrs. Abernathy stood, waving a hand at the table of food. "He loves my cooking, and with his wife gone, a home-cooked meal is always a treat."

"Be glad to, ma'am. Mind if I leave my satchel on your porch until I'm done for the day?"

Mr. Abernathy waved a hand toward the porch. "Not at all."

Before long, the missus had filled a plate full of food. She covered it with a linen napkin and handed it to him. "Thanks for delivering this. Now, husband, how about we take a trip to the Bay and buy some of those bombs or an extinguisher? The store here is out of stock."

George excused himself and hurried out of the cottage before he was privy to any more of the woman's unkind words. When he got to the hotel, Mary was sitting with Mr. Wiseman.

How providential. She'd surely never speak so disrespectfully to a man.

As he climbed the steps, Mr. Wiseman waved a welcome. Mary turned toward him, and her face lit up like a full moon, soft and lovely. But why was she not at the switchboard?

"Not working today?" He nodded a greeting to Mr. Wiseman and sat next to Mary.

Mary shrugged. "Charlotte stopped by and is covering for me while I get some fresh air. It's been a busy morning with all the fire calls."

"It was a terrible fire, to be sure." His pulse quickened at the chance to see her, then he set the plate on the table next to his old friend and pulled off the cover. "The Abernathys sent this over, but I'd wager the both of you couldn't finish this bounty."

"This is one meal? The three of us couldn't finish a plate so full." Mary blinked, and her perfect little brows rose.

Mr. Wiseman rubbed his belly. "Agreed. She always sends enough for a week of meals. Can I share this with you two? Stay awhile, son, and tell us about the fire."

"Sorry, but I've already feasted on her bounty. Besides, I must relieve the Bay crew. I've been gone far too long already, but I'll give you a quick update." He reiterated the fire's loss and his concerns, then stood to leave. He shook Mr. Wiseman's hand and leaned toward Mary. "May I escort you to the ice cream parlor when your shift is done? We both may be ready for such a treat by then."

"That would be lovely, sir." Mary's eyes lit up like fireflies in the dead of night.

He gazed at the pretty face before him.

Lovely, indeed.

Chapter 7

Mary disconnected her last call before turning the switchboard over to Charlotte. She'd heard too much for one long day and grumbled her frustration as she took off her headset. "Mrs. Brooks has been calling everyone she knows, talking about the wrath of God and how the Park *deserves* the fires we've seen. Can you imagine?"

"That's not the God I know. My God is merciful and loving. Fire is a terrible force of nature, to be sure, but not God's wrath." Charlotte shook her head.

Mary folded her arms and rolled her eyes. Hearing God blamed for man's folly and nature's fury wore her out. "Exactly. Hopefully, the woman will busy herself with dinner preparations and stay off the telephone so you won't have to deal with her. I also heard that the Greens' Gables cottage was the fourth one to burn, and the fire also scorched and slightly damaged the Otis, Waddington, and Pratt houses."

"I saw, and it was a terrible sight. And poor Miss Evans was inconsolable. She just stood in front of her ruins and wept, waiting for it to cool so she could look through the rubble for anything that might have survived. I doubt she'll find anything, since it's nothing but hot ashes." Charlotte plunked down at the switchboard, her shoulders slumped.

Mary's heart ached for those who'd lost their cottages and belongings today—and in the days prior. How terrible that must be. What if something happened to her aunts' cottage with all its hand-made doilies and quilts and tatted pillowcases? Their handful of irreplaceable family photographs, and the few things she still had—like her parents' wedding picture and her mother's ring—would be gone forever. She had little, but that handful of precious possessions were all there, in that cottage. Except her papa's *Scofield Reference Bible* that sat next to the telegraph machine. Her pulse raced and beads of perspiration wet her brow at the thought of losing that too.

"Are you okay, Mary?" Charlotte tugged her from her fears with a tone of concern. "You've gone pale."

She blinked, took a deep breath, and planted a quivering smile on her face. "Yes, of course. Just thinking about those poor souls."

Just then, George knocked, almost filling the doorframe of the tiny office. A wide grin graced his handsome face. "Good afternoon, ladies. Ready for some ice cream, Miss Flynn?"

Charlotte giggled. Her eyes twinkled like a love-sick school-girl's, and her hand flew up to cover her mouth.

Mary's neck grew warm, but she straightened her shoulders and presented the fireman with all the professionalism she could muster. "Mr. Flannigan, you remember Charlotte Mullins, my switchboard assistant and friend from the dance?"

"Nice to see you again, sir." Charlotte popped out of her chair and curtsied, then plunked back down like a bobber on a fishing line.

A light blinked on the switchboard, and Mary pointed to it. "Better get that. I'll see you tomorrow, Charlotte."

Charlotte waved goodbye as she turned to address her caller. As they left the office, George offered his elbow, and Mary took it.

George smiled down at her, patting her hand. "How was your day?"

"Busy. No wires, but lots of calls and even more sadness." Mary heaved a breath.

"Aye. It's been a fiery furnace kind of day, for sure, but let's set it all aside for a few quiet moments and enjoy an ice cream before I head back to the mainland, shall we?"

She smiled and bobbed her chin. If only he were staying on the island. But at least he was in the Park during the week. For that, she was grateful. "Sounds divine. What's your favorite?"

"Strawberry."

She grinned, licking her lips in anticipation. "Mine too. The parlor mixes big chunks of strawberries into the ice cream, and the berries are a nice frozen treat."

"Really? I've not had ice cream with pieces of fruit still intact." George led her down the front steps of the hotel.

"Wait and see. You'll want no other. Ever."

Inside the quaint ice cream parlor, with its black-and-white floor, Mary and George sat at a table in the corner and requested two bowls of ice cream. When the waiter returned with the order, each bowl held two large scoops drizzled with strawberry syrup. On top of the ice cream sat a mound of whipped cream and a cherry.

George laughed. "I had no idea they were so liberal with their servings. We could have shared a bowl."

"It's been a few years since I've been in here, so I forgot. But it's all freshly made." She worked a whole strawberry out of her ice cream and showed him. "And as you can see, it has lots of chunks."

George picked up his spoon and dug into his ice cream. "Yum. I'll have to suffer through eating it all, and I simply must bring Robbie here."

"Thanks for the treat. Where is your son while you're here working?" Mary scooped a spoonful of whipped cream and grinned.

George dabbed his lips with a napkin before speaking. "Mother watches him most of the time. He's often out playing with the neighbor kids from sun up to sun down, except when he's hungry. Then she feeds him and sends him back out to play." He scooped another spoonful of ice cream. "I'm bringing him with me tomorrow so we can go to the band concert. Care to join us? I'd love for you to meet my little man."

"How wonderful. Will your mother join you too?"

A dark shadow passed through his eyes, as if a storm had sprung from nowhere. "No. She needs a break."

Mary shrugged. "Well, it's a lot of responsibility to take care of a rambunctious child of six."

"As Mother keeps telling me." George scoffed. "To be honest, I'm not sure you'd like her. She'd have us walking down the aisle of matrimony just to get rid of the responsibility."

Mary blinked in her surprise but quickly shrugged it off. Suddenly, she closed her eyes and massaged her temples. "Oh … ouch. The ice cream froze my brain."

George guffawed. "I know the feeling, and it's no fun."

"Well, hello there."

Mary turned. Archibald Richmond. Not him again. Just when she was looking forward to learning more about George and his son.

The man pulled out a chair at their table and sat. He didn't even wait for an invitation. Didn't acknowledge her. How rude could a man be? "Mind if I join you? I need to talk to you about today's fire, George. I hear a cigarette might have started the blaze. If so, we need to find the culprit to settle any insurance claims. And because the fire was on the same site where nine cottages burned just six years ago, I'm not sure we can cover this incident."

George's face reddened and his eyes narrowed. Clearly, he didn't like the man. "I don't see what a prior fire has to do with taking care of your customers. And as far as the cigarette, that may have been the cause, or perhaps it's just a rumor, but how would we ever know? I did a thorough investigation earlier this afternoon, and I deem that the cause is unknown."

"We'll see about that." Mr. Richmond huffed. "I'll do my own investigation, thank you very much. And Miss Flynn, you need to get your aunts on board with getting some insurance for their cottage, or they'll regret it, and the folly will lay solidly on your conscience. Do you really want that? This fire season is proving the demise of many here in the islands."

Mary swallowed her ire and pasted on a smile. "Thank you for your concern, sir, but my aunts are perfectly capable of making their own financial decisions."

George rose abruptly, his posture stiff. "If you'll excuse us, Mr. Richmond, Miss Flynn and I would like to finish our conversation and enjoy our ice cream before it melts. Good day to you."

"Oh, all right. But I am only trying to help." Archie smirked and slowly stood. "I'll expect your fire report in the morning, George." He turned and winked at her. "Miss Flynn. Good day to you."

The nerve of him.

~ ~ ~

George's temper raced through his veins, but he tamped it down. In earlier days, he might have decked the man and sent him packing right there. Especially after winking at Mary. And who was the man to demand a report?

After Richmond sallied out, George slipped back into his seat and dropped the napkin in his lap, avoiding Mary's gaze. He sensed her eyes on him, but he had to calm down before Mary detected his anger. Alma always said that an annoyance or a frustration—and especially rage—revealed itself in his eyes like a moving picture show. Right now, rage was an appropriate label for what he felt.

He'd heard of the outrageous premiums Mr. Richmond charged. Likely, to line his pockets. The man was unscrupulous. Mr. O.T. Green, the other insurance man in the Park, never expected such exorbitant prices. No wonder his business was flourishing.

"Your ice cream is melting, George." Mary's sweet voice yanked him from his thoughts and calmed his angst. Her voice held tenderness mixed with uncertainty. "If it's too much for you, perhaps I can help you finish it off."

Without responding or looking at her, he took a bite and closed his eyes as if to savor a delicacy. But the creamy treat soured in his mouth.

Let it go, George. Let it go.

After another few moments, George heaved a great sigh, opened his eyes, and apologized. "Sorry for that, Mary." He glanced toward the door where Archibald had exited and then shrugged. "And for my sullenness." He thumped his chest. "People like that get my back up."

Mary reached over and patted his hand. Then she held it, giving it a tender squeeze. "It's okay. He gets everyone's back up. I'm surprised anyone works with him, especially with Mr. Green serving the same clientele."

"Thanks for that." A bolt of heat rose from her hand straight up to the back of his neck. He finally found his smile again.

By now, his ice cream was soup, and his taste for it had waned. "Are you done? Shall I walk you home?"

"Thank you, and yes to both." Mary patted her lips and set her napkin on the table.

On their way down St. Lawrence Avenue, Mary chatted like a magpie. "In the myriad of telephone calls today, I heard many accolades about the bucket brigade and what a good job they did to save other cottages. But no one even mentioned Alexandria Bay's contributions. Didn't they bring the scow and equipment?"

"They did, and they helped a great deal. The fire scow that they built over the winter is amazing. It has two steam fire engines, seven thousand feet of hose, several chemical engines, a hook and ladder, and many grappling and plying instruments. Unfortunately, the fire had already consumed the four cottages by the time they got here, but they helped beat back the flames and stopped it from destroying more homes. I suppose folks didn't mention them because they want to encourage the Park neighbors who volunteered. Still, they should commend the Alex Bay Department as well."

"They should. Fire isn't a problem just here. When it happened, I read about the Triangle Shirtwaist Factory fire that killed so many in New York City last year, but the details are fuzzy. Do you recall the tragedy? I had a nightmare about it the other night."

George shuddered. "It gave me nightmares for weeks when I heard about it too. Almost a hundred and fifty workers, mostly young Irish, Jewish, and Italian immigrant women, died from fire, smoke, or jumping to their deaths. It was the deadliest industrial fire in the city's history, because the exits and stairwells were all locked. Hopefully, legislation will improve factory safety and that will never happen again."

"May it be soon." Mary moaned her words. As they neared the aunts' cottage, she squeezed his arm. "I hope my aunts don't barrage you with questions and their attempts at matchmaking. Aunt Stella tends to meddle."

George waved off her concern. "My mother does too. I'm used to it."

They climbed the steps to an empty porch. Mary sighed, her brow furrowing. "That's strange. My aunties are always on the porch at this time of day, visiting with neighbors or just watching the world go by. I wonder where they are." She opened the screen door and called for them. "Aunt Maude? Aunt Stella? Are you home?"

George poked his head in behind her before he followed her, stopping just inside the door. A large steamer trunk sat in the middle of the small foyer.

Mary pointed to it, her brow furrowing. Then she glanced at the parlor, which seemed rather bare but for the furnishings. The many knickknacks, doilies, and decorations all gone. "What's going on? Where are all the aunties' things?"

Footsteps and banging echoed from above, and suddenly, Aunt Maude poked her head around the corner of the upstairs wall, her soft voice quivering. "Oh, Stella, we have company. Come, sister."

The two elderly sisters slowly descended the stairs and bid them to sit on the porch. Mary opened her mouth as if to ask a question, but Aunt Stella almost pushed her out the door. "I'll explain everything presently."

Once they'd all settled into the white wicker chairs, Mary burst out with her question. "Why are you packing? Is something wrong? Are you sick? We just got here a few weeks ago."

Aunt Stella raised her double chin. "We are well, but we have decided to return to the city. The fires have given us far too many nightmares, and it is simply too frightening to be here any longer. Maude and I are leaving for the season." The determination in her voice was unmistakable. "And don't try to change our minds."

Aunt Maude's eyes brimmed with tears, and when she spoke, her voice sounded like a child's who had lost her doll. "The thought of losing our precious heirlooms is simply too much to bear, niece."

"What if I take the trunks of heirlooms back to our house in Watertown, and then you can stay here? I hate the thought of you in the city all summer with this heat. It must be ninety degrees or more inland." Mary shook her head. She leaned forward.

Aunt Stella huffed and then rubbed her hands together before folding them over her ample bosom. "We've decided. We are leaving tomorrow. You can stay here, Mary, but as you can see, we've cleared out our treasures, so the cottage is a bit empty."

Mary glanced at George as if asking for his support. He wouldn't disappoint. "Are you sure? Will you be all right there without Mary?"

"We'll be fine. We have plenty of friends, neighbors, and folks from our church who dote over us. Better there than burning here in our beds." Aunt Maude sighed, her face creased with resignation.

Aunt Stella stood and motioned toward the door. "Will you stay for supper? I've made plenty of chicken salad. Besides, we'd like to ask you about your thoughts on fire insurance."

"I'd be honored, ma'am." George smiled, though their announcement saddened him. By the look on Mary's face, she was too. He rose and let the women lead the way to the dining room.

Soon they were enjoying what he reckoned would be their last meal together. Would Mary feel safe in this cottage alone? Would it even be proper for a young woman to stay by herself?

Mary had barely touched her food. She continued to pick at the chicken salad aimlessly, a frown corrupting her pretty face.

Aunt Stella broke into George's thoughts. "Should we even bother with insurance? It's ever so costly these days. Mr. Richmond quoted us an outrageous price."

George swallowed and patted his lips with his napkin. "I think you have to decide if the insurance would be worth it financially and emotionally. Would it give you peace of mind, or would the cost steal your peace? If you decide to get insurance, I suggest you go with Mr. Green. I hear he's more reasonable and, if you ask me, more reputable."

"I imagine so." Aunt Stella scoffed. "Mr. Richmond makes my skin crawl. He stops by to hound us at least once a day with his thick eyebrows waggling condemnation. But aside from us getting fire insurance, what is the Thousand Island Park Association doing to improve the Park's fire safety? That's what I want to know."

"A good deal, I hope. After the Hotel Frontenac's tragic fire last year, the Association's executive committee met, and Dr. Goodale informed me they were ready to match any funds that the Park residents contribute up to ten thousand dollars. That would help to purchase more equipment, maybe even hire a seasonal firefighting team."

Aunt Maude buttered a piece of bread. "We heard that, but the neighbors rejected the idea. They felt the Association should provide it all."

Mary sighed. "Mr. Fitch, the treasurer, said that without the residents' help, they can't spend the money. Apparently, the tax structure doesn't bring in enough money to fund such a large purchase." As soon as the words left her lips, Mary's eyes grew wide, and she covered her mouth. "I'm sorry. That was a private conversation. Please don't share that. I should not have."

A small chuckle escaped his lips. "Mum's the word, eh, ladies?" He needed to bring a bit of levity to the conversation, or they'd all have bellyaches. "This chicken salad is delicious. Thank you for having me." He paused, waiting for the mood to lighten. "May I help you with your trunks and escort you onto the ferry and then to the train tomorrow? I'd be happy to."

"That would be ever so helpful, Mr. Flannigan. Thank you." Both aunts smiled and so did Mary, and with that simple offer of kindness, the gloominess lifted. Mary patted her lips with her napkin.

"You are most welcome. I should get home, but thanks again for your hospitality." He pushed back from the table and stood to leave.

Mary joined him. "I'll walk you to the door."

George said his goodbyes, and Mary led the way to the porch. Before descending the steps, he glanced at the cottage and touched her forearm. "Will you be all right here alone?"

"Perhaps I'll invite Charlotte to room with me. Or maybe I'll move into the hotel. I'll talk with my aunts about it all tonight. Thank you for helping them. And me." Mary shrugged, her face filled with concern.

"My pleasure, Mary."

Truly.

Chapter 8

M ary hugged both of her aunts before they boarded the ferry. "Please telephone when you get home. I want to make sure you make it back to Watertown safely."

"We will, dear. You stay safe too." Sweet Aunt Maude kissed her cheek.

Aunt Stella slipped her hand into the crook of George's arm and patted his hand. "And you, fine sir, must keep a sharp eye on our niece."

"Yes, ma'am. Be glad to." With his free hand, he saluted Aunt Stella. He tossed Mary a mischievous grin, sending her emotions dancing on the breeze. How Aunt Stella weaseled her way into the affections of the firefighter was a marvel.

Aunt Stella wagged a finger at Mary. "You listen to this fine young man, missy. These are uncertain times, and you need a strong man's support and influence in your life. Be a good girl, and we'll see you in September."

Mary waved, irritation prickling her scalp. That comment wasn't worth a rebuttal. After all, she was a woman of twenty-eight and perfectly capable of taking care of herself. And she didn't need a man to buoy her up. Still, if she had to choose …

"Safe travels, Aunties. And thank you, George, for escorting them to the train."

When the ferry had sailed, Mary hurried to work. She was already a few minutes late, but hopefully, it would be a quiet morning. Still, uncertainty pricked her nerves.

She loathed the idea of being alone in the cottage. Besides, it wasn't proper. Should she invite Charlotte to join her? The girl was sweet, but would she miss being with her father at the hotel? And after her evening shift, would she be brave enough to walk home alone? So many thoughts danced in her head, all of them without answers. Not a good way to start the day.

As she climbed the steps of the Columbian Hotel, Mr. Wiseman waved to her. She glanced at the door and then at him. Though she should get to her post at the switchboard, a few moments with him shouldn't matter and might even change her gloomy mood. She joined him at his usual spot, next to the chessboard which always sat ready for a round of friendly competition. "Good morning, sir. How are you today?"

Mr. Wiseman hesitated for several moments, his eyes kind, compassionate, almost sympathetic, as if he could read her mind. "Better than you, I believe. I'm sorry your aunts left you alone on the island. What are your plans?"

Mary sat down, her heart sinking into the pit of her empty stomach. In the midst of the final packing and getting her aunts to the ferry, she hadn't eaten a thing. "I'm not sure what to do. I know I can't stay alone in the cottage, so I thought, perhaps, I might invite Charlotte to join me."

Mr. Wiseman *tsk*ed, shaking his head. "That child is afraid of her own shadow. She won't leave her father's rooms here at the hotel,

I can assure you. No … you must move into the hotel, and I have a suggestion. My apartment has two bedrooms. My son isn't coming this summer, so his room is empty. You can stay with me, if you'd like."

Mary blinked at the kind offer. Could the solution to her problem be that simple? The man was like a grandfather to all the young people in the Park, so it would be proper. "That is so nice of you. Are you sure?"

"Been thinking about it all night and praying about it, ever since George told me about your aunts' plans." Creases fanned around the outer edges of his eyes when he smiled. "I'd enjoy the company, and you'd be in excellent hands. Besides, you're like a granddaughter, so it would be like having family here."

Mary pondered the suggestion. The cottage would be like a tomb without the chatter of her aunts and the clutter of their memories, even if it was socially acceptable for a young lady to stay alone. Mary leaned forward and repeated herself. "Are you sure?"

Mr. Wiseman chuckled, his eyes turning into tiny slits. "I wouldn't have offered if I wasn't. I'd be delighted, my dear."

"Then I accept, and thank you so much. I'll fetch my things after my shift ends."

Mr. Wiseman grinned, his eyes sparkling with joy. "Wonderful. You've made an old man happy. I was so disappointed to hear my son wouldn't be visiting, so your company will soothe my soul."

"Very well, then. I'd better get to work." Mary stood, a wave of peace filling her heart. She bent down and planted a kiss on his cheek. "Until this evening, Mr. Wiseman."

"You're now officially adopted. Call me *Gramps*." He shook his head, grabbing her hand to give it a tender squeeze.

Mary giggled, the term of endearment slipping off her tongue like a spoonful of honey. "Okay, Gramps. Have a good day, and I hope you beat all your chess opponents today." She grinned as she touched the black queen, causing it to wobble and fall, knocking down several chess pieces. Three of them fell on the floor. She bent down to retrieve them. "Gracious. Sorry."

Gramps stopped her. "Go on to work. I'll take care of this. I've little else to do." He shooed her off, and she obliged him with a wave and a smile.

When she entered the office, the telegraph machine was already tapping out a message.

Goodness! The first one in days, and she was tardy. She grabbed her pencil and paper and scratched out a part of the message. "…hospital. Come quickly. Sarah"

Someone was in the hospital? But who? She tapped out a reply, asking for the telegrapher to repeat the message in its entirety. She waited for it to begin again, doodling on the top of the paper.

To Martha Chester. Adolph Chester had heart attack. In Good Samaritan Hospital, Watertown. Come quickly. Sarah

Poor Mrs. Chester. The woman had seven children, three of them having succumbed to the flu the same year as her parents. She still mourned them. What would happen if her husband passed?

Mary telephoned the woman's cottage, and she answered. After relaying the information and trying to comfort her with words of hope, she hung up and prayed for the family.

The news spread quickly with several calls from neighbors to neighbors, and soon the Park was abuzz with worry over the Chester family. Mrs. Murphy offered to care for the children. Mr. Stanton volunteered to escort her to the hospital.

Despite the weaknesses of the community, when there was a need, folks always stepped up to help. Surely a plethora of meals would be at their door in hours. Here, people cared. Like Gramps.

Though it seemed everyone knew of the Chesters' plight, the phone calls kept coming. Too bad the Park didn't have a way to inform everyone in one fell swoop. Maybe one day.

Two hours later, George popped his head into the office. "I have safely delivered your aunts and their belongings to the train going to Watertown. I called a friend who will meet them at the station and take them to their home."

"That was kind of you. Thank you, George. I have news. Mr. Wiseman has invited me to stay with him in his son's room, so I don't have to be alone in the cottage." Mary swallowed back the quick wash of sadness, a smile crossing her lips. What a thoughtful man he was.

George slapped his thigh. "What a great idea! I've worried about that. Problem solved. I also heard of the Chester situation."

"Yes. News travels fast in the Park. Where's Robbie?" Mary glanced beyond George to find the hallway empty.

George shrugged and rammed his hands into his pockets. "He woke up with a sore throat and temperature, so he stayed home with Mother. Sorry, but you'll have to meet him another day."

Mary gave him a playful pout. "Too bad. I was planning for that to be the highlight of my day. Now I'll have to settle for answering dozens of calls."

"How about settling for lunch with Mr. Wiseman and me instead? I have research to do, and he's the man with the information, I'm told. I saw Charlotte in the parlor and already asked if she'd fill in for you, and she said yes. I hope that wasn't too presumptuous."

"That would be lovely. Thank you." Just then, two lights blinked their need of her, and she sighed. She could definitely use a break today.

"Until noon." George grinned and gave a quick wink, sending her heart fluttering.

Mary smiled before turning to the switchboard. "Can't wait."

He waved goodbye before disappearing into the hallway.

Was she hearing things, or did he mutter under his breath with a bit of extra emphasis? *"Nor I."*

~ ~ ~

George cut his roasted chicken and took a bite, savoring the juicy wonder. After swallowing, he opened the conversation with a glance at Mr. Wiseman. "I'm researching prior fires in the Thousand Island Park to learn more about the strengths and weaknesses of the community fire protection. Dr. Goodale said you could enlighten me a great deal, sir. And Mary, I thought you might lend your aunts' input, since they rushed off the island before I could ask them."

Mary nibbled her lip before responding. "They've not spoken of the fires, so I'm no help. But perhaps I can add a little from the scuttlebutt I've heard from my time here. What is proper to share, that is."

George waved off her concerns. "No matter. Your company is all the help we need."

"I agree." Mr. Wiseman leaned back a bit from the table and gazed at the ceiling for several moments. "Let's see … there were several fires, but none like on one in 1890. That was an especially challenging time at the Park with several natural disasters. By then, I lived here year-round. In January, a terrible windstorm badly damaged about fifteen boathouses, ripped the enormous tower clear off the hotel, and destroyed the hotel's roof. One cottage actually overturned, and two more moved off their foundations. The St. Lawrence River even rose a good three feet and flooded the shoreline rather badly."

"Goodness. Was anyone hurt?" Mary set down her glass of tea and groaned.

"Not to my knowledge. Few people stay on the island year-round even now. After the storm, the Association hired Mr. Dillenbeck, the hotel's original architect, to make repairs and enlarge the tower by adding two stories to it. He also installed a glass roof over the courtyard and put in new flooring."

"Wasn't that the same year the hotel burned to the ground?" George swallowed the piece of potato he'd been chewing.

"It was. I'll never forget it. It was August twenty-first, the day after my birthday. That's how I remember it so well. My wife and I celebrated at the hotel, and it was packed. About five hundred souls were staying there, and even more came to hear the Leonard's Silver Band from Lowville play that night. We had a delightful time." He paused, and a frown wrinkled his face even more than usual. "But then, tragedy struck. About one-thirty in the morning, three men were playing Pedro and noticed flames coming from the kitchen."

Mary tilted her head, her brows furrowing. "Pedro?"

Mr. Wiseman chuckled, waggling his dark eyebrows. "It's a card game. A violation of hotel rules forbidding card playing. But it was a good thing they were still up, else no one might have seen the fire."

George scoffed. "A very good thing. But isn't the kitchen in a different building?"

"Aye, the kitchen was in the adjacent annex. Fred Twitchell saw the flames first, and the three card players sounded the alarm, each one taking a hallway, knocking and yelling and sometimes breaking down the doors. About the same time, the night janitor noticed the fire and alerted the first-floor guests."

"Did everyone get out okay?" Mary leaned in, her eyes wide.

"All but one, I'm afraid. The glass roof they just installed acted like a ventilation shaft, and in a mere forty-five minutes, the fire totally destroyed the hotel."

Mary let out a small moan. "Poor soul."

Mr. Wiseman nodded. "I was awake, getting a drink of water, and saw the flames from my cottage blocks away. I threw on some clothes and ran to help. Some say the flames rose three hundred feet high, and the fiery glow was visible as far as Watertown."

Did he hear right? The old man must have misspoke. "But Watertown is twenty miles or more as the crow flies."

Mr. Wiseman shrugged. "It was a terrible fire, son, but many of the guests and cottagers tried to help. When I got there, it was chaos. I joined the bucket brigade that stretched all the way down to the river, but by then, the pavilion, the bakery, and the hotel annex were all lost. A fellow from Denver, Mr. Whitney, said he searched for a hose to put out the flames but couldn't find one. But even if he had, the water pressure from the reservoir wasn't strong enough to service more than one hose, and the hotel's water tower quickly became useless, the fire so hot it turned the water into steam."

Mary blinked back tears, her face sorrowful. "How did five hundred people escape a burning hotel so fast? Were there injuries?"

"Most of the guests left everything behind and ran to safety in their nightclothes. But some foolish people threw things into trunks and tried to drag them out, clogging the hallways and stairwells and almost blocking the escape routes. Their folly led to hundreds being injured. Mostly cuts, sprains, and bruises, though. The worst injury was the proprietor's daughter, Miss Warner. She burned her face and hands badly."

George cringed at the thought of such a disaster. He shifted in his seat. "Were there heroes who saved others along the way? I always like to hear their stories."

The old man swiped his face with a hand. "Aye, there were. Mary Miner saved four small children. Herbert Klock saved a woman on the stairs, to name just two. But outside the hotel, it was pandemonium. Terrified, half-dressed folks cried and screamed. Some frantically searched for loved ones. Others stood like helpless statues. A few tried to go back into the flames to save their belongings, but all failed."

Mary patted her eyes with an embroidered handkerchief. She seemed to experience it deep within her. But why?

Mr. Wiseman continued. "The nearby cottage owners packed their things, and some threw furniture onto their lawns."

"Did it become a conflagration?" George's skin crawled.

The old man nodded, closing his eyes as if to picture it. He kept them closed as he shared the details. "Unfortunately, it did. The wind spread the fire in two directions. Morris's store burned. So did the gas house. The meat market, a plumbing shop, Roger's boarding house, and the Association barn also burned. Thankfully, the bucket brigade threw wet blankets on Reverend Kinney's cottage and kept it from burning. We also saved the post office, the museum, and the New England Kitchen."

Both Mary and he stayed silent, so Mr. Wiseman finally opened his eyes and continued, his voice sad. "The employees, housed in the annex near the kitchen, suffered the most. Mr. Frank, the head cook, broke a leg when he jumped from the upstairs porch, and his assistant, Mrs. Rickman, was hurt, too. The laundress, Mrs. Mitchell, was severely burned and rushed to Watertown. Thankfully, though, the only death was Miss Morrow, the head laundress. Doctors believe she died of heart trouble."

Mary almost whimpered her question. "Did the fire get under control then?"

Mr. Wiseman paused, took out a handkerchief, and dabbed his forehead. The memories seemed to consume him. "Not quite. To the southwest, Reverend Dayan's cottage burned. The Park's founder had just finished rebuilding it the day before, and he lost everything, poor man. The Truro Boarding House was next, but thankfully, all thirty-five guests escaped the fire. Next was St. Lawrence Hall, and within minutes, it burned to the ground. So did our chapel and the Haddock cottage."

George stood and stretched out the tension in his muscles. His neck and back always seemed to take the brunt of stress, even when merely hearing of such tragedies. He sat again. "Didn't Alexandria Bay, Clayton, and Gananoque come to your aid?"

Mr. Wiseman bobbed his head. "As you know, navigating the river in the dead of night can be treacherous, but Captain Estes of Clayton showed up around three a.m. bringing a fresh crew and plenty of fire pails. A few more cottages burned, but they finally got control of the fire and halted its spread. Between them and the bucket brigade, we continued to put out spot fires the entire night."

Mary sighed and took a sip of her tea. The waiter took their half-eaten plates before Mr. Wiseman continued.

"When the sun came up, the devastation was disheartening. Hundreds of people fled the island on the first ferry out, and that afternoon, a violent storm arose and nearly killed several people trying to leave the tragedy behind them as they made for the mainland in boats."

The sweet lass wrung her hands. "Was there insurance back then to take care of the losses?"

Mr. Wiseman groaned. "The cottages and businesses had little to no coverage, and the owners insured less than half the value of the hotel. Hotel patrons lost tens of thousands of dollars in precious jewels, clothing, and the like, and all the hotel's records were destroyed. Pessimism reigned over the Park, but the general store owner, Mr. Morris, wouldn't give up. He restored the Park's hope by providing supplies the very next day."

"How … how did it start?" Mary's bottom lip still trembled.

Mr. Wiseman folded his arms over his paunch. "They suspected an arsonist, but they never proved it. A suspicious-looking character that folks called 'the tramp' appeared in the Park a few days before the fire. I saw the tramp horseback riding, and he looked rather dubious. At the same time, several folks said the Association had to stop him from what they called 'certain practices.' Never heard what those were, but the night of the fire, Mr. Warner, the hotel proprietor, caught him peeking through a window and muttering about the lack of fire protection. After the fire started, Mr. Warner's daughter reported that he ran through the halls shouting that there was no fire. But then he disappeared, and no one has seen him since."

George huffed. "Arsonists are of the evilest lot there are, and unfortunately, they often seem to vanish into thin air. Evil. Pure evil."

The three of them sat silent. Stunned. Sad.
What if it were to happen again? How could he prevent it?
Somehow, he had to find a way.
Especially for those he'd come to care about.
And soon.

Chapter 9

Mary connected her fourteenth call of the morning with seasoned professionalism. She loved her job and its import. But here was yet another call about a meeting time and place? Why couldn't folks just connect on the streets? Because the Park had swelled to almost ten thousand inhabitants and visitors, that's why. At this rate, she'd need a larger switchboard and more help.

"Got time for a chat, little lady?" Mr. Wiseman … er, Gramps entered and sat on the chair she kept there for him. "Don't want to interrupt you."

She still wasn't used to the familiar moniker, but she liked it. And the elderly preacher's company in the evenings helped her feel less alone. She'd never had a grandfather, but if she did, she'd want him to be just like Gramps. She held up a finger to signal him to wait and pasted on a smile as she connected yet another call.

After finishing the call, she turned to face him. "Sure. If *you* don't mind being interrupted when a call comes in. It's been a busy morning, mostly with people making plans to meet for a tennis match, or to watch the roque tournament this afternoon, or to join them at the concert tonight. Weekends are just full of excitement around here, aren't they?"

Gramps nodded as he eased onto the chair with the aid of his fancy cane. "Aye, they sure are, and with the constant stream of students filling the New York State Educational Building during its Summer Institute session, plus all the different conventions the Park hosts throughout the summer, the population swells even more. I've heard there are only two rooms vacant this weekend. One of them is at a boarding house, the other in a tent."

"Do you think they will build another hotel or add more boarding houses?"

He shrugged, scratching his head and sending wispy shocks of salt-and-pepper hair flying every which way. "Don't rightly know, but last August, eleven hundred men from the Buffalo National Guard came and slept in tents all weekend. The 74th Regiment regaled us with a forty-piece band and performed marching maneuvers on the green in front of the hotel. They camped along Centennial Avenue, and the postman boasted handling more than fifty-seven hundred postcards that weekend. Those cards were likely a boon for promoting the wonders of the Park."

She pictured the army of men, organizing and mustering as if preparing for war. "I was working in Watertown last summer. It must have been a marvelous sight."

Gramps nodded. "It was crackin'. And this weekend, the Gananoque ferry dropped off a slew of Canadians. I must say, I rather fancy the two-nation culture we enjoy here. With half of the Thousand Islands part of Ontario, Canada, and the other half in New York, I think there's a special affinity between the two countries."

Mary nodded. "Right, and I would never have learned to put malt vinegar on my fries had I not tried it from my Canadian friends."

"I love that too. Did you hear …" Gramps guffawed.

Just then, a caller's light blinked, diverting her attention. She inserted the phone plug into the jack and answered. "Good afternoon, Mr. Samson. How may I direct your call?" She listened and then responded, her interaction adept, just the way she liked it. "Here you go."

Plug and done.

She turned back to Gramps. "You were saying?"

The elderly man waved a hand. "Just that the Grange is coming next week, and then a large choir from Schenectady the week after. It's fixing to be a busy month ahead, but with no rain, the risk of fire only increases with every person who visits."

"You don't think an arsonist like the tramp would come to the island, do you? You scared me with that tale of the 1890 fire, and though that was twenty-two years ago, I don't doubt that it could happen again." Mary's heart raced as she verbalized her fears.

Gramps leaned over and patted her hand. "It could, but we'll pray it never does. You can't borrow trouble, Mary. Psalm 27 says, 'The Lord is my light and my salvation; whom shall I fear? The Lord is the strength of my life; of whom shall I be afraid?' Put your trust in Him, dear one."

Mary breathed in that truth. She had to admit that, too often, she borrowed trouble. She fretted and worried about things beyond her control. And when she didn't release them, bad dreams carried her to places she never wanted to go. It was foolishness at its worst. "I will, Gramps."

Charlotte stepped into the tiny office, a small volume clutched to the bodice of her starched, white blouse. "Mr. Wiseman, good day to you. Would you like a break, Mary?"

"Hello, my dear. I'll leave you two ladies to it. See you both later." The old man groaned his way to standing.

She and Charlotte said goodbye at the same time and giggled at their echo, then she turned to her friend. "A break would be lovely. You're so thoughtful, Charlotte. It's been busy, so I'll be back soon."

Charlotte waved off her concern. "No hurry. I have nothing else to do and am bored with the day. You can plan to leave early if you'd like. Say, at three?"

"Don't you want to get out and enjoy the sunshine?" Mary clicked her tongue.

She shook her head. "Large crowds make me nervous, and besides, I'm halfway through this thrilling story and just have to finish it." She turned the book she held to show Mary the cover.

Mary read the title aloud. "*Tom Swift and his Motor Car by Victor Appleton.* Isn't that a boy's book?"

"Oh, stuff and nonsense. Boys schmoys." Charlotte huffed. "The bellhop, Jimmy, lent it to me, and Papa approves. This is the twentieth century, Mary. Really." She crinkled up her nose, a hint of hurt in her eyes. "And it's very exciting."

"I'm sorry. I didn't mean to make fun. I was just asking. What's it about?"

Fervor returned to Charlotte's eyes. "Oh, it's ever so thrilling. It's Tom's first adventure. He buys a motorcycle, modifies it, and drives to Albany carrying his father's plans for a new invention. But he doesn't know that there are evil men who want to steal the plans following him, and he ends up in danger. The villains have just trapped him, and I have to know what's going to happen."

Mary laughed. "Good novels are like that. They get you hooked, and you can't stop reading until the end." She set her hat on her head and picked up her reticule. "It's been busy this morning, so you might not get much reading done."

"It's okay. I can relive what I've read in between calls. That's why I like books." Charlotte giggled as she sat down and slipped on the switchboard headset. "Better get going. See you soon."

She waved goodbye to her friend, who fidgeted with her book. Waiting for Mary to leave so she could open it and read, no doubt. Well, good luck with that.

Mary scooted out of the hotel and into the warm summer sunshine as fast as she could. Was it her imagination or did a faint smell of smoke linger in the air from the four cottages that had burned down? Although it happened two days ago, it hadn't yet rained and cleansed the air. Despite the recent tragedy, as she glanced at the bustling town, everything seemed to be moving on as though it had never happened.

But it had, at least to the Arthurs, Greens, Captain Brown, and Miss Baker and Miss Evans. They had lost everything, poor folks. Mary felt sorriest for the two single ladies who'd seemed so forlorn and hopeless when she passed them yesterday. Miss Evan's bottom lip had quivered when she said hello, and her eyes had been red and swollen. Miss Baker, always the strong one, looked as if the life had gone out of her. Yesterday, the two women returned to their mainland home, and she would surely miss them.

Mary shook herself from her sad thoughts as she passed the needlecraft shop, glancing in the window at several completed works of art. She loved how people created all kinds of wonderful crafts. Perhaps, one day, she'd pick up one such skill.

The nearby glassblower mesmerized her as he blew a molten piece of glass into a beautiful swan. So did the interesting items she quickly perused in the Japanese bazaar and the Oriental goods shop. Hand-painted fans. Funny little statues. Elegant silk kimonos graced the shops.

She greeted the turbaned men standing outside the Persian and Turkish rug shop and American Indians who owned the basket shop. But her favorite shop of all was the candy kitchen. She loved to try new and interesting treats whenever she had an extra penny. Which she didn't have right now.

She returned to the office to let Charlotte go. But before she the younger woman could leave, Mary tapped a note sitting on the desk. "Is this for me?"

Charlotte spun on her heels. "Oh, I almost forgot. Fireman Flannigan called to see when you'd be off work. I told him at three. He sounded happy and said he'd stop by then and hoped he could escort you on an afternoon stroll and to an evening concert. I told him you'd be delighted." She giggled, a mischievous twinkle brightening her eyes.

"You didn't. How would you know I'd say yes?" Mary planted her fists on her hips and feigned offense.

Charlotte mimicked her, dramatically placing her fists on her hips, the book tucked under one hand. "I have eyes, don't I? You light up like a sunbeam when he's around." She pursed her lips as if to hold back a hearty laugh and then exploded in a rather unladylike guffaw.

Mary joined her in a less boisterous manner, unsure how she felt about her date. "Well, thank you, Miss Cupid, for managing my social calendar. Mr. Flannigan said he'd be bringing his son to visit soon, and I've wanted to meet the little tyke for days. Maybe he'll be with his father."

"My pleasure, friend." Charlotte curtsied.

Mary smiled as she turned her attention to another blinking light.

No, the pleasure will be all mine.

~ ~ ~

George waited on the veranda, chatting with Mr. Wiseman and keeping his eye on Robbie as he played with his dog, Cooper. Well, sort of his dog. The black-and-white Dalmatian was officially the Clayton fire dog, but since George kept him, Robbie claimed him as his own. The two were inseparable.

Does Mary like dogs? Children?

His nerves twitched in hopes she did.

Mr. Wiseman pointed to the child and his pet. "That's quite a dog you have. Jumps higher than your boy to fetch the stick. Did you train him?"

"A little. Cooper seems to have an instinct for fetching and finding things. Even found a dead body among the ashes of a burned-out barn once. We call him the fire dog, but he's become a splendid companion for Robbie."

"Good afternoon, gentlemen."

The sound of Mary's voice sent a pleasant shiver up his spine. He'd had his back to the door, watching his son, and his heart skipped a beat. His blood surged. His palms sweated.

"Hello, Mary."

Why was he so nervous? He could charge into a burning structure with more composure.

Mr. Wiseman stared at him and chuckled, which didn't help one bit. Diversion. That's what he needed. He pointed to Robbie and Cooper. "There's my son and our fire dog."

Mary smiled, her eyes dancing with delight. "Finally. I've been waiting ever so long to meet your little man." She turned on her heel and scurried down the steps to the child's side, not waiting for him to introduce them. She put out her hand to Robbie, who shook it. "Hello, Robbie. I'm a friend of your father's. And who is this?"

Robbie glanced at his father before answering. "This is Cooper. He's my best friend. Watch this." The boy threw a stick far and high, and the dog leaped up, catching it in midair.

"My, he's a quick one. And you are a strong young man to throw so high." Mary put a hand to her chest.

Cooper returned to them, and Mary petted the dog, kneeling on the ground. Robbie plopped down next to her, staring.

"Well, Mr. Wisemen, I best be on my way." George put out his hand.

The old man's eyes twinkled. "Have fun, young man, and take care of that one. She's a keeper."

"I'll do my best, sir." George pursed his lips and shoved his hands into his pockets.

He joined Mary, Robbie, and the dog, ready to get away from the keen eyes of the kind old preacher. "Let's walk. Shall we?"

She nodded, and he helped Mary stand. To his surprise, Robbie took Mary's hand rather than his. George leaned toward her and spoke low, merriment filtering through his words. "I see you've made a new friend."

She glanced down at Robbie, who continued to stare at her with admiration. As smitten as his father. George swallowed hard. Was this a good idea? What if things didn't go well with them? Robbie would lose another woman.

He shook the thoughts from his head and focused on enjoying his surroundings. The Park was abuzz with activity. Players filled the tennis courts adjoining the hotel, laughing and sending balls soaring back and forth over the nets. A fisherman sauntered down the middle of St. Lawrence Avenue, sporting the largest muskellunge he'd ever seen. The man held his string aloft, shouting, "By cracky, ain't she a beauty? She's got to be a trophy winner if I've ever seen one."

George chuckled at the strangers excitement. "Congratulations, sir. Well done."

"It's bigger than me, Papa." Robbie tried to pull away from him, but he held the boy fast.

Mary joined them in joyful laughter. He loved that sound more and more by the day.

As they passed a lemonade stand, he turned to Mary. "Would you like a glass?"

"I would, thank you." Mary licked her pretty lips and nodded.

He purchased her a glass as well as one for himself and Robbie, who guzzled it down and continued playing with Cooper. They stood together under a shade tree, watching the pair as they enjoyed their tangy drinks.

George took the last sip of his lemonade, noticing a mural of the Olympics on the outside wall of the stand as he returned his glass. "Did you know that the 1900 Paris Olympic Games hosted firefighting as one of the competitions?"

"Really? I thought the Olympics were only for sports."

George shrugged. "Firefighting is a highly athletic activity, and competing in the events proves to not only motivate the men on the job but also develop new and innovative techniques."

"That makes sense, I suppose." Mary tilted her head as she regarded him. "How did the competition work, exactly?"

"Both professional and volunteer firefighters competed. Unfortunately, the International Olympic Committee could never figure out exactly what sports to include, so there was no official designation by the time the games began, so they let all them all play out. The Kansas City firefighters won the overall championship for their famous engine and hook and ladder company number one."

"What kinds of events were held?" Mary quirked a brow.

George plucked a leaf from a low-hanging branch and rolled it in his hand. "Firefighting requires skills in rescue, fire suppression, and hazardous materials mitigation. I suspect they also had races pushing heavy fire equipment, pulling down burning walls with hooks and chains, bucket brigade races, the use of fire bombs and ropes and knots, fire hose operations, and ladder competitions. Those sorts of thing."

"I've never thought about the complexities of firefighting. But don't you fear the danger?" Mary ran her finger along her glass, avoiding his gaze.

George let out a slow, long breath before answering. "Fear is a good thing. It warns us of danger and the need to stay safe. But when it paralyzes us, that's when fear becomes an enemy. When it takes over, we either flee or freeze. Or we fight. My job is to fight regardless of the fear."

"I'm not so sure I'd be able to do that." Mary put a hand to her chest, her eyes sparking alarm.

"Well, I can't do it in my own strength. When I first started fighting fires, the danger overwhelmed me. But then Mr. Wiseman challenged me to memorize Isaiah 41:10, 'Fear thou not; for I am with thee: be not dismayed; for I am thy God: I will strengthen thee; yea, I will help thee; yea, I will uphold thee with the right hand of my righteousness.' Now I recite it before going into any fire, large or small, and I think it has saved my life more than once."

Mary's eyes grew wide. This tiny woman with the big heart was so accomplished and composed, yet here again was an undercurrent of something heavy. A trace of fear that he wished to extinguish. But what lay at the root of her unease and why? And could her reaction to his mention of being in jeopardy indicate she might be beginning to care for him? That was for pondering at a later time.

The day was perfect. He'd not spoil it. Better to change the topic.

He turned to his son. "Robbie, can you show Miss Mary how you tumble?"

The boy stopped running in circles with Cooper and beamed. "Sure can. Watch this." He somersaulted not once, not twice, but five times—until he almost rolled into a picnicking couple. Seeing them, he stopped and stood upright. "Sorry. Hope I didn't scare you."

Mary giggled, leaning in and looking up at George. Her lavender scent was intoxicating. "He's a delightful child, George. Truly."

"Thank you, Mary." Her approval meant the world.

"Shall we watch the roque a bit? It's ever so interesting, I think." She tilted her head toward the street.

George smiled. "Let's. Come, Robbie. Cooper." He waved his boy close, and the child slipped his hand into Mary's.

Yep. He's smitten.

The roque tournament near the library was in full swing, the players evoking laughter as they jockeyed in a game similar to croquet for the prize of a big, fat ham. Robbie joined the children, who played with hoops and balls on the green gracing either side of

St. Lawrence Avenue from the hotel down to the river's edge. A few teeners flew kites in the gentle breeze and flirted with one another.

George led Mary to a wide shade tree. "Let's sit. I can watch Robbie and Cooper from here. Do you mind that I brought them?"

"I'm ever so glad you did. I've wanted to meet your son, and Cooper is a great dog. Growing up, I had a collie who followed me wherever I went. He was my best friend too."

"You might displace Cooper in Robbie's affections. I've never seen him so taken with anyone." George touched her forearm, a stream of heat flowing from his fingertips straight to his heart.

Mary looked deep into his eyes, as if to read his heart. She blinked, bit her bottom lip, and sighed. "And I must confess, I'm rather taken by him too."

What could he say to that? A mixture of apprehension and excitement swirled in his brain.

Did she feel the same about him?

Chapter 10

Mary glanced in the small mirror on her bedroom wall, adjusted a wayward curl, and rolled her eyes. She'd fussed with her hair for far too long for a Sunday morning.

She groaned and whispered, "Vanity. Vanity." Even so, today was a rather big day, wasn't it? She'd be meeting George's mother.

And just how much should she tell Gramps about yesterday with George? He'd surely want to know. Could he already see her growing affection for the humble fireman? Would he guide her, rather than push her into marriage before she was ready—as her aunts did? That was the last thing she needed.

Ever since losing her mother and father to the flu epidemic, she'd held the many concerns that arose in her life close to her vest. Staunch friends were hard to find, so she'd bottled up her thoughts and feelings and fears much too often. Her brothers were busy with their families—and quite uninterested—to bother themselves with their spinster sister's troubles. And both seemed to have moved on from the loss of their parents.

But her? She still felt deeply alone, even after coming to live with her two aunts last fall.

Truth was, she had no one. She was an orphan, adrift on the sea of life.

She pinched her cheeks before opening her bedroom door. Gramps sat in the sitting room at a small table reading his Bible. A settee and side chair, a table and lamp, and a elegantly carved sideboard filled most of the room. Piles and piles of books filled every available space. So did a small portrait of his wife, bless her soul, and grown son.

He looked up and smiled. "Good morning, Mary. And how did you sleep?"

"Very well, thank you. And you?" She joined him at the table near the window.

He cleared his throat. "Oh, well enough, but I'm sorry I fell asleep before you came home. These old bones don't like late hours anymore."

"I understand. I did not expect you to wait up."

He patted his open Bible. "I've been reading Second Timothy and thinking of you. It says, 'For God hath not given us the spirit of fear; but of power, and of love, and of a sound mind.' The apostle Paul was trying to encourage young Timothy to use his talents well. And I want to encourage you to do the same today and every day, Mary."

"Thank you. I will." She nodded, slipping her hand out from under his and giving it a gentle squeeze.

Gramps closed his Bible and sat back in his chair. "Now, tell me about your evening with George and little Robbie."

She chewed her bottom lip and glanced out the window. Who else could she talk to? She turned back to him and smiled. "Robbie's adorable, isn't he? And he sure loves that dog. He chatted like a magpie all day about his playmates back in Clayton, and he seemed to enjoy the Park's festivities."

"Aye, he's a sweet little lad." The twinkle in his eye told her he wanted to know about the adults' relationship, if there was one. "But what about his father?"

Was she jumping the gun here? George had been kind and gentlemanly, but he'd not declared any feelings nor made overtures of courtship. Perhaps he was merely interested in a friendship. Still, he'd invited her to his church and to dinner with his mother.

Maybe she should discuss her thoughts about George. But not yet. Not until she had a better handle on where their relationship stood. She'd stick to the facts. "We watched a round of lawn tennis, shared caramel corn from the popcorn stand, and even went roller skating. I'd ice skated before, but this was different and I didn't fall once. Robbie was just amazing, weaving in and out of other couples until George had to settle him down by making him skate between us and holding our hands. He didn't like it as much after that."

"Oh, I bet not."

Mary leaned forward, smiling. "Shall we go to breakfast?"

Gramps took her hand and squeezed it. Then he drilled her with a chastising stare. "Always in a hurry, you are. In a little we bit, my dear. I want to savor our chat first. How did you feel about being honored at the concert? I was rather proud of the two of you when they acknowledged your parts in keeping the recent fire from spreading."

"Oh, stuff and nonsense. I simply did my job and called in the fire. There was little need to make a fuss over me. George and the bucket brigade are the real heroes."

Gramps shifted in his chair and shrugged. "And after the accolades? How was the concert? As you know, I left early."

"The open-air bandstand has wonderful acoustics, and the music was heavenly. I loved viewing the canopy of stars twinkle overhead, as if they were dancing to the music. And you missed hearing the hundred-member chorus sing, 'Those in Peril on the Sea" and 'Nearer my God to Thee.' Did you know the *Titanic* survivors reported that the latter was the last song ever played on the ship? They sang the two hymns in honor of those who lost their lives in April. Can you imagine?"

"I cannot. I've crossed the Atlantic four times in my life, and it can be perilous. Once, a storm arose so furiously that my wife and I were tossed right out of our bunk. She was so seasick, I wasn't sure she'd live to see the dawn, but she did. It was the last time we sailed."

"I'm not sure I ever want to take to the ocean, but I do love the river."

Gramps *tsk*ed her, tilting his head in a mock scold. "You're evading the topic, my dear. I want to know your heart. The way George looks at you—and the way you look at him? I may be old, but I'm not blind."

Mary sighed. "You see rightly, and yes, we danced. It was wonderful being held by such strong yet gentle arms. Like a warm blanket."

"I knew it. But please be careful, dear. He has a young child watching. We don't want him to get too attached before the match is signed, sealed, and delivered." Gramps struggled to rise, a small chuckle escaping his lips.

She helped him rise and handed him his beautifully carved cane. "Robbie fell asleep during the concert and napped on the quilt while we danced. But yes. Robbie is my greatest concern. I'd never want to hurt that little fellow. Ever. But today, I'm catching the ferry to attend church with them and then have Sunday dinner with his mother."

Gramps let out a little groan, his eyes clouding over like an approaching storm. But just as quickly as it had come, the grimace vanished. He swallowed hard, pasting on a smile and taking her arm to lead her to the hotel dining room busy with the morning crowd. "I have more to say, but we can talk over breakfast."

What was he thinking? Was something amiss with George?

When they were seated in the dining room with coffee in hand, Gramps continued the conversation. "I want to warn you about something. George's mother is, shall we say, challenging. Without betraying a confidence, I've been told she's rather opinionated. I tell you this only to prepare you, for I don't want you hurt, child."

Mary waved off his concern. "Oh, George had alluded to something similar, but I've lived under Aunt Stella's opinions for years, remember? His mother can't be all that bad. I'm sure I've seen worse. At least I've heard worse in many a conversation."

"Yes, well. Just so you know." He paused, and his wrinkled concern melted into a loving smile. "I hope you have a lovely time, Mary."

The waiter delivered flapjacks and bacon for both of them, with sides of fresh berries. She grinned. "Those berries look delicious."

After grace, she swallowed a sweet and salty bite. "Tell me about your years in ministry, Gramps. I've only heard bits and pieces of your story."

Gramps pulled out his pocket watch, snapped open the cover, checked the time, and closed it, returning it to where it belonged. "That's a long, long story, and if you're to catch the ferry in time for church, you'll have to settle for a short version. I started preaching at the age of twenty, stayed in one church for three decades, another for twenty years, and retired eleven years ago to live here permanently.

My dear wife, God rest her soul, went to heaven five years ago, and this community has become my family. My only son is a banker in Albany, so getting away to visit me isn't easy for him. And my traveling days are done."

"Does he have a family? Do you have grandchildren?" A pang of sadness pierced her heart.

Gramps shook his head. "His wife died in childbirth, along with their baby girl. Since then, he's plunged into work with abandon and is still angry with God for taking his family."

"I'm so sorry, Gramps. You don't have to talk about it. I didn't mean to cause you sorrow." The pang deepened to a heavy heartache.

He took a sip of coffee before continuing. "It's all right. I haven't told many, but it does a body good to share our grief with another. It lessens the burden, somehow."

Mary nodded.

That it did.

Hopefully, her coming days held more promise and joy than sorrow.

~ ~ ~

George caught Mary's eye as she stood at the back of the church at the close of the service, hands clasped tightly and shoulders slumped. As uncomfortable as a filly with its first halter. He weaved his way through the crowd to join her, never taking his eyes off her.

Why hadn't she come and sat with him?

"Good morning, Mary. Have you been here long? I thought you might've decided not to come." George rolled the rim of his hat in his hands to ward off his nervous energy. He'd fretted about her absence through the entire service.

"The ferry was late, and the service had started. I didn't want to make a scene." She shook her head, then nodded, as if confused.

"Miss Mary!" Robbie wiggled his way around a stocky gentleman and promptly wrapped his small arms around her legs. "I'm so glad you're here. I lost my first tooth this morning and want to show it to you, but it's at home. So now I'm a big boy."

"Are you, now? Well, congratulations." Mary giggled and patted his head. She put out her hand, and the boy shook it, standing tall and proud.

George chuckled and shooed him outside. "Go and play with your pals, but don't muss your Sunday best, young man. I'll be there in a minute."

George searched the room for his mother. There she was, whispering to her two best friends, Eleanor and Gertie, already judging poor Mary with a narrow-eyed glare. He knew that look. She hadn't even met her yet, but more than likely, she'd already made up her mind that this beautiful woman would not pass muster with her.

Then again, no one ever did. Not even Alma.

George gestured for Mary to head outside ahead of him. He needed to get her out of his mother's line of sight. She complied and made her way through the crowd, pleasantly shook the hand of the pastor, and descended the steps. He followed, but his friend, Sam, stopped him halfway down the stairs.

Sam snapped his thickly bearded chin toward the river. "Want to go fishing? It's a nice day for it."

"Not today. We're having company for dinner." George slipped on his hat. He motioned toward Mary, who waited for him on the grass.

Sam followed his gaze and oogled Mary longer than he should. "Better not keep her waiting. She looks to be a keeper."

George clapped him on the shoulder and hurried to Mary's side. "Sorry about that. Let's find Robbie and head to the house. It's just a few blocks from here."

Mary pointed at four little boys playing tag. "Robbie's right there. What about your mother?"

He chuckled, slapping his forehead with his palm. "I almost forgot about her. She's talking with her friends and should be out shortly. Do you mind waiting? We can stand under that big oak." He ducked his chin toward it.

"Certainly. I'm looking forward to meeting her."

George swallowed his angst and led her to the generous patch of shade. Several neighbors and friends gawked at Mary, but she seemed not to notice. Thank the good Lord for that. He needed to keep it that way. "Were you here for the entire service?"

"Yes. Everyone rose for the first hymn, so I couldn't see you until later. Your pastor is an excellent orator." Mary brushed a stray hair from her face.

Robbie now had a stick and was sword fighting with another boy. George mumbled to himself, "Don't poke anyone, child. Be careful."

Mary followed his gaze and grimaced. "Dear me. Little boys can get into mischief quicker than a mouse can scurry from a cat."

"They can, so if you'll excuse me, I'm going to fetch my little mouse before anything happens."

He left her under the tree, retrieved Robbie, and returned as his mother approached Mary, her two friends following arm in arm. George hurried to get there first. He arrived at Mary's side, ready to ward off any attacks the women might lob. To his surprise, Robbie unknowingly ran interference.

His son slipped his hand into Mary's. "Grandmother, this is my friend, Miss Mary. She's very nice and likes to skate, just like me. She knows how to tie shoes and everything."

Gertie chuckled. Eleanor guffawed. Mother scowled. But all three greeted her.

Mary curtsied respectfully. "Pleased to make your acquaintance. Your church is lovely."

Gertie and Eleanor excused themselves to join their husbands. Mother, however, had little to say.

George broke the silence. "Shall we head home? I'm hungry."

Robbie tugged Mary forward. "Me too. Come on, Miss Mary. Grandmother is making chicken and dumplings, and it's my favorite. She baked yeast rolls, and I ate two for breakfast. And she made a cake for dessert."

Mrs. Flannigan grumbled. "You needn't tell the entire world our menu, young man. Mind your manners and walk on." She took the child's hand and tugged him away from Mary. "I need your arm, Robbie. Come here and help an old lady out." She slipped her other hand into the crook of George's arm, leaving Mary to walk behind them alone.

What was he to do? The boardwalk wasn't wide enough for four, but Mother kept tight to both him and Robbie. He slipped Mary his most apologetic gaze and mouthed the word, *sorry*. What else could he do?

He had an idea. "Robbie, why don't you be a gentleman and walk with Miss Mary?"

His boy's face lit up with a smile, and he tried to pry his hand free, but … "Grandmother won't let go."

Mother frowned. "He'll stay right here, thank you very much. The boy gets into mischief far too often these days."

He turned to Mary and shrugged his failure. Mary, to her credit, mouthed back, "It's okay."

When they reached the house, Mother continued to shun Mary. She made Robbie set the table and kept George busy helping her.

Mary stood in the kitchen doorway unsure if she'd be welcome in the woman's domain. But she pushed through the awkwardness. "May I help with something? I'd be happy to fill the water glasses."

Mother shook her head. "No. You're George's guest. Sit over there in the dining room. We'll take care of everything."

Her tone slithered with condescension. Disapproval. Judgment.

Mary forced a smile. "If you don't mind, I'll just get some air on the porch." She sighed before slipping out the front door.

Robbie dropped a knife, picked it up, and placed it on the table. "Can I go too?"

"No!" Mother raised her voice as her eyebrows rose. "Stay right here, young man, where I can keep an eye on you."

George couldn't allow this behavior. Not even from his mother. He kept his voice low, in case Mary was within earshot. "You are being completely rude, Mother. She's done nothing to you. Change your tone now, or I'll take her and Robbie to dinner at the café."

Mother slammed her palm on the counter, her voice even louder. "That is no way to speak to your mother. She is not good enough for you. She's a working girl. And she sat at the back of the church like a heathen. She doesn't belong here."

Fury set his blood surging, and the little vein in his neck throbbed. "Enough. You judge that which you do not know, and you judge wrongly. Robbie, come with me. Mother, we'll be back later. Enjoy your dinner without us."

Mother stood frozen, her mouth open, her eyes wide. Robbie blinked at the interchange but he ran to his father's side, and the two left the kitchen.

The child stopped and looked up at him with a furrowed brow. "Are we not eating dinner? I'm hungry."

George led him through the living room and out onto the porch where he found Mary with the same aghast expression on her face, albeit much prettier than his mother's. He ruffled Robbie's hair. "Let's see what they're serving at the café, shall we?"

"But I like Grandmother's chicken and dumplings best." Robbie hesitated.

George knelt down and looked him in the eye. "Grandmother isn't feeling well and needs time alone. We'll eat her leftovers tonight."

"Perhaps I should say goodbye and let you two have dinner without me." Mary moved toward the front steps.

George shook his head. "No, Mary. Let her be. I'll give her your regrets later. After she's come to her senses."

Robbie reached for the front door. "But I didn't show Miss Mary my tooth."

"Another time, son. Let's go." George stopped him by taking his hand and tugging him toward the steps.

The three of them walked to the café. No one spoke. Not even Robbie. When they were seated in the café book, Robbie ventured to pipe up. "May I please have a malt? Do you like them, Miss Mary?"

"I do. Chocolate is my favorite."

George grinned. "Well, in honor of you losing your first tooth, we will all have malts."

Robbie cheered, but then he clamped his palm over his mouth. Slowly, he peeled his fingers away and whispered, "Yippee."

Mary and George laughed at the child's antics, dispelling a bit of the gloom. When a friend of Robbie's came into the café, he excused himself to say hello, and George took the opportunity to apologize.

"Forgive that back there. Mother doesn't think anyone is good enough for her son. Not even my dearly departed wife. I'm sorry she treated you so rudely." The last sentence almost croaked out of his throat as he tamped down his embarrassment, frustration, and anger.

Mary pressed her lips tight before replying. "It's all right. If I were her, I don't know how I'd feel about a working woman coming into my house with my son and grandson. And her an orphan, no less."

George's nerves quivered with angst. Would this be the end of their budding relationship? Few women would put up with such cold, heartless treatment.

He heaved a great sigh. "None of that should matter."

Mary let out a tiny moan. "Ah, but apparently it does."

Chapter 11

By week's end, Mary's thoughts had spun a web of confusion so tightly she didn't know what to say or do. Why would anyone treat another person as rudely as Mrs. Flannigan had her? If Mary had offended the woman, that would be one thing. But she'd barely met George's mother, and still Mrs. Flannigan and her cronies found her wanting.

The switchboard lit again, so Mary answered another call and plugged the telephone jack into the appropriate spot. She ran her hand over the machine with no small measure of affection. A switchboard operator held a modern and respectable job, for heaven's sake, but Mrs. Flannigan talked as if she worked in a brothel. She huffed her exasperation as the telegraph clicked to life.

She picked up her pencil and paper and jotted down the brief message. Truth be told, telegraphy was her first love, even if it was a dying art quickly being replaced by the telephone.

She read the message aloud. "'To Marilyn Petty. Mr. Petty returning from London by week's end. Gerard Petty.'"

A simple enough telegram, and one without drama. She called the front desk to send a delivery boy, gave the lad the telegram to deliver, and returned to her musings.

Would pondering the problem of Mrs. Flannigan's hostility over and over day and night solve anything? No.

Yet almost a week later, disappointment still tainted every encounter with George. He didn't speak of his mother's nastiness, and neither did she, but the quick conversations with him remained tense and uncomfortable, as if they were both lost in the awkwardness of the altercation.

Gramps had been right to caution her, but she still hadn't spoken with him about it. She'd grown so fond of George and little Robbie that she didn't want to write them off just yet. But was George dismissing *her* based on his mother's assessment? He sure didn't display the same warmth and affection he had a week ago.

"Good afternoon, Mary. Do you have a moment to speak?"

At the sound of George's voice, she startled. He stepped into her office, raking his hands through his hair. Her nerves prickled up and down her spine. She'd been thinking about him, and here he was!

She pasted on a smile she knew didn't rise to her eyes, but it would have to do. "Have a seat." She tapped the book on her lap. "Calls have been spotty today, so I've been catching up on my reading."

"Ah. What is it?" He leaned down for a closer look.

"*The Girl of the Limberlost* by Gene Stratton-Porter. It's about a poor Indiana girl named Elnora whose widowed mother blames her for her father's death and treats her terribly. But Elnora is smart in school and learns to play the violin. She also sells moths, of all things, to make money. Her mother thwarts her efforts at every turn, but then she meets a young man, Philip, and, well … that's as far as I've gotten."

George grinned, obviously amused at her prattling tongue. Nervous chatter was one of her many weaknesses.

She sighed and shrugged a silent apology.

His face grew serious, his eyes sad. "The woman sounds like my mother. Bitter. Mean. Manipulative. Opinionated. I'm sorry she hurt you, Mary. Truly. She had no right to say such things and to make unfair judgments. But Mother is a formidable woman, and as long as she takes care of my son and has such a powerful influence over him, I feel as though I'm always walking a tightrope around her so she won't seek retribution on Robbie."

Mary absorbed the reality of his confession. He bit his tongue and endured abuse for his son's sake. That put things into perspective. "Is there no one else who can care for your son?"

George shrugged. "Mother grumbles about having to feed him and watch him, but she'd explode if I sent Robbie to someone else. It's so much easier when he's in school, but in the summer, he has far too much time with her for his good. Nevertheless, you should never have to bear the brunt of her stormy existence. I'm sorry. Truly."

She nodded, pursing her lips and exhaling deeply. "I forgive you, and I'll try to forgive her, but that might take longer." She forced a smile, and to her surprise, the knot that had taken root in her heart eased a little.

A nerve near the scar on George's cheek twitched. "Moreover, I'm sorry I've been so melancholy with you this past week. I didn't know what to say, or how to say it."

The switchboard came to life with two lights at the same time, so Mary turned to take care of them. The distraction provided the time needed to settle her nerves.

George waited patiently until she'd finished. "You should be proud of how accomplished you are in this job." He pointed toward the telegraph machine. "And with that too."

Mary lifted her chin. "Thank you. Although your mother doesn't think so." That last admission just slipped out.

He fiddled with his pant leg. "She doesn't think any woman should work at anything but homemaking. Pay no mind to her narrow-minded opinions."

What could she say to that? She couldn't excuse what the woman thought, so she stayed silent.

George looked out the window, forehead wrinkled. He drew his lips into a tight, thin line, and his eyes changed to a deep cobalt blue, like the glassware her aunties collected. What was he thinking?

She let the silence fill the room as she measured the man before her. She wouldn't tolerate his mother's vitriol, but George did so for the sake of his son. What must it be like to live with such a woman? And how did she treat little Robbie?

George's voice broke the silence and pulled her from her thoughts. "Are you free tomorrow afternoon? Can Robbie and I take you on a boat ride and perhaps do a little fishing?"

Mary blinked her surprise. Such a change of topic, and for the better. "Will your mother be coming, too?"

He chuckled. "Never. She wouldn't step a toenail into a boat. Says the mighty St. Lawrence is far too dangerous and unpredictable for her."

"Then I'd be delighted. Please know that I don't hold a grudge against her or anything. I just don't want …"

He raised a hand. "No need, Mary. I quite understand. I promise you, I won't put you in such an awkward situation again. Robbie and I enjoy your company, and my son is ever so taken with you. If it means we can only spend time with you here at the Park or out on the water, then so be it. Until Mother comes to her senses, she'll miss out on getting to know you, and it will be her loss. Just like Alma was."

Mary tilted her head in confusion. "Alma?"

George's eyes flashed. Was anger? Or … fear? "My deceased wife. Mother never took to her. Because of it, Mother and I were estranged the whole time we were married, and we didn't spend time together until after Alma died."

Poor man. So much sorrow in his young life. "How did she die?"

Again, a flash of strong emotion crossed his handsome face. "That's a conversation for another time."

"Another time, then." Mary conceded.

That there would be another time filled her with hope.

~ ~ ~

The next afternoon, George and his son waited on the verandah for Mary. Such a perfect day for boating and fishing. The placid river had barely a breeze to ruffle its waters. Sunny and warm, but not too hot. A quiet afternoon on the St. Lawrence River with Robbie and the prettiest girl around.

Heaven.

Mary and Mr. Wiseman stepped through the doorway, chatting and laughing. The old man's cane clicked in syncopation as he walked, and Robbie drummed his hands on the verandah railing to the beat. George chuckled. His son often found the beat of whatever was around him, his rhythm impeccable. Perhaps he'd be a drummer one day.

Mary caught George's eye, and her face lit up like the Fourth of July fireworks. Today, her smile was genuine, joyful, and full. And oh, so beautiful. She gave him a little curtsy. "Good afternoon, sir. Robbie."

Robbie, who'd been watching children play on the nearby lawn, turned and ran into Mary's outstretched arms, hugging her tightly. "We're going fishing, Miss Mary. With you!"

She laughed as she lovingly stroked the boy's hair. "I know. I haven't been fishing all summer, so you'll have to give me lots of pointers, okay?"

Robbie nodded. "Okay, Miss Mary."

"Sounds like you're in for a wonderful afternoon, my dear." Mr. Wiseman chuckled.

George helped Mr. Wiseman ease into his chair. "Would you like to join us on our outing, sir? I'm sure we all would enjoy your company immensely."

"As I told Mary, my rheumatism is acting up today, so I'm in no condition to be in a boat. Sorry, but I'll stay on dry land and await your return."

"We'll miss you, sir. But I understand." George shrugged, taking Robbie's hand.

Robbie let go of his hand and hugged the old man. "I'll catch a big fish for you, Mr. Wiseman. Then you won't feel so sad."

Mr. Wiseman hugged him back. "That'll be just crackin', laddie. Have fun."

"Shall we?" George waved a hand for Mary to take the lead.

Robbie grabbed her hand and pulled her toward the stairs. "Let's go, Miss Mary. I'll show you how to catch a muskie."

Mary giggled, tossing a farewell over her shoulder. "See you later, Gramps."

After they settled in the launch, George eased the boat out onto the river, heading southwest. "I thought we'd skirt Grenell Island and fish closer to Grindstone Island."

"Whatever you think. You're the captain of this ship, sir." Mary nodded, a playful grin dancing on her lips.

"And I'm the first mate." Robbie sat up straight, poking his thumb into his puffed-out chest.

George chuckled. "On land and sea, that you are, Robbie."

He turned the boat toward Little Pullman Island, off the northeast corner of Grenell Island. "Do you know the story of Pullman House that used to be here?"

"I think I've heard it, but can't recall the details. Do tell."

George had reviewed its history the night before, just to be sure he could share the details accurately. "It was a beautiful fifty-four-room hotel built in 1890 that took up most of the space on the island. The four-story building had wide verandas and boasted much success for several years until other resorts brought a lot of stiff competition. But at two a.m. on September 14, 1904, it burned to the ground. They never rebuilt."

"Were there victims of the fire?" Mary's brow creased, and sorrow filled her pretty brown eyes, golden flecks sparkling in the sunshine.

Always caring about others, that one.

"No." George put her fears at ease. "There were only three guests and hotel employees there, but because the hotel occupied most of the space on the island, they fled by boat, leaving everything behind."

"I don't like hotels. They burn." Robbie scooted closer to Mary and took her hand.

Mary put her arm around the child and hugged him. "Not always, Robbie. The Columbian Hotel, where Mr. Wiseman and I now live, hasn't burned. Neither has the Crossmon House or the Thousand Islands Hotel in Alexandria Bay, nor lots of others."

Robbie whined. "But they might. And people might burn up like Mama did."

George cringed at the child's admission. He glanced at Mary, who blinked in surprise. And sadness. "Robbie. That's enough. Mama is in heaven with God, remember?"

"But if she's all burned up, how can she walk and talk?" His son scowled.

George's pulse sped up. He struggled to keep his voice calm and not alarm his son. "Who told you that, Robbie?"

Apparently, he hadn't sounded as calm as he wanted. Robbie curled up even closer to Mary. "Grandmother. And Tommy. He said she burned to a crisp in her bed. When I asked Grandmother, she said she died a terrible death."

Mary slipped Robbie onto her lap and cuddled him close. She stroked his hair. "No matter what happened to her, Robbie, she's with Jesus now. And in heaven, there's no more pain or sorrow or suffering. Only joy and peace."

"Promise?" Robbie popped his head off her chest and looked at her.

Mary smiled and nodded. She planted a long, sweet kiss on the child's forehead. "Promise."

His son hugged her tightly, then hopped off her lap. "That's good to know. Thank you, Miss Mary."

George heaved an enormous sigh of relief. What would he have said to comfort his son? He smiled and mouthed the words, *thank you*, to Mary, who nodded back.

To make sure Robbie didn't ask more questions like that, George called him to his side. "Come and help me steer, son."

Robbie complied, his little face scrunched up in serious concentration, but his smile wide, nonetheless.

George returned to playing tour guide to Mary and Robbie. "Grenell Island is a close-knit community that boasts of having one of the earliest island inns. Most of the cottages line the shore, as you can see here. But there's also a lovely chapel and a community house there where the islanders gather. And just like the other islands, mail delivery is by boat, though they also have a post office."

"When are we going to fish, Daddy?" Robbie kept his eyes keenly over the bow.

George smiled, shaking his head at the boy's impatience. "Soon, son."

Just then, a huge freighter came lumbering up on their starboard side. Far enough away to avoid its wake but close enough to enjoy the view, they waved at sailors who waved back. The captain tooted a salute, blowing the ship's whistle three times. Robbie waved both arms furiously, obviously delighted at the attention. He was done with captaining the launch for now.

George took over and skirted the south end of Grenell. "I hear the muskie are biting between Murray Island and Picton. Let's head that way."

He did, and soon they dropped anchor and settled in for an afternoon of fishing.

When Robbie complained of an empty tummy, George opened the picnic basket he'd brought and handed Mary a sandwich wrapped in wax paper. "I hope you like my chicken salad, though I'm sure it's not as heavenly as your aunts'. And there are carrot sticks and raisin cookies too."

"And lemonade. Can I have a cookie now, please?" Robbie put out his hand.

"Eat this first. It's a jam sandwich. Then you can have a cookie, son." George rolled his eyes, handing him the sandwich.

"Thank you. I hadn't eaten lunch." Mary giggled, unwrapping her sandwich.

"Me either." He took a bite and swallowed before speaking. "Daddy, why are Dalmatians used as fire dogs?"

George guffawed. "Now, why would you ask such a question out here in the middle of the river?"

"I was thinking about Cooper and just wondered." His son shrugged and bit his sandwich again.

George took a bite of his sandwich, chewed, and swallowed before answering. "Dalmatians are powerful dogs and get along well with horses. We train them to run in front of the fire engines to clear a path and guide the horses to the fire. Their long legs and sturdy bodies give them endurance, and they're obedient and good tempered. They are also very brave dogs, so they help keep the horses calm during a fire."

"Really?" Mary swallowed a bite. "Cooper can do all that? No wonder Robbie loves him."

George chuckled. "He's a great mascot too. Cooper guards the fire equipment while we're busy fighting fires. All in all, he's a valiant, invaluable asset to me as a firefighter, and he's a faithful friend to Robbie."

"He's my best friend." Robbie nodded, chewing a large bite. Suddenly, he jumped up, thrust his sandwich at Mary, and grabbed his bobbing pole. "I got a bite! I got a bite!"

He yanked his pole, and George helped him pull in his catch. Sure enough, his son caught the first fish, a large walleye.

"Well done, first mate. You're quite a little fisherman." Mary beamed. "I'd guess that to be almost ten pounds."

"Mr. Wiseman will be so proud of you, son."

Robbie sat tall in his seat. "Can I have a cookie now?"

Mary and George laughed together, but she didn't hand him a cookie. Didn't suggest he give his son the treat. She let him answer. So respectful. So … precious.

"Yes, you may. Mary?"

She shook her head. "I'm still working on the sandwich, thank you."

Soon, Mary's pole came to life, almost slipping out of the boat before he caught it. He handed it to her and let her wrestle with what had to be a large fish. When she finally got it in the boat, it was indeed a muskie.

George gave her shoulder a gentle side hug. "Well done. Muskellunges are a sport fisherman's favorite fish. And did you know they sometimes eat walleye?"

"Don't let him eat Wally." Robbie waved his hands over his fish.

Mary took his hand. "The muskie couldn't eat Wally. He's too small. Look."

The pair turned to compare the size of the mouths of their catches while he observed the woman who'd snared his heart.

Yep. She was a catch all right.

Chapter 12

Mary swept a wisp of hair from her eyes as she moved her bishop diagonally, taking one of Gramps's rooks. Her smile wouldn't leave her lips, but she tried to sound contrite, nevertheless. "Sorry about that. I'm sure you won't let that happen again."

"I'll try not to, but you just keep getting better every time I play you. You've become a worthy opponent, young lady." Gramps chuckled, swatting at a fly that tormented him.

She waved away the compliment. "Beginner's luck, I'm sure. I wonder how the Park Progressive Club meeting is going. George had to present his findings on fire safety and prevention tonight."

"Aye, I'm sure his report was ready, and he'll do a fine job." Gramps clicked his tongue. "Besides, Dr. Goodale has been very supportive of him, so he has at least one ally in his corner. I just hope the Association will finally be able to settle on a solid plan to reduce the fire danger around here."

She moved a pawn two spaces. "Me too. Except for that two-minute drizzle this morning, it's been almost seven weeks since we've seen any rain here. I doubt that smidgen of sprinkles helped even one blade of grass."

Gramps pointed toward the north. "Everything around here is so dry, and I've heard the Park's reservoir is at its lowest levels in a long while. I fear the fire danger is at a record high."

"I keep having bad dreams about the whole Park catching fire." Mary shuddered. "I pray those dreams never come true."

"Me too. Check mate, darlin'. You missed that one." Gramps nodded, then knocked over her king. He pointed to the opening she made by moving her pawn that gave his queen the pathway to victory.

George bounded up the hotel stairs, taking two steps at a time, pulling her attention away from the game. When he joined them on the veranda, he glanced at the board and raised an eyebrow. "Did he get you again, Mary? Good evening, sir."

Mary rolled her eyes. "Just when I think I've gotten the upper hand, I make a careless move. How did the meeting go?"

George wobbled his head back and forth as if trying to decide. "For a Wednesday evening, it wasn't too bad. And it was lively, I'll give you that. Dr. Goodale reiterated the suggestion for the Association to match private donations, and the committee unanimously agreed. But the problem still stands that the Park's tax structure limits how much money they can raise, so we've got to find another avenue to fund fire improvements and safety measures. I just don't know what that would be."

Mary put a forefinger in the air. "Perhaps we could engage wealthy benefactors who might help. Mr. Emery, perhaps? He lived through losing his very own Frontenac Hotel to fire just last year. Maybe he'd be sympathetic to our cause?"

Gramps shook his head. "That's doubtful, as he's moved on to other things. But other wealthy patrons who have stayed in the islands and have enjoyed the Park might be worth a try. Or organizations who have held conventions here, like the Grangers, the Templars, or the 74th Regiment? Anything is worth a try, I suppose."

Mary glanced toward the adjacent New York State Education Building. "What about petitioning New York State to help? After all, the Park is in the state, and so is their educational program."

"You two have presented me with more ideas in two minutes' time than the whole committee did in two hours. And good ideas, all. I'll take them to our meeting next week. Thank you."

A long silence filled the air until Gramps yawned and stood to leave. "If you'll excuse me, friends. These old bones are ready to retire for the night."

She stood and planted a kiss on his cheek. "I won't be long, Gramps."

"Take your time. It's still early. The sun won't set for another hour and a half." A twinkle crossing his dark eyes.

After Gramps hobbled into the hotel, George turned to her. "Care for an evening stroll before I return to the mainland?"

"I'd like that." Mary nodded.

Instead of heading straight down St. Lawrence Avenue to the main dock where George usually parked his launch, he led them up West Rainbow Street and then turned south onto Ontario Avenue. Strolling along quiet streets lined with pretty Victorian homes was a welcome and peaceful change.

She and George chatted about simple things as several neighbors waved their greetings when they passed by. Their topics of conversation were rather perfunctory. How nicely the Park folk kept their flower beds despite the drought. About the intricate gingerbread trim on the feminine Victorians. That Mrs. Town had just become a grandmother. Yet a much more important topic stirred in her mind. But how to broach the subject?

Finally, she got up the nerve. "May I ask something personal?"

George slowed his pace and glanced down at her with his sky-blue eyes, tender and receptive. "Of course. What do you want to know?"

Mary swallowed hard, hoping her inquiry wouldn't offend him. "When Robbie talked about his mother's death, I couldn't help but wonder what happened."

"I thought you'd ask about it sometime, so now is as good a time as any." He cleared his throat before sighing deeply.

Mary slipped her hand into the crook of his arm and gave it a gentle squeeze. "If it's too painful, you needn't."

"No." He shook his head. "You should know. I failed her, Mary. My job as a firefighter is to protect and save people from fire, and I couldn't even save my own wife."

She stopped walking, and they stood on the boardwalk for several moments in thick, uncomfortable silence. How could she console him when she didn't know what happened? Her blood chilled at the thought of being in a fire and not being able to breathe. "Oh, George. I'm so sorry for your loss. But I'm sure you would have risked your very life for her, if you'd had the chance."

George groaned. "That's just it. I wasn't even there. I was working at a barn fire out in the middle of nowhere, saving goats and pigs and chickens instead of my own family. Our neighbors saw the flames and got little Robbie to safety, but they couldn't save Alma."

Mary imagined the tragedy with too much clarity. She shuddered. "How old was Robbie?"

George glanced down the road for several moments before answering, his shoulders sagging like a popped balloon. "Just short of two years old. It was nap time, and apparently, Alma laid down with him and fell asleep. The neighbors saw him standing on the porch alone and crying. Then they saw the flames. By the time they got my son off the porch, the front room collapsed, and it was impossible to enter the house. It burned to the ground with her still inside."

Mary's throat thickened. Her eyes stung, but she blinked back the tears threatening to spill over. She had to be strong for him. "That wasn't your fault, George. You were doing your job, and she was doing hers. It was an accident."

The sound that escaped George's lips reminded her of a growl. Guttural. Grief-laden. "I should have been there."

How could she respond to that? "God save us from such a day."

"He didn't save my wife." Bitterness tainted his retort. "She died in a fire when I wasn't there. I failed her. I failed Him. I failed Robbie."

"But the tragedy made you who you are. Brave. Strong. Fearless. Yet kind and compassionate. A man who will risk his very life to help others." Mary turned to face him and shook her head. "There is no greater love, George."

George's eyes flooded with tears. "I wish I would have died in that fire instead of her. Then Robbie would have a loving mother to care for him and not a ..."

A couple stepped out onto a porch near them and waved hello. Mary waved back but tugged George to walk on, out of earshot of the couple. This conversation was for her ears only. "But God chose for you to live and be Robbie's father and take care of him. You can't wish away providence. You're a wonderful father, George, and no amount of regret or even wishing your son had a better caregiver will change that. I'm so sorry for your loss, but you must trust that God has a good plan for your future."

George worked his jaw back and forth before responding. "And what of Robbie's future with no mother?"

Mary hugged his arm tightly, trying to show as much compassion as she felt. "Jeremiah 29:11 is one of my favorite Scriptures. 'For I know the thoughts that I think toward you, saith the Lord, thoughts of peace, and not of evil, to give you an expected end.' When my parents died within days of each other, I felt so much anger and sadness I wasn't sure I could go on without them. I was angry at God and blamed Him for ruining my life. But after a while, I found my way back, only to realize that grief had severely tainted the way I looked at the world. I still miss them, and I always will, but I see life differently now. Through the lens of hope."

"Perhaps one day I will too." George tentatively smiled, but his eyes still showed pain.

"I'll pray you will."

~ ~ ~

George closed the screen door to his mother's house as quietly as he could. He didn't want to wake Robbie—or incur the wrath of his mother. The day had already been too confusing, frustrating, and stressful. Especially after opening his heart to Mary about Alma and his failures.

"It's about time you got home. Where have you been all this time?" Mother grumbled from the kitchen, banging pots and stomping her way into the living room. "I'm plumb worn out caring for your child. I wash my hands of it."

"I had the Park Progressive Club committee presentation tonight, remember?" George sighed. He hadn't the energy for this.

Mother wiped her hands on her dirty apron, her hair already in curlers and tied up with a kerchief. "You spend far too much time over there. Are you fraternizing with that working girl? You'd better not be. She isn't fittin' for you."

A spark of anger lit a fuse, just waiting to catch fire. It surged through him from his head to his toes. "Her name is Mary, and she's an accomplished telegrapher and switchboard operator. And I will speak to whomever I please, thank you very much."

His mother scoffed. "I've had to stop Robbie from speaking of that woman three times today, finally giving him a good swat with a wooden spoon to silence the name of her in this house. I'm tired of hearing his chatter day and night. I'll give you a swat, too, if I have to."

"You spanked him for talking about her? How dare you! And do you punish my son for talking about his mother too? Tell me. Do you?" George scrubbed his face with his hand, trying to calm his anger, to get control of his fury.

She straightened her shoulders and lifted her chin. "I most certainly do. There's no reason to speak of the dead. Especially someone who burned to death. It's not Christian. Only the heathens burn their corpses."

George had heard enough. He turned and punched the wall near the staircase, leaving it with cracked plaster and him with a sore hand. "You may never, ever spank my son. Do you hear me? And you may never, ever speak ill of my wife—or Miss Flynn, for that matter. If you do, we will leave, and you will never see me or my son again. I've left before, and believe me, I will do it again."

"Daddy? Is that you?" Robbie's sleepy voice called down from upstairs. "What's wrong?"

Without giving a moment for his mother to speak, George hurried up the stairs to his son and scooped him into his arms. "Let's go for a walk, Robbie."

Robbie's face scrunched up in confusion. "In my jammies? It's nighttime."

"Let's go for a nighttime ride in your little red wagon. You can look at the stars while I pull you. Doesn't that sound like fun?" George had to get out of there and take Robbie too. If only for a little while.

Robbie's frown turned to a sleepy smile. "Can I bring my blanket and teddy?"

"Certainly. It'll be a special adventure."

His mother just stood there with her fists on her hips, a scowl on her face, and eyes narrowed in disapproval.

Robbie scurried to grab his comfort items and returned quick as a wink. "Okay, Daddy."

"Okay, son. Let's go."

~ ~ ~

The next morning, George struggled to concentrate on playing chess with Mr. Wiseman. He moved a pawn aimlessly, but he really wanted to talk to the man, one on one. Perhaps the old preacher could help him navigate his complicated circumstances. "I need your advice, sir. I don't know who else to turn to."

"I'm all ears." Mr. Wiseman sat back, waving a hand over the chessboard as if to negate it. "Chess is just a way to break the ice with folks. Sharing people's lives is what I live for. It's what I've always lived for."

George tapped his forefinger to his chin, trying to figure out where to start. "I've made a terrible mess of things, sir. I've failed in so many ways and put my son in peril, and I don't know what to do."

"He seems like a happy little boy to me. What peril is he in?" Mr. Wiseman's forehead furrowed into a half-dozen deep lines.

"It's my mother. She's impossible. She's a bitter, vindictive, self-righteous woman, and I can't abide her caring for Robbie any-more." George ran his hand through his hair and squeezed the back of his neck that now ached with stress. "Ever since my poor wife died almost four years ago, Robbie and I have lived under my mother's thumb. In the beginning, it was simply irritating. But now, it's intolerable."

"Aye, I see. What makes it intolerable?" Mr. Wiseman picked up his queen and pressed it into his palm.

George reiterated much of what he'd told Mary the day before. The pain. The regret. And then he told the old man about last night's altercation.

Mr. Wiseman nodded. "This is quite a quandary, son. When a spouse dies, your world turns upside down. When my wife died, I wasn't sure I could go on, but somehow, I did. Still, it's all the harder when your loved one dies in a terrible accident like your Alma did. And if you have a small child to care for, you don't even have the freedom to mourn as you should. You must be strong for your child and care for him. Seems you've done the best you could, son."

"So many times, I've had to hide my sadness or my fear, paste on a smile, and pretend everything's okay when it wasn't. I've been angry, numb, shocked, and felt terribly, awfully guilty." George slapped his thigh. "But Robbie doesn't need to know any of that. He just needs to have a happy, carefree childhood, and my mother is making that harder and harder."

Mr. Wiseman leaned forward, his forearms resting on his thighs. "Why guilty?"

"I didn't save her. My wife died in a fire while I was fighting another fire. She'd still be alive today if I'd been there like I should have. And now, I can't even protect my son."

The old preacher shook his head and a forefinger simultaneously. "One thing at a time, George. First, you can't blame yourself for not being there. You were doing your job, and an accident happened. Guilt is too powerful an emotion to carry this long, and it can bring deadly consequences if you don't let go of it."

"Mother reminds me of my guilt regularly." George's voice cracked as he spoke. "And now she won't even allow Robbie to speak of Alma. She spanks him if he talks about his mother."

"That *is* a problem, and your son needs your protection. But first things first. You must forgive yourself." Mr. Wiseman clucked his tongue.

George swallowed hard and groaned. "Forgive myself?"

"Yes." Mr. Wiseman nodded. "You're so caught up in your own guilt and unforgiveness that you don't have the strength to move forward. But you must, not only for your son, but also for yourself."

George scoffed. "How can I forgive myself?"

"It's a choice, George, to face the reality that you are not perfect and this world isn't perfect either. Bad things happen to good people. You must let go and give up the right of self-condemnation, accept what happened, and choose to move on from it. Only then can you enjoy the freedom to live and find hope for your future. And Robbie's."

George rolled his shoulders and head, easing the tension and willing his body to relax. "That's a lot to ponder, sir."

"Aye. It is." Mr. Wiseman shifted in his seat. "But moreover, you should find a different living situation as soon as you can. Your mother isn't good for either of you, I'm sorry to say."

"I know, but I have to work, and Robbie needs someone to care for him."

Mr. Wiseman raised his palms to the heavens. "Let's put that to prayer. I'm sure God has an answer, even if we don't."

George patted the old man's wrinkled hand. "Thank you, sir. For everything."

Mr. Wiseman cleared his throat, his eyes somber. "There is one more word of caution I have for you, son. About Mary."

George sat ramrod straight. "Sir?"

The elderly man looked deep into his eyes until he flinched. "You can never truly love again until you fully forgive yourself, let go of your guilt, and find peace. Until then, you will only bring Mary heartache and incur more guilt. Go carefully with her, George."

He cleared the lump from his throat and took a deep breath. "I will."

"Can I pray for you?"

George swallowed back emotions he wasn't quite sure what to do with. "Certainly."

Prayer might be the only thing to help him get past this hard place and find the peace he desperately needed.

Chapter 13

Night after night, fire chased Mary in her dreams, lapping up every item she owned, melting the telephone, the telegraph, and everything in the Columbian Hotel.

She grew dizzy because her breath came in rapid, tiny, uncontrolled puffs, even in her dreams. Her heart raced faster than her feet.

Mary rolled over and shook herself, willing her eyes open, trying to stop the madness. After a relentless battle with her bedcovers, she finally woke up with a great deal of effort.

Safe in her bed. Secure and unharmed in the spare room of Gramps's hotel apartment.

She rubbed her temples, but her breath remained imprisoned in her lungs. For the past four days, the painful imaginings of Alma's demise had stuck in her thoughts, running over and over through her mind, draining her of energy and peace.

Every time she thought about fire—especially since George disclosed how Alma died—her heart raced and her lungs refused to work. The thoughts haunted her, so vividly she could almost feel the heat and smell the stench of the burning building. Even her eyes itched and watered until she removed her spectacles and rubbed them.

A knock at her door shook her from her fiery obsession. "It's time to get up, Mary. We should be at breakfast by now."

She scampered out of bed. "Sorry, Gramps. I'll be ready in just a few minutes. Go on ahead, and I'll meet you in the dining room."

As quickly as she could, Mary threw on her clothes and whisked her hair into a haphazard chignon. She'd fix it later. She pinched her cheeks and, within minutes, joined Gramps at the hotel dining room. "Sorry I'm late. Another bad dream."

Gramps patted her hand. "Fire again?"

Mary nodded. "Ever since George told me how Alma died, it won't leave my mind. I don't know how he does what he does, fighting fires and all that. I don't know how he goes on with such horrible memories."

"My dear, George has seen much loss in his young life, but he goes on for his son's sake—and for the high calling of serving and protecting others. That's what keeps him going, I believe."

She brushed a strand of hair from her face and hooked it behind an ear. She should've taken more care with it. "I honor him for all of that, and he loves Robbie so much. But being a firefighter …"

Gramps took a sip of his coffee before responding. "He cares for you, too, more than you realize."

Mary blinked, sucking in a gulp of air. Her hand flew up to her neck, massaging away the prickly heat. "George has been very kind to me, but I doubt he has any genuine feelings for me. We're just friends."

The waiter brought her coffee and refilled his cup. She added cream and sugar before taking a sip.

Gramps wouldn't let the subject go. "You need to guard your heart, my dear. George is a good man, but he has … some things to work through."

Mary rubbed an earlobe. It would be nice if he would expound on what those things were. She sipped her coffee in silence until the waiter brought them plates of eggs and bacon. By then, she could stand it no longer. "What things, Gramps?"

He shook his head and took a bite of crisp fatback. "That's not for me to say. But give him the time and space to figure things out, if he needs it, okay?"

Mary shrugged. "If you say so. Okay."

The way Gramps spoke, George had something mysterious in his past.

Would he tell her? Or would she have to find out for herself?

~ ~ ~

Settling into her office on this Fourth of July holiday, Mary grabbed her cleaning cloth and swiped a spot of dust here and there as the early morning sun cast a warm glow onto the telephone switchboard. The scents of linseed oil and beeswax proved that she kept everything shipshape. She nabbed a few dust bunnies around the telegraph keys too

She breathed in the clean smell as the telegraph came to life. After jotting down the message until the sounds ended, she reread the telegram.

TI Park. Beware of high heat, dry conditions, fire danger. Entire eastern seaboard seeing record highs. In New York City, four dead from heat.

Cold chills ran down her spine. Who sent this? And to whom should she confer this telegram? People dead? Was it a grim joke or the truth?

She responded with, "Who is sending? Who should receive?"

While she waited for an answer, the switchboard lit up. She inserted the phone plug into the jack and answered. "Good morning. To whom may I direct your call?" She smiled and her voice followed suit. "Here you go."

Plug and done.

She glanced at the telegraph. It sat silent. She sent her questions again. No response. Perhaps her aunts could guide her?

Mary rang her aunts' house in Watertown. Aunt Maude answered, her sweet, gentle voice soothing her frayed nerves. Mary explained her predicament. "Who should I give this to, Aunt Maude?"

Aunt Maude took a moment before answering. "Walter Brown is the Association chairman. Or Mr. Fitch, the treasurer? Maybe start there. Otherwise, Dr. Goodale would be happy to help, I'm sure."

Mary was still skeptical. "But could it be a joke?"

Aunt Maude groaned. "No. I was just reading the *Watertown Daily Times*. It's the top headline. Buffalo, Boston, Chicago, even Philadelphia are reporting high temps and deaths from the heat. And here in Watertown, they say it's over one hundred degrees in the sun."

Mary shifted in her seat and swiped her brow. "Oh, my poor aunties. Don't you want to come back to the river? It's cooler here."

Aunt Maude cleared her throat. "Stella wouldn't hear of it, dear. And on that note, we were going to call you today about the cottage. In case you hear of someone who needs a place to stay, you can rent out our cottage, if need be."

Two calls lit up. She'd have to cut the visit short. "Okay. If you're sure. Sorry, but I have other callers. I love you, and I'll telephone again soon. Goodbye, Auntie."

Disconnect. Mr. Brown. How providential. Plug.

"Good morning, Mr. Brown. To whom may I direct your call?"

Mary noted his request and told him about the telegram. Another light lit, beckoning her to connect the caller. "I'll have the telegram delivered to you right away. Here is Mr. Fitch. Thank you."

Plug. Connect. Done.

"Good morning. Whom do you want to speak to?"

Gananoque? An international, long-distance call. Excitement filled her to her fingertips as she connected the call to the Canadian operator. "Here you are."

Plug and done.

By the end of her shift, Mary closed her eyes, leaning her head back to stretch her knotted muscles. She stared at the punched tin ceiling, grateful that the hotel had so many fire-retardant features like that particular decorative finish.

"Good afternoon, Mary. I'm ready to take over."

Charlotte's cheery voice almost caused Mary to fall out of her chair. She giggled with embarrassment.

Mary slipped off her headset and handed it to her friend and co-worker. "Happy Independence Day, Charlotte. I'm on my way to Clayton for the parade and Fourth of July fireworks. Mr. Flannigan is walking in the parade with the firemen."

Charlotte clasped her hands together. "How exciting! Are the Quinn-Taylor Fireworks going to put on the show? Peyton is a friend of mine, though I haven't seen her in a long while."

Mary shrugged. "I believe so. At least, that's what the advertisement in the paper said. The parade is at six and fireworks at nine-thirty. There's a special shuttle boat that will bring us back at ten."

Charlotte wrinkled her nose. "In the dark? No, thank you. I'll watch from the safety of these shores."

Mary grinned at the gentle young lady. "Well, thanks again for covering the switchboard, Charlotte. I hope the lines are quiet for you."

Charlotte waved. "Enjoy the festivities. And Fireman Flannigan."

"Thanks. I will." Mary giggled.

I'm sure I will.

~ ~ ~

Mary entered the café where she was to meet George before the parade. There he was, near the window in the far corner. His gaze landed on her, and he stood, a grin spreading across his handsome face. Her heart skipped several beats. She gave him her brightest smile as she bobbed a little curtsy and joined him. "Good evening, sir."

George rumbled a "hello" with his deep voice, his Adam's apple bobbing up and down. He waved for her to take a seat, but his half smile didn't rise to his eyes. "Happy Fourth of July, Miss Flynn."

Mary sat, and so did George, but he wouldn't look at her. And why call her *Miss Flynn*? His crystal-blue eyes refused to betray his thoughts.

What had changed? In just four days, he'd gone from warm and engaging to distant.

He scanned the menu. "Care to eat something before the parade?"

Still no eye contact.

Mary assessed him from the corner of her eye. "Are you okay?"

His nostrils flared, and his jaw hardened as he glanced at her. "Me? I'm fine. Just don't want to be late for the parade, and I need to pick up Robbie."

A hint of vulnerability passed over his face, but just as quickly, he recovered, returning to his air of self-assurance. Mary handed him the menu. "We don't have to eat now. I wouldn't want to hold you up."

"No, no. It's fine." His clipped words almost seemed to indicate that she'd irritated him.

Her stomach shrank to the size of a pea. When the waitress approached, Mary requested only a chocolate malt. She didn't want to deter George from joining the parade on time or make him upset. He ordered the same. And the atmosphere hung as heavy as malt as well.

What in the world was wrong?

~ ~ ~

George marched in step with the other firemen, his helmet pressing hot and heavy against his skull and his rubber fireman's coat baking him in the July sun. His pulse throbbed as he craned his neck to find Mary in the crowd of spectators. He should have been kinder, more engaging at the café. What a dolt he was!

Yet, ever since Mr. Wiseman cautioned him to be careful with Mary's heart, guilt followed him around like a forlorn puppy. His brain fogged like a misty river's morn, and his pulse set to trotting every time he thought about her. How could he relate to her without engaging her heart? Hadn't he already done that?

Finally, he spotted Mary, her face soft and gentle as she knelt and spoke to Robbie, who laughed in response. As George caught her eye and nodded almost imperceptibly, a certain air of audacity overshadowed her full red lips when she smiled back. Her cheeks blossomed like the bloom of a perfect pink peony as she pointed him out to Robbie.

Robbie waved and hollered, "Hi, Daddy."

George waved back, then dipped his chin to Mary.

The tittering crowd pulled his attention back to the parade as he kept in step with his fellow firemen. Cheers and clapping rolled down the crowd of bystanders when the parade's master of ceremonies touted the brave men who kept their community safe. He called them heroes.

He could never be a hero. He hadn't even kept his wife safe.

He recalled what Mary had said and pondered Mr. Wiseman's counsel to forgive himself, but neither of their words rang true. How was he innocent of Alma's death? How could he let go of the guilt? A web of grief and failure ensnared him.

Would he ever be free?

~ ~ ~

As the sun dipped low on the river, George handed Robbie and Mary each a hotdog and a tumbler of lemonade. Almost two hours until the fireworks. Whatever would he do with Mary for that long? "Let's sit on the bench while we eat, okay?"

Robbie ran to the bench and plopped down, spilling lemonade on his shirt. "Oops. Sorry, Daddy."

George chuckled, wiping the spill from the boy's shirt. "It's okay, son. But let's be careful."

Mary took a bite of her hotdog. "Mmm … I haven't had one of these since last summer's Fourth of July celebration in Watertown. Thank you, George."

"Certainly. It's a Fourth of July favorite, to be sure." George nodded as he wiped mustard off his son's face.

Robbie took a bite and swallowed. "Is Grandmother coming to see the fireworks with us tonight?"

George shook his head. "She's staying home and resting. We'll go down to the shoreline in a little while. It's just us tonight."

"Good. She was grumpy all day. She spanked me and made me take a nap for ever so long." Robbie scrunched up his nose and bobbed his head. "But I couldn't sleep a wink, so I just made up stories in my head. Maybe her feet hurt again."

"Now, son, let's be kind. Are you done? Do you want to play with the boys over there?" George ran his hand through his hair, still wet from the post-parade dip in the river. He glanced at Mary, who pretended she wasn't listening.

Robbie wobbled his head up and down, a bright smile crossing his lips. "Yes, please. I'm full. Can I go now?"

George assessed Robbie's half-eaten hotdog and shrugged. "You may. But play nicely." Once Robbie was out of earshot, George groaned. "I've got to find another place for us to stay. Mother is simply …"

He gasped. Had he really spoken his thoughts aloud? Plus, he'd almost spoken ill of his mother after he'd told his son not to.

"I may have an answer." She raised a forefinger and her eyes twinkled. "I was talking with Aunt Maude just this morning, and they have decided to rent out their cottage. Perhaps that could be a temporary fix for you and Robbie? Mrs. Dowe, the next-door neighbor, has a boy Robbie's age, and I've seen her watch other children. Maybe she could watch your son?"

"Really? That just might work, at least until school starts. Mother no longer has the patience to care for an active little boy." George sucked in a deep breath.

That was kind enough. Right?

Mary grinned, her eyes lighting up. "Robbie may be active, but he's one of the sweetest little fellows I've ever met. I'm sure my aunts would agree to you staying at their cottage. And Robbie would be at the Park, even closer to you while you work."

George pondered the possibility. Mary was right. "I'll inquire about it tomorrow. Thanks for the idea."

Mary's smile pushed through his dark thoughts, the gold flecks in her eyes sparkling like the summer sunshine on the river.

Indeed, she was a beauty, inside and out.

If only *he* wasn't so … broken.

~ ~ ~

George's mood darkened again as the sun went down. He'd been able to carry on a half-decent conversation with Mary but said nothing about his deepest thoughts. They'd chatted about mundane things like the many boats on the river, the kinds of fish people were catching, the silliness of the boys playing all around them. What they avoided talking about was anything about the heat, the lack of rain, the danger of fire—or his mother.

As the hours ticked by, waiting for the fireworks to start, Mary grew quiet, pensive. Did she sense his angst, or was she pulling back too?

He checked his pocket watch and snapped it shut. His pulse galloped as he tried to find words to tell her what he was thinking. He shifted his weight on the quilt next to her, shrugging his shoulders as an apologetic half smile turned his lips up. "I'm sorry I've not been the best of company today."

"What's wrong, George? You've not been yourself all evening." A scant bit of color rose to her cheekbones.

He pushed back the desire to hug her. Conflicting emotions rose to almost take his breath away, but he fought them. Feelings wouldn't rule him. He had to think.

George leaned forward, wrapped his arms around his legs, and clasped his hands. Something in his heart had shifted, like a wildfire in a wind, an unstoppable, all-consuming blaze that filled his thoughts. His nerves twisted and tingled. He tamped them down too.

"Tell me. Please?" Mary laid her head on his shoulder.

Should he expose his very soul? He couldn't bear to be rejected by her, but he wouldn't toy with her either. One way or another, he had to divulge his feelings for her. When the tension finally broke, he blew out a ragged breath. "I can't be sparkin' with you, even if I wanted to. You're too special. Too worthy. It isn't right, Mary."

There. He'd said it.

Mary popped her head off his shoulder and scooted away from him as though he was on fire. "What are you saying, George?"

He pulled his gaze from her shocked face and stared at the moonlit sky, a twinkling pincushion of stars. The full moon sat in a cradle of clouds. Where were the fireworks?

He felt her eyes on him, but he refused to look at her. He'd lose the battle if he did.

What was he doing here with her? He'd lost his heart when Alma died. Could he bear to lose it again to this woman who lived so fully, so freely? A lovely lass who seemed to care for him more than he ever deserved?

A frightful mass of uncertainty mixed with a generous serving of fear set his palms to sweating. His stomach churned until he had to take several deep breaths to calm himself. "It just isn't right. *We* are not right."

Mary squared her shoulders. "I ... we ..."

A small groan escaped her lips. "Perhaps you may be right."

Chapter 14

Three mornings later, Mary rolled her abundant hair into a loose chignon held by a dozen or more pins. She poked her scalp as she placed one last pin. "Ouch!"

Seemed she couldn't get anything right these past few days. George's words bounced in her brain like summer hail. Three days of torment. Three days wondering what had happened to their growing relationship.

She collected her thoughts into a patchwork quilt, though it felt more like a crazy quilt than one of the perfectly designed ones. She couldn't talk to Gramps. He had warned her to guard her heart, and she hadn't. Hot tears threatened to spill, unbidden, as shame and guilt enveloped her.

Her nerves frayed like an unwound ball of twine, and her empty stomach roiled for lack of food. But she couldn't eat a bite. She couldn't risk Gramps questioning her.

After bowing out of breakfast, she made a plan. She had to talk to someone. Charlotte, perhaps? Her friend had proven to be a faithful confidant, a gentle young lady, and a non-judgmental soul.

Mary mustered all the courage she could as she rehearsed her speech on her way to Charlotte's apartment. She knocked on the door and found her friend still in her robe.

Charlotte raised an eyebrow but stepped aside for her to enter. "Good morning, Mary. Please come in. Tea?"

"Thank you. Are you sure it's not too early?"

Charlotte smiled, waving her hand toward the table. "No, Papa's already manning the front desk, and if you don't mind my robe, I welcome your company. Please have a seat. I was just reading the Psalms."

Mary went over to the table and slid her glasses up on the bridge of her nose. "Ah, Psalm 23. I've thought of those words often of late."

"It's quite comforting, isn't it?"

She didn't have time for small talk. But how to start the conversation? Perspiration misted her brow. Her pulse quickened, and her bottom lip trembled like a frightened kitten. She bit it into submission and forced her words to sound confident, though she withered inside. "I need your advice, or at least a listening ear. Do you mind?"

Charlotte snapped a glance at her, her furrowed brow and pursed lips showing compassionate concern. "Of course. I'm not sure about advice, but I'm a good listener." She set two teacups and a steaming pot of tea before them. "Go on, then."

Sweat clammed Mary up, but thankfully, a river breeze from the open window cooled her. She stared out the window into the distance. "This is all perfectly ridiculous. I'm such a ninny."

Charlotte reached over and touched her arm, pulling her back to her sympathetic presence. "Why do you think that?"

Mary still cringed as she thought about the July fourth encounter. Did George really mean to put her off like he did? Fear lassoed her heart, pulling tighter and tighter until she could barely breathe. "I don't know what happened. George and I have been enjoying time together, and I thought our friendship was growing, perhaps into something more. But he was perfectly icy when I saw him at the Fourth of July festivities. He rebuffed me and said we weren't right together. What does that even mean?"

Charlotte tilted her head. "Maybe there's another girl in Clayton who bats her eyelashes and has turned his head?"

Mary huffed her disagreement. "He's not like that. I think, perhaps, it's about his overbearing mother." She put a hand to her lips rather than speak more of her mind. "I'm sorry. I must keep my tongue tamed. I am tempted to say far too much of what I think about the woman when I shouldn't."

Charlotte shrugged, flipping to the back of her Bible. "I just read John 16 this morning too. It says, 'Howbeit when he, the Spirit of truth, is come, he will guide you in all truth.' What is the truth behind George saying you aren't right for each other? Surely, there must be more to the story. You and he are not unmatched. I've seen the way he looks at you, and you light up like a firefly around him."

Mary's skin crawled. "But he turned from warm to distant in the span of just four days. I thought we had something special. And I adore his son. But I cannot let him toy with my heart, Charlotte. *That* isn't right."

"Mr. Flanigan doesn't seem the type to toy with anyone's affections, does he? Something's amiss. But what?" Charlotte took a sip of her tea. "I think, perhaps, you should let the Spirit of truth guide you in this."

Mary groaned, confusion fogging her brain like a cool, misty morning. "But how? He's moving to my aunts' cottage to get away from his mother. That's why I think his mother may have something to do with his turn of temperament. But that still doesn't answer the question about us not being right for each other, and it hurts."

Charlotte pulled her into a warm embrace and squeezed her tight. "I'm no expert on love, but perhaps you should guard your heart and wait to see what the entire story might be. The truth will reveal itself, eventually."

Mary swallowed hard, almost choking on the sip of tea she'd taken. "That's what Gramps—er, Mr. Wiseman—said."

"That's Mr. Wiseman for you. I suggest you listen to him, Mary, and be patient with your Fireman Flannigan."

Mary shrugged. "I suppose you're right."

But no matter how wise her friend, the ache still filled her.

~ ~ ~

As Mary walked to her aunts' cottage, cotton-candy clouds dotted the cerulean-blue sky, but the heat of the late-afternoon sun was unbearably high and dry. She wiped the perspiration dripping from her temples and shook her skirts to ward off the material sticking to her legs.

She'd read the newspaper that warned of high temperatures and even higher fire danger, and several callers had discussed their worries throughout the day. What might the days ahead be like? God forbid there be another fire.

As she approached the cottage, she smiled to see Robbie playing with Cooper in the front yard. The dog chased the child, who giggled with joy. Such a pleasant, sweet sight. Then she glanced at the porch where George sat reading a book, and her stomach flip-flopped.

"Miss Mary!" Robbie squealed with delight and ran into her arms. "I love your aunties' cottage. It's right next to my new friend,

Paul. He's a nice boy, and I get to spend every day with him and his mom."

Mary laughed at the happiness this child exuded. She'd yet to see him sad or upset, unlike his petulant father. Oh, to be a child again, free from the fetters of adulthood and complicated relationships.

George stood and acknowledged her with a smile-less nod. His chiseled features sent her pulse jumping erratically. Even from where she stood, pinpricks of whiskers betrayed he hadn't shaved since the morning. "Good afternoon, Miss Flynn." His tone was flat, empty of warmth. "What brings you to this side of the Park?"

She climbed the porch steps and gave a little curtsy. Perhaps a bit of humility and social graces might ease the man's fractured emotions. "Aunt Maude asked me to stop by and see if you and Robbie have settled in all right—and if you need anything."

George shook his head, plunging his hands into his pant pockets. He even took a tiny step back from her. "Please tell her thank you, but we have everything we need and more. Your aunts left an abundance of kitchen utensils and linens, enough for a much larger family than just Robbie and me."

Mary nodded and pasted on a smile. "That's good. You probably already noticed that the back door sticks a little and the sink has a steady drip. Also, bats have found their way into the rafters for the past several seasons, so if you hear something strange up there, that might be it."

George looked down at the floor rather than at her directly. "I'll keep all that in mind. Now if you'll excuse me, I was just brushing up on my tactical firefighting manual." Then he caught her gaze, and for several long moments, he stared at her. What was he thinking? His expression baffled her until he broke eye contact and rubbed the back of his neck. "And I don't think we should be more than acquaintances. Ever."

Mary rarely lost her words, but the coolness of his comment stole them away. She bit the inside of her lip to hold back a flood of hurt. He returned to his seat, picked up the manual, and buried his face in it.

How rude!

The hurt turned to indignation as she stomped down the porch steps. Ignoring George, she opened her arms to Robbie. He ran into her embrace, and she planted a kiss on top of his head. "See you later, sweet boy."

The child looked up to her with eyes wide and questioning. "Can't you stay and cheer up my daddy? He's been sad since the fireworks, and I don't know why. I know he's glad to be here at the cottage, but he's … different."

Mary squatted down to his eye level and took Robbie's hands, almost whispering to him. "Sometimes grownups have a lot on their minds. Pray for him, and I will too. Okay?"

Robbie's adorable grin returned. "I will, Miss Mary."

Mary tussled his hair.

Was she fooling herself? Did the God of the universe really care about the prayers of a switchboard operator and a wee boy?

~ ~ ~

George peeked over the top of his manual as Mary interacted with his son. She was kind and loving to Robbie, and he obviously adored her.

Blathers! What a liver-bellied dunderhead he'd been. Hiding behind his book like a child behind his mother's apron strings.

But what could he say? He'd made a fool of himself with Mary and damaged the one friendship that might have blossomed into more. Most likely, he'd mucked it up for good, and for what?

Cowardice. Pure and simple.

Strike two.

What had he done? When Mary stepped onto the porch and he'd gazed into her melting caramel eyes and her sweet face, he'd lost his nerve. Her countenance should be on a priceless ivory cameo fashioned for the richest of wearers, not being tormented by him.

He'd put his own demons before this precious woman's heart, and he'd spoken to her with the rudeness of an unbred ship's hand.

Eejit.

Then, to top it off, he'd snubbed her, and she'd fiddled with an errant curl, then rubbed her ear. A habit he'd seen her do before when she was particularly upset or nervous. Yet her fragile expression frightened him most.

After Mary walked away with shoulders down and head low, his breath sped up too fast, too hard, until he stood and tottered like a drunken sailor. The pain he'd caused her lingered like the smoke of a fire.

He had to do something.

Fast.

Mary had already made it partway down the street when he bounded down the steps and took off running. "Stay here, Robbie. I'll be right back." He ran as fast as he could while cupping his hands around his mouth and hollering, "Mary. Wait. Please."

She stopped, but she didn't turn around right away. Afraid she'd resume her walk, he pushed on, even as neighbors watched from their porches. Even as he made a fool of himself.

When he got to her side, he stopped and heaved a breath, sweat pouring down the sides of his face and wetting his armpits and back. He swiped his face with both hands and wiped the moisture on his pant legs. "Sorry. Let me catch my breath, please."

She folded her arms around her chest and tapped her foot. Eyes narrowed. Mouth pressed into a severely pinched line. She swallowed hard but said nothing. She just stared at him as he heaved and struggled to catch his breath and tried to figure out what to say.

A mixture of deep frustration and dismay crossed her pretty features.

He ran his hands through his now-sweaty hair. "I'm sorry about the fool I've been, Mary. I would still like us to remain friends. Please?"

She stared at the ground and wouldn't look at him, so he grasped her shoulders and forced her to face him. Her pale skin and thick, dark hair made such a pretty sight that he almost recanted. His gut twisted, and he let go of her and mopped his brow.

A tight, ungenuine smile followed a withering glare. Her voice was thick with emotion, and uncertainty tinged her tone. "Friends? Acquaintances? You already said that quite plainly. Are there any particulars about our *friendship* that trouble you?"

He suppressed a groan. How could he tell her he wasn't worthy of her? That *he* was the problem? "No, but I think this is for the best. For Robbie. For me."

"Then, so be it." Her shoulders rose. Then she cast him a fiery glare, spun on her heels, and stormed off.

"See you around, Mary." With the common sense of a toad, his retort bordered on impolite.

The ache in his chest pulled taut, as if someone had roped him. The band tightened, choking him.

As he shuffled back to his son, he rubbed his temples to massage away the headache that had emerged. Halfway to the cottage, Archibald Richmond stepped off a neighbor's porch and into his path. Had Richmond seen his folly too? If so, he'd never hear the end of it.

The thick-browed rogue clicked his tongue, and his top lip curled. "Well, well. That was quite an exhibition, I must say. And quite entertaining." Richmond puffed his chest to match his ego. "A lover's spat, I presume?"

George sidestepped the man, but Archie matched him, blocking his path. "I see you and your son are staying in that old ladies' firetrap? You know it's not insured. You should purchase coverage, or you'll lose all of your personal possessions, and possibly your son, if it goes up in smoke."

His headache swelled behind his eyes, and blood rushed to his brain. Archie's taunts were the last thing he needed just now. He swiped his sweaty, scratchy face and swallowed his anger. "That is none of your concern, sir. Good day."

George pressed past Richmond, but not before the rogue butted George's shoulder with his, throwing him off balance. Thankfully, he continued his retreat with the slightest bit of dignity left.

When he returned to Robbie, the child sat in the grass cross-legged, hugging Cooper, wearing a crestfallen expression so sad that George's chest clenched.

He bent and gently lifted Robbie's chin. "What's the matter, child?"

Tears brimmed in the boy's eyes. "Don't you like her anymore, Daddy? 'Cuz I do. A lot. Miss Mary is kind and nice, and I think she should be my mommy."

Strike three.

He should never have let Mary get close to his son.

"I'm sorry, Robbie. It's not that simple. Grownups have a lot of complicated things to deal with. Things you don't need to worry about. Miss Mary is busy with her life, and we with ours. Besides, it's time for dinner. Now let's go in and wash up."

"But if you married Miss Mary, she could come and live with us. And she could cook for us, and we wouldn't have to eat sandwiches for dinner. And I'd have a mommy, and you wouldn't be sad anymore. I think that's a very good plan." Robbie stood and climbed the porch steps.

George huffed his exasperation. "Enough! I'll hear no more about it, Robert James Flannigan. No more talk of Miss Mary. Do you hear?"

Robbie blinked at the stern reprimand and whimpered, "Yes, Daddy," before scurrying off to wash his hands.

After they ate dinner, George put his son to bed, and the house was quiet. Sullenly, he reviewed the wretched day's events. Actually, the past three days of misery. How had things gone so wrong with Mary and now with his son? Robbie had barely said a word to him after he so impatiently scolded his innocent child.

He poured a glass of lemonade and stepped out onto the porch where it was much cooler. The day's heat still hung heavy in the air, and it alarmed him. So did the dry conditions. Perhaps Robbie and he should sleep downstairs where it was cooler—and safer. He'd make a pallet for the two of them when he was ready to call it a night.

His brain felt like an overcooked potato. Dry and mushy. But he forced himself to face the day's folly. Days' follies. Why couldn't he find his bearings with Mary? Why did he feel so topsy-turvy?

He pondered Mr. Wiseman's counsel to forgive his failures and move past them, but how? When he kept on failing—like with Mary and his son?

How could he have been so cruel to either of them? He wasn't an unkind person, but he'd pushed her away as if tossing her off the porch. And he'd hurt Robbie.

Words matter, and his had wounded the two people in the world dearest to him.

Strike four.

Chapter 15

Mary held onto Gramps' arm as they strolled to the small chapel for Sunday service, the cane aiding his syncopated hobble.

She grasped his arm a little tighter as he faltered momentarily. "You've seen a lot of special speakers in your years here, yes?"

Gramps resumed his slow gait. "Many. The most memorable, for me, was when the famous evangelist Billy Sunday came and gave an inspiring outdoor speech called, 'Christ Among the Poets.' He was known to be humorous and quite boisterous, but I found him surprising mannerly and mild."

Mary slipped the picnic basket into the crook of her arm, and with her free hand, waved her fan in front of her face, trying to fend off the heat. It didn't work. "I've read about him."

They stopped for a moment under the shade of a great oak.

"After the fire of 1890, the schedule of speakers was unending. They nicknamed Thousand Island Park 'the Chautauqua Institute of the Thousand Islands,' though we had no official connection to them. Our largest meeting place, the Tabernacle, and the Education Building were busy almost daily with special lectures. Topics ranged from history to national parks to theology to Darwinism. And I fondly remember when the South African Native Choir came and gave concerts for several days. My, but they were splendid."

Mary tugged him forward so they wouldn't be late for service. "I'm glad the Park still has a lot of educational programs, though I haven't been able to attend many that are held during the day."

Gramps patted her hand that now lay on his arm. "Perhaps, one day, you will. For now, you serve an important position in our community, keeping folks informed and connected."

"Thank you for that, Gramps. I've been feeling rather unsettled of late."

He stopped and gazed into her eyes. "Because of a certain fireman? I know you have misgivings and questions. Be patient, child. It may be that he has some sorting out to do. I believe things will settle in due time."

"I can only hope."

By the time they entered the chapel, Mary almost sighed in relief to be out of the blazing summer sun. Unfortunately, the church was almost as oppressive and stuffy as the outdoors, even though every window and door were open. Was there no respite from this blazing inferno?

The service commenced with two hymns and a prayer. Then Reverend Thompson stepped up to the pulpit. "Our text for today is from the prophet Malachi. 'Behold, I will send my messenger, and he shall prepare the way before me … for he is like a refiner's fire, and like fullers' soap: And he shall sit as a refiner and purifier of silver: and he shall purify the sons of Levi, and purge them as gold and silver, that they may offer unto the Lord an offering in righteousness.'"

Reverend Thompson closed his Bible and paused as the congregation waved fans and folded papers to cool themselves. Mary shifted in her seat, glancing at George and little Robbie, just across the aisle to her left. She sighed at the thought of what could have been.

The preacher interrupted her musings before they took a dark turn. "Most of us have watched Mr. Block blow glass and pound it into something beautiful. And many of you have seen a smithy heat metal to soften it so he can hammer and mold it into a useful product. Perhaps a few of you may have even seen a silversmith or goldsmith refine the precious metal to remove the impurities. Such a skilled metallurgist puts the silver or gold into a crucible—a container that won't melt. Then he puts the crucible into a fire and heats it to nearly two thousand degrees until the silver or gold melts." He let his words sink in. "After it cools, he scrapes off the impurities that have risen to the top. Then, he repeats the process again and again until there is nothing left that taints the precious metal. Only then is the silver or gold pure."

Reverend Thompson leaned over his pulpit and glanced around the room. "Can you imagine how blistering two thousand degrees must be? Remember the fire a few weeks ago? That fire might have been a thousand, maybe even fifteen-hundred degrees. But to purify precious metals, the fire must be even hotter."

Mary slipped her handkerchief from her reticule and swiped a stream of perspiration that ran down her cheek. She glanced around the room to see dozens of folks doing the same. What a topic for such a blazing day.

The reverend grinned. "I see you're rather warm today. Yes. It's been terribly scorching and dry these past few weeks, and we must guard against a possible conflagration, especially during this dry spell. But spiritually, we should do the same every day."

What was he saying? Mary leaned in, hoping to understand. So did many others around her, including George.

Reverend Thompson continued. "In truth, the difficulties and battles we face in our lives refine and purify us. That spiritual purification process removes the sin and impurities of our lives so we can better reflect Him. And sometimes that involves suffering."

He glanced over at Captain Brown and Harry Arthur. "Such as when you dear folk lost your cottages. Did your suffering draw you closer to God?"

Mary smiled as both men nodded fervently. Would she feel the same if her aunts' cottage had burned?

"Yes, you did. Your lives testify of it. I've spoken with several of you who have suffered loss lately, and I'm happy to say that you are refined and purified, and you shine like gold. The pounding, heating, and burning has made you better people, and I commend you for growing through those painful times."

Reverend Thompson sighed, swiping the sweat from his brow. His countenance turned somber. "We may have more refining fires ahead of us, and we must be on guard to never become bitter or unforgiving or hardened by those troubles. Our God is not a cruel God. Our troubles may be painful, but in the end, our experiences will purify us to reflect Him better—if we allow it. Is it easy?" Another pause. "Certainly not. But nothing God allows is pointless. He will work within our most difficult times so we can reflect Him better. May we stand strong in the midst of troubles and come out of it all as gold. Amen. Let us stand for the concluding hymn."

When the service ended, Mary and Gramps greeted several neighbors before joining the congregation for a picnic luncheon under a grove of shady trees. She laid out a quilt near a grouping of chairs where the elderly sat, including Gramps.

After making plates for both of them, Mary sat on the blanket, picked at her meal, and listened as her elders discussed the sermon.

Mrs. Vanderhoof sucked in a loud breath. "Gracious me. His sermon made me hotter than I already was. Would he have spoken about a blizzard, I'd have been much more amenable."

Gramps chuckled. "But he had many good points, especially with the trials we are facing this summer."

Leave it to Mr. Wiseman to bring balance and truth. Of all the blessings she'd experienced at the Park, he was at the top of her list.

And George? Was he a blessing too? That was yet to be determined.

Sunlight dappled through the trees, and by the time she'd finished her meal, a refreshingly strong breeze helped to cooled them. Mr. Nelson handed each of them a piece of horehound candy. Her aunts kept a crystal bowl of the sweet in the parlor. It was probably still there, tempting little Robbie daily. She glanced around to find George and Robbie sitting with a group of young families, including Mrs. Dowe and her son, Paul. They laughed at something George said, and her heart twisted.

She popped the hard candy into her mouth, instantly transported back in time to memories of her father's warm hugs and kind eyes. The feel of her small hand in his large one and his tender kiss on her cheek, a nightly ritual when tucking her into bed.

She touched her clammy cheek and felt eyes upon her. When she looked up, George stood over her.

He reached out a hand. "Care to take a walk? I have some things I'd like to share, if you'll permit me." His broad shoulders, slim hips, and handsome face made her pulse thump in her ears. His arm muscles flexed, sending her heart beating in triple time.

A fog of uncertainty replaced her initial surprise. Would this little visit be good or bad? Only one way to find out. Forcing a polite smile, she nodded and took his hand. He helped her stand and slipped her hand into the crook of his arm.

Before they left, George addressed Gramps. "Excuse us, sir. I'll return her soon."

"Take your time. We have all afternoon." Gramps smiled, a twinkle brightening his old eyes.

George nodded and turned to her. "Shall we walk?"

Mary smiled, her nerves firing. The masculine scent of balsam and soap and sweat quickened her breathing. "Yes. Let's."

But she'd heed Mr. Wiseman's words this time.

She would guard her heart from the one person who could break it.

~ ~ ~

George led Mary to a grove of elms shading a grassy sanctuary. "Shall we sit? It's too torrid to walk, don't you think?"

She inclined her pretty head in silent acknowledgment of his suggestion and settled with her back against a shade tree. A glimmer of exasperation—or was it confusion?—flickered in her caramel eyes. She tipped her chin to the heavens, and as if in a daze, and stared at the scant clouds dancing across the sky.

"I'd like to discuss the sermon first." He swiped his fingers through his hair.

A sheen of sweat glistened on her skin as she blinked in surprise and mopped her brow with her fingertips. "Very well."

He handed her his handkerchief. She took it and dabbed her face. "Thank you. It's so terribly sultry these days."

The thrill of her nearness sped his pulse. He nodded as a tiny muscle twitched in the side of his jaw. It always betrayed his nervous energy, even when he willed it still. He wiggled his jaw back and forth to release the tension and dug his fingernails into the grassy loam to anchor himself. "I'm in a fiery furnace at present, Mary. I'm being refined, and I have a lot of dross to get rid of. I just don't want to bring you into the refiner's fire with me."

He rubbed his hand over his jaw and gritted his teeth. Did he say that right?

Her expression changed, almost imperceptibly, as she filled the space between them with a warm smile and the scent of sweet sweat and lavender. The charming tiny lines at the corners of her large eyes accentuated her smile. Perhaps she understood, despite his total ineptness?

He cleared his emotion-thickened throat, but his voice still cracked. "That's why we must remain acquaintances. For now ..."

Her eyebrows tented, and she pressed her lips together as if to hold back a groan. For several long moments, she breathed deeply in and out as if he'd stolen her breath with his words. Sweat beaded on her brow, and again she patted it with his handkerchief. "I ... I think I may understand. I, too, have dross. Probably always will. We don't have to be perfect, you and I. We just have to be willing to ..."

Blood rushed to his brain at the sound of her lilting voice. "Willing to?"

As she turned her face, the flecks of gold in her eyes sparkled in the sunshine. Might he ever be worthy of her?

She colored to the shade of the crimson roses that once graced his mother's garden. Her eyes darted to a bird singing in the nearby tree. Another, probably his mate, answered just above their heads.

She forced a smile, though it shifted to a question. "Then there may be hope for us?"

He pressed a hand to his chest to calm the beating drum inside. He couldn't pull an answer past the lump in her throat, so he simply nodded.

Her eyes sparked, and a wide smile graced her lips. "Then, we'll leave it at that."

Beyond him, Mary's gaze darted to something that caused her eyes to widen and just as quickly narrow into tiny slits. Her mouth started to drop open, but she quickly snapped it shut and set her lips in a tight line.

George turned to see Archibald Richmond holding tight to Robbie's hand. What was that rogue doing with his son?

In an instant, George scooted to his feet and held out his hand to help Mary rise. But his eyes stayed trained on his boy. "Robbie? Are you all right?"

With much effort, Robbie wriggled free of Richmond and ran to him, holding out his fist. "I fell and knocked out my loose tooth, Daddy. Thee?"

Mary let out a small giggle, and Robbie showed her his tooth, the gap in his smile nothing short of adorable.

Richmond slithered up to them. "I saw your boy's mouth bleeding and thought I'd lend a helping hand."

Nerves full of suspicion tingled, tension coiling like a snake around his neck. But George snapped a polite nod. "Thank you."

Richmond's self-satisfied smirk turned into gawking as his dark eyes swept Mary from head to toe. "Hello, girlie. Aren't you looking rather fetching today." His waxed mustache and crooked nose hovered over a dark, twisted snarl.

Mary cast him a razor-sharp glare and squared her shoulders. But the corners of her lips quivered a bit. "Do not call me 'girlie.' I'm a professional woman. And twenty-eight is well beyond a girl, don't you think?" She thrust her hand onto her hip, an obvious challenge. Then she tilted her head, narrowing her eyes. "And I am *Miss Flynn* to you, sir!"

"She's right." George's heart thudded and he clenched his back teeth. The woman could hold her own, that was certain. But he had to defend her all the same. "You may not speak to Miss Flynn in such a manner, Richmond. Have you no manners?"

Richmond snickered, his mustache twitching almost comically. "Calm down, folks. I meant no harm. I'll be on my way, then."

Without another word, the scoundrel slinked back to the crowd, and Mary mumbled, "And good riddance."

"I don't like that man." Gap-tooth Robbie yanked his attention back to where it belonged. "Thorry, Daddy."

Mary bent down and studied the tooth. "Show me your smile?"

Robbie grinned wide, displaying a two-toothed open space. He ran his tongue along it. "It feels weird."

"But I think a big boy's toothless smile is the most handsome smile a young man can have. Ever." Mary chuckled.

Robbie laughed before planting a kiss on Mary's cheek. "Thanks. I think you have a pretty thmile too."

George nodded. "I quite agree, son. Shall we return to the picnic?" He offered Mary his arm, and she took it, a pleasant smile adorning her face. Might he be able to keep a measure of friendship with this woman without hurting her? He whispered a silent prayer that he could as they made their way back to the picnic.

Along the way, Robbie tugged on George's shirtsleeve. "Can I play thome more, please?"

George smiled. "Yes, but stay where I can see you."

The little boy ran off and joined several other children playing tag. His son could make friends with anyone and had fit into the Park community with amazing ease. If only he did too.

As they approached Mr. Wiseman and the others, Archibald Richmond's arrogant voice filled the air. "… and he's done nothing to help our plight of improving the fire protection around here. Giving speeches at meetings and poking his nose into the Park's private affairs. Why, he's not even from here. The Association pays him an exorbitant salary, and for what? To flirt with Miss Flynn and impose on those poor old ladies by living in their cottage?"

Mr. Wiseman addressed the man in a chastising tone. "Now see here, Mr. Richmond. Mr. Flannigan is a professional, an employee of this Park, and my friend. You shall not besmirch his good name. And furthermore, you may never, ever make false accusations against Miss Flynn. She, sir, is above reproach."

Several bystanders mumbled, "Hear, hear!" and "that is true," and, "the nerve of that man."

But Richmond was undaunted. He simply tossed them a sideways smirk and mumbled back, "If the shoe fits …"

Then he skulked off and disappeared to the other side of the church building. Probably to cause more trouble or spread rumors about him. Should George follow the man and have words with him? No, that would only taunt him more. With a huff, he delivered Mary to Mr. Wiseman.

By then, Mary was in quite a tizzy. More than a hint of color tinted her cheeks, and a strangled croak escaped her lips. "Who does that rogue think he is, saying those things about you? And me! I'll give him a piece of my mind. Excuse me, please."

She punctuated her words with a stomp of her foot and tried to pull away … toward Richmond.

But George held her fast, placing a hand over hers and shaking his head. "No, Mary. He's a bully and a troublemaker. If you cross him, you'll only get more of it. He doesn't deserve your time or your words. Let it go."

Mary took several deep breaths before nodding. "Very well. Are you ready to go home, Gramps? I sure am."

Gramps struggled to stand as Robbie joined them. "It's too hot to play, Daddy. Can we go for a swim?"

Robbie employed his most pleading pout. The child sure knew how to use that cute face to get his way.

"That's not a bad idea. Mary, would you like to come, too, and dip your toes in the cool river?"

Mary shook her head. "Heavens, no. I don't even have a bathing costume. Besides, I need to get Gramps … er, Mr. Wiseman … home and relieve Charlotte on the switchboard."

George released her hand and stepped back. "Certainly. And thank you for the talk."

"My pleasure, sir." She smiled, her long lashes fluttering as she spoke.

Was he fooling himself, or did that upward curving of her lips offer more than a polite ending to their time together?

Chapter 16

Mary sat with Mrs. Dowe, Paul, and Robbie, eating a juicy piece of ham and chatting happily. In the two days since the Sunday picnic, several who thought Mr. Richmond's insinuations indecent had invited Mary to visit. Funny how folks came to the aid of the underdog.

Robbie patted her arm. "Mith Mary, want to play checkers? Paul taught me, and I beat him. Twice."

"Sorry, little man, but I need to get back to the switchboard. Charlotte is just covering for me until one."

Mrs. Dowe glanced at the clock on the mantel. "Goodness. It's already one o'clock. Would you like to take a few of these ginger-snaps with you?"

"If you wouldn't mind. I'm sure Gra—Mr. Wiseman would enjoy them even more than I did."

Paul, a towheaded eight-year-old who stood a full head taller than Robbie, rose and held out his hand. "Can Robbie and I walk Miss Mary back to the hotel? It's the gentlemanly thing to do."

Mary laughed as she thanked her hostess. Mrs. Dowe nodded, and off they went. Paul would be a positive influence on little Robbie, of that she was sure.

As they walked, Paul pointed northwest. "Did you know that they're fixing the reservoir today? Mr. Jim is working on it. He said that since the water table is so low, it's a good time to do it."

"So that's why there was so little water pressure today. I wondered. Thanks for letting me know."

Paul grinned. "You're welcome. Mama could hardly get a trickle from the spigot this morning. If you ever need to know what's going on, just ask me. I know everything about everything around here."

Robbie pointed to her, a huge grin on his little face. "Mith Mary is the thwitchboard operator. I bet she knows even more than you do. Hey, wanna see if Mr. Wiseman can teach us cheth? I think we're big enough."

Paul kicked a stone in his path. "Nope. He says I gotta be nine. That's next summer. And three summers for you."

Mary interrupted the banter. "Mr. Wiseman is on the boat cruise today. The Park was taking a large group of older folks on the outing as a respite from the heat. He's not even at the hotel. Look. His place is empty."

Still a long way off, she pointed to the hotel veranda where Gramps always sat.

"Say, why is the chapel bell ringing?" Robbie put his hand to his ear.

"Oh, that's probably for Mrs. Benedict's funeral, I'm sorry to say."

Paul scrunched up his face. "The Indian lady who owns the basket shop with her husband?"

"Yes. And several businesses have closed so employees can attend the service, including the Park Department Store."

Robbie kicked a stone in his path. "Too bad. I had a penny from the tooth fairy and wanted to buy some candy."

"Weren't three gingerbread cookies enough, young man?" Mary patted the top of Robbie's head.

The child's face scrunched up like an old man's. "I suppose. I'll get my treats another day. But why is the bell still ringing?"

"The service begins at one-thirty. I suppose they are calling mourners to the church."

Paul picked up a stone and tossed it. "I don't like funerals. They're sad. Granny died last year, and we had to go. I cried and cried."

Robbie tried to one-up him. "My mama died, but I was real little, though, so I don't remember if I went to the funeral or not. I'll have to ask my daddy."

As they approached the hotel, several people scurried here and there. Something wasn't right. Did someone get hurt? Or was there a robbery? She turned to the boys. "It's time for you two scallywags to head home. Thanks for escorting me back to work."

She bent down and hugged Robbie, and Paul put out his hand. She shook it. Eight-year-old boys must be too big to be hugged.

Robbie waved before sprinting off to catch Paul. "Bye, Mith Mary."

Mary waved back but quickly turned to observe even more people scurrying about. Yet when she entered the hotel, no one seemed alarmed. The front desk waited on patrons. Women sat in the parlor talking.

Mary passed Dr. Harriett Sheldon and her daughter Stella on their way to lunch. Dr. Sheldon grasped Stella's arm. "You packed your trunk, right? If that *was* a fire bell, I want you to be ready."

Fire bell? Did he think the funeral bell was for a fire? Perhaps that was the fuss outside.

When she got to her office, Charlotte was speaking with someone, her voice an octave higher than usual. "Should I call it in?"

Pause.

Charlotte sighed. "Oh, all right. If you're sure. Goodbye."

When she disconnected the call, Mary stepped forward. "What was that about?"

"Mr. McGuire said he saw smoke and wondered if the bell was to alert us of a fire. I told him it was probably for the funeral procession."

Something deep inside her set her own warning bells ringing. Mary's pulse sped to a gallop. "Shall I inquire about it, or do you want to?"

"You go ahead. I'll stay here. I've been reading this book, and it's so good. Take your time." Charlotte patted a book beside her.

Mary glanced out the office window and saw nothing. Perhaps a small kitchen fire? "Okay. I'll be back soon. Thanks, Charlotte."

Mary left the cookies and her reticule in the office and wove her way through the hallways to the back entrance of the hotel. Just outside, she almost bumped into Mr. Rothschild, the hotel barber. The man's face was white as a ghost's and he panted like a racehorse.

She stopped him. "Sir, are you all right?"

"The Haller store is full of smoke, but it's locked. Mrs. Benedict's son, Frank, works there, so he's probably at the funeral. I rang the chapel bell to get help, but everyone is ignoring me."

Mary's hand flew to her chest. "Oh no."

"Tom and Grant Mitchell and Tom Stewart tried to get the fire engine out of the laundry building, but the door sill was blocking the way. They've gone for help. I'm looking for help too."

Mary took his arm and prodded him in the direction of the store. "Please, show me what you're talking about. I need to know if I should call for help."

Mr. Rothschild nearly dragged her to the store. Mr. Tousey peered in the store's window, holding a pile of blankets and linens. Sure enough, smoke filled the inside. Beside him sat two fire extinguishers.

Where was George? As the only official fireman on the island, he should have heard about this by now.

Mr. Tousey thrust a pile of linens at Mary. "Soak these in water." He pointed to a nearby cistern, and she complied. After she returned the heavy, wet blankets to him, he and Mr. Rothschild wrapped themselves in them and broke into the store.

Soon Mr. Hardenbrook came running. "I've got to get the safe closed. Haller says it's open, and he'll lose a fortune if it burns."

The man rushed into the store, but within seconds, a thud signaled trouble.

Mr. Sweeny, who had followed him in, yelled, "He's fallen. Get the fire extinguishers, Rothschild!"

Before long, all three men backed out of the store, heaving and gasping for air.

Mr. Tousey peered into the shop. "The smoke is like pea soup, but I don't see any fire. What's going on?"

Sweeny waved off his concern. "Probably just some old greasy rags smoldering or something."

Or something.

Suddenly, the store exploded into flames. Mary pointed. "Fire!"

They backed away as the flames popped and crackled and sparks shot out the door, carried on the breeze. Mary couldn't move. Couldn't think. Couldn't speak. Someone gave her a little shove.

Mr. Sweeny. "Get out of here, Mary. Call for help!"

Mary blinked and took off running. High on the Columbian, the cloth awning and some roof shingles caught fire.

She gasped. "No!"

Then, suddenly, the nearby Wellesley Annex was on fire too.

Mary ran inside the hotel, screaming, "Fire! Get out! Fire!"

Where was George? He wasn't at the aunts' cottage. She'd been next door with Robbie. But the boy hadn't mentioned where his father was. Neither had Mrs. Dowe. Who could she call?

She got to her office where Charlotte sat reading, peacefully unaware the hotel was on fire.

Mary grabbed the headset and shoved her out of the chair.

Charlotte's face turned ashen. "What's wrong, Mary?"

"The hotel is on fire! Get everyone out. Tell your father. Get to safety. Hurry!"

Charlotte didn't seem to understand. She just stood there with her mouth open.

Mary screamed at her. "Go! The hotel is on fire!"

Charlotte blinked and began crying, but finally, she ran out the door, her mousy call for help ineffectual. "Fire!"

Mary took a deep breath and connected to her aunts' cottage. The line rang and rang. She tried the Dowes' house.

Mrs. Dowe answered. "Good afternoon, Mary. How may I help?" Her tone was too calm. She didn't know.

Mary's voice cracked. "The hotel is on fire. Where is George? We need his help."

Silence.

Mary prodded her again. "Where is George?"

Finally, Mrs. Dowe spluttered, "H-he's just outside talking to Robbie. I'll get him."

It felt like an hour, but in mere moments, George answered. "Mary? What's going on?"

Mary whimpered like a small child. "Oh, George. The hotel is on fire."

"What? When? How?" Without waiting for an answer, he took control. "Call for help. All the surrounding stations. With this wind and heat, any fire may be a doozy."

Mary nodded, though he couldn't see her. "I will. Be safe, George."

"You, too, Mary."

~ ~ ~

George hugged Robbie before heading to the fire. "You must stay here with the Dowes. Do not leave this cottage. Hear me? Do not leave Mrs. Dowe's side. Understand?"

"Okay, Daddy." His poor son's body quivered with fear.

George kissed his forehead. "I love you, son."

Robbie clung to him. "You, too, Daddy. Thay here with me. I don't want you to go to another fire."

"I'll be back. You stay here."

Without allowing his son to tug on his heartstrings a moment longer, he took off in a full sprint toward the hotel. Even blocks away, he could see smoke billowing up into the cloudless sky.

"Dear God! Keep everyone safe. Please!"

When he got to the hotel, scores of people were already out on the green space. Furniture, bags, and trunks littered the grounds.

Others tossed belongings off the verandas, smashing on impact. The Association's treasurer, Mr. Fitch, stood at the bottom of the hotel's front steps in a daze.

George stopped to address him. "Are you okay, sir?"

"I tried to save the Association's records from the Annex office." He showed George his severely blistered hands. "My hands are burned."

"We'll get medical help here shortly. Don't go back into the hotel."

George took the hotel steps two at a time and entered the lobby. Chaos reigned. No one was at the front desk. Bellboys hollered "fire." People raced to get out of the hotel.

He dodged several folks wandering aimlessly, as if in a daze. He prodded them to get out.

In the parlor, he almost ran into Mr. Tousey, who grabbed him by the arms. "George. Glad you're here. It's a mess, but Sweeny, Van-Lengen, and Delaporta are sweeping the hotel to make sure every-one is safely out."

Mr. Sweeny joined them, carrying a woman who clung to his neck, sobbing. "This is Mary Bush of Watertown. I found her on the top floor at the end of the south wing. Smoke got her, but she's breathing now."

"She'll be okay. Get her out into the fresh air." George patted her arm.

Mr. Sweeny took a step toward the door and stopped. "Sanford Kemp and twenty men are up there now trying to save that wing."

"No! It's no use. Everyone must leave. Now!" George huffed.

Wait. Mary. Surely, she'd left the hotel after making the calls for help.

But what if she hadn't?

Fear gripped him in a vise. Bolting like a stallion, George ran to Mary's office, praying he'd find it empty.

It wasn't.

George's fear turned to anger. "What are you still doing here? Get out. Now!"

"I'm still trying to contact Gananoque. Clayton and Alex Bay are on the way. But the Canadians won't answer." She paused. "Oh, hello. Is this the Gananoque Fire Department?" Pause. "The Columbian Hotel at Thousand Islands Park on Wellesley Island is on fire. We are requesting immediate assistance." Pause. "Thank you very much. Good day."

Just then, the telegraph clicked to life, and Mary began deciphering the message. To George's horror—and amazement—Mary calmly jotted down the message.

He had to get her out of there. As he hadn't done with Alma. Now!

He stomped over to her and tugged her, but she resisted. "I can't leave just yet, George. The telegraph. And look at all those lights. People need answers."

He yanked her headset off and pulled her out of her seat, scooping her up into his arms. "And I need you to stay alive. This hotel is being consumed!"

Mary struggled in his arms, but he didn't care. He ran with her as if she were a mere toddler, fear surging through his veins, every nerve on high alert. When they got outside, Mary seemed to comprehend his purpose.

She hugged his neck and planted a kiss on his cheek. "Thank you, George. How can I help?"

Softened by her kiss and gratitude, George set her down and palmed her cheek. "Just stay safe and help where you can, my love."

He didn't wait for her to respond but turned to a group of men who waited for instructions a hundred feet away to avoid the intense heat. Heat that was building by the second.

When he joined them, Mr. Delaporta gave him an update. "Everyone is out of the hotel, including the Kemp crew. We did a thorough search."

"Aye. The hotel looks to be a total loss. Get back, men! It may collapse at any moment."

He stared up at the structure that was now fully ablaze. All four wings. All four floors. Everything.

But not Mary. She was safe.

Suddenly, she appeared in front of him. Her eyes flashed fear. "Where are Charlotte and her father? I don't see them anywhere."

"Don't worry. Everyone is out of the building. Where's Mr. Wiseman?"

Mary touched his sweaty arm. "He's on the boat tour."

"Thank God. Charlotte must be here somewhere. I need to organize this. Promise me you'll stay safe, Mary. Promise me."

"I will. Now go, and you stay safe too." Mary squeezed his arm.

He nodded and ran to the west of the Columbian, where the Wellesley Hotel was in danger of catching fire. Several men stood on the hotel roof stomping out tiny fires started by sparks and embers tossed by the wind. Another climbed a ladder, carrying a hose.

George hollered at the men on the roof. "Mr. Knapp? Mr. Kaufmann? Get those barrels of paint off that roof. If they catch fire, they will doom the hotel."

The two men complied, sending barrels of paint crashing onto the ground below. Then the two attempted to wet down the roof of the building, even with low water pressure impeding their progress.

George addressed a young man about to climb the ladder to the roof with a shovel and wet blanket. "Your name, son?"

The teener snapped a nod. "Paul Crouch, sir."

George saluted him. "Thanks for helping. Carry on."

Young Carroll and Robert Fearon helped, too, pumping water from the well. It was slow going, but thanks to them and others, the Wellesley Annex was saved. George clapped the boys on the back. "Keep up the good work, boys."

Next, George hurried to the north, where the fire spread along St. Lawrence Avenue, devouring the shopping area and catching cottage after cottage on fire as though they were made of tinder. Sweat soaked his shirt, but his jaw set as he faced the flames and drove volunteers to do the same.

The fire's roar sounded in his ears. Flames popped and cracked, like a celebratory fireworks display turned devilish.

Crews took up their positions at St. Lawrence and Paradise to stop the northward advance of the fire. Other crews positioned northeast of the fire.

George groaned as hope plunged to the bottom of the river, deep into the abyss where things would never be the same. The Columbian gone. The shopping district gone. The blaze spreading to the north and east, out of control.

In less than an hour, the fire had become a conflagration.

Where were the fire departments? Without their help, the Park's townsfolk were but a pinprick in the sea of ravaging flames. The buckets of water like throwing pebbles at Goliath.

George hurried back to a spot where he could monitor the main boat dock. When several launches and steamers pulled up to the docks, he sprinted down St. Lawrence Avenue to assign jobs as help came.

The next hour was a blur.

As the Gananoque Fire Department approached from Canada, he snapped a glance to the river, hoping a barge would follow close behind their launches. "Where are your engines and hoses and equipment?"

Sergeant Vollmer replied, "We hurried here to help, sir. Thought you'd have enough equipment for us to use."

His heart sunk. They had left their equipment in Canada?

Soon Clayton pulled up with a barge of equipment waiting on the waves. George cupped his hands and shouted to the captain of the steamer *Newsboy*, who sat at dock. "Can you tow in that barge, sir?"

The captain nodded, waved, and shouted back. "Right away, sir."

George sent the Canadians to cover the eastern flank and the Clayton department to the north. Before long, the Alexandria Bay department appeared with the *Zilpha C* cruiser towing their fire scow. Three other boats, the *Keywadin*, the *Coloso S*, and the *Oberon,* followed close behind, full of volunteers.

After they disembarked, George made a plan. "Thanks for coming, men. Take your positions along St. Lawrence Avenue and hold the fire. Perhaps, with your help, we may beat this thing yet."

Perhaps.

But highly unlikely, barring a miracle.

Chapter 17

Mary hovered near the burning hotel, hoping to spot Charlotte or George or Gramps—or anyone she knew—to find comfort in their presence. Until she did, she'd help where she could.

The ash-filled sky—no longer blue, but autumn-orange, hazy, and sinister—rained poisonous particles all around her. Tiny fires lit here and there as the sparks flew up and then dive bombed like bats on the prowl. She stamped out the flames as fast as she could, but they seemed to light faster than she could get to them.

Large embers glowed red and rose high in the air. Then they dropped from the sky, one burning the nape of her neck. She swiped at it furiously, but it immediately blistered her skin. Then a strange, rancid smell accosted her. Her hair was on fire! She slapped it out, but she suspected a small spot near her right ear would leave evidence of her battle.

With a growl, she stopped and stared at the grand hotel that had been her home and workplace. Vicious flames danced their wicked war dance, consuming the once-beautiful structure with abandon. Fire rose higher and higher, roaring like a freight train. Hotter than Hades—or so she thought.

Hair rose on her forearms, bristling from her fear. Who or what could win over this heinous monster?

Like a steamer's smokestack spewing white-hot steam, the livid red flames overwhelmed the dying hotel. Glass cracked and shattered. Furniture popped and crackled. Wood groaned and collapsed. Walls fell.

Then something exploded, deafening and foreboding. The nearby gas factory, perhaps? Mary covered her ears and fell to the ground, hiding her face and head with her arms.

Cinders and ash floated on the wind, falling on her clothing and hair, making tiny holes in her dress as if it had been chewed on by fire-mouthed moths. She swatted at them, furiously protecting herself.

Then terror dug its talons into her as, in one last act of surrender, the hotel's roof heaved and groaned until it imploded onto itself—and the grand and beautiful Columbian Hotel became nothing but an enormous pile of ash and debris.

She wheezed as her throat choked at the emotion of such loss, and the thick, poisonous smoke enveloped her like a foggy night. Smoke and dust stung her eyes and tickled her nose as if a hundred tiny ants crawled inside.

She swallowed a bitter burn of bile. Everything she owned was in the hotel. In Gramps's apartment. And in the switchboard office. Forever buried in the rubble and ruins before her.

Confusion enveloped her. Panic strangled her. Anguish taunted her.

Parched beyond what she thought possible, she crawled to a muddy puddle in the street and took a sip. She tried to wash the soot and sweat from her eyes, but that only made them sting more. Instead, she swiped her face with the sleeve of her dress.

It didn't help. Nothing did.

As the dust settled, Mary blinked back tears to survey her surroundings. Sack-suited men and fancy-clad women covered with ash stumbled all around her. Children cried for their mothers. Loved ones frantically searched for each other. Smoke- and sorrow-induced tears made rivulets down the cheeks of the passersby—hollow-eyed homeless whose sadness was palpable.

The nightmare seared itself into her brain. Forever.

"Mary? Is that you?"

Charlotte touched her shoulder, sending quivering, shaking shock waves through her traumatized body.

Mary studied the girl's ash-covered face. "Charlotte! Oh, Charlotte! Look what happened to our home." She pointed helplessly to the ruins that was once the Columbian Hotel. "What will we do?"

Train tracks of tears ran down Charlotte's face, too, her lips cracked and bleeding. She'd lost everything as well.

Mary stood and hugged her tightly, thankful to have someone to share her sorrow. They wept in each other's arms for several moments.

Charlotte clung to her with a strength that surprised Mary. "Is your father all right? Have you seen Gramps?"

Charlotte pulled back but kept hold of her hands. "Both are fine." Her tone was uncharacteristically calm. "Mr. Wiseman is safely on the touring boat with the other older folks. Papa is helping fight the fire. And I saw Robbie with the Dowe family down by the riverfront. People have been jumping into the water to protect themselves from the cinders and sparks, Mary. What a terrible day!"

Mary sighed her relief. All the people she cared about were safe for the moment. Everyone except—possibly—George. But she quickly shook off that worry and squeezed Charlotte's hands. "Let's help where we can, you and me together."

Charlotte agreed, still holding Mary's hand as they walked north on St. Lawrence Avenue. She pointed to her left. "The Wellesley Hotel survived, but look at all the businesses ahead of us. The chapel is gone. So is the school. And the post office."

Mary grimaced as the ruins of a dozen or more shops lay before them. "The grocer. The china shop. The Oriental shop and Japanese Bazaar. So much loss."

North and east of the business district, cottages lit like birthday candles. Mary groaned as the boardwalks acted like fuses, catching fire and burning up to a cottage's steps, then the porch, and finally, destroying the entire structure in mere minutes.

As they walked along the cement sidewalk, the heat grew unbearable under Mary's feet. She pulled Charlotte onto the dirt road. "Let's head east and see if we can help there."

Charlotte hesitated. "I don't know how the firemen can get as close as they do. Even from here, this fire is hotter than the preacher's sermon described. Won't we be in the way and hinder the men's work?"

"We have to help our neighbors." Mary tugged Charlotte onward. "I can't stand here and do nothing." Sweat slid down her forehead and into her eyes, burning them worse than they were, but she swiped it back and pressed on. "Coming with me?"

Charlotte's silent nod and resigned step served as her reply.

Hot ash continued snowing down on them, choking and burning. On the side of the road, Mary found a dirty apron and a discarded man's handkerchief. She handed Charlotte the handkerchief.

"Cover your hair so it won't burn like mine did." She pointed to the spot where her hair had burned. Then she tied the apron over her head and around her chin.

To their right, the fire burned brilliant, blazing in the afternoon haze. As they walked east on Oak Street, folks carrying sheets and tablecloths of food and belongings looked like the hobos she'd seen near the Clayton train station. Somehow, she had to help these poor souls save what she could not.

Suddenly, to her right, flames shot high in the air and then died down suddenly, consuming another cottage. The brave firefighters hollered and worked, doing what they could to keep the fire at bay. Was George in their midst, helping to lead the troops?

She stopped and searched for his tall frame and wide shoulders under a dome-shaped leather helmet. But there were so many other firefighters dressed like George, and the helmets' brim that rolled to a long back tail hid most of the wearers. So did the rubber duck coats, making it impossible to identify him. The smoke and haze and chaos of the moment made it even worse, so she plodded on, whispering a prayer of protection for George. For all of them.

When they got to the corner of Oak and Garden, Mary spotted Mrs. Chancery, a friend of her aunts'. The elderly woman struggled to toss a chair onto her lawn, tears forming rivulets on her ashen face. Her lips cracked and blistered. Her hair covered in ash.

Mary tugged Charlotte forward. "Let's help this poor old lady."

"Is it safe?" Charlotte held back.

Mary shrugged, tugging her forward. "It may be smoky, but the fire is still blocks away. See?" She pointed south, where flames blazed barely a hundred feet from them. Without waiting for her friend, Mary hurried to Mrs. Chancery's side and gave her a hug. She righted the chair and patted the seat.

"Sit, missus. We'll save what we can." Mary ran into the smoky house, looking for valuables and something to carry them.

Charlotte joined her but stopped at the doorway. "She wants the picture of her husband on her dresser upstairs and her special reticule that is in the drawer."

"I'll get them. You gather what you can down here."

Mary ran up the smoky, steep steps and easily found the requested items. But then, a cat meowed in the hallway. She followed the sound, but she couldn't see the cat through the smoke. "Here, kitty. Come, kitty."

The floor creaked and groaned under her slight weight, the windows in the bedrooms exploding into flying chards of sharp debris.

Pop. Crackle. She hurried into the closest room, searching for the animal. Pop. Crackle.

Smack.

Then everything went dark.

~ ~ ~

Over the roar of the inferno, George heard his name called. It sounded like a woman. He squinted through the smoke, searching for the caller.

Firebrands wafted on the breeze, landing on nearby rooftops, setting house after house on fire. They were completely losing control of the fire—if they ever had it at all.

Adrenaline surged through his veins. Sweat poured from him. Passion pressed him on.

The wind shifted, sweeping the fire north, engulfing the cottage nearest him. "Retreat, men! Back to Oak and Garden, and hold the line there. Create a firebreak. Clear the street, and we'll defend the other side."

The high-pitched scream begged his attention. "George! Fireman Flannigan! Help!"

George turned toward the sound and almost ran into Charlotte. "What are you doing here? You should be at the shoreline."

Charlotte shook like a leaf. Her voice quivered with fear. "Mary is trapped in the house. Upstairs. Save her."

"*My* Mary? Where?" Terror coursed through his veins. Dread twisted in his gut.

Charlotte tugged his arm. "Come. Hurry. The roof caught fire, and she's upstairs. I couldn't go in and get her." She dropped his hand, hoisted her skirts, and ran like a deer from a wolf.

George kept up with Charlotte as sparks rained down on them, landing on anything they could attack with a vengeance. The wind shifted, then shifted again, as if they were in a whirlwind. The sky hazed over, an eerie, evil orange.

"God, please keep her safe. Help me get to her. Help her. Help me. Please."

George's lungs burned from the exertion, from the smoke, from the fear of losing her. But he pressed on, surprised how fast Charlotte could run. Surprised he had the strength to continue.

This fire. This wicked fire. How could he fight such a Goliath? It seemed to chase them toward Oak Avenue.

When they got to the house, Charlotte pointed at the roof alight with flames high in the air. "She's upstairs! Hurry!"

Smoke puffed out the door, but he didn't see flames inside. "Where is she? Where are the stairs?"

Charlotte wrung her hands and closed her eyes, as if trying to recall. "The stairs are to the left of the door."

He shouldn't. He might very well lose his life. But he had to try. For her sake. For Alma's.

He heaved a couple of deep breaths and rushed inside. Smoke made everything dark, but he felt for the stairs and hurried up, eyes closed and feeling with his hands in case she was on the steps. "Mary? Mary?"

He breathed in the smoke and choked, but still he listened, hoping he would hear her voice, hoping beyond hope he'd find her alive. When he got to the top, he remained on his hands and knees, feeling, feeling, praying, praying.

What was that? Fur? An animal? Yes. Cloth. A body?

Mary!

His lungs screamed for air.

Pop. Crack. Glass breaking. The roof was going to fall.

Hurry!

With all his strength, he scooped Mary's limp body onto his lap and the cat onto hers. Then he felt for the stairs and slid on his backside all the way down, clutching his precious Mary, holding onto the animal's tail. Neither moved. Neither seemed aware of the bumpy ride.

At the bottom of the steps, his feet hit the wall hard. He kept low as he held Mary tight in his arms, the cat's tail still in his grip, and scurried out of the house, heaving in the air as soon as he crossed the threshold.

The glorious, half-smoky air.

He coughed, dropping the cat onto the porch, and stumbled down the steps onto the grass with Mary still in his arms. His lungs burned and so did his eyes, but he had to help her. He laid her on the grass and patted her cheek. "Mary! Mary!"

She didn't move. Didn't respond.

He put his ear to her chest. Her heart thumped, although too faintly. He put his ear to her mouth. Her breathing was fearfully shallow.

He pinched her nose and blew into her mouth. Again and again. Still no response. After what he seemed an eternity, she finally, wonderfully, heaved a deep breath and coughed.

Crash!

The roof imploded, causing the lower-level windows to break and fire to shoot out of them. The cat was gone, but Mary was alive.

He picked Mary up and retreated into the neighbor's yard, where an old woman sat in a dining room chair, rocking back and forth. He lay Mary on the grass and tended to her. Kneeling, he patted Mary's face. "Mary. Oh, my precious Mary! Are you all right?"

Mary heaved and coughed but wouldn't open her eyes or answer. She needed help, more than he could give her.

George lifted her into his arms and turned to Charlotte. "Tell the firemen I've gone for help and for them to carry on. To hold the line. Then take this woman and get to safety." He gestured toward the old lady on the lawn. "The fire is out of control."

Charlotte opened her mouth to speak, but he didn't wait to hear what she had to say. He must get Mary to a doctor.

As fast as he could, George hurried down Oak Avenue toward St. Lawrence Avenue. Through thick smoke, he somehow stayed on the road. "Help her, Lord. Please let her live."

He headed for the tabernacle where Doctors Wilbor, Bruce, and Place had set up a triage station. Dozens of men, women, and children sat in the pews, some bandaged, some crying, some staring silently into space. Dr. Wilbor wiped his hands on a towel. "Doctor, please help. She's fallen to smoke inhalation and is unresponsive."

"The switchboard operator?"

"Yes." George gently laid her on an empty pew and brushed the hair from her face. Only then did he see the blood staining the apron she wore over her hair. "She has a head injury, sir. Please come."

At that, Dr. Bruce turned the patient he was working on over to his assistant and hurried to their aid. He listened to Mary's heart, her breathing, and checked her pulse. Then he examined her head wound. "Something must have hit her, knocking her unconscious. Not good in combination with smoke inhalation."

"Will she be all right, Doctor? Please say yes." George's voice cracked.

"Can't say for certain, son, but I'll do all I can. Now you better get back to fighting this battle. I'll fight hers."

George kissed her on the forehead and whispered, "Please, Mary. Wake up and be all right. I need you." At his admission, his throat thickened until he thought he'd choke. But he swallowed the lump. "Thank you, Doctor. Please take care of her."

"Drink this." A nurse thrust a tumbler of water into his hands. "You must be dehydrated by now."

George guzzled the water, rushed from the tabernacle, and returned to the firebreak at Oak and Garden. But nothing had stopped the angry tongues of fire. An updraft took the flames higher and higher.

George helped as the firefighters tried to hold their ground at a natural firebreak on Central Avenue, but the fire simply hopped over the street and continued burning east. Reverend Thompson's cottage went up in flames next.

A hose burst. Then another. The little water pressure they had faltered.

The fire spread past them and south toward the shore. It had to stop there. It had to. Weary firemen wiped sweaty brows but kept up the battle. Without water pressure, all George—and anyone—could do was watch in horror as the fire won this terrible battle. Ash fell like snowflakes. Embers rained down and started more spot fires, the resulting flames lapping up cottages like a thirsty behemoth.

Cart-draggers pulled the fire carts to the new lines, but the pumpers were no match for the firestorm, especially with so little water. And it was blocks to the river.

Stiff summer winds whipped the fire like a bellows. Tornados of flames ripped down the rows of homes. The fire swept through the streets with the roar of a dozen freight trains. They used axes, shovels, whatever they could find to dig trenches and create a firebreak, but it still didn't help.

Cottages ignited simply from the heat. One moment, the structure appeared secure. The next, it burst into flames and burned to the ground before anyone could stop it.

Pieces of paper, cloth, and wood fell from the sky like dead pigeons, landing on piles of belongings that the neighbors desperately tried to save, only to have them set aflame by a burning napkin or something else. Women and children scurried to the shore, to the docks, anywhere away from the monster set on destroying their peaceful existence.

For two hours, the firefighters failed to get the steam engines to work and had to resort to useless bucket brigades. Finally, by four forty-five, the pumps built up enough pressure to wet down the buildings still standing. The wind shifted again, turning the fire back onto itself and saving a few cottages. Within the hour, the blaze died down to smoldering ruins, and the devastation became all too real.

Through smoke and sadness, George surveyed the damage.

Utter destruction met his eyes.

The eastern half of Thousand Island Park was gone.

Chapter 18

Mary groaned at the hardness of her bed. A blanket covered her, but a lumpy pile of cloth seemed to be her pillow. Her aunts' spare bedroom didn't have such a hard bed or lumpy pillows. What had happened to it while she slept? Was she dreaming?

She struggled to open her eyes, but her lids felt like lead and refused to comply. With all her might, she gave it one last try, and slowly, her eyes blinked open, fear wrapping its evil arms around her, pushing her into the hard bed.

Had she died? Was she in a coffin? On either side of her were wooden planks, as well as beneath her. But … the coffin seemed to be open. Several distant voices engaged in a cacophony of unrecognizable discussions. Then a baby cried nearby.

Ouch!

Her head ached something fierce, so she squeezed her eyes shut. Surely, with such piercing pain, she must still be alive. But if she was in a coffin, the voices needed to know she was still alive before they nailed her inside it—and buried her alive!

She took a deep breath and yelled as loudly as she could, but nothing came out. Her throat was parched, her lips cracked and dry and bleeding. Pain stabbed her lungs with every breath, but she pushed past the pain, heaved a deep breath, and hollered again. Her voice came out weak and gravelly. "Help me, please!"

Someone touched her, and she flinched. She forced her eyes to open. Blurry at first, a face hovered above her.

A man in a white coat. "I'm Dr. Bruce, little lady. Welcome back. You gave us quite a fright. I wasn't sure you would see the light of day."

Mary cried — a soft whimper at first, but soon it grew into deep sobs that hurt her chest and head. "I'm alive? Where are my aunts?"

Dr. Bruce held back a frown and gently patted her shoulder. "There, there. Lie still and let me examine you."

He put a stethoscope to her chest and checked her head. When he touched the crown of her head, knife-sharp pains pierced her brain.

"Ouch! It hurts so badly. Please stop." The light hurt her eyes, too, so she shut them, tears leaking out of the corners and running down her cheeks. "What is wrong with me?"

Dr. Bruce rubbed her forehead. "You've been injured, and your head will smart for several days, my dear. I had to put a dozen stitches back there to patch you up. Do you know what hit you?"

"I … I can't remember. Where am I?" Mary furrowed her brow, but even that hurt.

The doctor spoke with deep tenderness. "In the Tabernacle. There was a fire and …"

Mary tried to sit up, but she hardly had the strength to lift her head. That made her woozy, so she dropped it back onto the hard pillow and squeezed her eyes shut. "My aunts' cottage? Did it burn down? Are Aunt Stella and Aunt Maude all right?"

"Shh … relax. Their cottage is fine. They are safe at home in Watertown." The doctor brushed the hair from her face with his thumb and patted her shoulder. "I must take my leave and help others. Nurse Reff is here."

Her brain tumbled with confusion. "What? Where was the fire, then? I live with my aunts on Ontario Avenue."

Mary heard shuffling and murmurs, and then a woman's voice. "I'm Nurse Reff. I'll be helping you. Do you know your name?"

"Mary Flynn." Mary's head was fuzzy, but she knew that much.

The nurse touched her arm, her voice soothing. "That's right. And do you know where you live, what you do, and what happened to you?"

"I … I think I'm going to be sick." Her brain swam, her stomach roiled.

She was.

After she'd emptied her stomach of nothing but bile, Nurse Reff tucked a blanket tightly around her, as her mother had done when she was little. "You rest and let your stomach settle. Then we'll give you something for the pain. You are safe here, Mary. We'll take good care of you."

"Thank you, Nurse." Mary licked her lips. They had blisters on them.

What else was wrong with her, and how was she hurt? She'd been in her aunts' house. Upstairs. Looking for something. But what had happened? Had she fallen down the stairs?

Her head hurt too much to think any longer, so she willed herself to sleep. Perhaps sleep was all she needed. Just for a few minutes.

When she awoke, it was dark and quiet. Her eyes felt gritty, as though sand was in them, but they didn't hurt as they had in the light. She looked around. The Thousand Island Park Tabernacle.

She'd been here for several services and lectures. Perhaps she'd sat in this very pew.

But why was she here? Dr. Wilbor had an office next to the post office. Dr. Bruce practiced at the Pratt House Hotel on East Coast Avenue. Dr. Place had an office on the corner of Garden and Oak.

Garden and Oak. Why was that so familiar?

Her head throbbed. Slowly, she reached up and touched the crown of her head. They had taped a thick patch of cloth back there. Had they also cut her hair, her beautiful hair, to put in the stitches?

She felt all around her head. Most of her tresses seemed intact, although something was wrong with a patch of hair over her right ear. Had they cut it there? But why?

Her head swam again, and the piercing pain increased. She needed help. She croaked out her petition, barely above a whisper. "Nurse? Can you help?"

Footsteps approached and Nurse Reff appeared. "Hello, dear. How are you feeling?"

Mary tried to focus on the woman's face, but the darkness deepened her blurry vision. "My head hurts. Everything's blurry."

"Blurred or double vision is quite normal following a head injury. Let me get you something to help." Nurse Reff took her temperature, checked her pulse, and listened to her heart.

In a few minutes, the nurse returned and eased Mary's head off the bundle serving as a pillow. "Drink this. It will make you sleep and help with the pain."

The bitter medicine was almost intolerable, but she drank it, anyway. Soon, she slid back into a deep sleep and enjoyed vivid dreams of better days.

When she woke up, it was light, but her eyes refused to focus. Was she going blind? Panic set her heart racing, and tears filled her eyes. Bit by bit, she recalled where she was, but she still didn't know why.

She took a deep breath and called for assistance again. "Nurse? Can you help, please?"

Instead of Nurse Reff, Gramps appeared over her. "My darling Mary. How are you?"

"Gramps. What are you doing here?" At the sight of him, Mary burst into tears, heaving great sobs of relief.

Gramps took a seat on the pew next to her head and gently stroked her forehead—the part that was undamaged. "I've been here all night, praying for you and the others."

Mary shook her head. *That* hurt. "Thanks for being here. Gramps, I don't know what happened. I don't know how I got hurt. I was at my aunts' cottage and went upstairs to get something, but that's all I can recall."

"You don't remember anything else?" Gramps groaned, his face troubled.

Mary probed her muddled mind but came up short. "No. Why am I here and not in a doctor's office?"

Gramps sighed but said nothing for several moments. He simply stroked her hair, as soft and comforting as a gentle wind. "You don't remember the fire?"

"No." Mary pressed her lips together. Nurse Reff had mentioned a fire too. "Did I start a fire?"

He quickly put her fears to rest. "No, child, you did nothing wrong. But there was a fire. An enormous fire. You tried to help an old lady but got trapped. George saved you."

"Who is George?" Mary's mind grasped for the memory and the name he mentioned.

Gramps gasped. "You don't remember him? He carried you out of a burning house. He saved your life."

She didn't. Didn't remember anything. Her head pounded with the strain of trying to recall. "My head hurts. Please get the nurse."

Gramps called for Nurse Reff, and after another checkup and a glass of that awful-tasting medicine, Mary relaxed. But she had so many questions. "What happened to me, Gramps?"

He continued to stroke her forehead. "That is for another discussion at another time. But before you sleep, I want to encourage you with something. No one likes pain, Mary, and most of us go to great lengths to avoid it. You're dealing with a great deal of it right now. But pain can be a profound teacher. If you accept that life may be painful at times, those experiences can become opportunities for growth."

Mary mulled his words over, but they made little sense. He wanted her to be in pain? Her thoughts became confused and Gramps' voice distant. She needed to sleep, if only for a moment. "Okay, Gramps. I'm sleepy."

"Then rest, my dear, and I will pray for your quick healing."

Mary slipped into dreamland, where she searched for a man named George. He had saved her, Gramps said, so she needed to thank him. But who was he, and how could she know him? She searched far and wide, running through the streets of Watertown and Clayton and Thousand Islands Park, calling for her rescuer, calling for George. But no one responded.

Finally, tired and frustrated, she took a deep breath, cupped her mouth, and called out one last time, "George!"

She woke up to a strange face hovering over her. He was handsome, but his hair, eyebrows, and eyelashes appeared singed. Blisters covered his lips and face, but deep in the recesses of her memory, something seemed familiar, and his expression shone with compassion and concern.

"My love. I'm here."

She frowned. "George?"

~ ~ ~

George sucked in a ragged gasp, his pulse thumping in his neck as Mary's face contorted with bewilderment. A knot twisted in his gut. "You … you don't know me?"

"Should I?" Mary shrugged, innocent as a child.

He didn't know how to answer that, but thankfully, she drifted back to sleep before she could demand an answer. The doctor said that she might be in and out of consciousness for some time, that her prognosis was still uncertain.

He'd fought a ravaging fire. He'd risked his life for others, giving no heed to his own. He'd stayed up all night putting out spot fires that continued to taunt him. He'd even fought his final battle with Mr. Sheeley's barn fire last night—though he'd lost.

But he'd encountered nothing as devastating as this. Just when he realized she was his …

Suddenly, the rancid smell of smoke accosted his senses again, permeating everything. Though he'd washed in the river, even soaked in it, he still reeked right down to his undergarments. No, down to his skin. Maybe he'd forever smell of smoke—like everyone else at Thousand Islands Park.

Or was it Mary who carried the scent of her near-demise?

Though a blanket covered her, she still lay in the cinder-eaten clothes she'd worn the day before. The day she'd risked her life to help an old lady. The day she'd lost everything.

Someone had washed her face and hands, but that was all. Even her shoes revealed her trauma, their soles melted to ruination. He gently slipped them off and rubbed her small feet tenderly. Even as she slept, a slight smile crossed her cracked lips, so he continued to rub them for a long while as he reviewed the past twenty-four hours.

Though exhaustion threatened to take over, he willed himself to stay awake for Mary's sake. Robbie was safe with the Dowes, and her aunts' cottage—and the entire west side of the Park—were saved from the inferno.

But somehow, Mary had no memory of the terrible day—or of him!

How could he explain their growing relationship, what she'd done for Mrs. Chancery, and how she no longer had anything to her name, save the ruined clothes on her back? The Columbian fire took everything, including her means of income.

Yet she had made it through the night, and so had he. He and dozens of firemen had worked from dusk to dawn monitoring the smoldering flames, putting out spot fires, and dreading what lay ahead when the sun came up. Sometime before the dawn, thick fog swept in off the river, covering the ruins.

For one blessed moment, the Park appeared serene, peaceful, promising.

But then the fog lifted and revealed that their world had indeed turned to ash and dust.

He'd surveyed the damage in the early morning light. In those four terrible hours, the fire razed the Columbian Hotel, seven businesses, three schools, the chapel, and ninety-nine cottages—one hundred and ten buildings in all. Owners had released dozens of boats into the river for fear they'd burn, some likely never to be found.

In the fire zone north and east of the hotel, only five buildings remained. The Iron Cottage that survived the 1890 fire miraculously had survived this conflagration also. The two Tousey cottages still stood, as did the gas plant, thank heavens. But that was all.

More than five hundred people were left homeless, many of them spending the night in the open areas of the Park, huddled around the few belonging they still had. A hundred or so found shelter with unharmed neighbors to the west. Rescuers took another hundred to nearby hotels, such as the Murray Hill Park Hotel. Others left for Watch Island or went back to the mainland.

The memory of all this devastation took his breath away. Even the once-beautiful shade trees seemed to weep, their withered branches dry and brittle, scorched by the fire's fury. And the lush lawns were nothing but dust.

But still, it was time to count their blessings. Despite the devastation, a miracle had happened that day—though more than fifty people were injured, none died. Not one soul killed or fatally injured.

He looked at Mary's beautiful face. Could she be that one fatality? The doctors still wouldn't discount that possibility.

"Dear God! Please heal her. Please!"

Mary groaned and opened her eyes. "What did you say, Doctor? May I have some water, please?"

Doctor?

"Absolutely. Be right back." George jumped up, ready to help her with anything she needed.

He rushed to get her a drink, returned, and lifted her head gently to help her sip it.

After settling her back down again, Mary glanced around. She appeared much more alert. "Where's Mr. Wiseman?"

George grinned at her progress. "Gramps? I sent him to the Wellesley to get some sleep. He's been here praying all night for you and others."

"The Wellesley? But he lives at the Columbian Hotel." Mary frowned.

Oh no. How much should he divulge? He had no experience with amnesia, though he'd heard it could often happen with a head injury. He paused, fumbling for the right answer. But he was so tired, his brain wouldn't work.

"Is Mr. Wiseman okay?" Mary's voice cracked, and she fidgeted. "Nothing can happen to him. He means the world to me."

"Shh … he's fine. Just tired. He's not a young man anymore, you know." George patted her arm.

Dr. Place motioned that she'd be his next patient. When he'd made his way to Mary, he smiled. "Well, Miss Flynn, it's nice to see you awake." He took her vitals, checked her bandage, and nodded. "Looking good. Now let's see if you can sit up."

George eased her upright. "How are you doing, dearest?"

Mary gasped, snapping a frown at him. "'Dearest'? Who do you think I am, sir?" She recoiled at his touch. "Who is this person, Doctor?"

"I'm so sorry, Miss Flynn. I misspoke." George groaned.

"I should say so."

Mary closed her eyes and bent her head back, as if it was too heavy for her neck.

Dr. Place frowned, touching her arm to draw her attention to him. "Do you think you can eat something? I need to give you more medicine, but you need something in your stomach."

"Perhaps." Mary sighed, her eyes squeezing shut. "Can someone else help besides this stranger?"

"Certainly. I'll have someone bring you a bite. Eat slowly, then rest." The good doctor glanced at him and shrugged apologetically.

George excused himself and followed the doctor beyond Mary's hearing. His pulse pounded around his eyes, and now his head ached. "Doctor, how can I help her remember? She doesn't know me or recall anything about the fire. How much should we tell her?"

"You've been brave, George. You've rallied the troops and organized the firemen in the midst of this terrible devastation. Now you must be brave in this new battle. Please go home and rest. We'll take good care of her." Dr. Place clapped his shoulder.

George swallowed hard. "But Mary needs me."

The doctor shook his head. "I'm sorry, but when someone has a head injury and doesn't remember you, your presence may exacerbate their fragile condition and keep them from getting better. Give her time. Hopefully, she'll remember you before long. But if you push her, it might take even longer for her to recall her past. The mind protects itself when there's such trauma by forgetting what hurt her. The good news is, it's usually temporary."

"Are you sure?" George felt as if he'd been sucker punched.

Dr. Place nodded. "I am sure. Go. Rest."

George turned to say goodbye to Mary but almost lost his breakfast. None other than Archibald Richmond cradled Mary in his arms, attentively feeding her soup.

She smiled at him.

She knew *him*?

Chapter 19

Mary stood, her head fuzzy and her feet unsure. "I can go? Are you sure?"

Dr. Place touched her forearm. "You may still be a little dizzy for a few days when you change positions. Just take it easy, Miss. Flynn. Stand and sit slowly, and drink plenty of water. And take this medicine when your head hurts." He handed her several small packets of powders before continuing. "The hotel staff has set up your room at the Wellesley Annex, and you'll be much more comfortable there. Mr. Richmond offered to escort you to settle in."

The doctor called for the man who stood by the windows staring at her, a crooked smile sending unexpected chills up her spine. He wasn't a doctor or a nurse. But she remembered him at a dinner her aunts hosted, so he must be all right. There was another man at the meal, but no matter how hard she tried, she couldn't recollect anything about him.

Mr. Richmond approached her and offered his arm, and she took it. He smile never rose to his eyes. Instead, there seemed to be hunger in them. "Let's get you over to the Annex. You're a lucky little lady to be offered the last room there, I tell you. Every spare place is full of all the fire refugees. And it was a miracle the Wellesley Annex didn't burn with all the rest of it."

"What burned, Mr. Richmond?" Mary had heard there was a fire, but everyone seemed to avoid giving her any details. Perhaps the fire had been inconsequential, but somehow, she didn't think so.

The man groaned, as if irritated by her question. "Call me Archie. The fire decimated over a hundred buildings in a four-hour span of time. This Park will never be the same."

Her pulse sped up and her heart thumped. Why could she not recall such a terrible event? What else didn't she remember?

When she and Archie stepped into the bright morning sun, her eyes hurt as if stabbed with ice picks. She shielded them against the brightness with her free hand, tucking her face close to Archie's arm. Her head pounded with every step. "The sun hurts something fierce. How far is it?"

"Close your eyes, if you'd like, and I'll keep you on the straight and narrow. You're such a tiny spit of a thing that if you falter, I can catch you with but one hand." Mr. Richmond held her tighter, comforting even.

She giggled despite herself. "Thank you, sir. While we walk, tell me about yourself, please. Seems all the details muddle my mind."

Mr. Richmond sniggered. Several long moments passed before he spoke. "What can I say? I'm the most successful insurance sales-man on this island. We have had several outings together, you and I, and I'd dare to suggest that I'd won your interest. I was thinking about asking you to a concert before all this happened."

She grew frustrated with her memory or his arrogant account-ing—she wasn't sure which. Something wasn't right. "Are we …? Are you …?"

"Your beau? Yes, Mary, I am."

He bent down and pecked her on the forehead. But instead of experiencing the warmth of a beau's kiss, she felt even more confused.

As they walked south on St. Lawrence Avenue, to their left, block after block was nothing but rubble and smoldering ruins. Though it hurt to look, she had to see what had happened, and it was worse than she'd imagined. Smoke still billowed up from several places, and the air reeked of burned-out structures. What had been there? What buildings had burned? The more she tried to recall, the more her head hurt, so she gave up.

Her voice cracked when she finally responded to Archie's declaration. "I … I don't remember you being my beau, so please keep a proper social distance and be patient with me until I can recall things better."

Archie slapped his chest with the palm of his hand and pasted on a shocked expression she sensed was altogether disingenuous. His mocking tone confirmed her fears. "I'm offended at your insinuation, Mary. I am nothing if not a gentleman. And as your beau, I have earned the right to your affections, whether or not your feeble mind recalls the fact."

Her heart skipped a beat or two, and perspiration formed on her upper lip. She swiped it away with her dirty shirtsleeve. Why couldn't she recall such an important person as a beau? And how had she agreed to be his beau when he made her so uncomfortable now? Perhaps he'd changed from then to now? She tugged at his arm, trying to disengage, but he held her hand there even tighter. Like a prisoner. "I don't feel so well. Are we almost there?"

Archie smiled down at her and snapped his pointy chin to their right. "It's just over here."

Once in the Wellesley Annex, Archie led them to a large room with a bed tucked against the wall, a washstand, a large desk, and two chairs. "They will install the telephone and telegraph system in here tomorrow. You'll have to share your lodging with your workstation. You do recall your position of employment, don't you?"

"Yes. I work as a switchboard operator and telegrapher, and I remember all the dots and dashes perfectly. I just don't remember … us."

"Well, you better rest up and get that sweet little brain of yours working soon. I need to get to work. I'll see you later." Archie gave her a little nudge as they entered the room.

Mary stepped away from him before he could touch her. Something about him made her skin crawl. "Have a good day, sir."

Archie left, taking his inky darkness with him. How could he possibly be her beau? Though handsome enough, he wasn't the kind of man she'd ever be interested in.

Or did she even know anymore?

She plopped down on the bed. Now what? Where was her friend, Mr. Wiseman? And her colleague? She squeezed her eyes shut to try and recall the young woman with hair the color of ripened wheat. Her brown eyes, thick brown brows, and full lips. The girl was a little naïve and shy but very willing to work anytime Mary needed a break. Charlotte Mullins, that was her name. She remembered so much. Why not …

Just then, the stranger from yesterday knocked on the doorframe, his deep voice warm and kind. "Miss Flynn? May I come in, please? I have some things for you."

"Enter, sir. Your name again, please?" Mary stood, wobbling a little when she did.

The man motioned with his palm to the floor. "Sit, please, Miss Flynn. George Flannigan, at your service. You're still on the mend and should take it easy. I brought a few things from your aunts' cottage and clothes that were donated to those who were burned out."

George set a large basket beside her and stepped back, a gentle smile on his face. His brows and hair still bore singe marks, and several remaining blisters dotted his temples and lips. The poor man must've fought the fires bravely.

And saved her? That's what they said. Why couldn't she remember?

The doctor said she mustn't push herself.

She sighed, allowing a measure of peace to fill her soul. She turned to inspect the basket. From under a towel, she pulled out a pretty white cotton blouse with lace panels, pintucks, long sleeves, and a nipped waist. Under it was a simple navy skirt that looked to be just her size. Next was a soft pink cotton lawn with woven pinstripes. She ran a hand over the wide, open collar and puff sleeves. "These are just lovely, Mr. Flannigan. Thank you."

He grinned. "Call me George. There are boots I hope will fit you, and a nightgown and … well, other things you can peruse later. I also brought a brush, comb, and mirror set from your aunts' as well as toiletries and other necessities. And there is a small jar of petroleum jelly that will help soothe your cracked lips. I hope they are what you need, Miss Flynn. If there's anything else, please let me know, and I'll fetch them for you."

"Thank you, sir. I appreciate all this, but now, I must rest. The room is spinning." Mary's head throbbed.

George hurried to her side and helped her recline, tucking two pillows under her head and covering her with a blanket. "I'll get you some water and let Gramps and Charlotte know that you have arrived. They'll tend to your needs, and Charlotte is happy to work all the shifts—until you're well enough. She's ever so eager to see you."

"Thanks again. For everything." She closed her eyes and licked her cracked lips.

She listened as George's footsteps retreated. Who was this man? Even beyond the blisters and burned hair, he was handsome. And kind. And she didn't feel the least bit afraid of him. Why was Archie her beau and not him? Everything was all so terribly confusing.

Feminine footsteps entered, and Charlotte's sweet voice interrupted her thoughts. "Mary. It's so good to see you. Are you in pain? Can I help?"

Mary opened her eyes and smiled. "No. Just a bit woozy."

"Sit up and drink this." Charlotte handed her a glass of water. "George gave it to me for you and said he'd be back later to check on you."

"He's a fireman?" Mary sipped the cool water.

Charlotte's brows furrowed, and she sighed deeply. "He is. Papa said you have amnesia, and I should be careful how much information I give you. I'm so sorry, Mary."

"But I remember you and Mr. Wiseman and Archie." Her voice quivered.

Charlotte's furrow deepened into train tracks that ran between her eyes. "You remember Archibald Richmond and not George?"

"Of course. After all, he is my beau. Why shouldn't I remember him?"

Mr. Wiseman hobbled into the room before Charlotte could respond. "My darling Mary. Welcome to the Annex. How are you feeling?"

Mary stood, padded over to him, and gave him a hug before offering him the empty chair. "I'm so glad the fire didn't hurt you, Mr. Wiseman. Was it very terrible? I saw the ruins as Archie led me from the Tabernacle to here."

Gramps snapped a frown at Charlotte. "Call me, Gramps, my dear. Mr. Richmond brought you here?"

"Yes. Dr. Place said I was free to go, and Archie was there waiting to escort me." She turned to Charlotte. "Do you think you can help me wash and change? And I need some of that petroleum jelly on my lips. I'm a terrible sight, I'm sure, and the smell of smoke is making me nauseous."

Gramps chuckled as he stood to leave. "Aye, that's a good idea. I just needed to see you for myself. My room is across the hallway and two doors down. I think I'll take a little snooze while you get settled."

"Thanks for coming, Gramps. I wanted to see you too." Mary waved goodbye.

Once he left, Charlotte helped Mary wash, change, and settle into her bed. By then, she was ready to take her headache powders and sleep for a while. "Thanks for helping me, Charlotte."

Charlotte squeezed her hand. "I'm glad you're okay. And you can rest all you need to. In the meantime, I'll fetch something for you to eat. You must be famished."

"Some toast and tea, perhaps?" Mary whet her lips, a little less painful with the petroleum jelly slathered on them. "Thank you, friend."

Charlotte smiled. "I'll be back in a while. You rest."

Mary snuggled under her covers, more confused than ever.

Gramps was the same.

Charlotte was too.

But who was George?

~ ~ ~

"Fire at the Touseys'!"

George's pulse took to trotting as he ran toward the Tousey home, yanking up his suspenders. Still in motion, he threw on his heavy duck coat and pulled the strap to his helmet under his chin.

He panted a prayer as he sprinted to the structure. "It's only been a day since the conflagration, and it's barely nine o'clock. Please help us contain this fire, Lord."

When he got to the house, flames were already shooting through the roof. William Tousey and his family, still in their nightclothes, stood in the street, dazed expressions on their faces. Mrs. Tousey wept quietly.

Thomas Roberts, the night watchman, pointed to the roof. "It just burst into flames a few minutes ago. Must've been smoldering in the gables while the family slept. Could've killed 'em all in their beds."

George hollered to several volunteers nearby. "The Alex Bay fire department is still at the dock. Bring up the fire equipment. Let's get this thing under control."

Roberts saluted George. "Already did, sir. They're on their … Oh, here they are now."

George joined the department, grabbed a hose, and went to work dousing the fire. Before long, the blaze was under control. Given the sudden eruption of it, though, he was ill at ease. "Tear off the roof, men. We've got to be sure it doesn't flare up again."

Before going into the cottage to inspect it, George turned to the Touseys. "You were mighty blessed, folks. That fire must've been smoldering all night. God was watching over you."

"Thanks for coming so swiftly. Is it a total loss?" Mrs. Tousey sniffled.

George touched the rim of his helmet. "I'll go in to check now, ma'am. Please stay here, all of you."

Once he completed a thorough inspection, he returned to the family. "Sorry, sir. Ma'am. Your furniture looks to be a complete loss, but the basic structure is sound. I'll have one of my men escort you in to get your essentials, but the cottage will be off limits until we make the proper repairs."

Roberts joined George as he shed his coat and helmet. "I heard that Mr. Emory has called a meeting to discuss rebuilding—either the Columbian or the Frontenac Hotel—or constructing that ten-million-dollar hotel on the Clayton riverfront he's been talking about."

"He's not at all invested in the Columbian, is he?" George frowned.

Roberts shook his head, running a hand through his curly hair. "Nope, and that's what concerns me. He's got the money to rebuild the Frontenac or to build that fancy hotel. That could leave us out in the cold. We should send someone to plead our cause. How about you?"

George groaned, mopping his sweaty brow with his shirtsleeve. "Send one of the board members to represent the Thousand Islands Park. I need to stay here and oversee the smoldering ruins and the clean-up. Looks like the burned-out areas may be hot for days. Can't risk another fire erupting."

"Yes, sir. On it now." Roberts saluted him.

"You don't need to salute me, Thomas. We're in this together." George chuckled, slapping him on the shoulder.

Thomas lifted his chin and gave him an exaggerated salute. "Oh, but you've led us well, George, and you deserve to be honored as our leader. If you hadn't been here, I don't know what chaos would have ensued. We're all just untrained volunteers. You're the only one who knew what to do."

"Thank you, but it's not necessary." George shrugged, conceding to the accolade. "What other news has come your way in the past few hours?"

Thomas pointed toward the dock. "I heard that Commodore T.A. Gillespie and Herbert Coppelle are sending food for a bread line. The Park will set up a temporary kitchen in the steamer office."

"Splendid." George smiled, pleased that neighbors were stepping up so generously in a time of need. "There're still almost seven thousand people at the Park, many who need that kind of help. Even though the fire victims may have a place to stay with the generous cottagers who didn't get burned out, this will take the burden off everyone. Thanks for all your help in this terrible time, Thomas."

Thomas shook his hand. "Glad to be of service. These are my people. Been here nearly a decade, and I'd want neighbors to help me if I were in the same spot."

George headed toward the Tabernacle. He walked past the bandstand where farmers had already set up a milk stand. Long lines had formed dozens deep.

A young maid, still in her Columbian Hotel uniform, stopped him. "Excuse me, sir. Do you know where the post office will be? I simply must post this letter and tell my parents that I'm all right, or they'll die of fright once they read about the fire in the newspaper."

George pointed beyond her. "It's at the John cottage, miss. And the Columbian is going to pay for your passage back to your home since you're now out of work. Go and see your manager. He's at the Wellesley. He'll help you and the rest of the staff."

The girl cried, grabbing his arm and clinging to it. "Thank you, sir. I slept under that tree all night. All my belongings are gone. All the salary I'd saved for school. Gone. Burned up. Now I'll have to return to my parents and be under my father's heavy hand. He never wanted me to go to school, but I want to be a nurse, and I'll do whatever it takes to get there."

"I'm so sorry, miss." George waved toward the Tabernacle, gently slipping her hand from his arm. "After you've talked with your superior, perhaps you'd want to help with the injured? I know they could use any willing hands."

"Perhaps I will. Thank you, sir." A tentative smile crossed her lips.

As he passed the hotel ruins, junk dealers and clean-up crews were already picking through the edges of the rubble, even as it still smoldered. They'd not get to the deep interior for days. It was still too hot.

His thoughts turned to Mary and the loss she'd have to face—once she remembered it. Poor woman. Why could she not recall the fire? Was the trauma too much for her, or did the blow to her head cause it? When would she remember?

Well, at least he'd been able to bless her with the meagre basket of goods. He decided right then and there—he'd start all over again to win her heart.

Memory or not.

Chapter 20

Mary rubbed her hand along the switchboard in front of her. It was smaller and older than the Columbian Hotel version, but the familiarity offered comfort. So did the telegraph to her right. She tapped the machine a time or two. If only it would come to life and bring her a measure of satisfaction, as only it could.

She knew her job. She knew the intricacies of the dots and dashes.

But she couldn't remember the horror of three days ago or the man named George who was so kind. What was wrong with her?

She had always been one to remember everything. Teacher said she had a steel trap for a mind. Once she met someone, she never forgot their face or their name. When she learned something, it stuck like glue. But now …

She prayed her body would heal, her mind would mend, and she'd be able to remember again. She prayed for her heart too. For the past two days, frustration and fear had plagued her, especially every time Archie came by. How could he be her beau? His presence weighed her down with dread that grew daily. She tried to be friendly, and he scoffed. While he plied her with flattery, it felt false, and he insinuated that she was nothing but a frightened female who hid behind a loss of memory. He'd even hinted that if she didn't stop pretending not to remember him—them—she could be removed from her switchboard position. But she wasn't pretending. And that scared her most.

The telegraph came to life, and she jumped for joy. Taking her pencil to paper, she deciphered the information.

New York State Fire Marshall's deputy chief will visit the Park to investigate the fire. Arriving this afternoon.

Goodness! She needed to get this information to Fireman Flannigan immediately. She rang her aunts' cottage, where, she'd been told, the fireman had taken up residence. But there was no answer. Then she rang the Dowes. "Mrs. Dowe? Is Fireman Flannigan nearby? I have an important telegram for him."

Mrs. Dowe puffed a ragged breath into the phone. "No, I think he's conducting his investigation now that the fire has cooled. But I can send his son, Robbie, and my son, Paul, to fetch it and deliver it to him, if you'd like."

The Wellesley bell boys were so busy, it was hard to find a delivery boy. She sighed. "Thank you. That would be ever so helpful. Goodbye."

So … the fireman had a son? Where was his wife? There was no mention of her.

Soon, two little boys came tumbling into her office. The taller one laughed. "I won."

"Did not. It was a tie." The little one looked familiar.

Mary giggled. "Hello, boys. Thanks for coming. Could you please tell me your names?"

The little one ran up to her and hugged her. "Oh, Mith Mary, you know me. I'm Robbie. My daddy and you are friends. We've had picnics and boat rides and watched the fireworks together. I think you like my daddy."

"Your daddy is Archie?" Mary sucked in a breath.

Robbie shook his head. "No. His name is George. Don't you remember?"

George? The fireman?

The taller boy interrupted her thoughts. "I'm Paul Dowe. We're here to take the telegram to Mr. Flannigan."

"Pleased to meet you both. You'll have to forgive me. I had a bump on my head and am having trouble remembering a few things." She folded the telegram and handed it to Paul.

Robbie hugged her again. "It's okay, Mith Mary. I forget my numbers all the time. Especially subtraction. But Papa says it'll stick one of these days. I hope we stick and you remember soon."

Mary hugged him back. "Me too. Thanks, boys. Now be quick about it. This is a very important message."

The boys said goodbye and disappeared as abruptly as they came. Robbie. A tiny glimpse of a memory flitted through her thoughts but retreated before she could grab ahold of it. Something about the way he said, "Mith." What an adorable toothless lisp. He was the fireman's son?

The phone line lit up, so Mary plugged it and answered. "Good morning. To whom may I direct your call?"

The woman's voice quivered. "Mary? Is that you? Are you all right? I've been so worried."

"And you are?" Mary sat up straight.

"Mrs. Chancery, dear. Your aunts' friend whom you helped during the fire. You saved my husband's picture and tried to save my cat, though he didn't survive. You were hurt during the rescue. Fireman Flannigan saved your life."

Mary sighed. None of that sounded the least bit familiar. "I'm sorry, missus. I had a nasty gash to my head and can't recall that. But I'm glad you're okay."

"Thank you. I'm glad you're mending, but will pray your memory returns. I'm in Rochester with my daughter. May I speak with Mrs. Dowe, please?" Mrs. Chancery chuckled, waiting to be transferred.

"Right away, ma'am. God bless you. Here she is."

Plug. Done.

As she was disconnecting the line, Charlotte stepped into the room carrying a tray of food. "I brought you some lunch. Coffee, fruit, and a ham sandwich. The bread line has three hundred dollars' worth of food. Can you imagine?"

"That's a small fortune, and quite a blessing. Thanks for bringing this." Mary swallowed her surprise.

"Glad to help. Do you need a break?"

Mary shook her head. "I'm quite enjoying it, thank you. The state inspector is coming this afternoon to do an investigation of the fire. I hope they find the source."

"Me too." Charlotte sat on the empty chair beside her. "Go ahead and eat while I catch you up on all the news. The Association has announced that it will rebuild, and the Columbian Hotel employees are being sent home. Many of them were college students and lost everything but the clothes on their back. They depended on their salaries for the next year's tuition, so the hotel is paying for their trips home."

Mary swallowed her bite and took a sip of the weak coffee before speaking. "That is kind of them. You lost everything, too, didn't you?"

"A lot, yes. But Papa kept his money and valuables in a box that he grabbed as he fled the building. Providence was good to us, and though I lost clothes and such, we saved Mama's picture and jewelry and all our money."

"I'm glad. I suppose I'll never see my mother's wedding ring or my parents' photograph again. Or my father's Bible. It was all I had of them."

Charlotte touched her hand. "I'm so sorry, Mary. So many lost so much. But still, no one died in the fires, and for that we must all be grateful."

"What should we be grateful for?" Archie popped his head into the room and stepped in unbidden. "I trust you're talking about being grateful for me."

The ham sandwich suddenly soured in Mary's stomach. She nodded to him and glanced at Charlotte as a slight scowl crossed her lips.

"Hello, Mr. Richmond." Charlotte stood.

Mary stayed seated. "You don't have to leave, Charlotte."

She wished she wouldn't.

"Sorry. Papa needed me to run a few more errands. I best be on my way. I'll return at three to give you a break, okay?"

"Three would be fine. Thanks, Charlotte."

On her way out the door, Charlotte gave Archie a cool nod, and he nodded back. Charlotte didn't like the man either.

Archie took the seat Charlotte had occupied. "How's my little woman today? I'm glad to see you're working. Perhaps it will help you to get your mind back soon."

Mary glanced at the switchboard. If only it would light up.

It didn't.

Archie didn't wait for her to respond. "I have news. The Association created a volunteer police force to stave off looting, and they put me in charge. It is quite the honor, I'll tell you. So far, the thieving hasn't been near as bad as the Frontenac's. Do you remember the hubbub about all the stolen goods from that hotel fire last year? I suppose not. Well, the Columbian's silver and other valuables that they've recovered are being stored and locked in the library for safekeeping until they rebuild. The personal property they recover is being brought here to the Wellesley Hotel for folks to claim. What little is left intact, that is. But thanks to me and others, even two days later, piles of belongings along the shoreline are still untouched."

"That's good. I don't suppose I'll ever find my things."

Archie scoffed. "Don't be daft. You were on the bottom floor of the hotel. Charred ruins cover anything that might have survived."

Mercifully, the switchboard lit up. "I need to work, Archie."

He stood, pecked her on the cheek, and left without another word. Thank the Lord.

Mary plugged into the call. "Good morning, Mr. Sweeny. To whom may I connect your call?"

Mr. Sweeny cleared his throat. "Reverend Thompson, please."

She connected them but kept the line open, hoping to hear a little good news. If any were to be had, these two would deliver it.

Mr. Sweeny didn't disappoint. "Some folks want to close TI Park for good, but the Association will rebuild bigger and better. Just as Chicago and San Francisco thrived after their fires, so will our beloved Park."

"I believe the priorities should be the chapel, school, and stores to start." Reverend Thompson agreed. "And we must construct the buildings of concrete blocks so they'll be fireproof. Otherwise, we'll likely face another fire in our future."

Another fire?

God forbid.

~ ~ ~

George led Deputy Chief State Fire Marshall Ingram to the back of the Columbian Hotel ruins. The large, middle-aged man surveyed the piles of rubble, the mounds of ash, the standing chimney. "Here's where they spotted smoke first. The H.H. Haller store caught fire, and before long, the two-hundred-and-twenty-room hotel was a seething caldron of flames and smoke. The wind blew something fierce, and within the hour, only the brick abutments, burning rubble, and a mass of intensely hot, twisted ironwork remained."

He explained how they couldn't get the engine out of the Annex, how they broke into the store, but then how it ignited.

"What time was this?" The man took copious notes, groaned, and *tsk*ed. But he rarely said a word.

"One o'clock on July ninth, sir. The heat, the drought, and the reservoir repair were likely factors."

Deputy Chief Ingram raised his palm. "I do not want your opinions. Only the facts. I will make my own conclusions after my investigation."

George ducked his head. "Yes, sir. We called for help as soon as we could. The Bay, Clayton, and Gananoque came to our aid."

Upon careful inspection of the Haller store area, Ingram quickly ruled out faulty wiring. And since it was so hot, there was obviously no fire in the store's stove.

For the next several hours, they perused the site and interviewed dozens of people who waited in a long line to share their ideas, theories, and claims. None of them rang true.

Mr. Rusk believed a match dropped on the storeroom floor started the blaze, but he had no proof. Mr. Blanchett charged that stored paint and kerosene somehow ignited in the locked shop. Mrs. Fulton and Mrs. Wilcox accused deliverymen of smoking near the store's bedding, as they had done many times. Mrs. Pickett held to a theory that mice gnawed on matches and set the shop ablaze.

Two men who had publicly complained about an American Indian holding a funeral in *their* chapel had fingers pointed at him as a possible arsonist.

George spoke up in the Indian's defense. "That makes no sense. I'm acquainted with this man, sir, and I believe he would never stoop to setting a fire. That, I believe, is a purely false accusation and completely unsubstantiated. Perhaps the accusers are the guilty ones."

Deputy Chief Ingram clicked his tongue. "I concur. And the other theories of arson? The tramp? The other possible arsonists? What have you to say about them?"

Now he wants my opinion? George sighed. "I have no facts but, in my *opinion*, none of them have substance, sir. All are innuendo and guesses. I think folks are grasping at anything that will put the blame on something solid. But unfortunately, often there just aren't clear-cut answers to such tragedies."

Ingram continued to write in his book, page after page. George escorted him up to the reservoir to have a look while detailing what the men were doing there that day. Ingram shook his head. He harrumphed. He wrote.

Back in town, they walked the length and breadth of the burn area, east from St. Lawrence Avenue all the way to Grove Avenue. Then they trekked north of Oak Street and then south to Coast Avenue along the river. Walking the entire burned-out area made George even sadder than he already was.

One hundred and more buildings. Gone.

As they plodded through the ruins, Ingram asked a few more questions and discussed the boardwalks, the construction of the cottages, the inadequate hydrant system. Surely, this would be a black mark on the Park. But how bad would it be?

Next, Deputy Chief Ingram wanted to see the inside of a cottage, so George took him to Mary's aunts' cottage. The Deputy Chief pointed out the unsealed timbers finished with flammable varnish and scoffed at the flimsy shingles.

He swept a wide arc with his arm. "There is plenty of fodder to feed a fire in this small cottage alone, and I see several sources of ignition. As you know, candles, kerosene and oil lamps, open fireplaces, and wood and coal stoves are all triggers for combustion. And as for the fodder, bedding and clothing and doilies and afghans? This cottage is ready to fuel a fire, all right."

George swallowed. "Unfortunately, it's all too true. Most of the cottages have glass fire grenades, but they are no match for a conflagration. Some buildings had electricity, and many had extinguishers, but not all. Yet extinguishers were no help in this massive fire either."

Ingram wrote that down, but as they exited the cottage, he decried the dry and weathered boardwalks too. "These walkways are matchsticks waiting to catch fire."

"True enough. I watched that play out in real time. Once the boardwalks caught fire, they were like fuses running to the cottages and setting them ablaze."

"Why didn't you tear up the boardwalks to keep that from happening?" Ingram furrowed his brow, deepening his scowl.

George sighed. "We hadn't the manpower, sir. The Park is only now assessing the fire protection needs. I am the only paid fireman in the Park, hired to give my suggestions for improvement. Those who came to my aid were untrained firefighting volunteers, but they fought bravely and did as best as they could."

"And what of the wind?" Ingram shook his head, disgust prominent on his features. He wrote a whole page after that.

George's pulse ticked up a notch at the memory. "It started as a stiff breeze from the west at about fifteen miles per hour, pushing the fire east, but as the blaze grew, it created its own patterns, whipping back and forth several times and sending embers all around a fourteen-block radius. We retreated and took up new lines repeatedly, sir. We've had reports that the sparks and embers even spread to a stand of trees near Rockport, Ontario, a full seven miles across the St. Lawrence River."

"As I suspected."

Next, they inspected the hydrant system along the main roads as well as the side streets. "Two-inch pipes are not adequate for a population this size. Nor does the system reach the far edges of the Park."

More *tsk*ing. More harrumphing. More disapproval. There would be a scathing report when all was said and done.

The earth reeked of still-smoldering ruins. Pieces of the hotel, its foundation stones, its charred wood and bricks, its remnants of furniture—all stood as reminders of the fire's wrath. Debris, neck deep, still too hot to go near, shouted the conflagration's victory.

Junk dealers picked through the burned-out area, riffling through the mess to collect the iron and other scrap metal. Residents did, too, finding little worth keeping.

The clean-up and debris removal would take months.

He coughed, scratched the side of his nose, and a layer of ash on his face filtered to his chest. Everything had a layer of ash, including, he suspected, his lungs.

He pointed toward a hill beyond Ingram. "Until they can install a better system, I suggest the Association erect a standpipe on Sunrise Mountain to increase the pressure in the existing hydrants. At least they'd have a fighting chance if another blaze erupts."

Finally, Deputy Chief Ingram agreed. "Good idea. And you need to raise up a volunteer fire department and train them. This week. There can be no more putting off to tomorrow what should have been done years ago."

"I agree. I just hope the Association will."

"They will, or I'll shut down the entire Park." Ingram cleared his throat.

That statement made the hair on George's neck stand at attention. He sucked in a breath as he led Ingram to meet with the Association board.

As he spoke to the board, Deputy Chief Ingram was firm, if not offensive. "Gentlemen. I have concluded my investigation and find many problems here at Thousand Islands Park, some bordering on negligence. I cannot—and will not—cast natural occurrences like the drought, the wind, and the unbearable heat wave upon your shoulders, sirs. Neither, I suppose, can you be blamed for the work on the reservoir, although it would have been wiser to wait until the heat wave had passed and you'd had some rain."

Ingram paused for several moments, flipping through his lengthy notes. The longer he did, the more jittery the board became. But no one said a word.

Finally, the Deputy Chief concluded his findings. "Arson, though promulgated by several of your residents, may be a possibility, yet it cannot be proved. Therefore, I deem the cause inconclusive, and will so attest."

He stopped reading from his notes and bore a narrow-eyed glare into each of the men. "But, as the leadership of this Park, you are culpable for the lack of equipment, the absence of a fire department, and the pathetic hydrant system I witnessed. In these matters, prosecution is a direct possibility—if the department so deems."

Reverend Thompson wiped his brow. "What are the chances of that, sir? We are working on making the changes, raising funds, but we need time."

"We shall see." Deputy Chief Ingram scowled.

George suppressed a groan. After all their loss, they might face this burden too?

Chapter 21

Mary gulped in searing breaths of thick smoke as sparks flew all around her like devils on a mission, riding on the wind, settling on beautiful summer homes that smoked and kindled, ready to ignite. Ash peppered the wind and dusted everything in a deathly gray.

The air, dry as dust, choked her. Needles of heat pricked her face and hands. Her feet, immovable, stuck to the ground.

Fear sparked and flamed to life. Not another fire!

Her pulse thrummed at the base of her neck, and sweat tickled her scalp. Shrinking away from the flames, she shook like a dog cowering before a larger opponent.

Firebrands danced on the breeze. Flames licked up the grass, ignited the bushes. A spiraling column of flames trampled house after house like a giant on the move. A building collapsed. Rubble rolled into the street.

Children wailed. Neighbors cried. Screamed. Ran. Shoved. Prayed.

Older folks stared in silence as if turned to stone. Young people worked, fought, tried to save what they could. Grabbed their belonging and threw them into the streets.

Rats fled the barns. Cats meowed. Dogs barked. Horses neighed. Birds fell from the sky.

Glass melted, silver fused together, candles warped. Streets clogged with belongings. Chimneys stood like soldiers guarding the debris of people's lives.

The flames overpowered the raised wooden sidewalk and caught the next veranda ablaze. Her aunts' cottage? No! Angry clouds of smoke and ash whipped all around her. Fiendish flames of fire teased.

Terror mounted with every step, but she fought a rising panic. She had to save her precious aunts.

There, in the upstairs window, Aunt Maude and Aunt Stella banged on the glass, trapped inside their burning cottage. They screamed for help, but they couldn't make themselves heard over the roar of the inferno.

The wind took on a menacing power as her aunties' home exploded into flames.

Fear fluttered in her stomach and she fought nausea, gathering her courage. She hoisted her skirts, dashing up the burning cottage steps and through the front door. Felt her way up the steep staircase, barraged by the heat. Choking on the smoke. Her nerves stretched and strained.

A headache swelled behind her eyes, her nerves taut as piano strings. Fear poured over her like a torrential summer storm. She reeled back, the flames pushing her to retreat, away from her aunts, like the bully it was.

The fire whipped into a whirling dervish. Flaming wallpaper spiraled down, hitting her on the shoulder, burning a hole in her dress. Flying embers attacked her, scorching her hair. Still, she pressed on.

She had to find her aunts and save them. Where were they? She tried to call out, but her voice croaked, indistinguishable, useless.

Sparks rained down like hail. A cloud of ash covered everything in a layer of white powder, making it hard to see. Her nose filled with it. Her eyes burned with it. Her throat choked with it.

The flames spread before and behind her, surrounding her with heat so hot she wondered if she had entered Hades.

She called for her aunties, but nothing came out of her mouth. Then … there … Aunt Maude's paper-thin hand, a network of veins covering the back of it. She reached for her, but something pulled her back, kept her from saving her loved ones. She groaned, reached, pressed toward the hand …

"Mary. Wake up." Charlotte shook her gently, a tender hand touching hers. "It's a bad dream."

Mary sucked in a breath and blinked.

No fire. No smoke. No ash.

She was safe in her room. At her desk.

She had fallen asleep.

Charlotte rubbed her shoulders, trying to calm her. "There. There. You were having another bad dream. Breathe. You're safe."

Mary groaned and willed herself awake. Her heart raced and her nerves prickled. She hated to sleep, so she was always tired, especially since she'd hurt her head. When her body finally succumbed, she knew what would follow—terror. Like now. Her niggling doubts always crept into her dreams. Her fears—and possibly memories—taunted her.

"Are you going to answer that, or shall I?" Charlotte tapped her arm.

The switchboard was lit with a call beckoning her. Mary cleared her throat and plugged in the call. "Good morning. How may I direct your call?"

A gruff older woman scoffed. "It is the afternoon, young lady, *not* the morning. Have you been asleep at your post? If so, I shall have to report you. I've been trying to reach my son for ever so long. Connect me with Mr. George Flannigan at once."

Oh no! Mary steadied herself. "Yes, Mrs. Flannigan. Just a moment, please."

Mary glanced at Charlotte for a boost of support as she rang her aunts' cottage. After several rings, the fireman answered. "Good afternoon, sir. Your mother is on the line."

"Oh, all right. Thank you, Miss Flynn." George groaned loudly.

She smiled, her voice taking on a lighter tone. "You're welcome, sir. Here you go."

Though she knew she shouldn't eavesdrop, Mary kept the line open and listened. She just had to know if the woman would impute her character. She did. "That woman on the switchboard failed to answer my call for several minutes. Then she sounded like she'd been sleeping. What kind of person has the Park hired to do such an important job, and in the midst of a tragedy? They should find more reliable help, and do I hope you're steering clear of her."

"Mother, we're all doing the best we can. She had a severe concussion. It's a wonder she can work at all." George huffed.

Mrs. Flannigan snickered, then it turned into a cackle. "Stuff and nonsense. If she's not well enough, she shouldn't be at her post.

But that's not why I called. When are you and Robbie going to come home where you belong? A burned-out Park is no place for a child."

George grumbled, deep and low. Barely audible. "We've been all through this, Mother. Yesterday. This is my job, and I'm staying to help these people in their time of need. I'll come and see you soon, but until school starts, we're remaining here."

"Well, I've never known a more ungrateful son. Have it your way, but don't be getting mixed up with the likes of that switchboard woman." The lady grunted her disapproval.

George cleared his throat. "Goodbye, Mother."

The phone disconnected, and Mary turned to Charlotte, who was waiting patiently. "Mrs. Flannigan doesn't like me, but why?"

Charlotte blinked. She pursed her lips and shrugged.

"Tell me, Charlotte." Her friend knew something. "Please?"

~ ~ ~

George reluctantly escorted Archibald Richmond throughout the burn scar, just as he'd done with several other adjusters. As with all the insurance men, Richmond grumbled about the lack of fire prevention resources and cited its inadequacies as a reason for not paying out on the claims. With each passing minute, he liked the man less.

Archie scoffed, shaking his head. "I told all the Park residents, just like I told you. Without insurance, these nitwits will have to incur the cost of cleaning up their mess and rebuilding their cottages on their own. And some morons who finally insured their places only did so at fifty percent of the value—or less. Others didn't have the common sense to retrieve their policies before they fled the fire, and without the paperwork, I'll not pay them a penny. Fools!"

George's stomach clenched, and his blood surged hot. The scoundrel wouldn't pay on any policy if he could avoid it. He and his kind gave insurance men a bad name. Anger gnawed at his insides. He snapped his pocket watch open and surveyed the face. "Are we done here?"

"Not yet. We haven't walked down Grove Avenue to Coastal yet, so I'll tell you when we're finished.' Richmond smirked, his eyes turning to narrow slits. "And when we're done, I need to see to my girl, Mary Flynn. You do know she's mine, don't you? So don't be getting any ideas. I'm thinking she might make a pretty good wife once I work that independent spirit out of her. And she'll not be working the switchboard when I get a ring on her finger. No sirree. She'll be doing nothing 'cept working in my kitchen and doing as I say. Women like her need to learn their place in the scheme of things."

George held his tongue, pressing his lips together until they hurt. How had such a man weaseled his way into Mary's affections? Whenever Richmond came near her prior to her injury, she'd always turned up her nose.

Wait! Was Richmond taking advantage of Mary's memory loss? If so, Archibald Richmond would have to reckon with him. "Since when did you and Mary become so closely acquainted—that is, beyond the dinner at her aunts'?"

Richmond guffawed. "Wouldn't you like to know? She's taken a shine to me for some time now. We've had several … shall we say … encounters of the personal nature, and she's been quite free with her affections, if you know what I mean. That hair? Soft as a baby's. And those full red lips? Luscious."

"How dare you speak of such things about Miss Flynn? She is a woman of impeccable virtue and honor." Anger flared inside George. Blood boiled in his veins.

The scoundrel chuckled. "If you say so. She might have been a sweet little angel before, but people change, Flannigan. Especially when knocked on the noggin."

George stepped in front of him, blocking his path. Pulling himself to his full height, a head taller than Richmond, he stared him down. His hands clenched into tight fists. "Take it back, Richmond. And if I ever catch you disparaging Mary in public or otherwise, you'll be sorry you ever spoke of her."

Richmond folded his arms over his chest and stood a little taller. But the smirk never left his face. Instead, he boldly tipped his chin higher to meet the challenge. "Settle down, George." Sarcasm fairly dripped from his crooked mouth. "Would I say anything that wasn't true about my soon-to-be betrothed? Nae. You have it all wrong, sonny boy. You are the one who will have a reckoning if you chase the skirts of my girl."

George stepped toward him, ready to pounce, but thought the better. There were other ways to deal with a scoundrel and a bully. He bumped Richmond's shoulder with his own, hurling him off balance and sending him to the sooty ground. He feigned surprise. "Oh, I'm sorry, ol' chap, but I need to get to a meeting and train the volunteer fire department. So long, sonny boy."

Before the rogue could find his tongue, George took off in a sprint. Though he did have a meeting, it wasn't for another hour, and the training was an hour after that. But he had to get away from such a vile person before he did something he'd regret.

Like when he'd first met his wife, Alma.

Alma had a neighbor boy just like Richmond who toyed with her affections and insinuated things that weren't true. And George had pummeled the lad, breaking his nose and blackening both eyes. The boy's father threatened to have him arrested, but the sheriff knew the boy's reputation for troublemaking and only gave George hours of community service.

When provoked, George's temper could get the best of him. He couldn't let that happen again.

Yet he couldn't bear to have Mary's good name dragged through the ash heap of the Park. Concussion or no, he would never allow her character to be tarnished. But what could he do to stop a man set on spreading rumors and telling lies?

He'd have to think on that one. In the meantime, he had to meet with the Association board and then train thirty volunteer firemen.

Soon, he entered the Fitch cottage and joined the others. Mr. Fitch, the Association treasurer, hosted the meeting, and Dr. Goodale joined them.

Mr. Brown, the chairman, called the meeting to order, then launched into business. "We set the post office up in the John cottage on St. Lawrence Avenue. The bandstand has become a dairy store. Haller and Kendall have decided to work together to set up a grocery and meat store in the Association's storerooms. The other businesses are working out of their cottages or have rented cottages whose owners have fled the Park since the fire. But we simply must rebuild the shopping area and the Columbian Hotel as soon as possible. They are critical to maintaining a sense of normalcy here in the Park."

Mr. Fitch scanned the financial ledger he had brought with him. "Glad I had this at my place since all the other records were lost." He tapped the journal before continuing. "There simply aren't the funds, sirs. We are woefully lacking, and I don't see how we can raise enough for even clearing the rubble, much less to build new buildings."

George cleared his throat. "Don't forget overhauling the fire hydrant system and adding more equipment. That should come even before rebuilding. For your residents' safety."

"Let's prioritize our most pressing needs, gentlemen." Dr. Goodale put up a hand.

Mr. Brown shook his head. "Given the Thousand Islands Park charter that constrains us from raising more taxes, how are we to fund the necessary fire equipment and the rubble removal and the building? I don't see a way through this."

Dr. Goodale countered. "We can re-institute the matching funds' campaign and hope the residents will see the need to invest with us in equipment that can save their property—and possibly their lives. It was nothing short of providential that no one died in our most recent conflagration, but that kind of luck isn't likely to continue. Someone is going to die the next time, and then where will we be? The scandal might ruin the future of Thousand Islands Park forever."

Mr. Fitch tapped his ledger, shaking his head. "We've tried that, and where did it get us? Eighty-three dollars and forty-five cents. I'm afraid to say that doesn't work."

"As the Edward Hickson song says …," George puffed out his chest and belted out the chorus of a popular song.

"'Tis a lesson you should heed—Try again;
If at first you don't succeed, Try again.
Then your courage should appear; For if you will persevere.
You will conquer, never fear, Try again.'"

He paused as several men applauded. "I think we should put this to the test. Perhaps the terrible and ever-present fear of fire might move our neighbors and friends to forego a few extra luxuries to safeguard their properties and families."

"Hear, hear." Dr. Goodale pounded the table. "And to recall the rest of the song, I think, is rather appropriate for this discussion." He waved his hands like a conductor. "Join me."

And join they did. Off-key, off-tempo, even forgetting words. It didn't matter. The final chorus rang out, filling the room—and George—with hope.

"'Once or twice, though, you should fail.
If you would at last prevail, Try again.
If we strive, 'tis no disgrace. Though we did not win the race
What should you do in that case? Try again.'"

George chuckled. "That may be a children's lesson, but it is true, gentlemen. What can it hurt to try? Dr. Goodale, would you lead this charge?"

"I will, sirs." Dr. Goodale nodded.

Mr. Fitch shrugged. "That's all fine and good, but what else can we do?"

"If I may." George waved a hand. "I've raised up a thirty-man volunteer fire department, and I begin training them within the hour. I've also put out inquiries to see if there might be wealthy benefactors among the islands who would donate to our cause."

Mr. Brown clapped him on the shoulder. "Thank you, sir. We appreciate all you've done and are doing to help the Park. Your work has not gone unnoticed. And I think we should all join George in seeking benefactors who might help, given our situation. Who agrees?"

When all the men raised their hands, Mr. Brown declared the meeting adjourned. It was all hands on deck to find funds to solve the Park's dilemma.

As George passed the Wellesley Hotel on his way to his next meeting, Mary and Richmond stepped out of the hotel arm in arm. But instead of appearing to be a happy couple, Mary looked upset. Fearful, even. A deep frown tainted her pretty face, and her shoulders slumped. And was she trembling? What was wrong?

He had to find out. As quick as a pony's gallop, George stepped into their path. "Good afternoon, Miss Flynn. Richmond. What brings you out on this warm afternoon?"

He glanced at the blazing sun, hoping his concern was none too obvious. Truth was, he feared for Mary's safety with the likes of Archibald Richmond.

"I … we …" Mary's breath came out in little puffs, and her jaw quivered.

Richmond interrupted her. "The cat's got your tongue, little lady? What's it to you, anyway, Flannigan?"

"I don't feel well, Archie. I think I should go back and lie down." Her eyes widened and her mouth dropped open. She snapped it shut.

Richmond gave her a yank. "Not until we take our walk. That switchboard has kept you cooped up all day, jabbering. It isn't good for you. Besides, I have things to discuss."

George scanned Mary's face as fear clouded her eyes. Her mouth twitched, and her cheeks turned rosy as though she'd been outside on a cold winter's day. Her gaze shifted to Archie, and a sigh of resignation slipped out of her lips.

Archie swiped his whiskered face, then reached over and ran a possessive hand over her cheek. "I'm afraid I must insist, dearest."

"If the lady needs to rest, let her." George's nerves fired as his anger ignited. The scoundrel was forcing the poor lass's hand.

Richmond cupped her elbow tighter and pulled her out of George's path. "This is none of your concern, fireman."

George beseeched Mary with raised eyebrows. "What do *you* want, Miss Flynn?"

Mary stood there like a wilted, dying daisy. She pasted her lips shut as her eyes welled with tears.

"Get out of our way." Richmond gave him a shove.

George shoved him back. "Not on her life, you rogue."

Chapter 22

Mary worked her hair into a high rolled chignon to hide the bald spot where her stitches once were. Dr. Place had removed them days ago, and although the area was still quite tender, she had thoroughly enjoyed washing her hair and finding a little sense of normalcy in styling it again. But she could do nothing about the singed patch near her ear, and she'd have to wear the chignon this way for quite some time—or find a hat.

Satisfied with the results, Mary pinched her cheeks, then adjusted the pink cotton dress Mr. Flannigan had given her. What a thoughtful gentleman he was, but how strange that he'd think of her, a complete stranger. He'd even provided undergarments and shoes that fit. Her cheeks warmed at the realization he'd picked out unmentionables.

Yes, Mr. Flannigan seemed to go out of his way to pamper her and protect her. Did all firemen attend to the victims of a fire so conscientiously? If only Archie would be so kind. Wouldn't a beau treat a woman even better than a relative stranger might? He, on the other hand, seemed only concerned with his own well-being— and bullying her. Talking endlessly about what he wanted and how accomplished he was. He bragged and boasted until she thought him an insufferable boar. And the more she was around him, the less she liked him—if she'd ever liked him at all. He vowed that they had courted for some time, but why couldn't she remember?

She smoothed the wide, open collar and expanded her large puffed sleeves before picking up the navy reticule which Fireman Flannigan had also included in the gift basket. He—or whomever donated the purse—had enclosed a silver dollar inside and a pretty embroidered handkerchief. Priceless gifts when she had nothing else.

As she meandered up St. Lawrence Avenue to Sunday service at the Tabernacle, she shuddered at the naked, desolate limbs of charred trees, mute evidence of one of the worst conflagrations that had swept the islands in years, so said the newspapers. And the heaps of rubble? They would take months to remove.

Somehow, the damaged trees reminded her of Archibald Richmond. Bare, bleak, and lacking life—at least any life she could see. How in the world had he become her beau? No matter how hard she tried, she couldn't reckon it. And if, indeed, she had somehow agreed to a courtship with him, how could she possibly get out of it? In her circle, breaking a betrothal simply wasn't done.

As she entered the Thousand Islands Park Tabernacle and took a seat, she observed her neighbors. Some smiled, many frowned, and a few sat like forlorn orphans. They'd lost as much or more than she. At least her aunts' cottage remained standing and them safe in Watertown.

As the service began, Fireman Flannigan and his little boy slipped into the seat next to her. He smiled and whispered, "Good morning, Miss Flynn."

Mary nodded and gave the child a small wave as the minister opened the service. "Hattie Buell wrote the hymn we are about to sing after hearing a sermon right here in 1876. Let us stand and sing hymn number forty-eight, 'A Child of the King.'"

Mary opened her hymnal and sang with all her heart. George's deep baritone blended with her soprano voice rather nicely.

> My Father is rich in houses and land,
> He holdeth the wealth of the world in His hands!
> Of rubies and diamonds, of silver and gold,
> His coffers are full, He has riches untold.
>
> I'm a child of the King,
> A child of the King,
> With Jesus my Savior,
> I'm a child of the King.
>
> My Father's own Son, the Savior of men,
> Once wandered on earth as the poorest of them;
> But now He is reigning forever on high,
> And will give me a home in heav'n by and by.
>
> I once was an outcast stranger on earth,
> A sinner by choice and an alien by birth;
> But I've been adopted, my name's written down,
> An heir to a mansion, a robe and a crown.
>
> A tent or a cottage, why should I care?
> They're building a palace for me over there;
> Though exiled from home, yet still may I sing:
> All glory to God, I'm a child of the King.

Reverend Thompson prayed and bid them all to sit. "I chose this hymn today to help us gain perspective on our current circumstances. The conflagration of the past week has displaced many of us. Hundreds of you have lost much. Some have already fled our midst and are in exile, so to speak. All of us mourn the tragedy in our community.

"But this world is not our home, and our belongings, whether a cottage, an elegant house on the mainland, or any of the things in our dwellings—these are just temporal. Our true riches are in heaven, and people are all who really matter. Let us never forget this truth."

The preacher paused and scanned the congregation. "And speaking of people, I want to mention several heroes of our Park and thank the good Lord for putting them in our community for such a time as this. Who knows, but we might have had several deaths without their bravery, kindness, and courage."

Reverend Thompson spread his hand out toward the front row. "The first to come to mind is Fireman Flannigan, who rallied the troops, and the many brave firefighters, undaunted by the fire's fury." A polite clapping ensued, and many looked his way and smiled.

"Next is Grandma Tousey. At ninety-two, she is deeply loved by all. This dear woman calmly directed the efforts of so many of the volunteers, begging them to save everyone from harm before making any attempt to save property. From what I've been told, Mrs. Tousey personally saved at least two people. In an adjoining cottage that had caught fire, she found Mrs. Anna Nunn and Mrs. Eager unconscious and called for help to drag them to safety."

Mrs. Eager wiped tears from her eyes. Mrs. Nunn nodded, a bright smile crossing her lips.

A titter of *yes*es and *amen*s wafted through the crowd as Mrs. Tousey waved away the compliment with her fan. She never was one to be the center of attention.

Reverend Thompson smiled at the man sitting next to Grandma Tousey, then dipped his chin to three other men. "William Tousey, Robert Van Lingen, and Frank Sweeny worked together to clear the burning Columbian, rushing from room to room to evacuate everyone safely. Mr. Tousey even carried Miss Buster of Watertown to safety after finding her unconscious in the farthest room on the top floor."

He continued bestowing gratitude to his parishioners, stepping away from the pulpit to touch the arm of a child sitting in the front row. "And you, dear child? Miss Marion Mayer here, just twelve years old, was brave enough to save the Billings Hall boarding house with a garden hose. Well done, child."

The girl beamed at his comment while the preacher returned to the pulpit. "Paul Crouch of Cortland, who stood on the peak of the Wellesley with a blanket thrown around him, ripping the burning shingles from the roof for two long hours? He and other volunteers on the ground saved the Wellesley Hotel from destruction. There are too many others to mention, those who risked life and limb to save people and property, and we thank the good Lord for all of you."

At that, the congregation heartily applauded.

Reverend Thompson nodded at the applause, waiting for several moments for the crowd to quiet. "And though they're not here, we must show our gratitude to Joseph Wittman of the Isle of Pines and T. A. Gillespie of Basswood Island, who sent their private yachts to Clayton to purchase all the baked goods available and anything else useful for the fire sufferers. These goods totaled over three hundred dollars and helped us all in our time of need."

More applause and cheers. Mary had never experienced a church service where churchgoers clapped and hurrahed. It was rather wonderful.

Then the preacher grew somber, and so did the gathering. "And now, we must turn our hearts to pray for those injured. Let's bow our head and ask the Lord's healing touch on the following. We pray for Sanford Kemp, Herbert Huber, Mrs. Lena Kilmore, Roy Mitchell, Robert Van Lingen, Harry Roddenbeck, and Miss Mary Flynn. God, please heal these and all the injured, whether in body or soul. Amen."

Mary took out the handkerchief and dabbed her eyes.

Please, Lord. Let it be.

~ ~ ~

George patted Mary's hand to console her as the congregation prayed. A jolt of warmth crept up his arm when he touched her, but he ignored it. He focused on praying for her. Would her memory ever return? Would she recall what had blossomed between them?

When the service ended, Mary turned to him, and the beautiful smile he craved lit up her face like a sunrise. She touched her dress and presented her reticule. "I don't believe I've thanked you properly for everything you brought me in that basket. It was very generous of you. Especially the silver dollar."

"You're welcome, Miss Flynn. That's what friends are for."

Mary frowned. "Are we? Friends, I mean? I'm sorry, but I can't remember. If so, please call me Mary."

Robbie scooted between them, his gap-toothed grin impeding his speech. "We've been friends for ever tho long, Mith Mary. We went on a boat ride and watched fireworks togefer and everyfing."

Mary giggled, drawing questioning glances from two old biddies. Her eyes darted between the observers and Robbie. She cast them an apologetic smile.

George tossed them a dismissive head shake as Mr. Wiseman joined them. Robbie hugged the elderly man.

So did Mary. "Hi, Gramps. I didn't see you this morning, or I would have walked with you. When I stopped by your room, you'd already left."

"I wanted a little extra prayer time, and I needed to talk to Reverend Thompson. And as you know, it takes me a while to walk any distance these days."

George took his son's hand. "Would you do Robbie and me the honor of joining us for lunch, sir? I made a roast yesterday and have plenty. And you, too, Mary, if you'll join us."

"Oh yeth, Mith Mary. I want to show you my pet turtle, Timmy." Robbie grabbed her hand and pulled her toward the door.

"Now, really, how can you say no to that? Let's join them, Mary." Gramps chuckled as he mussed the boy's hair.

A tentative smile crossed her lips as she traced a finger along the woodgrain on the top of the pew. She leaned in close to Mr. Wiseman's ear and whispered loud enough for the four of them to hear. "If you think it's proper, given Mr. Richmond is my beau. He's off the island for the day."

Mr. Wiseman scrunched up his face into a plethora of wrinkles. "Ridiculous. My adopted granddaughter can join me and have lunch with whomever she likes. Is there a ring on your finger?"

"Of course not, but he said …" Mary glanced at her bare hand.

Mr. Wiseman slipped his hand through the crook of her arm. "I'm the elder here and I say let's go."

Mary shrugged one shoulder. "Yes, sir. Lead the way, Robbie." She let go of Robbie's hand and steadied Mr. Wiseman.

Her concerns for that scoundrel Richmond tugged at George's heart. Dr. Place had said he feared a shock to Mary's brain might disrupt the healing. He insisted on letting her discover things as her memory returned and not force it too soon. But in the meantime, Richmond was manipulating her, toying with her, playing her for a fool.

He'd have a talk with the doctor first thing in the morning. Richmond's lies could no longer go unchecked. She thought she had to kowtow to the rogue? Well, he'd put a stop to that, and soon.

Pale blue skies met the deep blue river as they walked to the cottage. Like the narrows upriver, the street meandered to the west, its banks of lovely unharmed Victorians waiting to be enjoyed.

Robbie stopped in his path, nearly tripping him. "Can I run ahead and thee if Timmy is awake? Please, Daddy?"

"Sure, son. We'll be there soon."

"Can I go with you? I can't run, but we'll walk fast. How about that?" Mary glanced at the child and back at George.

George and Mr. Wiseman laughed and nodded, and Robbie and Mary hurried off hand in hand.

George offered the elderly man his elbow, and he took it. How fortuitous to have some time alone with the man. "Mr. Wiseman, may I ask you something, please?"

"Please call me Gramps. Everyone I care about does, and you're in that number. Robbie too."

His heart warmed at the offer. "Thank you, Gramps. That means a lot. Truth is, I'm concerned about Mary. Richmond has her hoodwinked into thinking they have a romantic arrangement. That he is her beau. He's a rogue, sir, and I worry for her safety."

"I've gathered that, and I, too, am concerned." Gramps stopped and studied George's face. "I think we should address the matter with the doctor and see what he thinks."

"That's what I thought too. Shall we go together first thing?"

The old man shook his cane. "Pick me up at nine. We need to protect this lovely lass."

Hope rose now that he had an ally in his court. On the rest of the walk, he and Gramps chatted about the fair weather, the soon-coming concert, and the fun he shared with his young son.

When they got to the cottage, Mary and Robbie weren't on the porch as he'd expected. Hinges creaked as he opened the door. He called out, "Anybody home?"

Mary answered from the kitchen. "In here. Robbie and I are preparing lunch. You two sit and visit."

"We're gonna do everyfing, Daddy." Robbie scurried into the room. "Mith Mary knows how."

"That's wonderful, son, and I'm mighty proud of you being a good helper."

His boy nodded and disappeared into the kitchen while he and Gramps took seats in the parlor. What would it be like to have Mary care for his boy? Be his mother? And she be his wife?

Gramps interrupted his musings. "You're mighty deep in thought, George. Penny for it."

"One day, perhaps." George's face warmed, and he shook his head.

Gramps glanced toward the kitchen and cast him a knowing smile. "Yes, hopefully soon. So how long do you think it'll take to clear out all the rubble and rebuild?"

George sighed, glad for conversation to veer away from the pretty lady in his kitchen. "Depends on how much help we have moving it all. Seems folks are willing to help, but we need to be careful in case there are valuables in the midst of it. To save people's precious memories if we can."

"Dinner is therved." Robbie stepped into the parlor, a tea towel flung over his arm.

George helped Gramps rise and led him to the dining room set with the aunts' best dishes, ones he hadn't used since he'd come there. "This is lovely, Mary. Thank you for taking over, and you, Robbie, for being her sous chef."

"I like helping her." Robbie scooted into his chair and sat tall and proud.

Mary set a plate of sliced roast beef on the table. "And I like your help, young man."

Gramps reached out his hands. "Shall we pray?"

After he did, they enjoyed a dinner of cold roast beef sandwiches, potato salad, pickles, and sliced tomatoes.

Mary took a bite and smiled. "This is delicious. Few men know how to cook this well. Thanks for having us."

At the compliment, his pulse tripped over itself, and a chuckle gurgled deep within him. "Thank you. After Alma died, my mother taught me. She's a rather good cook."

Robbie took a crunchy bite of a pickle on the side of his teeth. Juice sprayed on him and the tablecloth. "Thorry."

Mary laughed, taking her napkin and dabbing his face, shirt, and the cloth. "It's a little hard to chew without those front teeth, huh? It's okay, Robbie. Enjoy the pickle."

His heart jumped at the maternal care Mary so naturally gave. Gramps took a bite of a pickle and sprayed the juice too. On purpose. They all laughed.

"It's so strange that I can remember so much but not you or details about Mr. Richmond." Mary glanced around the room before her gaze landed on George. "All of this is so familiar. So is the switchboard and telegraph. Why can't I remember *you*?"

Robbie answered her. "Maybe it'th like me and numbers. I keep getting the thix and nine mixed up."

"Maybe …"

Just then, a rap on the door interrupted them. George excused himself and answered it.

Richmond?

George didn't open the screen door. Instead, he kept it between them. "What do you want?"

The man pulled the door open and stepped inside. "I hear my girl is here. She's no business fraternizing with the likes of you. Where is she?" Richmond pushed past him and headed to the dining room. "What are you doing here, Mary? You're supposed to be home, resting. Where you belong."

Gramps raised a hand. "She's with me, Richmond. The Flannigans invited us for lunch, and she accompanied me."

Mary flinched, and the color drained from her face. She dropped her gaze in resignation before patting her lips with her napkin. Slowly, she stood. "I should probably get back to the hotel and rest, anyway." But fear thickened her words.

George would not see her bullied. "No, it's not all right. You don't have to go anywhere, Mary."

Gramps agreed. "That's right. Besides, I'd like to finish my meal."

Mary let out a deep sigh. "Me too."

Chapter 23

Mary shivered at the tension in the room. George and Archie were facing off again. Because of her. She hated being the center of attention, especially among men. Her cheeks flamed, and her heart pounded like a runaway firetruck. Why did Archie think he could barge in and demand she leave in the middle of a meal?

George swallowed hard and waved a hand toward the empty chair. "Join us, Richmond, while Mary finishes her meal. There's plenty of food."

Archie plunked down and folded his arms over his chest like a spoiled child who didn't get his way. He gave her a narrow-eyed glare. "I don't have time for this. I've had to search for her, and now I must wait until she picks at her food? I have more important things to do."

Gramps set down his glass. "On a Sunday? Today should be a day of rest. Relax, sir, or go and do what you need to. I will escort Mary back to the Wellesley."

"Oh no. Not with him around my girl." Archie scoffed and trained his glare on George.

Mary's stomach turned. After this rant, she couldn't eat another bite. She stood, pushed her chair under the table, and sighed. She needed some air. "I should get back to the switchboard and relieve Charlotte, anyway. Thanks for the lunch, Mr. Flannigan. Robbie. It was lovely."

Gramps laid his fork on his plate. "Do you want me to come with you? I'm not quite done here, but if you need me to ..."

"No, you stay and enjoy the afternoon." Mary went over to him and kissed his cheek.

George stood and patted Gramps on the shoulder. "I'll walk with you back to the hotel whenever you're ready."

"I don't want you to go, Mith Mary." Robbie jumped up from his chair and scurried to Mary, scrunching up his face and scowling at Archie.

"I'll see you soon, sweet boy." She hugged him. "I need to help people with their telephone calls this afternoon so Charlotte can enjoy the Sabbath."

The little boy cupped his hands around his mouth and whispered in her ear. "I don't like that man, Mith Mary. He's mean."

Mary's pulse quickened as the child confirmed what she felt. Was she safe with Archibald? She wasn't so sure. But one thing was sure—she needed to end this relationship—or whatever this was. She'd seen enough, heard enough to know Mr. Richmond was not for her. No matter what people thought of her.

As she walked toward the hotel with Archie, he kept a controlling hand atop hers, pasting it into the crook of his elbow. He glared at her several times before speaking, the atmosphere growing thicker than a humid summer's afternoon. She sensed his anger deepen by the moment, casting a pall over her previously happy day.

He cleared his throat. "You are never to go there again, Mary. I forbid it."

"But that's my aunts' cottage, and the Flannigans are my friends. Besides, I went there with Mr. Wiseman, and you are not my boss. I am not married to you."

"You are my girl, and you will do as I say." He squeezed her hand, tighter and tighter.

"You're hurting me."

Mary winced, trying to wriggle free, but he was too strong. Panic surged through her until terror stabbed her heart. Truly, she wasn't safe with him. Why hadn't she seen this before now? Dread gnawed at her insides until she had to get away.

"Let go of me, Archie." Her voice rose an octave too high. "Please."

He shook his head, his Brylcream-laden hair flopping onto his forehead. Sarcasm and threats dripped from his lips. "And let you walk alone? Oh, that wouldn't be right. You will do as I say, Mary. You are altogether too independent an old maid for your own good. Someone has to straighten you out, and that someone is me."

"Sir, let me go. Now!" The hair on the back of Mary's neck prickled. She almost hollered her demand.

Neighbors in the cottage they were passing looked their way, and an older lady stood, waving a hand toward her. "Are you all right, dear?"

That gave her just enough time to disengage from Archie and scurry to the woman's side. Mary had seen the woman in church but didn't know her personally, but she didn't care. She feigned her to be an old friend and kept her back to Archie. "Good afternoon. And how are you today?"

The gray-headed woman must have noticed the fear in her eyes, for she played along. "Come and have a glass of lemonade with me, will you?"

Mary took a seat, heaving a deep sigh as Archie skulked off without a word. "Thank you. I appreciate this."

"I'm Mrs. Pratt." The elderly woman held out her hand and shook her head toward the retreating Mr. Richmond. "Seems you needed a reprieve from that one."

How could she explain her concerns to a total stranger? She couldn't risk any prattle. "Oh, we were just having a bit of a spat, is all. I'm fine now, thank you."

Before the woman could dig deeper into her personal affairs, Mary stood. "Thanks for your hospitality, but I need to get back to the switchboard and telegraph."

Mrs. Pratt touched her arm, concern evident in her compassionate gaze. "Very well, then, but if you ever need another respite, my door is always open, day or night."

"Thank you again. Goodbye." Mary descended the stairs and hurried to the safety of her room, watching out for Archie the entire way. Thankfully, he had disappeared.

For the moment.

Upon returning to the switchboard, Mary placed her hands on her hips to emphasize her words she spoke to Charlotte. "You know things about Archie Richmond and George Flannigan that I don't. What are they?"

Charlotte's eyes flashed concern as she shook her head and nervously handed over her headset. She glanced at the switchboard as if looking for a distraction. "The doctor insisted that we must let you discover your lost past on your own. He said it might be detrimental for you if we give you the missing information too soon."

Mary pressed harder. "But I *need* to know. I feel as if everyone works very hard to hide things from me. As though I'm the only one who doesn't know the secrets of my life. Besides, Archie is pressing me. Trying to control me."

"But don't you see? If I tell you things, and it hurts you, I'll never be able to forgive myself." Her friend touched her arm.

Just then, the telegraph came to life. Charlotte looked at Mary for help. "Please, Mary. Can you decipher it? I still haven't learned it well enough."

Mary penned the information. Easy as a wink, she could decode the dots and dashes tapping in her ear. She finished writing the contents of the wire and set down her pencil.

Charlotte tilted her head. "What did it say? I only caught a few words."

Mary read it to her. "'Mr. Brown, announcement confirmed. Columbian Hotel and business district to be completed by next season. *Watertown Daily Times.*'"

Why was the more difficult task of telegraphy so easy for her, yet she couldn't remember pieces of her past? Day after day, it became more and more frustrating. And potentially dangerous.

Charlotte scoffed. "That's a mighty big promise. I hope the Park can follow through with it."

"Sorry. What did you say?"

Charlotte shook her head. "Oh, nothing."

"Were there calls I should know about?" Mary huffed at her friend's refusal to share her thoughts.

"Your Aunt Stella called. She and your Aunt Maude are coming to the Park tomorrow. They want to see the ruins and visit with you for a few days." Charlotte tapped the notepad. "They want to make sure you're all right, I think. I'd be happy to cover the phones while they're here."

Mary's eyes welled with tears. The comfort of her Aunt Maude would be a blessing, and she'd be the perfect person to share her concerns with. Her voice cracked as she responded. "It'll be good to see them. And thank you, Charlotte, for being so accommodating this summer. You've been a good friend and a wonderful colleague."

"You're welcome." Charlotte pursed her lips and furrowed her brow. "But what's wrong, Mary? I can see that something deep and dark is troubling you."

Mary wrapped her arms protectively around her middle. Frustration trickled down her cheeks in the form of two tears. "It's Archie. I have to be rid of him."

"As you should." Charlotte scrunched up her face and nodded.

Mary was so tired of these games. She slapped the desk with her palm, demanding answers. "*Why* should I? What do you know, Charlotte? Is he dangerous? What is no one telling me?"

Charlotte jumped, her mouth dropping open. She snapped it shut and seemed to consider her words for a long while before responding. "I probably shouldn't say anything, but I can't see you suffer under him any longer."

Mary leaned in and waited for her friend to speak. Maybe now she'd get some answers.

"Mr. Richmond isn't your beau. He never was."

~ ~ ~

By midafternoon, George escorted Gramps back to the Wellesley Hotel for his Sunday siesta, as he called it. Robbie ran beside them, kicking a ball back and forth as they went.

George and Gramps had shared their concerns for Mary as best they could with Robbie present, yet neither had bridged the topic of her feelings for either him or Archie. But he couldn't let the day go by without tackling the subject. He had to know Mr. Wiseman's thoughts on the matter. "I'm pretty sure Mary doesn't really care for Richmond a whit, but I'm not sure she cares for me as more than an acquaintance—or maybe merely as a friend? Women befuddle me."

Gramps chuckled as he paused on their walk. He tapped his cane on the hard ground, sending little puffs of dirt into the air. "Aye, son, women befuddle all men, but how blind love can be. Can't you see she's smitten with you down to her toenails? She bursts with joy when she sees you, and her eyes twinkle like Fourth of July fireworks. At least she did before she forgot what was growing between you."

George blinked, a grin widening at the thought. Then his jaw hardened. "And Richmond? What does she think of him?"

"I have half a mind to reveal her past to her, regardless of the doctor's orders." Gramps groaned, swiping a trickle of sweat from his brow. "It is all too clear to me that Mr. Richmond is not treating her well and is trying to control her. He's scaring her, and I can't have that."

George's hands drew up into fists, and the nerve on the side of his face twitched. "Nor I. I see how he treats her—like he owns her. And I'm tired of the secrets too."

"I don't like him either. He'th mean." Robbie kicked the ball into his path.

George sucked in a breath. He hadn't realized Robbie was within earshot. He had always taught his boy never to gossip, and here he was, talking poorly about Richmond. "Robbie, this is a grownup discussion between Gramps and me, and you are not to repeat it.

Any of it. Understand? Go and kick the ball ahead, but stay within sight of us."

"Okay, Daddy." Robbie wiped his face with his shirtsleeve and gave the ball a good kick.

Gramps's gentle smile faltered, and he took ahold of George's arm to steady himself. "You're a good father, George. And concerning the Richmond situation, leave it to me. I've seen more than enough to know I must do something."

As they approached the hotel, Robbie stopped short and pointed toward the Columbian's rubble. "Can I go hunting in the rubble with Paul, Daddy? Pleathe?"

In the distance, Robbie's friend, Paul, and his father were doing just that. Though he'd rather follow Gramps's tradition and take a nice, long nap, how could he say no to treasure hunting? You never knew what you might find. "Okay, Robbie. You may join them, but be very careful. There is likely to be sharp metal and broken glass around. And stay within sight."

Robbie hugged Gramps and ran off to help find other people's treasures. So far, buckets of jewelry, mirrors, watches, and other glass and metal objects that survived the fire were being stored at the Wellesley, ready to be claimed by their owners. Unfortunately, some of those people had already fled the island and might never return.

After escorting Gramps to the hotel entrance, George joined his son and the Dowes. He greeted Mr. Dowe and Paul, who were searching in the far northeast corner of the rubble, close to the area where the telephone and telegraph office once had been. "Finding anything interesting?"

Paul showed him the pail. "A pocket watch, a necklace, some coins, and two spoons that are melted together."

"We just got started a few minutes ago, but I suspect there's more to be found. Folks have been recovering all kinds of things throughout the burn area." Mr. Dowe shrugged.

George picked up a soot-laden coin. "The recovery has been layer upon layer, and we're just now getting to the hotel's first-floor rubble. I expect it'll be a few more weeks before we get to the bottom of it all."

"Sometimes it's hard to tell if it's valuable or nothing." Mr. Dowe looked at something and tossed it back into the pile. "Say, did you hear that the Park's events, programs, and entertainments are returning to normal scheduling this week? The Clayton Professional Band will start giving concerts tomorrow and every Monday for the rest of the season. My wife is in the Park chorus, and it has returned to practicing every week. I'm in the Roque Club, and they have just announced a tournament for early August. Looks like our Thousand Islands Park will go on undeterred, even with this mess still about us. We certainly are a hearty lot, don't you think?"

"You sure are, and it's been so nice to be a part of this community." George chuckled. "The Park is nothing like I've ever experienced before. Neighbors caring for each other. So much learning and so many events. And a community faith element that is truly inspiring."

"You and Robbie belong here, I think. Why not make this your permanent home? You'd certainly be welcome."

"It's something to consider, thank you." He rubbed his chin. "I've always lived in Clayton, but times are changing, and so have Robbie and I. Perhaps a new start is just the thing we need."

Mr. Dowe patted him on the shoulder. "The year-round school here is top notch, I can tell you that. We moved here from Watertown two years ago, and since then, Paul has learned so much that he's even skipped a grade. The teacher is wonderful, and the younger children seem to just soak up the lessons of the older students. They all help each other excel."

Dr. Goodale joined the men as they chatted. "You're thinking of moving here for good, George? That'd be mighty fine for the Park. It would save us from finding a new captain for the fire department and give us some much-needed stability. The problem of fire danger looks to be a long-term concern, and I'm sure the nearby community of Fineview would be happy to have you on the island too."

George smiled. He liked it here, but what about Robbie? Though he had made several friends this summer, what about his pals in Clayton? And what would it be like to live on the island year-round? Only a few hundred stayed all winter, but when the river froze over, it wasn't hard to cross. Perhaps it would be best to be a safe distance from Mother—and all the memories.

And what about Mary? Where would she go once the summer ended?

He turned to Dr. Goodale. "Are the post office, telegraph, and telephone services open during the winter? And the shops?"

"Yes. I live here year-round, and the general store services our community all the time. The post also runs throughout the year. As for the telegraph and telephone, I'm not sure. I've heard that Mr. Mullins and his daughter, Charlotte, are moving back to the mainland. He's taking a position in Alexandria Bay." The doctor paused, grinned knowingly, and snapped a nod. "As for Miss Flynn, I don't know what she'll be doing at the end of the season. But I'm concerned she hasn't recovered her memory yet."

"So am I. Why does Dr. Place insist we abstain from giving clues to her past?"

Dr. Goodale shrugged, turning his palms to the sky. "It's the popular opinion in medical circles that the brain needs to recover on its own. I'm not so sure that recommendation applies with Miss Flynn, given her … circumstances."

"Would you please talk to Mr. Wiseman? He's concerned for her and needs to hear your thoughts." George's throat tightened and his mouth went dry.

"I expect he's napping at the moment, but I'll look in on him around dinnertime, and we'll have a chat."

Hope lurched to life in George's gut. "I'd be much obliged, and so will he. Thanks, Doc."

Robbie ran to him, waving something in his little hand. "Look what I found, Daddy!"

George took a small ring that had to belong to a woman. Charred almost black. He dipped it in a nearby bucket of water and wiped it off as best he could with his shirttail.

Wait. There was something written inside. He cleaned it, scraping the soot with his fingernail, and looked closely. He turned to Robbie, who waited for clues about his treasure. "There's an inscription that might help us find the owner. It says, 'Martha and Patrick Flynn forever,'"

Could this belong to Mary? Could it be her mother's ring?

Chapter 24

The next morning, Mary waited for the boat to arrive at the main dock. She glanced at the clock in the ticket booth. Five to eleven. In just minutes, she would get to visit with her aunts again.

Yes, she'd spoken to them by phone, but she hadn't burdened them with her confusion. She'd decided to wait to talk face-to-face and only told them she had a minor head injury. Now, after two weeks of confusion, frustration, and worry, they'd be welcome company.

Perhaps her aunts could confirm Charlotte's announcement. Archie was lying to her? She'd wanted to confront him, but she'd not seen him since fleeing from him. The rogue needed a stern repudiation.

As the boat pulled up to the dock, a gentle wind plucked wisps of her hair from her chignon, slapping her face and sticking to the light film of perspiration. She swiped them back into place before waving a greeting. "Aunt Maude. Aunt Stella. It's so good to see you both."

Once they disembarked, she gave them big hugs before slipping her hands into theirs as she had as a child. She needed that security just now.

Inklings of memories flashed through her mind—moments with them when she was a girl. Story time with Aunt Maude. Helping Aunt Stella in the cottage kitchen. Knitting in the cool of the evening. Chatting with neighbors on the porch. Warm, fond memories that brought peace and joy, even though Aunt Stella could be ... well ... a bit too much.

All of her memories of her aunts were crisp and vivid. Why weren't the memories of George and Archie also?

Aunt Stella veered them up St. Lawrence Avenue. "We want to see the burned-out area first. Then Mr. Flannigan has invited the three of us to luncheon at noon. That way we can see our cottage too."

Mary's nerves prickled at the announcement. Her pulse quickened, but she swallowed her fear. Still, her angst tainted her tone. "I don't know if I should."

Aunt Maude stopped and studied her with a deep, wrinkled frown. "Why ever not?"

"Archie has forbidden me to. He doesn't want me to go to the cottage or to be around George. Ever." A small shiver ran down her spine.

"Who?" Aunt Maude clicked her tongue, her brow furrowing.

Aunt Stella scoffed. "That disreputable insurance man, Mr. Richmond, sister. What does he have to do with telling you where you can and can't go, Mary?"

She pursed her lips. Didn't they know about her relationship with Archie? Surely, he'd been around when they were still on the island, though her memory of it failed her. "He's my beau. Remember? He has been for some time, I guess. I just can't recall it."

"When did that happen?" Aunt Maude shook her head. "He's not the kind of man I'd choose for you, dear, and he had nothing to do with you before we left Thousand Islands Park just a few weeks ago."

Mary sucked in a deep breath. Everything was so topsy-turvy. "I thought you knew. That you approved. Archie said we've been a couple for months and months. Way before you left. Way before the fire."

Aunt Stella bellowed her disgust. "You most certainly were not, young lady. That man is trying to pull something over you. He's a wily one. I wouldn't trust him with a toothpick, and certainly not with my niece. What has happened to you that he caught you up in such trickery?"

"That's what Charlotte said too." Mary slipped her arms around Aunt Stella and hugged her tightly. "I told you about my head injury and how my memory was spotty. I remember everything about you and my work. I just can't remember anything about either Archie Richmond or George Flannigan, the fireman. With them, it's all so fuzzy."

Aunt Maude touched her arm. "I agree with my sister. That Mr. Richmond is deceiving you. When he was at dinner, you could barely tolerate looking at him, and you scoffed at his nastiness. On the other hand, Mr. Flannigan lit up your eyes and brightened your face so it almost glowed."

Mary rubbed her shoulder that had tensed into a hard brick. Her impressions of Archie being disingenuous and wanting to be rid of him were sound. What was she to do?

Aunt Stella stomped her foot. "Where is that nasty Mr. Richmond? I'll settle this here and now."

"I wish we could …" Mary's voice cracking in desperation. "But I haven't seen him since yesterday afternoon, and the ticket office said he was off the island today."

Aunt Maude's eyes blazed with anger. The woman seldom let things get to her, but when they did, watch out! "That coward! You're coming to lunch with us. Mr. Flannigan may be of service to us in this matter."

"All right, but I fear that Mr. Richmond may seek retribution if he hears about it."

Aunt Stella grumbled. "Stuff and nonsense. Mr. Flannigan will protect you. I'll see to that."

By now, they were nearing the ruins of the Columbian Hotel. "Good heavens!" Aunt Stella pointed, her voice surging with emotion. Somehow, the smoky stench still hung in the air. "Good heavens! Desolation all the way to Coast Avenue. And all the shops too? You said it was bad. The papers printed the details and pictures. But seeing it with my own two eyes is ... heartbreaking."

Aunt Maude agreed as tears rolled down her cheeks. "Will our wonderful Park ever be the same?"

Mary swiped the tears from her Aunt's wrinkled cheek. "The Association will rebuild and plans to have everything up and running by next summer."

"How can that happen?" Aunt Stella groaned, skepticism dripping from her words. "They hadn't the funds to buy the proper equipment to prevent these fires. Now they're going to rebuild? Sounds rather pie in the sky to me."

The three of them walked along Oak Street and then down Central Avenue, discussing and mourning the ruination of the eastern half of the Park. Now and then, they stopped to chat with neighbors who were busily cleaning up their properties. Her aunts offered their sympathies and concern and commented on how it must be a test from above.

How could the Lord allow such a test? Mary couldn't fathom it. He hadn't sent the fire, she was sure of that. But as with Shadrach, Meshach and Abednego, He was in this fiery furnace with them. She spoke encouragement to her aunts. "No one died, and only a few were injured. God was with us, even in the midst of this terrible fire."

Aunt Maude slipped her hand in the crook of Mary's arm. "Yes, child, but like in the book of Daniel, chapter three, God was testing them to see if they'd bow to evil. Perhaps this fire was to test the good people of Thousand Islands Park, to see where their priorities lie and to be a witness of God's protective hand."

"True. I trust God's goodness, but my faulty memory scares me. Will I ever get it back?"

Aunt Stella chuckled. "Patience, girl. You never were one to persevere in troubling times."

"We'd better head over to the cottage. We don't want to keep the fireman waiting." Aunt Maude checked her tiny timepiece pinned to her shirtwaist.

When they got to the cottage, Robbie was waiting for them on the steps. "Mith Mary, look what I found in the rubble yesterday. Daddy said I could keep it and show you. He thinks it might be yours." The child grabbed her hand and opened it, palm up. Then he placed a small, well-polished gold ring in it. "Look inside. It thays something."

Mary held it just right and read the inscription. "'Martha and Patrick Flynn forever.' It's my mother's ring!"

She showed her aunts, and they confirmed the find.

Before she knew it, Robbie had taken her hand and squeezed it. "I'm glad I found it for you, Mith Mary."

Mary blinked. As if waking from a dream, she recalled the Fourth of July in Clayton, eating hot dogs and watching fireworks. Holding Robbie's hand. Like now. Enjoying time with his father. With George. Memories of walking and talking so happily with him.

Not Archie.

She remembered.

Everything!

"Mary, are you all right? You are white as a seagull." Aunt Maude touched her arm.

Mary glanced at her and then at Aunt Stella. She nodded. Then she looked down at Robbie, who still held her hand, a large, gap-toothed grin on his adorable face.

She bent down and kissed him on the cheek. "Thank you, sweet boy, for finding the ring. But just now, you also gave me the greatest gift of all—my memory back."

Robbie giggled, let go of her hand, and ran into the house shouting, "Daddy, they're here and Mith Mary's all better."

George appeared in the doorway, a puzzled grin on his face. "Welcome to your cottage, ladies. And what is this news my son is bubbling over with?"

Mary wanted to kick up her heels and dance a jig, so excited she was. But she kept her composure. Her heart raced as she leaned closer to George. "I remember. Everything. Who you are to me. And who Archie is not. I'm so sorry, George."

"I knew your memory would return, but it sure was hard to oblige the doctor's orders." George took her hand, sending shivers through her body. He tossed her a quick wink, and the corners of his mouth turned up into the handsomest smile she'd ever seen. "There have been a dozen times or more that I've half exploded with the truth, but Dr. Place insisted we wait until you remembered on your own. Was it the ring?"

She tucked her hand into the crook of his arm and shook her head. "It was the warmth of Robbie's hand and his sweet smile. Something about him made everything click. But I'm sure the ring helped too."

"Let's celebrate your return, Mary." George led her and her aunts to the dining room.

She giggled with joy. "Yes, let's!"

~ ~ ~

George relished every moment with Mary and her aunts as they feasted on fried fish, potato salad, ripe tomatoes, and green beans. They laughed and rejoiced at the return of Mary's memory. Cringed at the cruel deception of Archie. Plotted and planned how to confront the rogue.

And Robbie entertained them all. He showed them his pet turtle, his drawings, his toy soldiers. And his toothless lisp kept them in stitches.

It was a busy afternoon.

As they sat on the porch sipping lemonade and greeting neighbors, Aunt Maude slipped a small oval frame out of her reticule and handed it to Mary. "In all the excitement, I almost forgot. This is the only picture of your parents that I have, but I know you lost yours in the fire. I want you to have it."

Mary burst into tears and hugged her aunt. "Thank you so much, Auntie. Of all the things I lost in the fire, what truly mattered to me have returned to me—my memory, my mother's ring, and my parent's picture. Everything but my father's Bible. What a glorious day! And to top it off, I'm so glad you're going to stay a while, Aunties."

Aunt Stella cackled as she swiped perspiration from her brow. "Did you think we'd make this trip from Watertown and return the same day? We're not spring chickens anymore, girl. Besides, we have some catching up to do—and apparently, to conduct an inquisition on a certain devilish insurance man."

They laughed at that, but then George inquired about their accommodations. "You should stay here instead of us. Robbie and I can go to the hotel, and you can be in your own cottage."

Aunt Maude shook her head. "No, you two have made a nice, comfortable home here, and we appreciate how well you keep it. We wouldn't want to disrupt that, would we, Stella?"

"No. Besides, we have reserved a room at the Wellesley and will be just down the hall from Mary. We can have meals with her and visit with her while she works."

George shrugged. "All right, if you're sure. We have enjoyed your cottage, ladies, and Robbie is so happy here. Thank you for sharing it with us."

"Can we live here forever, Daddy? I never want to leave." Robbie stopped playing with his soldiers and tilted his head.

George groaned. The child had been happier than he had in years. "School starts soon, son. And what about your friends in Clayton? I'm sure they miss you."

Robbie glanced at the ceiling for several seconds before answering. "There's a thkool here, and Paul says it's loads of fun. He says teacher is wonderful. Bethides, we can go and thee my friends and Grandmother when we want to. It's only a boat ride away."

George rolled his eyes, and the women tittered quietly. God had blessed him with such a precocious child to raise.

"It's time we head to the hotel for our naps. I want to attend the concert this evening. I hear the Clayton Professional Band is back performing every Monday." Aunt Stella stood, and Aunt Maude followed suit.

Mary smiled. "It is, and I need to relieve Charlotte for the afternoon so I can join you tonight." She stood, mussed Robbie's hair, and smiled at George. "Thanks for the delightful dinner and visit. You've made this a wonderful day."

Robbie hopped up and hugged her. "I'm glad I found your ring, Mith Mary. And I'm glad you remember us. It was hard to not thay anything."

Mary nodded. "I'm sure it was, but it's all settled, and everything will be back to normal."

Robbie glanced up at Mary. "Will you be done with that Mr. Richmond? He'th mean."

"Yes, Robbie, I will." Mary snapped a determined nod.

George sighed his relief. Perhaps they would find their way back to where they were. He would do everything under his power to make that happen. "May we walk you back to the hotel?"

Aunt Stella took his arm. "Why, yes, young man, that would be delightful."

Robbie offered Aunt Maude his arm, mimicking his father, and they walked ahead. "I'll walk you back, Aunt Maude."

Mary took Aunt Maude's other arm since holding the small boy's arm made her unsteady. "Robbie, why don't you take Aunt Maude's hand instead? I think she'd like that even more."

"Sure, Mith Mary. Be glad to oblige."

George hung back until it was convenient to stroll casually up to her side. He held his tongue, waiting for the appropriate time to question her. When he did, conviction filled his tone. "Would you be willing to deepen our acquaintance now, Mary?"

Mary blinked, and her cheeks turned rosy. "I'd be pleased to, George."

~ ~ ~

George couldn't wait until the evening's concert began. He bathed and shaved—twice. He donned his best suit and slicked back his hair with pomade. He'd look his best for Mary.

She remembered him!

He'd almost given up. Almost.

The community gathered as the Clayton Professional Band warmed up on the outdoor Thousand Islands Park bandstand. Many brought blankets and picnic baskets. Some brought chairs. Everyone ready for an evening of entertainment. Except Gramps. George had been told that he was under the weather and would miss this fine evening.

George and Robbie brought two chairs for the aunts and a blanket for Mary and the two of them to sit on. Robbie helped him spread the blanket under a large oak tree, and he placed the two chairs behind them. When the women arrived, George greeted the three with a warm welcome and a peppermint stick each.

Music filled the air, dancing on a gentle breeze as stars popped out on their velvety canopy. The band played several older sing-alongs as well as a few new tunes like "Down by the Old Mill Stream" and "Oh, You Beautiful Doll."

While enjoying the rhythm to the songs, George scanned the crowd to see if Richmond would show his surly face. If so, he'd not only protect Mary, but also deal with his deceit. A concoction of hope and anger ruffled his emotions. Once he got rid of Richmond, could Mary be his?

Mary sang and laughed, but before long, Robbie laid his head on George's lap and fell asleep. Mary reached over and rubbed Robbie's leg so lovingly that it took George's breath away. Would she make a good mother for his son? He reckoned she might.

When the band played "Let Me Call You Sweetheart," George couldn't help but glancing at Mary. His pulse quickened and his throat tightened as the lyrics mirrored his thoughts. She must have felt him staring, for she turned and met his gaze, her eyes sparkling in the twilight. For several long moments, she held it. Then she gifted him with a quivering smile.

Could she ...

Aunt Stella interrupted their wordless interlude, tapping Mary's shoulder and speaking to her. Mary turned back to him, the scent of lavender in her hair filling his senses. "My aunts are tired. I'll take them back to the hotel and return presently."

George glanced at his sleeping son trapping him where he sat. "Shall I escort you?"

Mary shook her head. "Don't disturb him. I'll be back soon."

When they were gone, George examined the feelings surging within him. After the fire, he'd tamped down those longings, holding them at bay, especially when Mary couldn't remember him or what had blossomed between them. And when she seemed so surprisingly taken by Richmond. But here they were, blooming again like a peony in the warm morning sunshine, opening its petals to a new day.

George followed Mary and her aunts with his gaze as they slowly made their way toward the hotel. But something niggled at him, causing the hair on the back of his neck to stand up and prickle. He strained to scan the area around the departing women through the growing darkness.

There, by the large maple. A lone figure followed them.

He could tell that swagger anywhere.

Richmond.

Chapter 25

Mary opened the door to the Wellesley Hotel and beckoned her aunts to pass through. "Goodnight, Aunties. May you sleep well. I'll see you at breakfast."

Aunt Maude touched her arm. "Go back to the concert, dear, and enjoy this lovely evening."

"I'm glad you're feeling better, dear. Goodnight." Aunt Stella nodded.

Mary closed the door and started to leave, but something to her right caught her attention. In the darkness, she could barely make out the form of a man, but soon she realized who it was.

Archibald Richmond.

He gingerly stepped in front of the door, blocking her escape into the hotel. She glanced toward the veranda steps a dozen feet away. Everyone was at the concert or tucked safely in their beds. Except her. And Richmond.

The sniveling snake was back, slithering out of the shadows and into the moonlight, his narrow-eyed glare and thin-lined mouth mocking her. His stiff stance and folded arms alerted her to trouble.

Her pulse took flight, and perspiration moistened her forehead. She swiped it away. Why was he here?

"I thought I told you to steer clear of that fireman!" He fairly spat his vitriol. "You've disobeyed my orders, Mary, and I will not tolerate it. I saw you there, sitting with *him* at the concert. You are far too independent for you own good. Something I shall rid you of soon enough."

Mary trembled inside. Like a vine strangling her, her throat grew thick, plugging her airway. She swallowed hard and shook herself free of the growing fear, but it kept a tight hold of her, terrifying her down to her toes. But she buoyed herself against it, pulled herself to her full height, and stomped her foot. "No, sir, you won't." Though her voice quivered, she stood her ground.

Archie took a few steps toward her, but she moved backward to maintain a safe distance. She didn't trust the man as far as she could sneeze. She took a deep, fortifying breath, and a tiny groan escaped her lips.

At that, Archie chuckled. Then, like Robert Louis Stevenson's Dr. Jekyll and Mr. Hyde, he softened his tone, almost cooing his rebuttal. "Well, now, aren't you the brave little woman I've chosen for my own? You needn't be afraid of me. Truly. I just want you to learn your place in the scheme of things."

"Liar!" Her voice sounded an octave higher, and her gaze darted furiously between the steps and him. If only she could make it down the stairs, she could pick up her skirts and run. Her pulse thrummed in her neck, and her heart galloped like a racehorse. She searched in the darkness for help, but everyone seemed to be at concert that continued in the distance. Even if she screamed, would anyone hear her?

Could she escape his clutches before he trapped her there on the veranda? Just ten steps to freedom. Could she do it? Gooseflesh prickled her arms.

With a defiant lift of her chin, she made it to the first step, but he snickered and took a giant step closer.

"Come now, what are you afraid of?"

She refused to wither under his malevolence. "Leave me be, you rogue. I remember everything. Everything! You are not my beau. You, sir, are a dastardly deceiver, and I want nothing more to do with you."

Archie scoffed, pandering a smirk so sinister her dinner wanted to revolt. "Oh, is that what you think? I'm only looking out for your welfare, miss. After all, you're a vulnerable, unmarried, working woman living alone without family. You need a strong man to look out for you."

It was her turn to sneer. "And you would be the last man on this earth to look out for me. Leave me alone, now, or I shall scream."

His devilish eyes snapped a glance toward the bandstand where the music blasted. He took another step toward her, his grin contemptuous. "And who do you think would hear you?"

She had to get out of there, and fast. She quickened her steps, but Archie matched hers, catching her at the top of the steps. She smashed her heel on his toes, but he stayed planted in place. Unwavering. She struggled in his tight grasp as his fingernails dug into her skin.

Archie held her so firmly she couldn't wiggle free. He had the strength of a monster. "Now, to have the prize I've been so patiently waiting for."

The miscreant pressed his slimy lips to hers and held them there, pushing her neck back and attempting to part her lips with his tongue. She bit it with all her might, causing him to disengage and step back. "Ouch! You little floozy. You'll pay for that!"

He rubbed the back of his hand over his lips as she fled down the steps, but he grabbed for her halfway down, sending her off balance, tumbling to the walkway in a heap. The rough cement burned her hands, bloodying them. Searing pain shot through her hip. Half dazed, she tried to stand, but her twisted skirts held her fast. She had to get away from the rogue. No telling what he'd do to her now.

"Mary! Is that you?"

George called to her, but her pulse surged in her ears so loudly she couldn't tell if he was near or far.

She cried out to him. "I'm here! Help me!"

"Are you all right?" In an instant, he was at her side.

She pointed up to the veranda, where Richmond had retreated like a dog. "This was Archie's doing. Apprehend him, George. Quick!"

George nodded and hurried up the stairs. "Stop right there, Richmond, if you know what's good for you. If you aren't too afraid of me."

Archie chuckled, folding his arms in defiance. "Afraid of you? Whatever for? It wasn't me. The clumsy girl lost her balance on the way down the steps, is all. I tried to help her, but she refused."

"He's lying, George. He—" Mary got to her feet and pointed to him.

George grabbed Richmond by his lapels and gave him a good shake. Then he shoved him against the hotel wall and held him there. "I saw what he did, Mary, and now I'll settle this once and for all."

"Wait! Let me deal with him first. Please." Suddenly, Mary's fear turned to fury.

Ignoring the pain, she stomped up the steps and faced her abuser while George released him, firmly motioning for him to stay against the hotel wall. "You move an eyelash, and you'll breathe your last, you reprobate."

Mary pulled back her right hand and slapped the scoundrel as hard as she could across his ugly face. "That is for all the villainous, contemptible lies." With her left hand, she slapped him with all her might. "That is for the shameful way you've treated me these past few weeks."

He grunted and whimpered.

Again, she slapped him with her remaining strength. "That is for the disgusting and detestable kiss you forced upon me. How dare you!"

That done, she wiped her hands on her skirts and took a deep, satisfying breath, folding her arms in victory. Even in the evening light, her handprint and streaks of her bloodied hands decorated both of his cheeks. The sight was most rewarding.

As George took hold of him again, a flicker of fear crossed Archibald Richmond's dark eyes as they darted from her to George. He shivered under their glares.

"He's all yours, George." Mary couldn't help it. An amused chuckle bubbled up and spilled out.

George's eyes sparked anger. He worked his jaw vigorously, eying the rogue for a long while. Archie withered under his ire. Then the man went limp.

Suddenly, George exploded into action. He shook Archie as if he were a rag doll. "You ever touch her again, and you won't live to see the morning." He stabbed a finger into the man's chest again and again, accentuating each word. "Apologize to her now!"

Archie glared at her for several moments, his thin lips pressed stubbornly together.

"Apologize!" George shook him again.

Archie mumbled an uncontrite, "Sorry."

George groaned. Like a toddler wanting his way, he stomped his foot to demand Richmond comply. "Not good enough. Apologize like a man, or you'll feel the full weight of my fury. Now!"

"Easy, George. He's not worth the effort." Mary swallowed. If he wasn't careful, George would get himself in trouble for murdering the man. She couldn't have that.

George glanced at her and grumbled, his eyes blazing. "My regrets, Mary, but he must apologize to you … or else!"

"I'm sorry, Mary." Archie whined, his voice sounding like a schoolyard bully's thrashed by the teacher.

"That's a little better. Now, you listen up, you blackguard. You will leave this island by dawn and never return. If I ever see your face here again, I'll have your head on a platter. Do you understand?"

By now, Archie trembled like a child. "Yes, sir. I'll catch the first ferry out. And Mary, I am sorry."

Mary's hands burned from the fall and the slaps, her hip throbbing. "I'll forgive you. Some day."

George groaned as he shook his head. "It'll take more than that for me. And to be sure you don't do any more mischief, I'm going to lock you in the hotel closet for the night."

"That sounds like the perfect place for him, George." Mary giggled.

~ ~ ~

After securing Richmond in the hotel's coat closet, George returned to Mary on the veranda. He fortified his nerves with a deep breath, but the anger had been growing in him all day—for weeks, really—and would not depart soon.

He struggled to hide his emotions as the sight of Mary's bloodied hands and pained expression caused the fire to rise in his belly all over again. And he sensed the embers sparking in his eyes. "I think it best that I stand guard over the rapscallion. Who knows what scheme he might have up his sleeve? In the morning, I'll take him to the sheriff in Clayton and let the law deal with him."

"That's probably wise. Thank you for coming to my aid, George. If you hadn't, I'm not sure what might have happened." Mary rubbed her hands together gingerly.

He brushed a hand over her forearm. When he touched her, warmth poured into his cheeks. "I saw enough to want to kill the man."

"I'm glad you didn't, or else you'd be the one in jail." Mary placed her hand on his.

He took her hand and turned it over. Scrapes and dried blood speckled her palms. "That must hurt like the dickens. You should have them cleaned and bandaged. Is anything else hurt?"

Mary shrugged. "Just my hip. I suspect I'll have quite a bruise, but it'll mend."

He kissed the palms of both her hands, and her eyes flashed surprise. "Anything else?"

Mary smiled. "My pride."

He chuckled. "That, too, will heal. If you're sure you don't need a doctor, let me get you safely to your room so I can hover over the villain."

"Thank you for protecting me. You truly may have saved my life." Mary slipped her hand into the crook of his arm and hugged it as they headed into the hotel.

He harrumphed. "I won't even think of that, thank you very much. I'm just glad you're okay."

Mary stopped and cast him an inquisitive frown. "Where's Robbie?"

George waved his free hand. "I left him with the Dowes. He and Paul were going to have a sleepover. When I saw Richmond lurking around, I had to make a plan."

"Oh good." Mary sighed, relief tainting her tired tone. "They've been a godsend to you, haven't they?"

"They have. This entire community has. Save one rogue."

Mary laughed. "And soon we'll be rid of him. I'm glad he's locked up, and I'll be even happier to have him exiled from the island. Thanks again."

"You are most welcome." George grinned as he opened her door. "Now, tend to your hands, sleep well, and please, lock your door this evening."

Mary placed a hand on her chest. "I will. Until tomorrow."

"Until tomorrow, sweet Mary."

~ ~ ~

Throughout the night, George pondered what might have happened to Mary had he not intervened when he did. Several times, he thanked God for nudging him to notice that Richmond had returned, for keeping Mary safe, for helping him to hold his temper enough to save Richmond's hide.

George asked God to help him overcome his tendency to lose his temper, for he feared he might never tame that emotion. But he shuddered at his rage toward the scalawag, and he prayed he'd forgive the man.

Yet with each snore from Richmond through the bolted door, George couldn't figure out how he *could* forgive him. Why, horse-whipping should be the punishment for any man who would treat a woman so uncivilized, so dishonorably. Hopefully, the law would teach the miscreant a lesson or two before they even thought about letting him out.

When morning finally dawned, George unlocked the door and tied Richmond's hands securely—and perhaps a bit roughly—behind his back. "Richmond, you listen carefully. We're going to take the boat to Clayton, and I'm going to turn you over to Sheriff Lafave. If you give me one iota of trouble, if you create the least bit of fuss, if you say even one word to anyone, I'll unleash my pent-up anger on you, and you'll be very sorry I did. Do you understand?"

Richmond nodded, his eyes sparking fear, his lips pressed into a thin line. The scallywag's mussed hair testified of his rough night, and his shirttail hung half out of his trousers, but George had no intention of correcting his bedraggled appearance. And the smudges of dried blood on his cheeks? His marks of guilt. For that matter, a black eye as a keepsake would serve him right.

But George delivered Richmond to the sheriff without incident, gave him his testimony of the entire situation, and left the law to deal with the scoundrel. And by God's great grace, he left his anger there too.

George had another delivery to make that morning as well. He headed to his mother's house and walked through the screen door. "Mother? Are you home?"

She mumbled from the top of the stairs as if she had cotton in her mouth. "Up here, son."

George climbed the steps to discover his mother indeed had cotton in her mouth—and a bruised cheek. Alarm seized his soul and sent his pulse racing. "Mother! What has happened to you? Are you all right?"

"I'm fine. I had three teeth pulled two days ago. The doctor said they were so infected it could have killed me."

Confusion muddled his thoughts. "But you never complained of your teeth. How could that be?"

"Who knows? They've ached for a while, but I'll be fit as a fiddle before long. What are you doing here?"

He told her the story of Richmond and Mary, and he blanched at the thought of his response. "I've never been so angry in all my life, Mother. It scared me."

"You've always had a trigger-hair temper, but you've kept it under control. I suspect you got that from me. I'm sorry, son."

He gasped at her confession. His mother never apologized for anything. Ever.

She continued. "I'm sorry about a lot of things. My surly disposition. My sharp tongue. My opinionated ways. My treatment of your son. I've become a grouchy old lady that no one wants to be around."

George couldn't contradict any of that, but he couldn't condemn her either. "No matter what, Mother, I love you and so does Robbie. We are family and always will be. I'm grateful you took us in after Alma died and cared for Robbie while I worked."

His mother wept. Really sobbed. George couldn't recall her ever shedding a tear in front of him before. Not even when his father died. What had happened to her?

He wrapped his arms around her and let her cry in his arms like a child needing a parent. It felt so strange but so wonderful at the same time. Her rock-hard exterior had vanished. The stubborn stoicism was gone. In its place was a repentant woman. "There, there. It's okay. Are you in pain? Can I get you some powders?"

She nodded. "Perhaps they would help, though it's not from the pain in my mouth but the pain in my heart that I weep. Since you and Robbie left, I've seen how miserable I've become, and I don't like it one bit. Am I too old to change?"

"Never. God can change anyone, if you let Him." George shook his head.

She smiled, bloodied cotton slipping between her lips. "That's what the preacher said too. I'm certainly going to try." She blew her nose and wiped her eyes, putting on her usual stoic exterior but with a gentleness that he remembered from his childhood. "Now, I was going to call you today, George. My sister, Mary Ellen, is coming to visit in a few days. She's allergic to dogs, you know, so I was hoping you can take Cooper."

George chuckled. "I was going to ask you if I could bring Cooper back to the island with me. Robbie misses him a lot. So do I."

Mother sighed. "Well, that's providential. How are things at the Park?"

"Clean-up is going well, and Robbie is thriving there. Everyone loves him. And the Association has invited us to stay there year-round and oversee the restoration and development of the fire department. What do you think?"

Mother was quiet for a long while. "Perhaps a change might be good for you two. Would you like breakfast?"

"I'd love some, Mother, and I'll even cook." George grinned.

She rose from the bed. "It'll be soft food for me, but I have bacon and eggs, and my neighbor brought muffins over this morning. Let's eat."

George helped his mother up and gave her a kiss on the cheek. "Let's."

Chapter 26

Mary glanced at her hands while waiting for another call. Finally, they were almost healed. But the bruise on her hip still reminded her of that awful night a week ago. She squeezed her eyes shut tight and pinched the bridge of her nose. The nightmares had ceased, but she still struggled with the memory of that terrible man and thoughts of what might have happened had she learned the truth too late. She shuddered at the thought of marriage to such a beast.

When the phone line lit up, Mary answered it. "Good afternoon. Thousand Islands Park. How may I direct your call?"

The caller asked for Mr. Fitch, the Association's treasurer, but after several rings, he didn't answer. "May I take a message, sir?"

The gruff-sounding man clipped off the message. "The St. Lawrence River Concrete Company will be on the island tomorrow to set up for business. We will supply sand, crushed stone, cement blocks, and brick for the reconstruction of fireproof buildings, as requested. I will meet Mr. Fitch at the docks promptly at eight a.m. with the first barges."

Mary scribbled down the message. "Yes, sir. I'll get this to him immediately. Good day."

Click. Done.

Charlotte stepped into the office and plopped down in the chair. "How's your day going, Mary?"

She folded the missive and handing it to Charlotte. "It's been a busy day of calls, but nothing earth shattering. Would you please have this delivered to Mr. Fitch?"

Charlotte opened it, read it, and refolded the message. She nodded. "Things sure are progressing around here. Papa said the Association will begin rebuilding the shopping area first with cement blocks, concrete interior walls, stamped metal ceilings, and a metal roof. The Armenian Oriental Bazaar is the first building on the schedule. They have also planned for winter construction of a new chapel and school, all with cement and metal fire protection. They have no intention of letting another fire destroy our beautiful Park—ever again."

Mary stood and stretched. After sitting so long, she needed the break. "That's wonderful. Have you heard how the matching funds campaign is going? The Association wants to raise more than half of the money needed to rebuild by the end of the summer."

"I think it's going well. At least, that's what I've heard." Charlotte slipped an errant strand of hair behind her ear. "But it sure is a lot of money to raise. Unlike the rich folk who own castles and mansions here in the islands, our Park residents are mainly middle-class dwellers, and most of them didn't have their burned-out cottages insured."

"Terrible luck, to be sure." Mary sighed, swatting at a fly that buzzed around them. "Most of the calls I've had for the past few days have been to inquire about the insurance money—or lack thereof. I wonder how many people will sell or simply abandon their property."

Charlotte glanced at the ceiling before returning her gaze to Mary. "Who knows, but isn't it interesting to be on the phones and hear so much of what goes on around here? We get to learn all the scuttlebutt before anyone else."

"We do, but sometimes it's hard to keep that information to myself, especially when I'm with George." Mary tossed her a sheepish grin and allowed a chuckle to escape her lips. "He's so inquisitive and interested in everything about my thoughts and my day. He asks me the most interesting questions about my dreams and fears, and he wants to know about my past and my family. But what I love most about him is how much he cares for his son. He never stops talking about the boy."

Charlotte's eyes danced with mischief. "Ooooh, you're smitten all right. Has he kissed you yet?"

"What? No, and he wouldn't, I dare say, without a deeper commitment." Mary sucked in a surprised breath and sat down. "He's quite the gentleman and very patient with me. After all, it's only been a week since I got my memory back, and a little of that still seems fuzzy. Yes, I care for him deeply, and I think he feels the same, but he hasn't spoken of such things yet."

Just then, the telegraph came to life, and Mary pointed to Charlotte. "Want to try? I'll back you up."

Charlotte nodded, grabbed the paper and pencil, and started transcribing the message. She spoke it aloud as she wrote. "'To Mr. Fisk. Mrs. Stengle and Mr. Roseboom requested the New Geneva and Pratt House to begin reconstruction immediately. Confirmed. On the list. SLR Concrete Co.'"

After finishing the message, Charlotte grinned. "I've finally mastered it, Mary. Thanks for being patient with me. I'll have this message delivered with the other."

"I knew you'd get it." Mary patted her hand, tossing her a proud-of-you wink.

A satisfied grin creased Charlotte's face. "Say, I wanted to talk with you about something. Even though Papa is going to work in Alexandria Bay, I'd like to stay here in the Park. He said I could if you agree. I love it here and would like to keep on working with you, if you'll have me."

Mary took her friend's hands in hers and squeezed them. "*Have* you? I'm honored you want to stay. You've covered for me so many times, I couldn't do this without you. And, if you'd like, we could add a bed in here and room together. There's plenty of space." She waved at the far wall. "That would save us both some money on our room."

Charlotte nodded furiously. "I'd love that, Mary. Thank you. But what if you and Mr. Flannigan marry? Will you have to leave all this behind to care for your home?"

Mary shrugged, punctuating the gesture with a sigh. "As I mentioned, George and I haven't spoken of such things, but if it happens, I hope I can continue working. At least until a little one joins us."

Charlotte tilted her head and furrowed her brow. "But if you marry him, won't you already have a child? Robbie?"

Mary blinked. Why hadn't she thought of that? Indeed, she would have the responsibility of being an instant mother to Robbie. Would that mean she'd have to leave her work behind to care for him? "I hadn't really considered that. Silly me."

She and Charlotte shared a hearty laugh before returning to the conversation. Mary picked up the pencil and twirled it in her hand to expel some nervousness. "I suppose in a month or so, most of the summer folk will be long gone. I'm told there are but a hundred souls who stay in the Park year-round, so the telephone switchboard will be much quieter throughout the winter months. And the telegraph is becoming less important, except for maritime use or if folks need to communicate with someone overseas in Europe or elsewhere."

"True. I expect in a year or two, my telegraphy skill won't matter all that much." Charlotte giggled. "But I'll keep on learning, Mary, I promise. You can count on it." The young woman glanced at the notes in her hand as if she'd forgotten they were there. She stood and waved them in the air. "I'd better deliver these. I'll see you at five."

"Thanks, Charlotte. Enjoy the lovely afternoon." Mary waved her off.

The hours flew by, and when Charlotte returned, she came with company. George and Robbie.

With each passing day, Mary enjoyed the anticipation of seeing the two of them more and more. What would it be like to be a wife—and mother? She'd pondered it most of the afternoon, and the possibility both intrigued and scared her. Could she care for Robbie as her own? Would George welcome that? He'd been a single father for so long.

"Hello, Miss Mary. May we men take you on an afternoon stroll to stretch your legs after your day of work?" George dipped his chin as he greeted her, then flashed a grin as wide as a summer rainbow.

A giggle bubbled up, and she swallowed it. "Hello, Robbie. George. You may."

"Wonderful." The deep tones of his bass voice encompassed her like a warm blanket. "It's a mighty fine afternoon for a jaunt along the shore. Shall we search for shells, son?"

"Yeth. You can help me, Mith Mary." Robbie grasped her hand and pulled her forward.

An amused grin tugged at George's lips, and his eyebrows spiked. "Shall we?" He offered her his arm, and she took it, the feel of his hard muscles sending a tingling tease to her heart.

Such a thoughtful man. But could she keep her apprehensions at bay long enough to grant George her heart?

A distinct possibility.

~ ~ ~

George handed Gramps a plate of egg salad sandwiches. Another plate of sliced tomatoes and dill pickles sat on the table. "It's a simple dinner, I know. I'm not the greatest cook, but I hope these will do."

"It's great, son. To be honest, I tire of the rich food at the hotel and enjoy a simple meal now and then. Thank you."

Robbie reached for a sandwich, but George stopped him. "Guests first, son. And let's pray."

After they prayed and filled their plates, George broached the question that had haunted him for days. "How do you think Mary is faring?"

Gramps took a sip of his tea before answering. "Very well, I think. She seems to have her memories fully intact. *All* of them."

The way he said the word *all* made George think that Mary must've talked to Gramps about their relationship. Should he pry into the old man's thoughts and dig for details? Perhaps. But not in front of his son. That would have to wait.

Cooper laid between them, hoping for a dropped morsel or a piece of table food. Gramps rubbed his head. "You're a good boy, Cooper."

Robbie scooted up on his knees. "I mithed my dog so much. I taught him to catch a ball in the air."

"Did you, now? That's great. Now your family is almost complete."

"Almost? Am I missing something?" George furrowed his brow.

Gramps' old eyes twinkled with mischief. "You sure are, son. The most important part, I think. Best get on with acquiring her before she gets away."

Mary. Of course.

George snapped a glance at Robbie, who was busy trying to eat a large slice of watermelon without his front teeth. Juice poured down the front of his shirt. "Careful, son. You're making quite a mess of things."

Robbie gave up. "It's too hard to eat."

George cut up the fruit into small pieces and lovingly mussed his boy's hair. "This should help."

Gramps wouldn't let it go. "You're staying in the Park, aren't you?"

"I've decided to, yes. I even told my mother, who gave us her blessing."

Gramps set down his fork and steepled his fingers together. "Good. You'll be an asset to restoring our community and a great comfort to us all. But you need your own comfort, son. And I think you know what I mean."

George took a slow sip of his tea to bide his time to think while Robbie busily munched his pickle slices. "I'm not sure I'm ready. When do you know?"

"Who can truly be sure? Sometimes you just have to take a leap of faith. And I believe she's worth the leap."

But how to proceed? He wasn't one for flirting and had only ever courted one woman. Alma. They were so young and free, and her parents quickly consented to the union. If there were rules, he didn't remember them. And with Mary, things were complicated. He had a son. She had a job she loved and two elderly aunts to watch out for. And where would they live? Could they truly find comfort and companionship together? His mind spun with questions.

Gramps dabbed his lips with his napkin and interrupted his musings. "Why don't you take a walk and see where it leads? I'll stay here with Robbie and teach him chess."

Robbie's head popped up, and a huge, toothless smile crossed his lips. "Cheth? Am I big enough? Paul thaid I had to be nine."

The old man laughed. "That's often the case, but you're an unusual young man. Let's give it a go, shall we?"

Robbie wiped his mouth with his napkin and hopped down from his chair. "I'm ready."

George wagged a finger at him. "Not so fast, young man. Clear your place first, please."

The child groaned. "Awww, Pa. Do I gotta?"

"Yes, son."

Gramps waved a hand. "We men will take care of this. You take your walk, George. And if you're late in returning, I'll put Robbie to bed."

"As you wish."

And, oh, how I wish!

~ ~ ~

George found Mary sitting on the Wellesley Hotel veranda reading a book, deeply engrossed in it. He stood back and watched her as possibilities danced in his head. Like a kite soaring on the breeze, wonder soared. Might he be able to love again? Could she love him and his son as deeply as Alma had? His heart took flight, skipping several beats.

Just then, Mary looked up and blinked in surprise. "Why, George. How long have you been standing there?"

George swallowed, warmth rising from his chest to his neck to his jawline. "Just a moment. You looked so beautiful sitting there with the setting sun on your face, I hesitated to disturb you."

Joy sprinkled her laughter. Mary removed her spectacles and cleaned them with her daisy-embroidered handkerchief. "Join me, will you?"

She didn't have to ask twice. He did, pulling up an Adirondack chair close enough so they could talk privately. He glanced around. Thankfully, no one was within earshot. A few people milled around the hotel, but everyone seemed engrossed in their own worlds.

"Where's Robbie?" Her brows rose with her question.

George wiped his sweaty palms on his trousers. He felt like a schoolboy. "Gramps is teaching him chess. They're quite a pair, those two."

A grin tipped up her lips. "And I adore both of them, young and old."

But does she adore me? George could only guess.

Nervous energy coursed through his veins. "Would you like to walk? We can see the sunset better from the shore."

Mary slipped her spectacles into a small leather case and tucked it in her reticule. She snapped her book closed. "That would be wonderful. I almost took a walk by myself but wanted to finish this chapter."

She showed him the book spine, and he read it. "'*Where Angels Fear to Tread* by E.M. Forster.' I'm not familiar with it."

She stood, and George offered her his arm. She took it with her small hand. The warmth of her touch sent his blood surging. They descended the steps and strolled down St. Lawrence Avenue toward the shore.

"It's about a widow who falls in love with an Italian man while in Tuscany." Excitement laced her words and lit up her eyes. "They marry, but her former husband's family causes trouble for them and tries to take her baby away to raise him English. That's as far as I've gotten, but it's quite an interesting read."

"Sounds rather mysterious." George chuckled.

Mary's tone turned blustery. "Yes, but if they kidnap that child, I'm going to stop reading it. No child should be a pawn for anyone."

George smiled. What a sweet thing to say! "I quite agree. Children are a gift from God, and we should treat them as such."

Mary turned and glanced up at him with a tenderness that made his heart thump in his chest. "That's how you treat your son, and I admire you for it. So many men ignore their children or treat them harshly. You're a wonderful father, George."

"Thank you, kind lady. I try." He rubbed a hand over his whiskered cheek, trying to wipe away the blush. It didn't work.

They arrived at the shoreline just as the setting sun painted a myriad of yellows, oranges, reds, and purples across the rippling river. Seagulls squawked goodnight. Crickets chirped. Fish jumped and splashed, as if celebrating the day.

Mary's wistful gaze looked as if she'd tasted the most delicious cake ever. Her voice was soft, winsome. "It's just magical, is it not? I never tire of seeing the sun set on the St. Lawrence River. It's as if the two are a meeting of heaven and earth."

"That's a wonderful way to describe it, Mary."

They stood in silence as the sunset shifted its colors again and again. Soft and subtle. Bold and beautiful. Gentle and genial. When the performance ended, her gaze shifted to him. "Thank you for sharing this with me."

George's throat grew thick and tight, so he simply bobbed his chin. Oh, how he wanted to touch her angelic face. He reached out but thought better of it. He didn't want to frighten her with any brash moves. Memories of Richmond turned his dinner sour.

Her tender gaze slid from his eyes to the scar that ran from his left ear to his jawline, and a wispy look of longing crossed her gold-flecked eyes. She reached up and passed a tender hand over it. "What happened?" She almost whispered, her voice wobbly.

A small groan escaped his lips. If she understood the dangers of his profession, she might flee. "A fire mishap several years ago. It's ugly, I know."

Mary caressed the scar and shook her head. "Your scar doesn't mar you, George. It makes you even more handsome than you already are. It's a badge of courage. A sign that you've overcome the worst life can bring and served others valiantly in the process."

He'd forgiven himself for what happened with Alma, but could he risk loving and losing again? Oh yes. With Mary, he'd risk it all.

Chapter 27

Night after night, Mary barely slept. Her excitement grew to hope. Hope to longing. Longing to prayer.

A prayer that God himself indeed orchestrated this relationship. Deep in her heart, she knew it to be true. But was George ready to put the past behind him and step into the future with her?

It had been a week of growing closer day by day. She and George had enjoyed picnics and dinners, concerts, and church gatherings. They'd flown a kite with Robbie and taken a boat ride in the early morning mist.

Gramps had joined them for several outings, too, always encouraging, an impish twinkle casting forth his all-knowing optimism that they were meant to be together. He seemed as excited as she. Would George speak of it to her aunts today, after their arrival for another visit? They'd not been here for any of the drama of the past weeks.

When the boat docked, Mary reached out to help Aunt Stella disembark. She hugged her, then turned to Aunt Maude, whom George had already aided. "It's good to have you back in the Park, Aunties. How I've missed you!"

The three of them stepped away from the boat to allow other passengers to disembark while George stood watch.

Aunt Stella, always the stalwart one, nodded curtly. "You, too, niece. But we are here on official business."

"We're selling the cottage, dear." Aunt Maude shrugged, her voice low. "We can't care for it any longer, I'm sorry to say. Stella's rheumatism is getting worse by the day, and my eyes bother me greatly. Besides, after the fire, our desire to be here has gone up in smoke, so to speak."

Mary frowned, her heart plummeting. "I'm so sorry to hear that. I will miss you being here, and I'm sure you will miss the Park and the river too."

Aunt Stella sighed deeply. "We will miss the river and our neighbors, but we've made our decision, niece, and that is that. You can't live there alone and unmarried. It's just isn't proper. And we can't leave it abandoned for the mice and other critters to destroy until you find yourself a man. I'm sorry you won't have a cottage to call your own one day, but now … no more talk of sadness and longing."

Mary touched her aunt's arm. "That's okay. The hotel is fine, but …" This certainly put George into a fix.

She glanced at him as he aided a young mother and her children from the boat.

Where was George's mother? They'd expected her on the same launch.

George's deep tones wafted on the breeze, even from several feet away. "Welcome, Mother, it's so good to see you."

Mary turned as the elderly lady appeared behind the mother and children. She gasped. The woman looked like a—a new woman! Mrs. Flannigan wore a cheerful hat bedecked with flowers. A light blue dress.

And a smile.

George kissed his mother on the cheek and led her to join them. Then he nodded to the circle of women. "Mother, you already know Miss Mary Flynn."

Mrs. Flannigan smiled. "Hello, dear. It's so nice to see you again."

Dear? Mary's tongue tied in knots. She merely curtsied.

Next, he introduced her aunts. "And these are Miss Flynn's aunts who have graciously rented their cottage to Robbie and me. This is Mrs. Stella Everson and Miss Maude Armstrong. Ladies, this is my mother, Mrs. Bertha Flannigan."

Mrs. Flannigan held out her wrinkled hand. "Pleased to meet you both."

Her aunties reiterated their pleasure in making her acquaintance, but Mrs. Flannigan seemed distracted, searching her surroundings with a slight frown. "Where's my grandson?"

"Playing with his turtle, I expect. I left him with the Dowes. He and young Paul have become inseparable." George rumbled a chuckle.

George's mother sighed. "Just as well, I suppose. Three old ladies can be a bother to a little boy."

They all laughed at that, dispelling the tension that meeting people for the first time can bring.

George gave a slight bow. "Shall I escort you fine ladies to the hotel and get you settled? Then I'll take you to see Robbie, Mother."

Aunt Stella nodded but took the lead, walking up St. Lawrence Avenue ahead of the Flannigans. She and Aunt Maude joined her. Such an independent soul. How was she ever married? Uncle Edward must've been a saint.

Aunt Maude glanced at Mary. "Do you have to work the switchboard today, dear?"

She shook her head, lending her arm to her aunt for support. "No. Charlotte is giving me the entire day off. She's become a good friend and is so helpful."

As they walked, George and his mother stayed behind several feet, talking quietly together, smiles on both of their faces. What happened to the surly woman she'd met in Clayton?

Aunt Stella stepped up her pace. "Come along, sister. We mustn't be late for our meeting with Florence."

Mary kept her voice low. "Mrs. Kinney? I'm happy to hear that you're using a woman as your realtor. Though Mr. Green is a nice man and an honest realtor, women supporting women is a fine thing, I think."

"'Tis only fittin'. Come along, ladies." Aunt Stella set off at a determined clip.

George escorted his mother on his arm, speaking up to be heard from behind them. "This is a perfect Thousand Islands' morning, is it not?"

The four of them mumbled their affirmation until Mary interrupted the murmurings. "Why don't you stay at the cottage with your family, Mrs. Flannigan? I'm sure my aunts would be amenable."

"My son said that the staircase to the bedrooms is too steep. I ain't a young chicken any longer, and my knees bother me greatly." George's mother cackled at her comment.

Aunt Stella agreed. "That's another reason we're selling. Maude and I have struggled with those stairs for some years now. You're wise not to tackle them."

George's head snapped toward Aunt Stella. "Selling? The cottage?"

Aunt Maude blushed at her disclosure. "I'm sorry you won't have it for a home, Mr. Flannigan."

Mary squeezed Aunt Maude's arm. "I guess there's a season and a time for everything. I'm sorry to hear of your decision, but I'm sure you'll get a good price for your place. Folks who lost their cottages have been calling and calling, hoping to purchase existing ones instead of rebuilding. I hear there may even be a waiting list."

Aunt Stella shot a glare at her. "Enough chatter about money in front of strangers, Mary. It isn't proper."

"Sorry, auntie. I do tend to prattle too much." She blanched under her aunt's reprimand.

Aunt Stella nodded. "Yes, you do. Now hush."

By now, they were at the hotel, where George surprised them all. "Mary, would you please escort my mother to the dining room for a cup of tea while I speak to your aunts?"

"Is that all right with you, Aunties?" She sucked in a breath but nodded.

Both of them waved her off without a word.

What a strange request. "Certainly. This way, Mrs. Flannigan."

Mrs. Flannigan glanced at her son, and the two exchanged a silent conversation that befuddled Mary.

She opened the door to the hotel. "After you, missus."

In the dining room, she and Mrs. Flannigan sat near a window. A waiter served tea as quick as a wink. What should they talk about? When they'd first met in Clayton, the woman was curt. Mean, even. But today she seemed … different.

Mrs. Flannigan took a sip of her tea and set the cup on her saucer. "I'm glad we have these few moments alone, dear. When we first met, I was rude. And I apologize for that. I was dealing with some rotting teeth and was in a great deal of pain. Not that it justifies my treatment of you. But when the doctor pulled them, he said the infection was so bad that it may have altered my mood. Could have killed me, even."

Mary blinked in surprise. "Goodness. I'm sorry to hear that. But isn't it wonderful that the medical advances of our day can solve such things? I'm happy you're all right, Mrs. Flannigan."

"Yes, well, shall we start over and make our relationship a pleasant one?"

Mary's heart skipped a beat. She had worried about George's mother accepting her … if they were ever to marry. That concern was now put to rest. Silently, she thanked God for the gift. "I'd love that."

Mrs. Flannigan glanced around the room. "So … you're a switchboard operator and telegrapher? Tell me about that."

Mary did, sharing her joy of helping others connect. "I've had the blessing of helping a young mother announce the birth of her first child, and the sorrow of informing a family of the passing of their loved one. Though most of the calls are about business, I take great pleasure in bringing people together."

The corners of Mrs. Flannigan's eyes crinkling into starbursts of wrinkles. "That's nice, dear. And how do you like my grandson? He's a bundle of energy, that one."

She giggled. "That he is, but he's a treasure, all the same. He says and does the funniest things, and he sure loves his dog, Cooper. The two are inseparable. And little Robbie makes friends wherever he goes. He and his buddy, Paul, are masters at coordinating kickball and stickball and hide-and-seek games with all the neighbor children." She put a hand to her mouth, her cheeks growing warm. "Oh, goodness. Here I go, prattling away. Sorry."

Mrs. Flannigan guffawed, the gap in the back of her mouth where her teeth once had been on full display. "Oh, that's all right.

I see he's captured your heart, and that makes me happy. And what do you think of my son?"

Mary's heart raced, and the unwelcome blush deepened. What should she say? How much had George told his mother about their blossoming relationship? "He's a kind man and so concerned for the community. When the fires were happening, he unflinchingly ran to help whomever needed it without thinking of his own life and has been a bright spot in the Park's reconstruction. He has such good ideas for improving our fire protection system and has been so helpful to the Association, always fighting for what's best for everyone."

She paused, glancing at Mrs. Flannigan to assess if she'd appreciate something more personal. The woman bid her to continue with a simple nod.

"What I appreciate most about your son is how caring he is with Robbie. I've never seen such a wise and loving father as he. He seems to know instinctively how to raise an energetic boy while showing him love and security, even as he works a job as dangerous as being a fireman."

Mrs. Flannigan tilted her head and sighed. "And does that bother you? Him working in what could be a dangerous job?"

Before Mary could formulate her reply, George interrupted their conversation with his presence. "Hello, ladies. Enjoying your tea?"

She and his mother both nodded. Then they smiled at one another.

They were friends.

~ ~ ~

George had donned his Sunday best for dinner at the Wellesley Hotel that night. He made sure Robbie wore his best clothes, too, and he talked to his son at length about how to behave in a fancy dining room.

His mother had taught him the proper social graces, but he had to admit that he'd yet to teach Robbie thus, and he'd never taken him to a restaurant other than Ann's Café, a casual Clayton establishment, to be sure. Why had he neglected such an important lesson for so long?

After seating the ladies, George adjusted his tie and unbuttoned his suitcoat before taking a seat next to Robbie. When he removed his hat, locks of hair celebrated their sudden freedom, waving in the breeze that floated in from the open window. He should've gotten a haircut. He placed his hat under his chair and heaved a great sigh. If only they could get through this meal without a spill, a spat, or some other disaster.

The bastille of Mary's chignon let a stray curl escape. Suppressing a chuckle, he motioned for the waiter and requested that he lower the window a bit. The man complied.

Once they'd ordered, George spread his arms, turning in a slow circle, as if presenting a fine orchestra to a crowd at a command performance. "So … will you miss it? All of this, I mean."

Aunt Stella shrugged, setting down the roll she'd just buttered. "I will, but we have the fancy Hotel Woodruff in Watertown. They have an orchestra and dancing almost nightly, and we have a lifetime of friends in the city. We will be fine."

Aunt Maude didn't seem so sure. "I will miss my friends here." Her small voice faltered and cracked, and she looked as if she might cry. "I guess that I'll be writing many letters in the years to come. There's more than one way to maintain friendships, I suppose."

Robbie chomped on a roll while he fiddled with the many utensils before him. But he was quiet and content, so George let him be.

Aunt Stella scolded her sister. "Don't be so melancholy, Maude. We can always visit and stay in the hotel or in a boarding house when we fancy visiting the Park. It's not like going to New York City, for heaven's sake."

The tense undercurrent of the aunts' exchange grated on his nerves. Mary traced a finger along the china's gold-trimmed rim, a frown marring her pretty features, her cheeks tinted pink. The banter embarrassed her, he was sure. Aunt Stella needn't be so snippy.

Yes, the mood was growing too somber for such a special night.

He turned to his mother. "Tell us the news of Clayton. And just the good news, please."

Mother glanced out the window for a moment before answering. "The Sandersons had a new baby boy. Mr. Carlson is repairing a St. Lawrence skiff they found abandoned on Murray Isle, and we're finally getting a new railroad manager."

George clicked his tongue a little too enthusiastically. "Well, I'll be. A manager after all this time of searching. That *is* good news."

The conversation halted, but Robbie jumped in. "I have another loothe tooth. Thee?" He wiggled his bottom tooth, sending everyone into quiet giggles that they politely muffled with their napkins. His childishness banished the sour mood instantly.

"And what new tricks are you teaching Cooper, young man?" Mary smiled, her tone gentle.

Her mysterious and mischievous smile had planted deep in his dreams of late, popping up night after night. There it was again. Beautiful.

Robbie scooted onto his haunches. "Well, I'm trying to teach him to bow, but he'th not too good at it yet."

Mary reached over and patted his hand. "Be patient. You're an excellent teacher, and he'll learn."

Robbie scrunched up his face and pointed to his utensils. "What are all them for?"

A grin tipped up her lips, and her eyes twinkled. She patiently pointed to each item as George motioned for him to sit back on his bottom. "Here's the first-course fork and the main-course fork. Over here is the soup spoon, first-course knife, and main-course knife. And these are the dessert fork and spoon. You just start using the ones on the outside and work your way in."

"But I can't eat all that. I'm not that hungry." Robbie's eyes grew wide.

Mary patted his shoulder. "You don't have to eat everything, son. These are just here in case you need them."

The child wiped his forehead as though he'd run a race. "That'th good newth."

More laughter.

By the end of dinner, Robbie had fallen asleep in George's arms, the aunts and his mother had become fast friends, and he released a contented sigh. "This has been a delightful evening, ladies, but I'd better get this little man home. Would you mind if we said goodnight?"

Aunt Stella nodded as she slowly rose.

Like always, Aunt Maude followed her lead. "We are tired, too, aren't we, ladies? We've had a busy day, so we'll bid you young folks adieu."

Mother stood and kissed Robbie's forehead tenderly. "Goodnight, child. Sweet dreams." Then, to George's surprise, she kissed his cheek too. "Goodnight, son."

He thanked her and nodded to the aunts as Mary stood and kissed her aunts' cheeks. But instead of joining the elderly women, she stayed behind. "May I walk you out to the veranda? I want to thank you for a lovely evening."

"I'd like that. Very much." He smiled, his nerves firing and pulse quickening at the mere thought of having a few moments alone with her.

Robbie never stirred as they slipped out onto the terrace. He set his son on a cushioned wicker settee, and the child curled up like a cat into a sleepy ball. Perhaps George would have more than a few moments with Mary if his son stayed asleep.

Mary went to the railing and stood there, gazing up at the full moon. "What an enchanting night this is. I feel as if I could unfold my wings and fly."

She spread her arms wide, closed her eyes, and tilted her chin to the sky, a placid smile covering her lips so tenderly he thought her an angel.

He joined her, a grin lifting one side of his mouth and his chest vibrating with his deep laugh. "Wouldn't that be wonderful? I wish we could fly away together, soaring over the mighty river. Swooping in and around each one of the Thousand Islands, skittering along the river's waves, teasing the mighty ships that sail its waters."

Mary turned to him and sighed. "Exactly."

He wanted to continue the dream, but he felt the earth's pull. "But back to tonight. I'd say we had a rather successful evening, don't you think?"

"I'd say so. I think the three of them will be forever friends. And Robbie was a perfect gentleman the whole time." Mary nodded, the gold flecks in her eyes reflecting the moonlight.

He reached for her but thought the better of it. Not yet. "Such a wonder you are, Mary." The tremor in his voice revealed his nervousness.

She inclined her head, a dimple appearing just below her now-rosy cheeks. He dared to run a finger along the side of one. Her dark lashes fluttered, and a small moan escaped her parted lips, as if she longed for his tender touch.

He studied her face, and his heart skipped several beats. Her eyes glinted with hope. Love?

She inched nearer, pressing her cheek into his hand, a bright smile dancing on her lips. "Do you think we might have a future together, you and me?" Her brows rose with the question.

His heart slammed in his chest, and his face flushed warm. His palms grew clammy.

Was now the right time, after all?

"Love is a most stupendous thing, I think. It burns from the inside out, consumes your mind, and engulfs your heart into flames so intense that nothing can quench them."

Relief flooded her eyes as her face beamed hope. "Always the fireman. I think you mean, yes?"

George let out a breath that ruffled her hair as he wrapped her in his loving arms. "Oh yes, my love, yes!"

Chapter 28

Mary couldn't sleep a wink. George had declared his love for her, yet he hadn't proposed. Sweet Robbie had awakened just when she'd expected George to ask her to marry him. Thus, she'd tossed and turned the night away, wondering what he'd say—and when. Just the promise of it sent her tummy tumbling and pulse surging. In the wee hours of the morning, she gave up trying to rest. She didn't want to wake Charlotte, so she quietly dressed and tiptoed out of the room.

The pink dawn trickled through the trees as Mary stepped onto the veranda. The morning mist cast the perfect quiet tranquility she needed to expel the nervous energy pent up inside her. She must pray and ponder all the possibilities before she opened the switchboard and started a busy day of work.

Oh, the trials of being in love!

A giggle escaped her lips. She *was* in love. With George. And, she had to admit, with Robbie too.

As the dawn of a new day slowly stamped long shadows onto the Park, a cheerful whistle wafted on the wind. She surveyed her surroundings through the hazy morning light. A gardener tended the pathways. A maid swept the terrace a good distance from her.

But no guests were in sight. So … who brought the tune to her ears?

There it was again. The whistle in the distance. She stood at the railing and listened to the familiar tune. "Let Me Call You Sweetheart" trilled in perfect pitch. She grinned at the memory of the last time she'd heard it. The night the band played the song was the first time she'd realized she loved George.

She had half a mind to go to George's cottage and declare her undying love then and there. But she rolled her eyes at her foolishness. No. She had to be patient. She had to wait for him.

The whistling drew nearer and nearer. The tune repeated. To her right, the whistler's footfalls ascended the steps, but the corner of the building hid him. She prepared to flee in case the whistler was a miscreant. Her heart sped up, and she turned toward the melody.

When he rounded the corner, her heart skipped several beats.

George!

His sun-kissed skin betrayed his wholesome island work. He smiled wide as he stopped whistling and looked at the rising sun. His brows rose in surprise when he caught sight of her, but he stopped a respectful distance away.

"Good morning, sweet Mary." His velvety voice soothed her, and his air of confidence bolstered her. "I didn't expect to see you out here so early."

"I … I couldn't sleep, and neither, I suspect, could you. And I didn't know you could whistle so well." She held her chin high, even as it quivered.

He directed an impish smile her way, his brows lifting. "I expect there's a lot you don't know about me. If I may, I'd like to rectify that condition as soon as possible."

"I'd be much obliged if you would, sir." Her pulse took to trotting, and pure joy exploded into a plethora of giggles she couldn't contain.

The tease in her tone surprised even her.

When he closed the gap between them, he smelled like a warm spice cake hot from the oven. "Have you been baking this early? You smell like cinnamon and nutmeg."

George chuckled, taking her hands in his. "Gramps brought still-warm cake from the hotel's kitchen. He came to watch Robbie and to send me on an important errand."

Confusion paused her playful banter with alarm following close behind. Her voice rose an octave. "An errand this early in the morning? Is Gramps okay? Whatever could be so urgent at this hour? The boats aren't even in service yet, and the dining room is yet to open." A lump rose in her throat as her mind whirled with the possibilities.

"Shh … sweet Mary. Everything is fine." He bent his head close to hers, a tender grin calming her nerves.

He let go of her hands and cradled her face in both of his. His touch, so gentle, that it reminded her of a warm summer breeze. "Just now, the sun's rays are caressing your features in a magical dance. It makes you so beautiful, I can hardly breathe."

His words ruffled the curls near her ear. What could she say to that?

"I love you, my dearest Mary. I want us to be a family."

His velvety voice soothed her as a forefinger trailed along the side of her cheek, tickling her.

"I'd like that too. But what about Robbie? Would he?" A happy giggle escaped her lips.

George wrapped her in a hug that unknotted the tension from the sleepless night. "Oh, Mary. That's what I love most about you. You always care about others above yourself. That's what the Bible calls genuine love, I think. But you'd actually give up on us if it wasn't best for Robbie? That makes me love you all the more."

Mary placed her cheek against his chest and held him tightly. She couldn't look at him just now for fear he'd give her a negative answer. "But would Robbie truly be happy with us being a family? I have to know."

George pulled her back to look into her eyes. He studied her for a long while, but she failed to read his expression as the tiny tick near his ear jumped to life.

Finally, he smiled and nodded. "Yes, Mary, he would. When I put him to bed last night, he asked me if you would be his new mommy. I asked him if he would like that, and he said he would. Does that answer your question, my darling?"

Her worries faded into the dark corners of her mind. Her cheeks warmed. Her dream was coming true. Right here in the early morning mist. An old maid no more.

"I love you, too, George."

Her voice wobbled with emotion. She'd thought it. She'd dreamed it. But this was the first time she'd ever declared it. And it wouldn't be the last!

His grin rose higher than a fireman's ladder, and his eyes sparked in acknowledgement. A deep baritone chuckle burst from his lips, and he threw back his head. "Thank you, God, for this gift from Your hand!"

She was God's gift to him? Could anyone say anything thing better of a person? She thought not and repeated those precious words. "And thank You, God, for the gift of Fireman George Flannigan."

They burst into joyful laughter as if there wasn't a soul about, and at that moment, she didn't care who was around. He slipped a lock of hair from her chignon and twirled it around his finger, his features growing somber. "I want you to know, although Alma was my first love and the mother of my child, I will never compare you to her. I love you for who you are, and I'll not look back."

"Thank you for that, George."

He hadn't finished. "And I need to know if you have concerns about my profession and the dangers that come with it."

Mary pursed her lips before a great sigh escaped them. "I've thought about that for some time. I've concluded that I must trust God with your life, but I will pray for your protection every day."

Suddenly, he got down on one knee and slipped something from his pocket. He held it out to her. "Marry me, Mary Flynn, and make me the happiest man in the world?"

Pinched between his thumb and forefinger was a lustrous white-pearl ring in a golden setting. She'd seen strings of pearls on wealthy women who had stayed in the hotels, but this lone pearl in a ring of gold called to her. Her hands flew to her chest, and tears filled her eyes. "For me?"

He stood and slipped it on her finger. It was too big, but that didn't matter. He kissed her hand. "I want you to have this. It was my mother's, and before that, her mother's. That's why Mother came to visit me yesterday. She knew I'd need it. For you."

Mary sucked in a breath as a large tear slipped down her cheek.

George gently swiped it away with his pinky finger. "A pearl is strong, formidable, and beautiful. And pearls differ from other gems because they are born of the sea. They don't require cutting or polishing. They are beautiful just as they are. Like you, my love."

Mary swallowed her emotions enough to whisper her thanks as she peeked at the ring on her finger. She'd dreamed of this moment her whole life, but her dreams had never come close to the wonder of this moment. When she looked up, George's expression had changed. It was longing. Hungry.

He took her in his arms, tipped her back, just a little, and brushed his lips on her temple, sending shivers through her body. His lips moved to her cheek, as soft as a feather, searching for his prize. Slowly, excruciatingly and wonderfully, he found her lips.

And time stopped.

~ ~ ~

George heaved a ragged breath as the citrusy scent of Mary's lemon verbena perfume tickled his nose. Enticed him. The warmth of her body so near sent his blood surging through his veins.

When he found her lips, they were soft, like his feather pillow. He swept his mouth over hers in a feeble attempt at self-control. Another kiss, more deeply, as passion took the lead. He had vowed to be gentle, but the fire within him warred with his pledge.

A groan escaped, deep from his chest, as he pressed another kiss against her luscious lips, her breath coming in short puffs.

Innocent. Untouched. Yet longing.

His pulse quickened, his heart banging against his ribs as if wanting to escape and take flight.

Steady, old boy.

He pulled back, just an inch or two, to glimpse the beauty before him. Her eyes fluttered closed. Long lashes quivered. Her skin was unmarred and soft as a baby's.

To his surprise, she opened her eyes. They sparked desire, longing. For him.

She pressed her lips to his and demanded a kiss, fast, passionate, burning.

George softened the kiss and turned to her cheeks, kissing them with all the constraint he could muster. A Scripture danced through his head. The Song of Solomon. He spoke it aloud. "'I charge you, O daughter of Jerusalem, that ye stir not up, nor awake love, until it please.'" He took a deep breath and shook himself, setting her upright. "We'd best not stir our passions until we're wed."

Mary blinked and swallowed hard. Then her eyes danced with joy, sparkling in the day's dawn. "You're right, of course." Her voice was breathy. "But that kiss … I've never been kissed before."

He planted a playful peck on the tip of her nose and chuckled, stepping back. He wanted to stay here forever, to kiss her over and over and bask in their love, but that wouldn't be wise. Besides, they'd soon have an audience of guests and townsfolk starting their days. "Shall we celebrate with a hearty breakfast? Perhaps Mother and your aunts will be there, and we can share the news."

When they entered the hotel dining room, George grinned. His timing was impeccable.

Mary stopped short and gasped. "They're all here? How?"

"Oh, I've had this little plan in the works for some time now. Robbie delayed it last night, but it seems to have sorted itself out just fine." George slipped his hand into hers and kissed it.

He led her to the table where Mother, Aunt Stella, and Aunt Maude sat there with grins as wide as Lewis Carroll's Cheshire cat's. Gramps smiled, too, but Robbie hopped off his chair and ran to Mary, wrapping his arms around her. "Are you gonna be my mommy?"

Mary squatted down and looked him in the eye. "Would you like that, little man?"

"Yeth! Oh, yeth. Can I call you *Mommy* now?" Robbie hugged her again, throwing her off balance and causing them to tumble onto the dining room floor.

After George untangled them, Mary addressed the boy's question. "How about you wait until the wedding, and calling me mommy will be your wedding gift to me?"

Robbie scrunched up his face and then shrugged. "Okay, but it will be hard for me to wait. And don't be mad if I thlip up."

Everyone chuckled quietly at his son's response. As they took their seats at the table, the older folks all voiced congratulations. Mary fairly glowed with the accolades, while his heart simply brimmed with ecstasy.

Once the waiter had taken their orders, it was time to reveal the rest of his plan. He couldn't wait. He snapped a nod at Mary's aunts.

Of course, Aunt Stella spoke first. "Congratulations, George and Mary. We have a surprise for you and Robbie. Instead of selling, Mrs. Kinney suggested that Maude and I give you the cottage as a wedding gift."

George groaned. "But I offered to buy it, ma'am. That's too great a gift."

Aunt Maude grinned. "Stuff and nonsense. We were going to give it to Mary anyway, but now we get to bless all three of you."

Aunt Stella punctuated the announcement. "No arguments. It's yours, free and clear."

"Thank you, aunties. We'll take good care of it." Mary's eyes brimmed with tears for the second time. Her voice came out raspy but joyful.

George murmured his agreement. "I've already begun plans to winterize it and add a bedroom and bathroom on the first floor so that when you two come to visit—and you, too, Mother—you won't have to tackle the steps."

Aunt Maude smiled. "That is very thoughtful, son. Thank you."

Gramps, who had been silent until now, spoke up. "And I should like to officiate your wedding. As a retired preacher, I have that ability, if you'll give me the chance."

Mary's eyes twinkled with delight. "That would be wonderful, Gramps. But can you walk me down the aisle too? Please?"

"Well, now, in all my years as a preacher, I haven't had the privilege of doing both. I would be honored." Gramps chuckled, patting his lips with his napkin.

Just then, the waiter brought their food. After Gramps said the blessing, Mary put out her hand to show the ring. Her aunts *ooh*ed and *ahh*ed.

His bride to be turned to his mother. "Thank you for sharing your family heirloom, Mrs. Flannigan. It's so beautiful. I promise that I shall take good care of it and pass it on one day."

"Happy to, my dear. But you may call me *Mother* from now on. After all, we're family."

Robbie waved his fork in the air. "Can I have a baby thister like Paul has? He really liketh being a big brother, and I would too."

The entire table burst into laughter, sprinkled with a small dose of embarrassment. Mary's cheeks turned as rosy as the flowers on her teacup.

George patted Robbie on the shoulder. "One day, perhaps, but first, I'd like you to be my ring bearer, son."

"Thure, Daddy. What do I do?"

Mary answered him. "You get to carry my ring down the aisle so your daddy can give it to me during the service."

"But it'th already on your finger." Robbie's face scrunched up.

More titters and giggles. His son sure had a way to bring gaiety to life. What a gift.

Just then, Charlotte entered the dining room and waved to them.

George rose and grabbed an empty chair from a nearby table and set it next to Mary. "I'm glad you joined us. Welcome."

"Good morning, everyone. Are we having a party here so early in the day?" Charlotte took the seat, a bright smile adding to the group's happiness.

Mary's eyes lit up, and she thrust her hand toward her friend. "Look! We're engaged!"

"Really? I never would have guessed." Charlotte giggled, her tone sassy.

"You knew?" Mary's eyes narrowed, a smirk crossing her lips.

Charlotte shrugged. "Your husband-to-be is quite the planner. To that end, he spoke with me yesterday, and I agree if you agree."

Mary's brow furrowed. She glanced at him and tossed him a playful head shake before turning back to her friend. "Agree? To what?"

Charlotte paused for several moments before answering. "A swap."

"Swap what?" Mary still didn't understand.

"Positions. I take the lead switchboard operator position and you back me up. That way, you can still work *and* run a household. We can adjust your hours to when Robbie is in school."

Mary threw her arms around Charlotte. "That would be absolutely wonderful. Thank you. Will you be my maid of honor?"

"Of course, I will." She inclined her head in George's direction. "But this swap was all George's idea. He thought of everything."

"Except the wedding date." He crossed his arms and raised a questioning brow. "How about today?"

Mary blinked, and her jaw dropped. "Today? You mean, *today*?"

George chuckled. "There's no time like the present. Why wait? Our loved ones are already here, and my cousin Sam will be on the noon boat. He can be my best man."

Mary took a sip of tea and pondered the plan for several moments. "Well, why not? But what about a dress?"

Charlotte grabbed her hands and squeezed them. "I've got that all sorted out, and you will love what I've chosen. Mrs. McReady will be here at one to do your hair. By this evening, you'll be Mrs. George Flannigan."

Mary glanced at him with such love and desire he couldn't wait for the day to end. "Okay. Let's get married."

"Okay. Let's!"

~ ~ ~ The End ~ ~ ~

ABOUT THE AUTHOR

Susan G Mathis is an international award-winning, multi-published author of stories set in the beautiful Thousand Islands, her childhood stomping ground in upstate NY. Susan has been published more than twenty-five times in full-length novels, novellas, and non-fiction books. She has eleven in her fiction line including, *The Fabric of Hope: An Irish Family Legacy, Christmas Charity, Katelyn's Choice, Devyn's Dilemma, Sara's Surprise, Reagan's Reward, Colleen's Confession, Peyton's Promise,* and *Rachel's Reunion. A Summer at Thousand Island House* comes out July, 2023. Susan's book awards include two Illumination Book Awards, three American Fiction Awards, two Indie Excellence Book Awards, and two Literary Titan Book Awards. *Reagan's Reward* is a Selah Awards finalist.

Before Susan jumped into the fiction world, she served as the Founding Editor of *Thriving Family* magazine and the former Editor/Editorial Director of twelve Focus on the Family publications. Her first two published books were nonfiction. *Countdown for Couples: Preparing for the Adventure of Marriage* with an Indonesian and Spanish version, and *The ReMarriage Adventure: Preparing for a Life of Love and Happiness*, have helped thousands of couples prepare for marriage. Susan is also the author of two picture books, ***Lexie's Adventure in Kenya*** and ***Princess Madison's Rainbow Adventure***. Moreover, she is published in various book compilations including five ***Chicken Soup for the Soul*** books, ***Ready to Wed, Supporting Families Through Meaningful Ministry, The Christian Leadership Experience,*** and ***Spiritual Mentoring of Teens.*** Susan has also several hundred magazine and newsletter articles.

Susan is president of American Christian Fiction Writers-CS (ACFW), former vice president of Christian Authors Network (CAN), and a member of Christian Independent Publishing Association (CIPA). For over twenty years, Susan has been a speaker at writers' conferences, teachers' conventions, writing groups, and other organizational gatherings. Susan makes her home in Colorado Springs and enjoys traveling around the world but returns each summer to the islands she loves. Visit www.SusanGMathis.com for more.

BOOKS BY SUSAN G MATHIS

Visit: www.SusanGMathis.com/fiction

A Summer at Thousand Island House
(coming July, 2023 with Wild Heart Books)

Addison Bell serves children of the Thousand Island House guests on Staple's Island. Part nanny, part entertainer, she's full of creative energy and endearing love for children. While thriving in her work, Addi's vivacity attracts the attention of the recreation pavilion's manager, Liam Donovan, as well as the handsome Navy Officer Lt. Worthington, a lighthouse inspector, hotel patron, and single father of mischievous little Jimmy. When Jimmy goes missing while in Addi's care and former President Chester Arthur finds the child a stowaway on his fishing boat, her job and reputation are endangered. How can she calm the churning waters of Liam, Lt. Worthington, and the President, clear her name, and avoid becoming the scorn of the community?

~ ~ ~

Mary's Moment
smWordWorks (2023)

Mary Flynn is christened the community heroine for calling in a fire and saving dozens of homes. As the first telephone switchboard operator for the Thousand Islands Park, she basks in her fame but hides a secret that haunts her. Less than a month later, Mary must risk her life to call for help when an even worse fire blazes through the Thousand Islands Park Commons. Widowed fireman George Flannigan is enamored by the brave, toffee-haired lass and takes every opportunity to connect with Mary. But he has secrets of his own, and when he can't stop the Columbian Hotel—and almost a hundred cottages—from being burned to the ground, Mary is left homeless, and she withdraws from him. Will she be consumed by her painful past or embrace the future?

Peyton's Promise
Heritage Beacon Fiction (2022) 978-1645263449

Peyton Quinn is tasked with preparing the grand Calumet Castle ballroom for a summer gala. As she works in a male-dominated position of upholsterer and fights for women's equality, she's persecuted for her unorthodox ways. But when her pyrotechnics-engineer father is seriously hurt, she takes over the plans for the fireworks display despite being socially ostracized. Patrick Taylor, Calumet's carpenter and Peyton's childhood chum, hopes to win her heart, but her unconventional undertakings cause a rift. Peyton has to ignore the prejudices and persevere or she could lose her job, forfeit Patrick's love and respect, and become the talk of local gossips.

Devyn's Dilemma
Heritage Beacon Fiction (2020) ISBN-13: 978-1645262732

Devyn McKenna is forced to work in the Towers on Dark Island. But when Devyn finds herself in service to the wealthy Frederick Bourne family, her life takes an unexpected turn. Brice McBride, Mr. Bourne's valet, tries to help the mysterious Devyn find peace and love in her new world, but she can't seem to stay out of trouble—especially when she's accused of stealing Bourne's money for Vanderbilt's NYC subway expansion.

Katelyn's Choice
Heritage Beacon Fiction (2019) 978-1946016720

Katelyn Kavanagh finds herself in the service of none other than the famous George Pullman, and the transition proves anything but easy. Thomas O'Neill also works on Pullman Island and tries to help her adjust to her new world, but she just can't seem to tame her gossiping tongue—even when it could endanger her job, the 1872 re-election of Pullman guest President Ulysses S. Grant, and the love of the man of her dreams.

~~~

Rachel's Reunion
smWordWorks (2021) 978-1737936640

Rachel Kelly serves the most elite patrons at the famed New Frontenac Hotel on Round Island. She has wondered about her old beau, Mitch, for nearly two years, ever since he toyed with her affections while on Calumet Island, then left for the high seas and taken her heart with him. Now he's back, opening the wound she thought was healed. Mitch O'Keefe returns to claim his bride but finds it more difficult than he thought. Returning to work at the very place he hated, he becomes captain of a New Frontenac Hotel touring yacht, just to be near Rachel. But his attempts to win her back are thwarted, especially when a wealthy patron seeks her attention. Who will Rachel choose?
~~~

Colleen's Confession
smWordWorks (2021) 978-1737936688

Colleen Sullivan conceals secrets when she works on Comfort Island and awaits her betrothed's arrival. She loves to draw and dreams of growing in the craft. But tragedy strikes and her orphan dreams of finally belonging and becoming a wife and an artist are gone. What will her future hold? Jack Weiss is smitten by the lovely Irish lass. Perhaps introducing her to the famous impressionist, Alson Skinner Clark, will brighten her opinion of him. But rumors of war in Europe means Jack must choose between joining his homeland's army or staying safe in the Thousand Islands as he makes a life with Colleen. If she will have him.

Reagan's Reward
smWordWorks (2020) 978-0692686645

Reagan Kennedy assumes the position of governess to the Bernheim family's twin nephews, and her life at Cherry Island's Casa Blanca becomes frustratingly complicated. Service to a Jewish family and tending to eight-year-old mischievous boys brings trouble galore. Daniel Lovitz serves as the island's caretaker and boatman. When he tries to help the alluring Reagan make sense of her new world, her insecurities mount as her confidence is shaken—especially when she crosses the faith divide and when Etta Damsky makes her life miserable. As trouble brews, Daniel sees another side of the woman he's come to love.

Sara's Surprise
smWordWorks (2019) 978-1087235714

Sara O'Neill works as an assistant pastry chef at the Thousand Islands Crossmon Hotel where she meets precocious, seven-year-old Madison and her charming father and hotel manager, Sean Graham. But Jacque LaFleur, the pastry chef Sara works under, makes her dream job a nightmare. Sean has trouble keeping Madison out of mischief and his mind off Sara. Though he finds Sara captivating, he's jealous of LaFleur and misreads Sara's desire to learn from the pastry chef as love. Can Sean learn to trust her and can Sara trust him—and herself to be an instant mother?

Christmas Charity
smWordWorks (2017) 978-0578207797

Susan Hawkins and Patrick O'Neill find that an arranged marriage is much harder than they think, especially when they emigrate from Wolfe Island, Canada, to Cape Vincent, New York, in 1864, just a week after they marry—with Patrick's nine-year-old daughter, Lizzy, in tow. Can twenty-three-year-old Susan Hawkins learn to love her forty-nine-year-old husband and find charity for her angry stepdaughter? With Christmas coming, she hopes so.

The Fabric of Hope: An Irish Family Legacy
smWordWorks (2017) 978-1542890861

After struggling to accept the changes forced upon her, Margaret Hawkins and her family take a perilous journey on an 1851 immigrant ship to the New World, bringing with her an Irish family quilt she is making. A hundred and sixty years later, her great granddaughter, Maggie, searches for the family quilt after her ex-pawns it. But on their way to creating a family legacy, will these women find peace with the past and embrace hope for the future, or will they be imprisoned by fear and faithlessness?

Other books by Susan G Mathis

Countdown for Couples: Preparing for the Adventure of Marriage

The ReMarriage Adventure: Preparing for a Lifetime of Love & Happiness

Lexie's Adventure in Kenya, a children's picture book

Princess Madison's Rainbow Adventure, a children's picture book

Susan is also an author in various book compilations including five *Chicken Soup for the Soul* books, *Ready to Wed, Supporting Families Through Meaningful Ministry,* and several more.

Visit her at www.SusanGMathis.com

sign up for her newsletter

and please consider writing an Amazon review. Thanks!